DAVID WILLIAM PEARCE

THE FIST INSIDE THE GLOVE

A MONK BUTTMAN MYSTERY

Black Rose Writing | Texas

First printing

This is a work of fiction. Names, characters, businesses, places, events, and incidents are either the products of the author's imagination or used in a fictitious manner. Any resemblance to actual persons, living or dead, or actual events is purely coincidental.

ISBN: 978-1-68513-082-4
PUBLISHED BY BLACK ROSE WRITING
www.blackrosewriting.com

Printed in the United States of America
Suggested Retail Price (SRP) $22.95

The Fist Inside the Glove is printed in Chaparral Pro

*As a planet-friendly publisher, Black Rose Writing does its best to eliminate unnecessary waste to reduce paper usage and energy costs, while never compromising the reading experience. As a result, the final word count vs. page count may not meet common expectations.

By David William Pearce

Monk Buttman Mysteries

Where Fools Dare to Tread
A Twinkle in the Eyes of God
Too Many Women, Too Little Time
In the Service of Others

Available from Black Rose Writing

THE FIST INSIDE THE GLOVE

PROLOGUE

"History in and of itself is neither friend nor foe; it is merely the poetics of the means to an end. Whatever is made of any particular passage is predicated on the understanding that it is first and foremost an instrument of coercion, a mechanism to parade human failure, human grandiosity for whatever ends are deemed necessary to advance an agenda and play upon the ignorance of the populace. To be ahistorical is advantageous not as a slight but as an introduction to a false or premeditated history meant to evoke emotion rather than thought. A bias towards a truncated history only indicates a prejudice towards a particular narrative, however authenticated. The true history is illusion, the key by which the zealot and the functionary are controlled. The iconic image, whether philosopher-king, conqueror, tyrant, or prophet, is only imagery whose sole purpose is to provide reason, which is also false, towards the application of power..."

"Legitimacy is immaterial, so long as the means of law rest in the hands of those who understand its value to coercion. We value the image of legitimacy more than its actual execution simply because its definition is ephemeral and malleable to ahistorical minds attuned to nothing more than the present or to a fictional past..."

"The question before you is one of resolve, of application... any other narrative has no more value than that of Oz..."

"The only true measure is to act..."

–Excerpt from the book, *The Court Jester*, by Ashley Carmichael

1

He was screaming.

I, on the other hand, was pondering the damage to my beloved 1964 Ford Falcon Futura Sport convertible. Sixty years of service to me and a man named Gunther, and in all that time barely a scratch. Now the rear-end was crumpled, the bumper left twisted, disfigured. The trunk deformed and half open. Around the sides, the fender wells were pushed deep into the tires. It was possible the rear axle was bent; certainly, the frame was.

The screamer wouldn't let up.

My neck and back were doing a little screaming of their own as I tried to shake my head in disgust. I was getting too old to be rear-ended in a car with no lumbar support or a headrest.

The idiot and my neck weren't the only ones screaming.

The mass of humanity trapped behind our mutilated cars was not amused; normal traffic being bad enough. Horns flared, and I lost count of the number of middle fingers and the illiberal comments hurled at us as they inched past. In response, I shrugged and motioned towards the screamer, who was getting on my nerves.

Good times.

It wasn't my fault he carelessly swerved in behind me, misjudged how fast I was going, and trashed his precious new BMW. The fuzz wasn't any more sympathetic, handing him a ticket and telling him to watch his mouth. When he pointed at me, I pointed at the two frightened children shaking by the aid car.

"Watch your language, dumbass."

He appeared genuinely amazed that they might be further traumatized by his crazed behavior.

It was also hot out.

I wiped my brow and pondered my options. There was only one. I pulled the phone from my jacket pocket and winced in pain.

"Are you sure you're alright?" the medic asked.

I didn't understand the question. "I'm alright, just sore," I assured him.

"It's possible you suffered whiplash, or worse, when your car was hit. I really think you should have that checked." He noted I was rubbing the back of my neck.

"I appreciate the concern, thanks," I mumbled, brushing him off. He shook his head and returned to the screamer and his two frightened children.

I called Bernie. If anyone could put the Falcon back together, his shop was it. Javier answered; Bernie wasn't there. Javier listened, and, after a moment, told me a tow was on the way. A weird feeling crept over me that something was wrong beyond the damage to the Falcon and maybe my neck. I thanked him, hung up, and called my beloved wife, Agnes.

"You're an accident waiting to happen, Buttman," was her response to my tale of woe. I chose to ignore her poor attempt at comedy.

"Yes, however, I'm going to need you, or your representative, to pick me up at Bernie's here in a little bit." Agnes groaned. "What?"

"Did you get hit in the head?"

"No... why?"

More groaning. "Then why don't you remember that everyone is here at the big house?"

Big house?

"Buttman?"

I was trying to think... Oh, yeah, Barron, Agnes' son, was getting married, and it was decided that the big house with its glorious panoramic views of LA and the Pacific was the place to have the ceremony. It was Agnes who first suggested the house as the perfect venue, which somewhat surprised me. She was always going back and

2

forth about how she felt about my owning Judith's beautiful house. It was, after all, the place where Judith and I would enjoy each other's company before... It was also a glorious place for Agnes to rub her ex-husband's nose after he'd left her for another man.

"You really need to get over that. It's been years now," I would complain, following another of her swipes at Simon.

"Yeah, yeah, yeah..." she would say.

Tonight was the ceremonial meal before the next day's big event.

As I rubbed my neck, the pain grew sharper and began migrating north.

"I didn't do this on purpose." I was trying to remember where I was.

Agnes grumbled some more, and I heard muffled sounds before she rather indignantly informed me that Fidel, my son-in-law, had volunteered to come get me. I thanked her, told her to lighten up, and to let everyone know I'd be there as soon as possible.

"Did you pick up the flowers?"

Flowers? I looked in the Falcon. No flowers. "I don't see any... no, wait. Theresa will bring them over herself."

"Yeah, she's more reliable, if you know what I mean. Try not to get into any more accidents, ok?"

I shook my head and cried out in pain. The medic looked over and stepped towards me, but I waved him off. "I'll do what I can," I croaked into the phone.

"Are you hurt? You said it was no big deal... Are you ok?" I noted the concern in Agnes' voice.

"Just a twinge," I said. "No worries."

"You do know that I know that 'no worries' is Buttman code for I'm lying my ass off, don't you?"

Damn!

"I think that's a misrepresentation of the facts, beautiful."

"Don't lie to me, Monk. Are you hurt? Does Fidel need to get you to the hospital? Aren't there any medics there?" Agnes was asking too many questions.

"I'm ok, honest," I lied. "Just have Fidel meet me at Bernie's."

More groaning. "Fine. I worry about you, Buttman, I really do."

Yeah, I picked up on that.

It took the tow truck forty minutes to get to me and my damaged car. It took another forty minutes to get to Bernie's, which wasn't that bad given LA traffic and my part in making it worse. Javier was there to greet me, as was Fidel and Zachary, my grandson. They all marveled at the damaged to the Falcon. Javier directed the driver to where he could dump the car. The weird feeling I had when I talked to him earlier crept back in as I watched him. Javier was a sly character; quiet if he didn't know you, but sneaky-clever once he did. That Javier was not here today. When I asked about Bernie, he furrowed his brow, something Fidel noticed as well, and cryptically told us that Bernie was out of town for a while. I was tempted to ask more questions, but my head was throbbing and I wanted to lie down.

"Have him give me a call," I said. He assured me he would. I gingerly got into Fidel's Jeep and carefully eased my head against the seat, hoping for a moment of respite from the pain enveloping my head. Fidel eyed me as he put Zach in his car seat. I noticed the two of them looking at me.

"No worries," I assured them. Zach laughed.

Fidel did not. "You sure you don't want to go to the ER?"

I stupidly tried, again, to shake my head and, again, cried out in pain. Fidel gave me the same grim face he gave Zach when he misbehaved, which Zach immediately recognized.

"Uh-oh, Gamps," he admonished.

Fidel ratted me out and called Agnes to let her know that we were, despite my protests to the contrary, going to the ER. I whined to no avail and soon enough, we were waiting for the good folks at the UCLA Medical Center to look me over. We didn't have to wait long. Fidel casually mentioned I was executor of the Judith Delashay Memorial Trust, which had donated a fair amount of funding to advance cancer research here at the medical center, and was it possible to get me in sooner rather than later. I protested that I should wait like everyone else, but was ignored.

A common thread of late.

It took the doctor ten seconds to have me ushered off to diagnostic imaging for an X-ray that revealed two cracked vertebrae and a concussion. After an MRI revealed no damage to the spinal cord, I was doped up and fitted with a neck brace and Fidel, much to my annoyance, assured the doctor that I would follow this up with additional trips to those in the medical industrial complex that specialized in cracked necks. I groused to no avail.

Agnes, much as my duplicitous son-in-law had, frowned as I was carefully brought into the house. What was supposed to be a big family dinner was now the freak show with Monk Buttman as the headliner. I apologized to all assembled, and it was quite an assembly. Agnes' mother, father, and brother were there. As were her ex-husband Simon and his husband, Eric. Anna, Agnes' daughter, stood with Barron, Gerta, Barron's fiancé, and Gerta's parents. Fidel, Rebekah, and their growing brood were also in attendance. Anna, with help, wanted or unwanted from Simon, was catering the affair, as she would the reception down at the Manifesto after the wedding.

All were hungry and I, Monk Buttman, was holding up the show.

"You didn't have to wait," I said. Agnes just shook her head. I was deeply envious.

For once, the dining room was utilized for its intended purpose. I had never seen it used as a place to dine in all the years I'd come up here since first meeting Judith, and for reasons unknown, marveled at how well it accommodated the crowd. Of the few times we had a large group over, the pool and cabana were where the action was at, but Agnes decided that an important function such as this should be held in that part of the house so designed. I chose not to argue the point. Simon was rousted from the kitchen and forced to sit at the table, which allowed Anna, with help from Rebekah, to delight the table with what she had prepared. It smelled wonderful, I think. I carefully tugged at my annoyed wife's sleeve, motioning for her to move closer to me.

"What," she whispered.

"It's possible the pain meds may interfere with my ability to consume without drooling, so I'm commending myself into your loving care so I don't come off looking like a complete ass."

She thought that was cute.

Rebekah, as if on cue, slid in between us with two plates.

"This one," she pointed to the plate in front of me, "is so you won't choke. Fidel said the doctor told you to be careful the first few times you eat, till you get used to the restrictions caused by the brace."

How thoughtful. Why didn't I remember that?

The rest of the dinner was thankfully free of questions about my debacle on I-5, and centered more on the happy couple, their plans, what a wonderful house this was, and many other topics that I drifted in and out of. As much as the food enticed my olfactory senses, hunger did not absorb me, which was probably for the best since choking would only exacerbate my poor showing, and tarnish Agnes' eagerness to show off her good fortune to those she felt slighted by.

"Judith would be proud," I told her as we graciously said goodnight to those of our guests leaving for accommodations elsewhere. Agnes decided the best response was to elbow me in the ribs.

Her parents, Jerry and Denise, Barron and Gerta, and Gerta's parents, Jürgen and Eva, were staying here for the night. Jerry was fascinated by the large projection TV out by the pool, and Jürgen by the architecture of the house. While Barron dutifully kept his grandfather company, while he scrolled through the thousand or so channels and complained that I didn't have any regular beer, I pulled out the drawings and history of the house in the library, something Judith had been keen to preserve.

"And the woman in the painting?" Jürgen asked in a heavy German accent. I looked up at the woman I had loved and thought of an appropriate answer.

"She owned the house before me. Her name was Judith Delashay."

He pondered the beautiful woman. "Did you know her well?" A sly grin came to the German.

"I did." I think the brace hid my sly grin.

I stood there, lost in memories of Judith.

Jürgen laid out the plans on the library table. "I know of this architect; he was quite famous for his houses here in California. I see that the owners have kept the house and property much as it was when it was built..." He waved his hand across the room and out towards the garden.

"Yes, Judith bought the property because of its pedigree, and when the house was remodeled, she made sure it retained its distinctive character. The kitchen, obviously, has been updated, and the pool as well; the original was not a waterfall design, but the footprint and the design of the house have not changed since it was built."

We then, with prints in hand, walked the interior of the house with Jürgen making comments here and there. Agnes, Denise, Gerta, and Eva watched as we encroached upon their space and conversation. After a few comments Jürgen made in German, we left them to whatever they were taking about.

I was running out of gas.

I tried to direct him to the funfest out by the pool, but his interest in Jerry's complaining was right there with mine. I understood now why Agnes had made no real effort to involve him, and by extension, Denise, in our lives. I thought that was unfortunate, because I found Denise to be quite funny in her own quiet way. We returned to the library and put the prints away. He sensed my fatigue.

"Would you mind if I take these papers to read?" Jürgen was holding Judith's history of the house.

"Not at all," I said as we returned to the living room and the women.

I apologized for being tired and sore and for the screamer and his two frightened children who kept me long from so delightful a party. I was abandoning them for the safety of my room, which was once

Martin Delashay's, and the faint hope that sleep would come and relieve me of the pain in the neck the day had given me. Denise, hearing her Jerry bloviating to Barron, patted Agnes' arm and headed out towards the pool to free Barron from the trap he had so foolishly stepped into. Eva, whose English was almost non-existent, had Gerta relay how much she loved the house and how grateful she was that we were letting her and Jürgen stay with us.

I assured her it was our pleasure.

Barron, freed from his grandfather, latched on to his lovely bride to be and directed her, Jürgen, and Eva to their rooms. Denise, with a half in the bag Jerry, said goodnight. We watched as she maneuvered him down the hall.

"You have a very interesting family, beautiful."

"Yes," she groaned, "I certainly do." She turned to me and kissed the side of my face. "How are you holding up, Sunshine?"

"I'm very sore and very tired, but other than that, I'm ok." I motioned towards our room.

"You know it's bad form to lie to your wife?"

"Oh, honey-bunny, when have I ever lied to you?"

Agnes slapped my ass. "You're lying now, Buttman. How many of those pain meds are you on?" she admonished.

"Apparently, not enough."

We made it to our room, and I tried lying down, only to discover the bed wasn't going to work. Agnes helped me get undressed and ready for the lounger that we ordinarily used for sex, but that I would have to sleep on till I figured out how to get rid of the neck brace. It was a very comfortable chair. I took some more dope and smiled at Agnes, who had pulled up next to me and was sitting on a stool from the closet.

"Are you going to be alright for tomorrow?"

"We already got married, remember?"

Agnes responded as I expected her to. She rolled her eyes. "A broken neck doesn't make you any funnier, Buttman."

"No?" I was certain it did.

"No!" She apparently was just as certain. "Everything is ready, right?"

I laughed. "For the fourteenth, and last time, yes, everything is ready: food, flowers, transportation, all of it. Relax, ok?"

"I'm pretty sure I've only asked ten or eleven times, loverboy, and with you, it's always good to make sure. I mean look at you..." She stood up and spread out her arms, making a big production out of my being laid up in the sex lounger as if the accident was my fault. "I think if the shoes were reversed, you'd be just as concerned."

I reached for her hand. She offered it, and knowing my intensions leaned in and kissed me.

"Goodnight, beautiful."

"Goodnight, Sunshine. Get some sleep. It's going to be a long day tomorrow."

Yeah, just what I need.

2

Agony best describes how the next morning chose to greet me.

Agnes was looking at me as I tried, unsuccessfully, to move. Her face betrayed her obvious concern for my well-being, and her exasperation that, somehow, even if I didn't intentionally mean to, I had managed to make the day that much more fraught with whatever she decided was important to fret about.

I just wanted to be put out of my misery.

The pain was right up there with the time I rolled the tractor and broke three ribs and my right leg. Agnes gently got the chair to its upright position while I moaned loudly for effect.

"Oh, for chrissakes, Monk, you're not dying."

"You don't know that," I whined, then added an aggrieved "ouch" to punctuate the point. Agnes simply ignored me. She got behind me to lift me out of the chair.

"Oh, my..." she gasped.

"What?"

She lightly kissed my forehead before shaking her head. "You have bruises all over your back, Monk!" She then made a disapproving face. "But hey, no worries, right?" She eased me out of the chair and helped me to the bathroom, where she made me look in the mirror and acknowledge that I had lied my ass off the previous day.

"Ok, so maybe I was a wee bit disingenuous. I just didn't want you to worry..." I admitted as I washed down a few more pain pills.

"Oh, brother!" was all she would say.

In a scene that echoed Judith's last days, Agnes got me in the large shower, filled a basin with water and cleaned me up. Apparently, the neck brace was not to come off anytime soon.

"The doctor said six to eight weeks, remember?"

"Six to eight weeks?" I groaned. A deep gloom enveloped me as Agnes merrily washed away. "I should sue that bastard; six to eight weeks... that's almost two months!"

Agnes shook her head in a very condescending fashion. "Yes, you should, because if there's one thing you need, it's more money."

"It's not the money, it's the message it sends," I harrumphed.

"I'm sure it is."

"You could be a little more supportive, you know." I was searching for some sympathy...

"I know and yet here I am washing your ass."

... And finding nothing... "Thanks," ... but bitter defeat.

After drying and dressing me, Agnes carefully walked me to the living room and called for a committee to ascertain the level of my functionality concerning the day's activities. Members of the committee included Rebekah, my again pregnant daughter, the traitorous Fidel, and new to the party, Denise, who was oddly sympathetic to my plight.

"It's such a shame this had to happen now," she exclaimed.

My thoughts exactly.

Those who knew me better were more circumspect.

"Of course, if you'd gone when I asked you to, you'd have been home already and not there to be run into by that guy you now want to sue," Agnes pointedly noted.

"I was being a loving grandfather," I replied.

"Fidel was already watching the kids, Dad. You didn't need to stay." Rebekah was enjoying this more than usual.

"Ah," I sniveled, "you're addled by hormones."

Rebekah just laughed. "This from a dope fiend."

"A prescribed dope fiend, if you don't mind," I muttered.

"Anyway," Agnes continued, "I think it's obvious that you need to rest, and for at least the next few days you're going to have to take it easy. Given how much work it was to get you here to the living room,

I think it might be best if you stayed here instead of going to the reception—"

"What about my speech?" I demanded. I didn't actually have a speech prepared.

"Yeah, well, as much as we all enjoy being embarrassed by your attempts at humor, your health and our willingness to deal with you when you're hurt trump any of your foolishness." Agnes had her arms crossed, which I knew meant I was to have no say in the matter.

"I don't think I like you anymore!" I snorted.

Agnes just smiled. "You know you love me more than ever."

"You're just guessing." She was, of course, right, which only darkened my mood.

"Uh-huh..."

They drew straws as to who would be left behind. Fidel, sensing his position as low man on the totem pole, volunteered. So did Zach, who had wandered in unbeknownst to us all. I knew him well enough to know he just wanted to stay behind so he could play in the pool. This was possibly Fidel's ulterior motive as well. And if Zach was staying, then why not his sister Lizzy, too? It worked out to everyone's benefit.

"Don't I get a say in this?" I objected.

"Of course, you do, Monk." Which was Agnes' way, again, of saying no. She noticed the unhappiness plastered across my face. "Now don't be like that."

"Bah!" was all I could think of.

The wedding was a beautiful thing, but then again, I was doped up and vulnerable to memories that during cross-examination might not jibe with the memories of, say, Agnes, or Barron, or anyone else. That said, nature was on its best behavior as we gathered for the ceremony. The sky was an unusually beautiful azure, the few soft clouds there were drifted merrily above us, and a cool Pacific breeze caressed, as Barron and Gerta promised to love and cherish and not do stupid things that would make their lives together a recipe for disaster.

A man named Revis administered the vows and both Barron and Gerta read prepared statements, which they spoke so softly that I didn't understand a word from either. But given the Oohs and Aahs from those around me, specifically Agnes and Rebekah, I presumed they were quite lovely. Agnes wiped her eyes several times and mentioned just as often how beautiful they looked, which was true.

I did my very best to look composed and alert and kept my mouth shut much to Agnes' great relief. I did not fall down and only groaned a couple of times. I considered it a personal triumph that I would use in my defense the next time my wife was unhappy with some aspect of my character.

After the ceremony, the various family permutations were subjected to a photographer with way too many ideas about how best to frame these special moments. Group after group were hustled to positions by the pool or the garden with the magnificent views in background for shot after shot. Agnes scolded me when I foolishly said I didn't need to be in the pictures with everyone else, and with a neck brace, I'd stand out like a sore thumb. She simply removed the brace and told me if I had to cry out to do so quietly. Once our fifteen minutes were up, she reattached the brace and had the traitorous Fidel remove me from the festivities. I watched from the couch until I could watch no further and fell asleep to the sounds of the photographer barking instructions.

It's only money, I told myself, and Judith told me I could do whatever I wanted with it, which in this case was what Agnes wanted in Barron and Gerta's name.

Rebekah woke me later as they were preparing to head to the reception. I wished her well, which she took umbrage at, admonished me, stood there next to Agnes as *she* reminded me to take it easy, and then turned to the traitorous Fidel, informing him to keep me in line. He smiled and promised to do her bidding. Zach, still in his wedding finery, sat next to me and positioned his head so he looked like his doped-up grandfather.

I was impressed.

The phalanx of those in the wedding party mouthed sympathy as they passed me on their way to the door, Eric being the only one who seemed sincere. Finally, the house emptied, save for me, the grandkids, and the traitorous Fidel.

With what little energy I could muster, I fumbled my way to the bedroom, managed to arrange the pillows so I could lie down, and took a well-deserved nap. The nap, however, devolved into weird dope filled dreams of Agnes chasing me at our wedding and a stoned Moses blaming us all for Jacob's death. After a few hours and another round of pain soothing medications, I fought the good fight to get out of the clothes Agnes chose for me and put on a Hawaiian shirt and a pair of shorts. It only took ten minutes, a great deal of discomfort, and a lot of foul language.

Fidel and the kids were, as they always were when I allowed people at the big house, in the pool.

Zach, who had now mastered flotation devices, was floating along the edges of the deep end. We had taught him basic swimming, and in the hands of the traitorous Fidel, or even me, when I wasn't doped up on pain medication, was quite confident, but on his own not so much. Lizzy was napping in the pen that formally housed her brother. Zach had figured out how to escape its confines and so required, at times, adult supervision. But mostly, he took a nap when Lizzy wore out. Here at the big house, Zach did not nap in order to maximize his pool time. This generally meant no quiet time in the afternoon, but gave his parents a break when he flamed out in the early evening.

I grabbed a beer and sat in the lounge chair next to Fidel. Fidel, who was reading a slender book, promptly took the beer and returned it to the fridge. He graciously returned with a bottle of water. I was not amused.

"I can't believe how quickly you've turned on me, man!"

Fidel shrugged, but I detected a fair amount of discomfort in his expression. "Sorry, but I promised. And much as Becks and Ag give you grief, I know they would be heartbroken if something happened because you were mixing alcohol and opioids. Sorry."

I was touched that he said sorry twice.

"Fine, I officially absolve you in this matter, but I plan to bitch loudly once the women return."

Fidel laughed and sat down. "Works for me."

He picked up the slender volume.

For some reason, I was curious and asked the obvious, "Whatcha reading?"

"It's called *The Court Jester*. I found it on the library table. It's by someone named Carmichael." He turned the leather-bound cover towards me. It was then that I remembered where it came from.

"Yeah, Dunkle gave it to me. He said now that I'm exceedingly wealthy, I need to upscale my conspiracy theories to better reflect my station in the world. He finds that to be the stuff of great humor and ridicule. How is it? I only looked at it briefly and considered it gobbledygook."

Fidel nodded while contemplating my question. "It certainly is wordy and kinda dense, but once you get used to it, it's not too bad assuming you can figure out what he's talking about."

"And what *is* he talking about?" I chided.

"Well, it's written in numbered paragraphs that supposedly deal with the chapter's title. This one is *Modes of Democracy*, which, if I'm catching his drift, is either elegant if it's exercised by the right people, or vulgar when exercised by the ignorant masses." He raised his eyebrows as he said the last.

"Hum, sounds like the conservative version of a French book I read years ago that talked about Marxism in the twentieth century and how everything we do is a great big scam meant to turn us into unthinking, easily manipulated lemmings. It too was overly verbose and sounded like Moses' rants writ with an elevated sense of importance." I tried to lean back and find a comfortable position while wearing the goddamned neck brace. I wasn't having much luck. "I didn't know you were into that kind of thing?" I said this hoping happenstance would save me and my aching head and back.

"Not really, I just picked it up thinking it would be a quick read while the kids were napping..." He again smiled, as he said this. "But apparently not."

"So have you figured out how it would involve an unworthy rich guy like me?"

He quietly laughed at that, which prompted Zach to laugh loudly, which woke up Lizzy who didn't want to be woken up. We all became very quiet as she flopped around before closing her eyes and going back to sleep. Fidel and I glared at Zach. He sheepishly paddled off.

"I wouldn't put money on it, but if I'm reading it correctly, because you're wealthy, you have a greater stake in the direction of the country, better access to a proper education, which therefore affords you a greater sense of probity in where that direction should take us. Consequently, that puts you in the rarified air of national leadership, which middle class shlubs like me shouldn't be a part of because we're ignorant and too easily manipulated by emotions to know better; sort of like your lemmings." He obviously was proud to be a middle class shlub.

"Interesting, and that does sound like the kind of nonsense Dunkle would find worthy of his contempt," I observed.

Having sated my interest, I closed my eyes and hoped to join Lizzy in a languorous afternoon nap. Fidel was good with that, too.

The clan returned home late. Agnes had the thousand-yard stare of a combat veteran or someone exposed to Jerry for many unending hours. Her mother wore weary across her face, but also resignation, as she hauled the inebriated Jerry to their room. Jürgen and Eva followed Rebekah, who had that knowing look on her face, which was her way of telling us that we'd all been here before, whether with her ex-husband Farrell's family, or any other drunken yahoos at a community or church sanctioned function. They were all exhausted.

Those of us left behind and still awake; Zach flamed out hours before and Lizzy had been in bed for an hour, were just hitting our stride. I was finally feeling a little better and Fidel was in his own little heaven, having completed his appointed tasks and actually having some time to himself. I pestered Agnes about the reception as she got herself a tall drink, and then whined that her goon, Fidel, wouldn't let me drink any beer.

"Monk," she said.

"Yes?"

"Shut up!"

And while a number of rather pithy rejoinders came to mind, recognizing the gravity of the situation, I shut my trap, sat her on the couch, and to the best of my abilities, and limitations; aided ably by the opioids cruising through my body, massaged her shoulders and neck. After a few minutes, she leaned back into me and let out a long sigh.

"Jerry?" I asked. Agnes let out another long sigh. "Care to share, vent..." I looked over as Rebekah and the rested Fidel sat down at the other end of the long white couch.

"It was ok till he started drinking. Then it was one long rant after another, mostly at my expense." Her head sank into her chest. Rebekah moved in closer and took Agnes' hand.

"Same old stories?" I knew Jerry harbored an odd resentment against Agnes for "turning" Simon gay. Eric found it supremely funny, which only added to Jerry's resentment. Simon had no interest in arguing with Jerry, which made things worse.

"I told you it was pointless," was his comment the one time it was brought up in my presence.

"Oh, there a new twist. He had to spend the evening giving Jürgen and Eva an earful, saying it's a good thing Barron doesn't come around much cuz who knows what influence I might have. After all, look what happened to Simon... ugh!"

"Maybe Johnny D knows some guys, you know..." I winked at Rebekah and Fidel, who started laughing while Rebekah frowned and shook her head.

"What about Denise, Dad?"

I was surprised she cared. "Oh, she'll get over it," I answered. "And the rest? The band, the food? Was Mikal there?" I had to ask. Rebekah continued to give me the face of familial disappointment. "Oh, come on, you guys got to feast while Fidel and I had to make do with crumby old pizza."

"Tomassa's Pizza?" she asked. "The best pizza in town!"

I looked at Fidel, who shrugged. "Maybe…"

"Yes," Agnes admitted, "Mikal was there, but he mostly stayed out of the way, taking care of the setup and supervising the people helping Anna. And other than my goddamned father, it was very nice. There was a lot of singing and dancing. Oh, and Mikal told me to tell you that he hopes you feel better."

How sweet.

Mikal was the former lover of Joanie, who had once been my lover, however briefly, and the presumed new lover of Anna, though both continued to play coy. This vexed Agnes to no end, but as with most of her interactions with her family, it had no noticeable effect on their actions.

Joanie had run off to marry Brian Thalen, the prince who would take her away to Suburbia and the perfect life she thought she wanted. She called and left messages asking about Mikal, intimating both happiness and concern, of which she didn't say, and finally hoping that I really did understand why she did what she did.

Everything was ok, really, she insisted.

Too bad her calls didn't convince me…

3

After venting, Agnes retreated to the bedroom, while Rebekah and Fidel wandered out to a quiet place by the pool. I picked up the instructions from the ER, deciding, finally, that it might not be a bad idea to see what they had to say. I groaned at the prospect of multiple doctor visits, being forced to wear this stupid brace for months, and noted what I could and could not do. Apparently, tackle football was off the table! However, if I was careful, I was allowed to shower. Agnes was in bed, staring at the ceiling as I organized the pillows in such a way so I could sleep. This included a wedge pillow that, like the recliner, hadn't actually been used for sleeping, but I knew I had to be somewhat elevated or I'd snore Agnes out of the room.

She reached for my hand as I slowly lowered myself onto the bed.

"Next time I stupidly think to invite my father to anything we do, please stop me."

"So, it's probably bad form for me to remind you that the *only* reason you invited him in the first place was to rub his nose in our fabulous wealth." I squeezed her hand.

Agnes let out a long sigh. "Bastard didn't even seem to care. Seriously, what was I thinking? I knew he'd do this! I knew it, and yet..." She let that linger. "Quite frankly, I'd have been less mortified if you'd invited whatshername and everyone watched her give you a blowjob!"

"So..."

"NO," she stated rather emphatically. "That's just an example, so don't get any ideas. Besides, you said she was running around with some Saudi guy." Ah, Monika Danalek, she of the fine figure and offers hard to refuse.

"That's what I heard." Agnes squeezed back as if I needed a reminder of how she felt about such things, but my conscious was clear. I'd been good. "Hey, it could've been worse, could've been like our ceremony up at the farm."

Agnes let out a snort. "You know that's not true; everyone had a great time. It may have been unconventional, but everyone knew that going in."

I tried to turn to see if she was smiling. But the brace wouldn't let me.

"Yeah, it was a blast, and it was worth the wait, right?" I waited for her rebuttal. Didn't take long.

"You're a jerk, Buttman."

"Yeah, well, we can't all be perfect."

Agnes sighed, but cozied up next to me all the same.

· · · · ·

To say our wedding, and that of Rebekah and Fidel, who were married along with us, was a raucous affair, might not adequately describe the occasion. Add rollicking for good measure.

Every oddball family member and friend was there except for Jerry, who was invited, but had tickets to the 49ers game that he refused to give up, and Jude, Astral's hubby, who claimed there was too much to do at their farm in Virginia. I did not miss the weasel who stole Astral from me, and Agnes, as well as her mother and brother, Todd, likewise did not seem to be the slightest bit put out that *Jerr*, as Denise called him, couldn't make it, probably because Simon wasn't invited.

It was the first time I met any of Agnes' family save her two kids.

Denise was disarmingly sweet, and Todd, a divorced accountant with two grown daughters, was amiable as well. Physically, Todd, like Agnes, took after their mother, stout rather than rail thin like Jerr, which was then passed down to Barron but not Anna, who favored her father, Simon.

Fidel's mother was there with her paramour, a man named Rodrigo. Ellen, who preferred El, had a thing for Latin men, something she presumably discovered after dumping Fidel's father, a man named Phil, who lived in Missouri. He apparently had no interest in Fidel after he left California.

Fidel didn't seem bothered by this.

"Every family has its ups and downs," he said with no apparent ill will. Rebekah later informed me that Philip Montaigne had been invited, but had respectfully declined after learning the "Crazy Bitch" El would be there. In fact, though he claimed no interest in Fidel, Phil was none the less keenly interested in his grandchildren, which made no sense to me. Rebekah added that when Phil and El's marriage blew apart, Fidel was stuck in the middle, and given his rather even temperament, chose not to pick either side, which infuriated both sides, which, again, made no sense to me.

That is, till I met El and Rodrigo and extrapolated Phil into the mix and came to understand why Fidel was more than happy to be out of that combustible stew.

Both El and Rodrigo were flirts of the most fascinating kind. El would approach the men, arch her back and tilt her head as she spoke to them, often placing her hand on theirs arms or sleeves. She tended to coo more than speak. The Mackinaw brothers and I had a good time with it while Sterling and Moses, when he wasn't stoned, were disconcerted, to say the least.

I was surprised to see Moses flustered, but not Sterling. The more I got to know Sterling, the odder I thought he was. Rodrigo, for his part, felt the need to proposition every woman there to dance. This included my mother, Rebekah, Meredith, Emily's mother, Calista, Calista's wife, Andrea, Agnes, Denise, Emily, and, naturally, Astral, who hated to dance. That he was, more often than not, rejected did not deter him from continuing to avail himself of all the womenfolk.

When I mentioned this, Agnes reminded me I hadn't been much better at Calista's wedding the year before.

"It's important to be delightful," I reminded her.

Agnes smiled and shook her head.

The contingent from Virginia surprised me even more. Not only did Astral, who I was continually told to call Lilith, show up, but so did my mother, Rebekah Sr., who dragged along her husband, Donald, who I didn't expect to be there, and to my delight, had a great time. This might have had something to do with Moses being stoned for most of the weekend, which mortified my mother and aggrieved Meredith, Moses' common-law wife. Carlton and Leslie also came out, which led to a lot of arguments, mostly amenable, concerning politics, drugs, guns, and tobacco.

"You got quite a family here, Willie," he marveled to me after a fairly playful exchange between him and Moses on the virtues and vices of dope versus smokes.

"Yeah, I noticed that, too," was all I could think of.

Barron, Gerta, and Anna rounded out Agnes' side of the family, and the unexpected return of one Isaac Bohrman rounded out mine.

Isaac, having spent the last six years in Africa, nearly stole the show, much to the consternation of Meredith, Agnes, and possibly Rebekah. I couldn't say for sure, as her biggest concern was how much religion to put into the ceremony. The folks from Virginia were far more religious than those on the farm, and she and Agnes didn't want to offend them by being too out there, but didn't want to be too churchy either, which Rebekah didn't really believe in anymore. That also meant I wasn't allowed any extemporaneous comments during that portion of the show when I was to be permitted to speak.

"I don't think that's fair! I should be able to say what I like," I whined.

"No one wants to hear you make some goofy comments about this or that! Just be good, Buttman!" Both Agnes and Rebekah made a point of telling me this.

On the plus side, Isaac showing up early allowed Moses to get most of his crying over Jacob's death out of his system, and he perked up measurably when Isaac stated that his adventure in Africa had come to an end and he wasn't going back. He had gone to Africa because he was lovesick and over time discovered that love wasn't stronger than his desire to not spend the rest of his life in Africa. That and his wife had discovered her own affinity for African men that superseded her affinity for him.

The ceremony itself was a rather breezy affair that between us took no more than twenty minutes. This allowed more time to be devoted to the consumption of food and wine, of which there was an abundance, and the required embarrassment of family and friends. The four of us promised to be good to our respective spouses, as God would like us to be, and to not run off with younger, hotter babes, although that wasn't explicitly stated out loud. To love and cherish, and to put up with one another during those times when we got on each other's nerves.

The reception consumed the afternoon and evening with lots of toasts and commentaries. Moses, drunk and stoned, deciding this was the time to wax eloquent on the good works done here on the farm as well as out in Virginia, which surprised the Virginians, and then rant about the government that he felt had a hand in Jacob's death. Beyond that, there were the usual arguments that families get into when they drink too much, lots of dancing and laughter, and at the end of it all, a resolution that an intervention was needed the next day because Moses was getting out of hand.

The intervention was basically a shaming that, for the first time anyone could remember, had both Meredith and Rebekah Sr. giving the, for the most part, sober and contrite Moses an earful about his recent behavior and that just because dope was now legal in California didn't mean he could devote his time to being a stoned pest. Everyone was saddened by what happened to Jacob, but enough was enough. I pulled the Ezekiel and Dorothea card; his long-departed parents, and noted how disappointed they'd be if they were still alive. Chagrined at being the person who made the biggest ass of himself at a gathering of some pretty odd characters, he promised to do better.

The weekend came to a close with the usual promises to get together at some vague point in the future, Astral wanting to spend more time with Zach and Lizzy, my mother's serious concern that I was up to something, Donald not caring, and El and Rodrigo unhelpfully sharing why the Latin way, is the only way, to truly experience amour. It was the only time I noted Fidel rolling his eyes and shaking his head. Car and Leslie came back with us to experience the deviltry of LA, while Fidel and Rebekah left the kids with Meredith, Emily, and Astral, who decided to stay a few more days, so they could have a honeymoon camping at Yosemite.

All in all, an interesting weekend.

. . . . .

A week later, Meredith, Sterling, Isaac, and a less than thrilled Moses, were standing at our door in West Covina with thoughts on their minds.

"I thought you had some fancy-assed Beverly Hill mansion?" grumbled Moses.

"Moses!" Meri admonished him. Moses furrowed his brow, which made me laugh.

"Yes, I still have a fancy-assed Beverly Hills mansion, but I save it for business and family getaways," I answered.

"That doesn't make any goddamned sense!" More grumbling.

"Then my work is done." I looked at Sterling and Isaac, neither of whom seemed particularly thrilled either. I assumed that Moses had whined the whole way down. "First of all, welcome. And what can I do for you?"

They followed me through the house and out to the backyard where Zach was splashing his sister in the kiddy pool. Lizzy howled when she realized I was back and would ease her agitation with her brother by telling him to stop. Zach, well aware of this, stopped splashing her and instead made a face.

"Look who's here?" Meri cried.

Lizzy flopped out of the pool, much to Zach's relief, and crawled over to Meredith, who picked her up. I directed them to sit at the table under the neighbor's big tree.

"Didn't you know we were coming down?" Meredith asked.

"I must have missed that, but now that you're here…" Did I know they were coming down? I'd have to ask Agnes.

Meredith got right to the point.

"Well, Agnes said you were setting up a foundation in Jacob's name and I, we, thought that with Isaac back and needing something to do, and he does have experience with charities and foundations with his work in Africa, that there might be a place for him."

I looked at Moses, Sterling, and Isaac. It dawned on me that another dynamic might be in play.

"Am I then to assume that you don't want to return to the farm?" I directed this to Isaac. The look on all of their faces answered that question loud and clear.

"I'll probably spend some time there, but I feel like I can do more if I'm out in the world, and given what's happened, I think I can help. And because he was our brother," he motioned towards Sterling, "I think it would be a good thing if a family member was a part of it."

I raised my eyebrows at that but understood the message: a family member who actually knew him. "Yes," I said, trying hard not to be offended, "I can see how that would be important."

Meredith caught the joke. "I don't think he quite meant it like that, Monk."

"That's alright, and yes, Agnes is correct, I am setting up a foundation in Jacob's name to assist service members, particularly those who fall through the cracks, and fortuitously, the first meeting with my money man, a Mr. Macklgrew, is scheduled for tomorrow up at my fancy-assed Beverly Hills mansion. You are more than welcome to join us, and we'll see where Isaac can be of assistance." That sounded reasonably fair, I thought. "Where are you staying?" I knew the answer.

"Agnes said we could stay with you, Monk."

I imagine she did. "Then I assume she meant at the big house. I'll find out. In the meantime, can I get you something to eat or drink?"

They all grudgingly accepted.

My duplicitous wife deflected any admonitions about not giving me a head's up that we'd have company with the bromide that she was sure she told me and I simply wasn't paying attention, which I didn't admit to, but was occasionally true. However, in matters concerning Moses and the gang, I knew, as did she, that I would not be inattentive.

Once Agnes returned home from work and Rebekah came to claim her children, we loaded up the Bohrman gang and made our way to my fancy-assed Beverly Hills mansion. None of them had been to the house, mostly because they were busy with their own lives (Sterling), off to exotic continents (Isaac), or disinclined to leave their comfortable plot of land (Moses, and by extension, Meredith). I had food delivered and *allowed* Agnes and Meredith to make dinner for the always-discerning Moses.

"I don't know where this 'food' comes from," was his ready defense when pestered about such matters.

"You're becoming a bigger and bigger crank, old man," was mine.

Agnes gave them the grand tour of the house, including the library where Judith's portrait dominated the room. The usual murmurs ensued. I simply smiled as Agnes shook her head, but the Judith thing had lightened, and neither of us chose to bring it up much. For those who had never met Judith, or knew what she looked like, the portrait answered some questions while posing others that tended to go unspoken. Moses remarked that she was indeed a beautiful woman, while Sterling and Isaac took another look at me before nodding in agreement. Meredith wisely chose not to comment.

With the tour concluded, we sat out by the pool, had a glass of wine from the stash that Sterling had thoughtfully brought with him, and took in the sights below. It was odd to see my people, my family, some place other than on the farm. They weren't dressed for this part of town, nor were they comfortable in these posh digs, but death was still pushing hard on them, forcing them from their comfortable spaces and propelling them to my door and Judith's money.

Isaac was the one closest to being at ease. I hadn't asked too many questions about his time in Africa, other than where he had been. All over was his answer, though I didn't believe him. It didn't matter. He was, of Meredith's three boys, the most handsome; the only one to inherit her light blond hair. Though he was close to the same height as Jacob, Isaac was a touch lighter, wirier, and as he became more relaxed around me, the more subtle and more interesting aspects of his personality came to the fore.

He was, as Agnes noted to me later, far more at ease with women than his two brothers, and far more sexual in his demeanor, which made me wonder whether the story he told of his former wife, Allison, was the whole truth and nothing but the truth. He was also far more interested in the foundation that the others, certainly its intended value.

"If you don't mind my asking, how much money are you putting in?"

"A hundred million, and that's being matched by a grant from a fellow rich guy named Dunkle. There are a number of other donors putting in smaller amounts, so the total will be around two hundred and fifty million to start. The money, oddly, won't be the hardest part. That'll be getting the foundation up and running and finding or starting organizations that can have a direct impact on veteran's lives." I went on to explain the main focus was on assisting homeless vets and those who did not get honorable discharges and therefore didn't qualify for the same VA services as those who did. Like most people, they seemed surprised by that.

"How do you know they won't just steal the money or waste it on other things?" asked the always suspicious Moses.

"If they do, then they're doing it now because it'll be administered by the same people who take care of all my other oligarchic money concerns, and they're far more knowledgeable and craftier than I'll ever be in such matters. However, I think if they were thieves, sooner or later they'd be found out because I've discovered that all us oligarchs are extremely sensitive to what happens to our ill-gotten wealth."

Moses gave me his most severe look of disappointment.

"A smart-ass to end, Sunshine, to the end," he intoned.

That made me smile. I noticed Isaac was as well.

I began to wonder if Isaac would be more trouble than his father.

4

A gauzy morning light woke me from my slumbers. Stiffness and a lack of desire forced Agnes to prod and then assist me out of bed, and two phone calls, one from Bernie and one from Joanie, cast a long shadow on what should have been a fairly quiet day.

In retrospect, I don't know why I thought that.

And then there was Agnes and her father, Jerry...

Jerr, already on thin ice with his daughter and, I assumed, nursing a hangover, decided that the best way to start the day was by complaining about what Agnes and Denise were making for breakfast. I normally commandeered the kitchen, but with my mobility temporarily thwarted by the Screamer in the Beamer, a pun that had thus far elicited no laughs, I was firmly told to go sit on the couch. From there I had a front-row seat to the conflagration that ensued.

Agnes was already upset that Barron and Gerta, who had spent their honeymoon night down at the posh Beverly Hills Hotel, were taking Jürgen and Eva with them on their trek up the eastern side of California and not us.

"We can always go, but Jürgen and Eva are only here for a short time, so they're combining their honeymoon and her parent's visit," I told her.

That did not placate her growing frustration with her son and daughter-in-law.

"I don't need you making excuses for him, Buttman!" she ranted.

As so often happens in these matters, Jürgen and Eva, joining us from their room, and Barron and Gerta, returning from what I assumed was a night of glorious passion, arrived just in time to hear

Jerr bitch about his eggs and witness Agnes let loose with forty years of frustration and anger towards her father.

First, she took his plate, a rather expensive one at that, and slammed it down, causing it to shatter. She then did the same to his cup of coffee. Jerry foolishly stood and tried to speak. Agnes cut him off.

"That's it. That's it! THAT'S IT!" she screamed. "OUT!"

Jerr, like the rest of us, was stunned.

"I am done with you, you understand me?" She continued, her face beet red and spittle flying out of her mouth. "For as long as I can remember, you have cursed and complained and belittled me, and I am sick of it, and sick of you! Get out of my house, get out of my life, and FUCK YOU for blaming me for Simon and Barron and all of your other stupid fucking problems. I'm done with you, done with you, DONE WITH YOU!!"

Everyone stood there, unable to move except Agnes, who was shaking badly at this point.

That got me off my duff. Denise tried, as she had for far too many years, to calm the situation, but Agnes would have none of it.

"Don't you dare defend him! Don't you dare! He's been just as horrible to you—"

"Honey, please..." Denise cried, while the oblivious and offended Jerry stood there.

"You can't talk to me that way, Agnes Jean!" the moron whined.

Agnes Jean Duquesne grabbed the rolling pin from the drawer and threw it at her father. Fortunately, or unfortunately, her athleticism failed her and the pin sailed off towards the couch and bounced harmlessly to the floor. I moved in to keep Agnes from grabbing a knife and actually killing the moron while Barron wrapped his arms around his grandfather.

"Get out!" she continued, her voice hoarse from screaming.

"Let go of me, boy!" Jerry demanded of his grandson.

"No," was Barron's answer.

Jürgen, Eva, and Gerta had no idea what to do. Barron, holding tight to his idiot grandfather, had an expression of admiration for his mother that I'd not seen before. Denise was crying.

"Goddammit, Denise, all you do is cry anymore!" Jerr bellowed at his wife. "Let go of me, Barron. How am I supposed to leave this happy little party if you don't let me go?" Barron reluctantly eased his grip. Jerry shook himself, as if making sure he was actually unfettered. He then turned to me.

"She's not worth it. If you're smart, you'll find someone better." He followed that asinine remark by barking at the crying Denise. "I'll be in the car. You have five minutes to get our stuff or be left behind!" Having made himself plain, Jerry left the house.

And true to his word, he left the still crying Denise five minutes later.

To say that Agnes was mortified once the anger, grief, and frustration faded, and the Hated Jerry Fannis had left the building, would be something of an understatement. Denise couldn't stop crying to the point where Jürgen, still composed, gently urged his wife and daughter to help Denise back to her room. He then patted Barron on the shoulder, spoke softly to him in German, and excused himself, saying he wished to further investigate the house. Barron kissed his mortified mother on the cheek and began packing for their trip.

That left Agnes and me to the eerie quiet of the living room, interrupted only by the sound of chirping birds and the occasional aircraft high above.

"Maybe he's right," she said at last, her head deep in her chest.

"If you say anything that stupid again, I will brain you with this!" I held up the rolling pin I had retrieved from the floor. Agnes tried to smile, but failed.

"I ruined everything…"

"Well, possibly the eggs, but I didn't get a chance to taste them, so I'll have to withhold my judgment." Agnes glared at me. "Wow, tough room!"

"This is serious, Monk! I'm serious." Her head was in her hands.

"Sorry, but an occasional laugh can't hurt. As for ruining everything, I'm going to have to call bullshit on that." I put the rolling pin on the counter. "Now if you had started screaming in the middle of the ceremony, then maybe, yeah, but that didn't happen and let's be honest, you've been more than a little angry with your father, and as you almost always do, you've been holding it in for far too long. Maybe this was the perfect time to let loose. The wedding is over, as is the reception and the dinners and all that. This was just breakfast." I put my arm around her and tried to kiss her, but the brace got in the way. Agnes looked up at me, found a small smile at my predicament, and leaned in and kissed me.

"What's wrong with me, Monk?"

As I couldn't shake my head, I rolled my eyes. "You know exactly what's wrong with you. You have a very hard time confronting people you love or think you love or think you're obligated to love. Did you ever yell at Simon for jerking you around about being gay and sleeping with Eric?"

"No. Well, not till that time I went to San Francisco."

"And before this, have you ever said anything so direct to your father?"

Agnes leaned into me. "No."

"And all the others?" I didn't want to mention Jordan, who nearly beat her to death, by name.

"You know the only person I ever really raised my voice to was you."

"Yes, I remember," I said, "and it was long overdue." I remembered us sitting in the Falcon. Judith had died, and I was lost to self-pity. Agnes, tears running down her face, actually yelled at me. Told me to get my shit together, and that I wasn't going anywhere without her. "And I'm still here and still hopelessly devoted to you."

"Don't joke..."

"I'm not joking. I might be an ass at times, but some things are sacrosanct."

"I don't know what that means," she teased.

"Oh, I think you do…"

"So, what do I do now?"

I was surprised by the question, but the answer was clear.

"Like I would know, but I do think we should see how your mom's doing." She nodded, and we got up to find Denise.

Denise was still in her room, still blubbering, and it was obvious that Eva and Gerta had done all they could do and were anxious to get on with their trip. Barron and Jürgen hovered uneasily by the door. We took the watch and wished them a safe trip. I saw them to the door as Agnes consoled her mother.

It was then that Bernie called.

But the Bernie I knew wasn't on the other end of the line. The Bernie I knew would have had a field day with my reticence over going to the ER, and would have offered a half-assed eulogy for the damaged Falcon, knowing full well that I loved that car. Instead, all I got was someone telling me I should come down to talk about what could be done and whether it was even worth it.

"It's not exactly a collectable," he said in a flat monotone.

"Uh-huh. And you?" I asked.

"I'll think about it. Ten o'clock good?"

"Yeah," I muttered, disturbed by the tone of the call. "Should I be worried?"

After a long silence, he said, "Yes" before hanging up.

Agnes brought Denise out by the pool, where I was trying to figure out what was going on with Bernie. Denise tried to apologize, but instead began crying again. Agnes, again, apologized for starting this whole mess and I, having had enough, told them both to stop apologizing.

"It's got to stop because neither of you has anything to apologize for, alright? Denise," she looked at me while Agnes had her arms around her, "why don't you stay with us for a few days, give yourself a break, rest, and a chance to think things over, ok?" Denise nodded and wiped her eyes.

Agnes was confused. "You mean here or at our house?"

"Our house," I answered. "Plus, the kids will be coming over and they're always good for lifting one's spirits."

Agnes thought this over. "You know you have to see the doctor tomorrow?" Damn!

"When? I already have to meet with Macklgrew about Jacob's trust, and then Bernie about the Falcon—"

Agnes rolled her eyes at that. "There are more important things than that old car," she harrumphed. "You meet the doctor at nine tomorrow morning down at UCLA. We should just stay here tonight."

"But I need to watch the kids and you have to work..." I was clutching at straws. I did not want to go to the doctor's tomorrow.

"Rebekah can watch them and Johnny's decided to wind down his operations so it'll be ok if I'm not there."

"What do you mean, wind down?"

"Monk," she was becoming exasperated, "you're not getting out of it."

"I don't want to go!"

"Tough," she said in a voice I knew meant I had no choice. "You're such a baby sometimes."

I smiled at that. Agnes frowned for a moment until she realized I was just being an ass to lighten the mood around the pool. She smiled back at me. "You're still going."

Damn!

I phoned Bernie to say we'd have to move our meeting to the afternoon. He didn't seem to care. Agnes poured Denise and herself a glass of wine and before long, they were both napping by the pool, exhausted by the morning's traumatic events. I wanted to nap, but that was when Joanie called.

"Buttman," I groaned.

"Why won't you talk to me?"

"I never said I wouldn't talk to you..." which was correct. I was avoiding her. "I simply assumed that now that you have your new life with Brian, there was no need for me to be offering any more unsolicited advice, that's all."

It was her turn to groan. "Jesus, Monk, I…" She hesitated, and I half-expected her to hang up, but no such luck. "I'd like to talk to you. I'm sure you're busy now with everything, but you know I don't have many friends and that, well, that… You know what I mean. I'd appreciate it."

I wanted to make a very loud exhibition of my lack of desire to hear about how her latest relationship was going down in flames, but Agnes and Denise were asleep…

Damn!

"I should have some time on Tuesday. Lunch maybe?" I offered.

"Just you, right? No kids or anything like that?"

Oh brother! "Just me."

"When?"

"Around noon…"

"Where?"

Good lord! "Our old sandwich shop."

She groaned again. "You're kidding, aren't you?"

"Nope. See you then." I hung up and sighed.

The rest of the day was mercifully quiet and uneventful. With the house empty, save for the three of us, it was easy to let it pass without comment. Jerr didn't call, but no one expected him to. He had beer and frozen pizza in the fridge, so why would he need Denise and if he got lonely? He had plenty of porn, this from Denise, which did and did not surprise me. I made a light dinner, and we sat around the pool listening to Jazz and taking in the evening light show from the city below. It still hurt to move around, but not so bad that I still needed a lot of pain medication; a lesser amount was doing the job. This allowed me to have a long-desired glass of whiskey as I sat with the Fannis women.

The Court Jester was still on the table next to me. Fidel must have tired of it or was too often pulled away by what the kids were up to. I picked up the book and decided to try one more time to get through it.

After two chapters and a glass of whiskey, I gave up.

The next morning an invigorated Agnes dragged both Denise and me through breakfast, then hauled my whiny ass down to the UCLA Medical Center so I could be examined and prodded by a preeminent quack.

"You should be so lucky!" was her response to my idle quack comment. "If you'd prefer an actual quack, I'm sure we could find one for you, one that specializes in leeches and blood-letting."

"That's pretty harsh, Aggie!"

Aggie smacked my arm. "Tough." She parked the car and helped me out. "I expect you to behave, Sunshine. Understand?"

"You're a jerk, Duquesne!"

"I learned from the best," she smirked.

The doctor, an intense young woman named Sunita, examined me, reviewed the images on the computer, and despite my protestations, informed me that the brace would have to stay on until the bones healed. Agnes frowned and rolled her eyes only a couple of times while I complained, but spent most of the time going over the instructions for my care. It was going to be a long eight weeks. We thanked the doctor, scheduled our next visit, and headed back to the big house. Agnes was already making plans for Denise's stay with us and I was wondering whether the percolating concern for Isaac, by Dunkle, and possibly Macklgrew, was growing or abating.

That they were all there when we arrived, intimated more friction in the house of Judith.

5

Macklgrew warned me, but I had Meredith to deal with and didn't expect Isaac to be the locus of various people's ire.

"While I do appreciate that you feel an obligation to your family, and that perhaps there is merit in having a family member as part of the foundation's board, you yourself would fulfill that obligation…" He paused to make sure I was listening. "Having pointed that out, my experience is that caution early in the process will save any number of headaches later." Oddly, Carson Macklgrew did not have that playful glint in his eye that normally complimented his advice to me.

I knew he was right, but as I said, my hands were tied.

I rationalized my way out of that wet paper bag by giving Isaac the job of scoping out the entities that would, upon hearing of our foundation, make a play for some cash. That part was working out. The part that wasn't became evident at the first meeting when I thoughtlessly introduced him to Natalya Constantinescu, who, growing more confident as my front in the world of art patronage, maneuvered her way into the position of my executive assistant, whatever that meant.

Xavier Dunkle II was also present and by the end, given Isaac's attentions towards Natalya, not pleased that this interloper might make a play for his gal. He, naturally, did not make his concerns known to Natalya because he was still treading on uneven ground and at that point, their relationship consisted only of a few dates and meetings. Instead, he made his fears and jealousies plain to me.

"How could you do this to me, Monk?" he growled under his breath. "You know how I feel about her!"

I did a poor job of hiding my disdain. "For chrissakes, Xavier, you're a grown man, not some fourteen-year-old. Have some faith and a little inner strength."

He didn't care for that, but held his tongue.

Today's gathering, much to my relief, was without Isaac, who I was told was in DC collecting info from the VA. Natalya, tasked with preparing the house for the meeting, was surprised to find Denise there, but not overly concerned. That changed for her and for Macklgrew when they set eyes on the man with the neck brace. Dunkle, who had arrived moments before Agnes and I, spoke for the group.

"What the hell happened to you, Monk?"

"I hurt my neck pleasuring Ms. Duquesne," I said. The group then turned to Agnes, who shook her head.

"You wish, Buttman. Now tell them the truth." Apparently, Agnes was in no mood for mirth.

"Wow," was all I could think of. "Alright fine, I was in a car accident the other day, broke a few bones, that's all."

Dunkle started to grin. "In the heap?"

I frowned at his suggestion that the Falcon was a heap. "It's a classic, dude."

"No, the Jag is a classic. That old Ford is a heap."

Why was he here again? Natalya must have noticed my annoyance and ushered us towards the library.

"We have work to do, boys." This from a woman barely in her twenties.

Without Isaac, the meeting lacked any real frisson and instead, as meetings with Mr. Macklgrew often did, marched along with military precision. It turns out that Carson Macklgrew was also a vet, having served a stint in the Air Force.

"Operations," was his reply when I asked what he did in the Air Force, which answered nearly all the questions I might have previously had.

Dunkle spent the meeting mooning over Ms. Constantinescu, who ignored him. He knew she was all business when it came to business, especially mine, but he mooned away just the same.

"It's embarrassing," I told him pointedly.

"Yeah," was his sheepish response.

During the meeting, it was decided that modest office accommodations for the foundation were in order. After all, Macklgrew noted, philanthropies of this size shouldn't be run out of someone's home. Or, he added, the house would have to be turned into the foundation's headquarters, which the neighbors would never approve. Xavier was more than happy to provide the necessary office space for the foundation and, more importantly, Natalya, who felt she needed her own office now that she was a bigger cog in the Buttman machine. I rolled my eyes, but said nothing. Agnes smirked when I mentioned it.

"Serves you right, loverboy." Probably.

With the business at hand completed and the participants scattering, it was time to gather up the despairing Denise and head to our much smaller house in West Covina. She was out by the pool, thumbing through the small leather-bound book. Macklgrew had followed me and asked what she was reading.

"Reading? Oh, heaven's, I scarcely understand a word of it," she said, handing it to him. He looked it over and smiled.

"Have you read it?" I asked. He raised his eyebrows before handing me the book.

"It's the answer to a good many prayers," he said, "assuming, of course, you know the right kind of prayer to ask." The smile disappeared.

"I don't know. You need a prayer just to get through it," I glibly replied.

"Then imagine yourself as Socrates and his Philosopher Kings." The smile returned as he said his goodbyes. Socrates?

Denise looked at me and the book. "Who's Socrates?"

"Greek philosopher. The main character in the dialogues of Plato, another Greek philosopher." She stared blankly at me. "It's not important."

Agnes gathered the meager belongings of her mother after lunch. I tried to help, but was told to sit down. "No lifting, Buttman; you heard the doctor."

"I don't like this," I muttered.

"Don't care. Help mom to the car."

"I thought I was supposed to sit down..."

Agnes crossed her arms. "Is this how you're going to be?" she demanded.

"I'm always like this. It's in the contract."

She wanted to be miffed, but that made her laugh. "Sometimes, Buttman, sometimes..."

That made me laugh.

With nothing left to say, I escorted Denise to the car. I didn't like taking the Mercedes, too ostentatious for the other house, but there was no way to fit the three of us, and our belongings, into the Jag. Denise settled in, caressed by the fine leather seats. I got in the driver's seat as Agnes closed the door to the garage.

"You're not driving!"

"Oh, yes, I am. Get in."

"Monk!" I ignored her.

"Agnes!" She stood there for a moment. "Let's go."

"Ugh," was all she said as she got in.

The afternoon and evening were shot through with Agnes and Denise arguing over what Denise ought to do concerning the omnipresent Jerry Fannis. I smartly grabbed a beer and attempted, for the third time, to read the leather-bound volume that I had absent-mindedly brought with me. Since tries one and two were failures, I took Macklgrew's advice and presumed a need for beknighted oversight. It worked until my attention was interrupted by the two women arguing just inside the kitchen. I had taken my sorry ass to the backyard, but more often than not, my attention was lured back by the conflict inside. Having scaled new heights by getting through the first three chapters, short as they were, I put the book down and joined the wife and her mother in the kitchen.

"What do you think, Monk?" Denise was staring at me.

I think it was a mistake to leave the backyard.

"Yeah, Monk; what *do* you think?" Agnes had joined her mother in the stare down.

"I think I need a nap."

"Monk!" No laughs today...

"Well, given that I know only what Agnes has told me and what I've observed over the last few months, it seems to me that this might be a good time to step back and try to evaluate your relationship with Jerry. Think about what you want, what you feel you have, and whether the two can come together."

Agnes shook her head. "That's what you think?"

"Hey, I'm not a professional, you know, but I do what I can." I raised my eyebrows for effect.

"You're a jerk, Buttman."

"Perhaps, but a jerk that loves you." I smiled. Agnes simply frowned. "I know you want me to tell your mom that it's time for her to dump the Jerr, and maybe she should consider it. I'm sure you also told her not to worry about money because quote, 'Buttman is loaded'." I looked back and forth between them. "Still, it's your mom's decision and if she wants to wait and see if Jerr is going to come to his senses, or something like that, then I think we should at least give her some time."

Agnes was undeterred. "He treats her terrible. He's mean and spiteful. He doesn't do anything to help at home. He just sits there while she does all the work—"

"You make it seem like there's no hope," Denise countered.

"You can find someone better—"

"Like you did? What good did it do you? *I don't want that.*"

Agnes recoiled at her mother's words.

I quickly realized she wasn't talking about me, but Jordan. It didn't occur to me that her parents were well aware of her disaster with him. Agnes stood up, tears rolling down her cheeks.

"That's not fair."

"But it's true and you know it!" The pleasant Denise I knew morphed into someone I didn't. Agnes started to shake.

"Then go back! Go back to your sad life and your dead heart!" She stormed out of the kitchen.

Denise looked at me, not knowing where to go with what she had started. "Doesn't it bother you knowing what she did?"

I tried to shake my head.

"No. Agnes has paid and paid for her mistake, and it's not my place to judge her. Besides, she's always been good to me. And before you get into any more of a knot over this, remember that it won't change how I feel and it won't help your problems, either."

She looked out towards the backyard. "Maybe I should go," she said at last.

"That's up to you."

Denise retrieved her belongings and stood by the backdoor staring out at Agnes, who was sitting with her back to the house. "Goodbye, dear," she said. Agnes didn't answer.

It was a long quiet drive to the house Denise shared with Jerr down in Anaheim. I wished her good luck and waited until she was inside. Agnes was still sitting in her chair under the neighbor's tree when I got back. I poured a glass of wine and handed it to her as I sat down in the chair next to her.

"Are you mad at me?" she asked.

"Why would I be mad at you? Usually it's the other way around."

"I don't know. I don't know anything anymore." Her head was back in her chest.

"At least you're not stuck wearing this thing." I lightly tapped on the brace. Agnes turned towards me.

"Does it still hurt?"

"Yeah, but it's tolerable," I assured her.

"Kinda like me..."

"Kinda."

"I just wanted to help." Her voice trailed off. "I don't know, something..." She took a drink from the glass.

"Yeah, but I also think you wanted them to see that you were ok, that you weren't the fuck-up everyone thought you were."

She took another drink. "They still do..."

"Have you ever talked about any of that other than with me? I mean really talked about what happened?"

Agnes gave me the queer eye. "To my family?" She turned back to the wine. "I was too ashamed... I still am. Besides, what difference would it make? You heard what they said. I'll always be Agnes Jean, the big disappointment. The fuck-up."

I leaned over and kissed the fuck-up's cheek. "Well, you're still ok with me, Agnes Jean, and you are doing much better with Anna and Barron, which says something about how far things have come."

Agnes Jean smiled. The tears were back, making their journey, once again, down her sorrowful face. "You're the best thing that's ever happened to me, Sunshine, and I love you more than you'll ever know..." She tried without success to stop the tears. I smiled back.

"I knew there was a reason you put up with me." I reached out and held her as best our being in two chairs and confined in a neck brace would let me. I let her cry for a while before taking her into the house. She cradled in next to me as we sat on the couch listening to the radio. She continued to tell me she loved me until she fell asleep. I just wanted this goddamned brace off. I tried to concentrate on something other than the stiffness radiating across my shoulders, but it won out as cramps began digging into my back. I woke Agnes, and we made our way to bed, where she held on to me for dear life. The bed and the strategically placed pillows kept the cramps at bay till the dope sent me to la-la land.

A false move woke me at three in the morning and after a moment, I realized Agnes was gone. Concern and a full bladder got me out of bed and I found her back in the chair under the tree. I sat down next to her, not wanting to state the obvious. A lifetime worth of sadness lined her face that was once more wet with tears. Agnes Jean Duquesne pondered the stiff with the neck brace before returning to rubbing her hands and compulsively wiping her eyes.

"I once told you I wasn't a very good person, remember?"

"I remember. Is that what drove you out of bed?"

She stood, took a step, and then dropped to the ground. I got up to help her, but she waved me away. "Don't..." Agnes sat up, stared at her dirty hands, and wiped them on the tee shirt she was wearing. Her hair was in her face, which she made a half-hearted attempt to brush away before staring up at me. "I think you'd have been much better off with Judith..." I wasn't going there. She must have recognized that and moved on. "Did I tell you that MaryAnn took me to a therapist?"

She hadn't.

"It was after Jordan and before you. I'd been drinking, and she was late to meet me one night at the bar, so I... I hooked up with a guy who was there. After he finished, he left me on the curb, which is where she found me. She wasn't angry, just disappointed. I had promised to stop, but... Anyway, she dragged me to talk to this woman. Turns out I have a lot of anger issues that I've avoided through bad relationships, drinking, and self-loathing..." She tried again to move the hair out of her face, but wasn't having any success. The frustration was getting to her as she brushed at it again and again. "I just want to be a good person, I just want..." Agnes put her face in her hands and started sobbing.

"Let's go inside..."

"NO," she spat. "Just leave me alone."

I went into the kitchen and made a pot of coffee.

There was nothing else to do.

6

Rebekah arrived at eight with the kids. Zach was his usual bundle of energy and Lizzy, who, unlike her brother, was not a morning person, just wanted to go back to sleep. Rebekah looked around, expecting to see Agnes.

"She's still asleep, bad night," I explained.

"Oh... Is this about the other day? I heard she got mad at Jerry." Interesting how the word gets around.

"That and more."

Rebekah pondered that. "Is it ok if we're a little late for the next couple of days? Some of the shoots have to stretch into the evening."

"It's ok."

"Are you ok?"

"I'm ok, sore and tired, but that's the way it goes." I don't know if she believed me. She leaned in and kissed me as she handed Lizzy to me.

"We'll see you tonight." She didn't seem too sure about that either. The three of us waved as Rebekah reluctantly returned to her car. Zach was itching to get out his box of goodies that were stored in the hall closet. I knelled down, so we were face to face.

"Grandma Ag is sleeping, so I expect you to play quietly, capeesh?" I put my finger to my lips. Zach responded in kind. I put Lizzy on the couch and she promptly clocked out. It amazed me how quickly she could fall asleep. Zach and I played with his Lego set while the women slept. Agnes shuffled out of the bedroom a couple of hours later.

Earlier, while Zach was pulling his box out of the closet, I had called Johnny D to let him know that Agnes might not make it in today. Johnny didn't seem either surprised or terribly concerned. There were other things going on.

"It's good you called. I wanted to talk to you. Rey is sick."

"Is it bad?" Rey was no spring chicken and had developed an alarming cough over the last few months.

"It's not good. He's in the hospital. Ask Agnes to call me when she has a moment."

"I will."

"Thanks, Monk." That left me with images of Rey standing in the bar, the TV glowing behind him.

Agnes got herself a cup of coffee before carefully sitting next to the napping Lizzy. I made a mental note that it was time to wake her up. Agnes must have thought the same thing because she picked up Lizzy and cradled her until she woke up. I watched as she held Lizzy and whispered into her ear, causing her to laugh. Other than adding a robe, Agnes looked just as she did when she called me back out into the yard while I sat in the kitchen some six hours before.

"Monk, I need you," she whispered. I was surprised I heard her.

She was lying on her back with her panties in her hand and her legs apart. I looked around thinking this probably wasn't a good time for sex in the backyard.

"Why don't we go inside...?"

"No," she said, reaching for my hand. "I'll be quiet, I promise."

I was skeptical. Agnes was not a quiet woman in the sack, unlike Judith, who was far more controlled. But they did share a common trait in that they both shook violently when they reached orgasm. Agnes pulled me down, tore at my pants, and with an unusually urgent tug, put me inside her. It felt as if all her anguish and frustrations were powering her desire as she grabbed and clawed and held on to the point where it was hard to breathe. She cried as she shook and climaxed, refusing to let go or stop apologizing no matter how many times I asked her to stop. Finally, her strength gave out, and I had to use what was left of mine to get her back to bed.

Except for the hard breathing, she didn't say a word other than sorry.

She sat there with Lizzy as I was trying hard to shake the memory of our early morning tryst out of my head.

"How's your neck? I didn't think about whether you were ready for..." She looked at Zach, who was busy with his Legos. "I was kinda—"

"Yeah, I picked up on that. It's ok. Still sore, but it's going to be whether I like it or not. Last night didn't seem to do it any more harm."

Agnes smiled and kissed Lizzie's forehead. "I'm glad to hear that."

"I'm going to meet Joanie for lunch at twelve, and then I have to go over and talk to Bernie about the Falcon. Is that alright?" Usually, whenever the name Joanie came up, Agnes would reliably provide a glassful of whine for me to enjoy, but this day she simply nodded.

"Do I have time to get cleaned up?" she asked

"Sure, and I'll make some lunch before I go."

"Ok." She kissed Lizzy again before putting her back on the couch, rubbed Zach's head, which made him look at me in wonder, and returned to the bedroom.

It was grilled cheese and tomato soup for lunch. I pushed the envelope a little by trying to use the best bread and cheese the kids would actually eat; same with the soup. Agnes loved the stuff and was always a happy camper on those days when grilled cheese was on the menu. Even today, when she was so obviously mired in sadness, she brightened as I handed her the sandwich and soup.

"Aren't we lucky today, kids?" she enthused.

"Yep!" shouted Zach.

The best Lizzy could do was, "Ep."

I had concerns about leaving, but I didn't want to have to reschedule or drag out either the car or Joanie. I kissed the kids and Agnes, who started to tear up.

"I'll be back this afternoon, alright? There's water in the pool and snacks in the fridge. And everyone takes a nap. That means you too, Zach!" I pointed at my recalcitrant grandson, who stuck out in tongue in protest. Agnes got out of her chair and hugged me. She started to say something, then stopped. "I'll be back," I assured her.

"Ok."

I stopped just as I got to the door. "You need to call Johnny."

Joanie texted twice. I was late, and she was oddly fearful that I was blowing her off again. As with the good folks at the board meeting the day before, Joanie was shocked to see me in the neck brace. It was as I expected. The first time was always, "Oh my God, Monk, are you ok?" which morphed into, "Oh my God, Monk, what have you done now?" I used to wonder if I was that bad, but now I've kind of accepted that I am.

"Car accident," I replied. I figured there was no point in alluding to injury during the act of lovemaking.

"In the beater?" she asked.

"It's a classic," I admonished. What was with everybody?

"Uh-huh. You know if you'd been driving a normal car, your neck wouldn't be in a brace."

"Yeah, yeah, yeah. So, what's so important that you needed me to talk to?"

She didn't care for that. "Be nice for once." Her brows furrowed. "You know I don't have many real friends, and like it or not, you're one of the few..." The sadness of that statement radiated between us.

"My apologies. How are you this fine day?"

"That's better." She sat back and turned her eyes to the menu, which was no different from the last time she was here with me, the day she left the Moonlight Arms for those of Brian Whalen. "I hear you *finally* married Agnes."

I rolled my eyes.

"Did you *finally* marry Brian?"

Joanie waved her ring-adorned finger at me. "I did!"

A period of silence, save for the construction going on across the street, divided us as we decided what to eat for lunch. It would be a Rueben and onion rings for Monk Buttman. Joanie flip-flopped between a pulled pork sandwich and a salad before going with the

Caesar. I peered through the window at the massive structures being raised on what was once a quiet couple of city blocks. The buildings were at least five stories high and there were six that I could see and count. It appeared that they were surrounding a center courtyard that was, as yet, nothing more than a large dirt pit. Gloom overtook me.

Joanie was looking out as well. "Have you heard from any of the people who used to live at the Arms?"

I was surprised by the question.

"I can't imagine why I would. I'm the ogre who sold the place out from under them."

"Well, that's true," she laughed, knowing full well her complicity in the matter.

"Yes…" I was not so amused. The waitress arrived to take our order.

"How's Mikal doing?" was the next question once the waitress had left.

"He's having the time of his life. He wants for nothing and gets to do all the things he's longed to do for years, and he's getting paid for it, too. He considers me the greatest guy around. There are concerts and open mics, seminars from local artists and luminaries; this is LA after all, and Mikal seems to know everyone in town. The big names help keep the books from being overly in the red, and the classrooms and rehearsal rooms are almost always full. We have shows and concerts booked through next year. He has rewarded my willingness to spend some of Judith's fortune by making a lot of people very happy to have a place to do their thing. It's too bad you don't sing anymore—" I caught myself. "Do you still sing?"

"Not lately," she said, pretending it was no big thing, but as one of her only friends, I knew she was lying. Prior to meeting the man of her suburban dreams, Joanie did nothing but sing. It was the reason she was even in LA to begin with.

"Then you should come down. Mikal would love for to you sing with his group. They perform every other Tuesday at seven. I'm sure he still has the arrangements he made for you."

"Yeah, maybe..." Mikal was the one big fly in the ointment of her new life, and both of us knew it. I was still disappointed that she ran off with Whalen. Maybe she felt obligated since she helped him finagle me into selling the Moonlight Arms, and it put a substantial amount of money, something she'd never had before, into her possession. Fucking money!

"Think about it and then come down," I told her as the food arrived. Her eyes tightened, which, as I knew, meant she knew I was right.

"I said I'd think about it..." Fake peevishness.

"Uh-huh." I rolled my eyes. More silence followed as we consumed our lunch.

• • • • •

The drive to Bernie's, slow as it was, mingled with the replaying of Joanie's words in my head. She looked better. The strained, thin woman was gone, replaced by the quiet dyspeptic one I had lunch with. The common trope dancing around with her words was that of a songbird in a cage, but I wasn't so sure. Maybe she was just lonely. I couldn't imagine Brian being the kind of guy who spends a lot of time at home and where else would Joanie spend her time? It's possible he made the same suggestion to her that I did: Sing!

But what about Mikal? My head and neck ached.

Bernie's shop was in view. Joanie's problems would have to wait for another day. My beautiful Falcon sat forlorn at the end of the lot next to the frame of what had once been a hotrod. I parked the Benz and stared at it. The damage was far more significant than I remembered. The back of the car was smashed in, the tires flat. I looked in the trunk; the spare was flat too. After a minute of mournful silence, I noticed Bernie and Javier standing off to the side.

"It's not good, my friend." Bernie put his hand on my shoulder. "The rear-end is cracked, as is the drive shaft and the clutch. The frame is bent, and given that it wasn't the most popular car of its time, not really worth what it would cost to fix it. And yes, I'm aware you have a few extra dollars in your pocket should your sentiments get the best of you. But I would gently move you towards buying something else to replace it."

"Like what? I already have the Jag and the Benz, but those were Judith's. There's the truck, but it's a truck. I liked having my cheap little Ford convertible..."

"I have a car you might like."

Ah-ha! "Oh, I see where this is going! You're just looking to make a sale," I joked.

"No, nothing like that," he replied with deadly seriousness.

They both stood there, composed, yet nothing like their ordinary selves. For a brief moment, I was certain the world was tilting and we would all fall down.

"Alright, what's up with you two? You were odd on the phone the other day, and Javier was the same way when we dropped off the car. And now, you don't even try to blow off one of my asinine comments. That ain't the Bernie I know. And while we're not intimate buds, I know something's not right here. We're talking about the Falcon! You have dogged me for years about that car and now that it's finally on the trash heap, you're acting like a used car salesman with no life and no future."

Bernie turned to Javier, who shrugged. Bernie nodded and tried to smile.

"Let's go in the office," he directed. We followed him in. After Bernie and I sat down, Javier excused himself. Bernie stared at me while tapping a pencil he had picked off the desk.

"What?" I asked.

He continued to tap the pencil on the desk. "How strong do you think our democracy is, Monk? Do you think it could survive an assassination, a coup?"

I waited for a smile or a laugh. Nothing. He was serious.

"It has before," I answered. Whatever I had thought might be bothering him did not include politics.

"True," he sat back, "but that was when we had stronger leadership and a more organized and less fractured political environment. We live in a time of actors, not statesmen, and that historically breeds trouble."

"Yeah, but we've survived that, too. What's so different now?" I had my own ideas, and I certainly didn't expect to be talking about society coming apart, but Bernie rarely weighed in on such topics, and both my concern and interest were piqued. That, and given my suspicions as to his real occupation here at Bernie's Repair Shop, I wanted to know what he'd heard.

"The high levels of distrust in our leadership and the government are deeply troubling. The lack of brevity in the national news, the proliferation of fake news, and the speed with which it travels. An ennui that we're not what we think we are, and a business elite very concerned with the direction the country is taking," he said.

"Isn't that the SOP, anyway? Everyone bitches, but the moneyed class still pulls the strings?"

"Normally yes..." He stopped and focused on the pencil in his hand.

"But?"

Bernie Schoor continued tapping the desktop, the clandestine gears whirring behind his light brown eyes. He'd never actually confirmed my suspicions as to the depth of his information gathering inclinations. I knew they were far more extensive than the little he did for me concerning Desiree Marshan and my other misadventures. Whether he spied on the government or worked for them with the shop as a front, I didn't know, and up to this point, didn't care. Maybe I shouldn't have asked?

"There have always been individuals unhappy with the way this country is governed and invariably there has been talk, mostly idle talk, of changing that," he said to the pencil. "But there has also always been a small contingent of individuals or societies, whether overt or covert, that have actively sought to subvert or radically change how our democracy works."

Bernie put the pencil down and leaned in towards me, those brown eyes focused behind the wire-rimmed glasses. "I have made it my life's work to monitor these individuals and groups, and that's not easy because for the most part they are very secretive and not prone to advertising their views publicly, but word always filters out. There's no way around that if you're searching for confederates to your cause, and lately, especially with the tenor of our politics these days, we've discovered a more determined effort to subvert our democratic process."

Really?

"To what, a dictatorship? A Kleptocracy? Seems kind of farfetched, if you ask me."

Bernie smiled at that. "And they would ask you! For you are what they would see as more enlightened, more engaged, not just intellectually, but, more importantly, in a financial sense, as a person of wealth."

"Sounds like they've been reading that silly book Dunkle gave me," I quipped.

Bernie's smile disappeared. "Silly only to those who think the author is a crackpot. But if you're referring to *The Court Jester*, then you deeply underestimate Ashley Carmichael and the people who finance and believe what he writes."

"How do you know about that? Dunkle and the book, I mean?" I was beginning to wish I hadn't broached the topic of Bernie's obvious funk.

"Our Mr. Dunkle likes to play the two sides of many coins. He finds it stimulating, and it allows him to indulge his internal conflicts over his family's wealth as well as agitate others, but he is playing a dangerous game with these people. The book is no joke, nor are the people associated with it."

"Ok, so they're serious about subverting the democratic process and putting themselves in charge, but one, isn't that treason, and two, rather fantastical in actually trying to make it happen?"

Bernie continued to bore in on me. "What of your friend, Mr. Jones, and the young politician he asked you to support?"

What? "Montgomery?" I asked.

"Yes, Jontaveus Montgomery. He's an intriguing young man, isn't he?"

"I suppose... What are you suggesting, that he's in league with these people you say want to overthrow the government?" This was nuts! It was time to go. Bernie picked up on my incredulous vibe and sat back.

"I'm saying something isn't right in any of this, and yes, I'm saying he's involved with the people associated with Carmichael and his followers." He got up. "Why don't we look at the car I'm trying to force on you?"

"Yeah..." Anything other than this!

7

My head was spinning...

For many reasons.

The car was sweet and Bernie knew I couldn't resist, even if I tried. It was an emerald green 1968 Dodge Dart GT convertible with a white interior.

"Something of a restomod, but only so far as the drivetrain and brakes go. We rebuilt the engine, a nice 426, which we retrofit with fuel injection, updated the electrical, and the brakes are all discs. The body's clean, no rust. Take it for a spin."

I did, and, despite feeling oddly manipulated, drove it home. At some point, I had to get the Benz, but Bernie offered to deliver it. It was all taken care of. I didn't know if Agnes would care for the bucket seats in the front; she liked the bench seat in the Falcon so she could sit next to me, but it was an automatic, no more grinding the gears.

Too many changes too quickly.

The spinning only got worse.

I hadn't expected to find MaryAnn at the house, but Agnes had had a bad night and MaryAnn was good for commiseration when Agnes needed it. They'd met at a support group years before for families dealing with sons and husbands coming out of the closet. Like Agnes, MaryAnn equivocated about her son's sexuality, or more precisely, his sexual activity and its relationship to love.

"It's not the sex per se," she replied when I pressed her on how it was anymore discomforting than sex between two women, something she had owned up to participating in. "It's the lack of desire for the opposite sex that I don't get." That and she considered her son's husband a priss.

"Rey's gone, Monk." Agnes looked up at me.

I was shocked: I thought Rey would live forever, but not surprised. After all, none of us do.

"Sorry. Johnny said he was in the hospital and that it was bad." Agnes got up and put her arms around me. Zach and Lizzy, who were on the couch with Agnes and MaryAnn, came over and hugged my and Agnes' legs in solidarity. "We knew Rey was sick, and it's not like he suffered a lot..." I was babbling.

"Johnny's shutting everything down: the business, the bar. He said he's already got a buyer for the property." Agnes was crying. "I don't have anything to do now."

"Why don't we sit down?" I suggested. MaryAnn came over and we moved into the kitchen. Zach was tugging on my pants, his non-verbal means of saying he was hungry. "The kids need to eat. Do we cook or just get something?" I knew the answer...

"Pizza!" shouted Zach. He knew it, too.

"I'll order." MaryAnn was taking charge. It all works out.

. . . . .

"I like it," was MaryAnn's response to what she thought of the Dodge.

"Too bad it doesn't have a bench seat," bemoaned Agnes, who was in a better mood after three healthy sized slices of pizza and two glasses of wine.

"It's an automatic," I said.

"So, I can drive it?" What a question.

"No."

Both Agnes and MaryAnn frowned.

"You're a jerk, Buttman."

I just laughed. "It goes with the shirt."

"What you two need, what Agnes really needs, is a vacation. Why don't you take her on a road trip in your new hotrod, Monk?" MaryAnn had her arm around Agnes' waist. "Go to the desert. It's nice this time of year, get away for a while. I know I would." She added a wink, so I'd get the message.

MaryAnn was what my reformed hippie conservative mother would call a wild woman. Thrice married and now single, she had men friends; her euphemism for lovers, and was more than happy to fill Agnes in on what was the hip new thing happening sexually in the great wide world. She was tall, five-ten, shapely, with sharp green eyes and a penchant for colorful highlights in her "blond" hair. Today she was sporting purple. Before I sauntered into Agnes' life, MaryAnn did what she could to keep Agnes from her demons as concerned abusive and thoughtless men. Given that, she considered me to be an ok guy.

"For a jerk, he's not so bad," was her typical response when Agnes would rag on me for reasons unknown.

"I spose," was Agnes rejoinder.

"Are you sober enough to drive?" I directed this to Agnes, who was surprised.

"But you just said—"

"Yes or no?"

"Yes!" She smiled as I handed her the keys. We piled in. I sat in the back with the kids. Lizzy had to sit in my lap due to her being too small for the lapbelts common to cars of that age. Agnes only screeched the tires twice before getting a feel for the throttle and the drivetrain. "It's got some pep!" she noted as we took off down the street.

Half an hour later, we pulled up to the home I so generously bought for Rebekah and Fidel. Becks had texted that she was at the house and where were we? Racing around was my reply, and that we'd be bringing the kids home.

She and Fidel came out to pick up the kids and find out what was making all that racket. I just stood there and smiled. The exhaust had a nice throaty tone, but was not loud, certainly not by hotrod standards.

"So, this is your new heap?" My daughter quizzed me as I handed Lizzy to her.

"I don't own heaps. I own classics!"

Rebekah merely smirked. "Uh-huh. It's nice though," she mumbled as she wandered around the car. "Seems to have more room that the Falcon." I noticed Fidel running his hands along the straight lines of the hood.

"Want to take it for a spin?" I held out the keys.

"Sure!" His eyes lit up.

"Great, it needs gas," I informed him. He just smiled and jumped in. Rebekah, with Lizzy in arm, joined him. Zach hadn't left the backseat. We waved as they zoomed off.

"Do we wait or walk back?" asked Agnes.

MaryAnn pointed to the heels on her feet. "I'm not walking back in these," she groused.

Fortunately, there was a bench on the front porch, something else I had so generously paid for.

"Enough with the whining about a few bucks, Buttman," admonished the woman sitting next to me.

"A little support would be nice." Wishful thinking on my part.

"Yeah, yeah, yeah…"

MaryAnn's mind, however, was somewhere else.

"So," she had that mischievous grin on her face that I knew meant trouble, "have you reconsidered my proposal? You know, the three of us?"

"No!" was Agnes' stern reply. I merely shrugged when she looked at me.

"You shouldn't be so closed-minded, my dear." MaryAnn laughed as she patted Agnes' thigh.

"No," Agnes repeated.

Fate, in the form of the young family who lived in this house, interrupted any further talk of threesomes and the like.

The rest of the evening involved more somber thoughts of Rey, what would happen to Johnny D's hole in the wall, and its effect on Agnes. Neither MaryAnn nor I were terribly concerned. Agnes would be all right. She duly noted that we were probably correct and then complained that we could be more supportive.

"I know how that goes," I said.

"Oh, be quiet, Buttman!" Man, what a grump. MaryAnn bid us farewell.

"Well?" I asked as we closed the door, just because.

"I said no and that's that," she huffed.

I laughed. "So how long has this been a topic of conversation between you two?" Tonight was the first I'd heard of it.

"I don't want to talk about it, ok?" Agnes glared.

"Ok." I saw no point in poking the bear.

• • • • • •

The sunrise woke me, and with the previous day's conversations merrily bouncing around my thick skull, I had no option but to get moving. Agnes had no problem staying in bed. A shower and coffee allowed me to better concentrate on the verbosity and obtuseness of the book I had so cavalierly mentioned to Bernie and Mr. Macklgrew. It wasn't till the fifth chapter, nicely titled *The Way,* that the pieces began falling into place.

Impulsively, I rang up the dear Mr. Jones.

"Are you up?" I asked.

"I work for a living, Buttman. Of course, I'm up." I found his mild irritation comforting.

"My apologies. I was curious. Have you heard from Mr. Montgomery lately?"

"Jontaveus?" He seemed surprised.

"Yes."

"Hmmm, last I heard, he was in DC making noise and pressing the flesh. Why do you ask?" Why did I?

"His name came up in a conversation I had with Bernie Schoor yesterday, and like I said, I was curious." I could picture Orville looking me up and down, wondering what I was up to.

"He's the intelligence guy runs the car shop, right?"

"Yep." I don't think he liked that.

"I don't like this, Buttman! He's a good kid, lots of promise."

"I'm not making any aspersions, merely noting his name came up, so, anyway..."

"Uh-huh, you busy Thursday night?"

Was I?

It was then I noticed Agnes standing by the door. "I don't know? I leave all that to Agnes and Natalya..." Agnes was smiling. I cupped the speaker on the phone. "Am I busy on Thursday?" She made a big show of checking her phone.

"Yes, we're meeting Mr. Jones at the Manifesto," she smirked.

Groan. "Apparently, I'm meeting you at the Manifesto on Thursday," I said to Jones, who laughed.

"You're something else, Buttman. Tell Agnes I said hello and I'll see your sorry ass Thursday." He hung up.

"Thanks," I grumbled to my delightful wife. She shrugged as she got herself a cup of coffee.

"It's kinda different to see you wearing something other than a shirt and tie." Agnes had moved next to me, running her fingers along the collar of the Hawaiian shirt I had on. "Did you take off the brace when you showered?" I noted a slight change in tone as she asked.

"It's easier that way and it's only for a few moments," I was aware this was breaking the rules set out by the Doctor.

"You're supposed to keep it on, Monk; even when you shower. It's so your bones will heal."

"Yeah, yeah, yeah..."

Agnes smacked the top of my head. "Don't you dare yeah, yeah me, Monk Buttman. You're going to follow the doctor's instruction, is that clear?"

"You're not my mom, you know!" I protested for effect.

"Tough! Did you eat yet?"

"No, I was waiting for the kids to get here. Are *you* going to make breakfast?" Agnes rarely cooked at home.

"Be nice for a change," she demanded.

"I don't know. Sounds like a lot of work."

Agnes stood there, contemplating the doofus in the chair. "Ugh!" was all she had.

As I suspected, my daughter was in a rush and assumed that we, Agnes and I, could feed the kids. "Have you eaten anything?" I inquired.

"They'll have something there," she said.

"Uh-huh." I handed her a mug of coffee and an egg sandwich that Agnes had made. "Late again tonight?" Rebekah smiled and kissed my cheek.

"Sorry," and off she went. The kids jumped in their chairs, or Zach did. Lizzy still needed a boost.

"Well, at least they're busy and making money," I said to no one in particular as Agnes was serving up breakfast. The three of them looked at me as I stood there. With nothing left to say, I sat down and enjoyed Agnes' morning grub.

Having successfully made an ass of myself to Jones, I felt the need to repeat the exercise with Dunkle. It was he who had handed me this silly book, or what I had assumed was a silly book, and now that the picture had darkened, I had some questions. The kids were in naptime and Agnes was over at Johnny D's.

"Monk," Xavier, glib as always, "I'm honored."

"As you should be, but beyond that, I'm finding some very interesting reactions to that book you gave me, *The Court Jester*."

Silence.

"Are you there?" I asked.

"What kind of reactions?" his voice had softened.

"That depends. Have you ever met this guy, Ashley Carmichael?"

More silence.

"Are you at your little house?"

"Yes," I assured him.

"Maybe I'll stop by. Later." And with that, he ended the call.

．　　．　　．　　．　　．

Agnes was sitting in the lawn chair opposite me, her eyes flitting between me and the two kids splashing in their dinky plastic pool. She hadn't said anything about Johnny after coming home. She hadn't, in fact, said anything; she simply came out and sat down. The kids made a few noises in her direction before going back to their play. My two previous attempts at questioning having gone nowhere, I decided not to push my luck any further.

"Johnny's taking Rey back to Colombia with him. He's having a small service tomorrow if you'd like to go." Agnes reached out for my hand.

"I'd like that," I said as I took her hand.

Zach, usually generous with his sister in the pool, was becoming agitated. Lizzy had grabbed his favorite flotation device called a torpedo bandit. He stood there ready to rage against this grave affront to his pool time. With a furrowed brow and an indignant pout, he turned to me and shouted, "I wanna go to the big pool, Gamps!"

Agnes and Lizzy turned my way as well, all of them looking to me for the answer.

"Thursday," I informed them. Zach didn't know his days yet. "The day after tomorrow." His grimace did not lessen. "Lizzy, let Zach have his torpedo..." Lizzy laughed and held the torpedo close before offering it back to her brother. Zach grabbed the toy and sat down, somewhat mollified.

Agnes tugged at my hand. "You're not going to ask?"

"About what?" Johnny? Rey? The bar?

"From yesterday," she said while watching the kids.

"You seemed pretty emphatic that you had no interest in discussing it, if that's what you're referring to."

"Yeah, but I changed my mind."

"Talking or doing?" Seemed like a fair question to ask.

"Talking," she replied rather sternly. "I don't want you getting any ideas."

"No, we wouldn't want that." I expected a rebuke, but...

The doorbell rang.

8

Xavier Dunkle II entered the "little house," his term for our home here in West Covina, after checking for any suspicious activity in the neighborhood. I didn't notice any. He made nice to Agnes, who *was* suspicious, and the kids, who ignored him. I offered him a beer, and we retired to the living room, which was the only semi-private place in the house except for the bedrooms and the bathrooms.

He was oddly anxious.

"Penny for your thoughts" seemed appropriate.

"Clever," he mused, "but it might take considerably more than that."

I laughed. "I was under the assumption that you had that consideration taken care of." I picked up the small leather-bound book. "Have you read this?"

He seemed surprised by the question.

"I read it."

"If I remember correctly, you were far more animated and, I don't want to say dismissive, but somewhat contemptuous of its contents and assumed I would be too. It appears that has changed."

"Have you read it?" was his response.

"Most of it. All that's left is the final few chapters—"

"What did you think?"

"About what?"

"About its premise?"

"That decline is inevitable, as is change, as is the need for those in possession of their faculties to utilize them for what is best for the republic by whatever measure is required? That?" I leaned in.

My visitor did as well. "Yes."

I sat back and took a swig from my bottle. "Carmichael is hardly the first savant to conjure the end of the American experience. The more interesting aspect is this wave of angst I'm finding in normally bubbly subversives. Bernie believes there's more to all this than a self-published polemic that very few people have read. I mean look at you and your reaction." I tapped the top of the book. "Is your phone off?"

Dunkle smiled. "It is, and yours?"

"It's in the kitchen, too far for prying eyes, or ears."

Dunkle simply shook his head. "That's what they want us to believe," and he was serious.

I wasn't sure now how to pursue this. I was looking for a few laughs, possibly at Bernie's expense, but like everyone else I'd encountered lately, the laughs were few and far between. "So, what happened? Something, otherwise why even stop by? Why the concern for eavesdroppers on our idle talk?"

Xavier Dunkle II was thinking, thinking hard. This wasn't our usual repartee, and he had yet to bring up Isaac, something he had not failed to do from the first day Isaac made his presence known.

"Times change," he began. "Circumstances, events, the kind that call into question, *for some*, whether we're drifting into decay as a country." His voice was nearly a whisper.

"Really?"

"Really! Look at the atrophy in Washington, or its dysfunction. Little gets done, and now this new administration that's borderline lunacy is making a mockery of what this country is supposed to stand for. There are a lot of very unhappy campers out there, Monk, and I'm not just talking about college kids or the morons in the media..." Dunkle looked out towards the kitchen as though half-expecting someone to pop out before looking back at me. "I know you think this is bullshit, but the people I refer to are the people who own this country, whose lives and fortunes are built on it, and who have been very unhappy with its direction for some time..." His eyes were losing their focus.

"Are you one of those people, Xavier?"

That brought him back, but not his unctuous smile. "No, but I live with them and have heard this rant for most of my life. I thought it was cute, given the source; the very people pulling the strings whining about a lack of control, but this is different. It feels different, out of control."

"Is something up? Are there plans afoot?"

"I won't say."

I didn't think he would. "Would Carmichael say? Of course, he doesn't actually explicitly state that the jig is up, but it's certainly implied."

Dunkle shook his head. "No, he likes to be careful..."

"Then you've met him?"

Xavier turned his head slightly. "Yes, he lives out in the desert, off the grid. I got an invite through my uncle, so I went with him, thought it might be fun to be the fly in the ointment, but I lost my nerve. Sometimes even I have to be careful around certain people..." He stopped, picked up his warming bottle of beer.

"Like?"

Dunkle raised his eyebrows before speaking, "Ever heard of a man named Delton Manaforte?"

"Nope."

"That's not surprising. He's very much a behind-the-scenes type. He isn't interested in being in the public eye, but he comes from money, big money, and has backed a considerable number of startups in the tech biz among others; startups that are now worldwide players. In fact, most of the companies he's aligned with have worldwide holdings and do business across the globe. He also has little tolerance for nativists and isolationists or for government intrusion and regulation. Anyway, he is, if I am to interpret the signals correctly because no one will say it out loud, Ashley Carmichael's chief benefactor and champion."

"Sounds like a typical A-type."

Dunkle grinned at that. "They all are, but Manaforte is different. You should ask Durant about him sometime. As for Carmichael, he enjoys acolytes, but you can't just show up; he requires a letter of introduction in advance before he'll let you into his compound." Dunkle set down the beer. "Are you interested?"

"It's been recommended that I take a vacation to the desert. Maybe the answers are there," I said, not thinking it all the way through.

"Maybe." He stood up.

"You didn't say what exactly you're concerned might happen in our democratic twilight?" I thought that clever.

"That night is falling, my dear Buttman, that the experience is over."

He wasn't joking. No one was joking.

Xavier said goodbye to the still suspicious Agnes as I picked up the unenjoyed beer. We bid him farewell under the bright California sky.

"Did he come to complain about Isaac hitting on Natalya?" Agnes thought that was both funny and deserved. Older men should not be pining for young girls.

"Nope, never uttered the name Isaac. Or Natalya, for that matter. He had other things on his mind..." I let the phrase linger.

"Like what?"

I smiled lasciviously at her. "Like what your good friend, MaryAnn, was getting at."

Agnes groaned and smacked my arm. "It's a good thing I love you, Buttman."

"Yes, it is, my love; yes, it is."

. . . . . .

As with the previous day, dinner would have to be provided, but unlike the previous day, that dinner would not be pizza. Zach sulked, Lizzy was unperturbed, and Agnes consoled him by saying that life doesn't always go the way we want. On the plus side, the kids were not terribly finicky about what they *would* eat, and I made more healthy approximations of the glop they found alluring on TV or that they were introduced to by Agnes, queen of a certain brand of American cuisine: hotdogs, PBJ's, mac and cheese, grilled cheese, burgers, and of course her favorite, pizza.

"You're a real buzzkill, Buttman!" was her standard refrain on such matters. She was right, but I refused to be a party to producing fat, unhealthy grandkids.

Moses would be so proud.

Rebekah, pregnant and exhausted, shuffled in around ten. The kids had long gone to sleep by then, something their mother desperately needed.

"Did you eat?" was *my* standard refrain to my petulant daughter.

"No," she pouted, as only an exhausted, pregnant woman can do.

"You know," I felt compelled to continue, "you don't need to pump out a child every year; it's what killed off the women-folk of yonder times."

Rebekah was not amused. "Are you done?"

"He's done!" Agnes interrupted before I made the situation more amusing. "There's still some dinner," she added, leading Rebekah to the kitchen. I followed at a safe distance.

"Fidel's still working?" I asked, though it was patently obvious he was unless he had cravenly deserted Rebekah, and she was keeping it from us. For the time being, I considered that patently absurd.

"Two more nights. The schedule for this shoot has been insane, but they're almost finished. I get a break tomorrow, so I can watch the kids."

"Why don't you let them sleep here tonight and once you get some rest, we can bring them over," Agnes advised as she refilled Rebekah's plate, the first having been consumed in literally minutes.

"You sure?" For some reason, she looked at me.

"Absolutely," I assured her.

"I really appreciate that." She then returned her attentions to the food before her. After thanking us once again, she shuffled off to her car and drove the two blocks to her house. If it had been any further, we wouldn't have let her go.

The day was over. Agnes was running her finger along the contours of the brace.

"How's the neck doing?"

"As long as I don't dwell on it; it's ok. I'm tired of it, it gets in the way, but so long as you and all the other health Nazis keep pestering me, it's not going anywhere!" A trapped man's lament.

"I know you don't like it, but I can't see how obstinacy and paralysis are a better option. Besides, it's important even if it is cutting into our love life." I noted the disappointment as she spoke.

"Speaking of which, can we talk?" I turned my head as far as I could so I could see her face. She smiled and leaned in and kissed me.

"I don't want to talk about it," she purred as a tease.

I decided not to bring it up anymore.

•   •   •   •   •   •

The remembrance for Rey, held at a better class of bar down the road from Johnny D's, was quite interesting. Reymondo Alonzo Melendez d'Orr turned out to be a far more colorful figure than I would have ever thought. He was eighty-six when he died, the lost member of a fairly well to do Colombian family, a onetime revolutionary, and cousin to one of John Dulcimer's great uncles. Several long-time patrons of Johnny's bar were there, but the more fascinating were those who had known Rey long before he made his home behind the counter serving drinks and watching the place.

Agnes and I dropped off the kids at noon. Rebekah looked a little more with-it, but was a touch cranky on the assumption that a crass remark was on the lips of her beloved father. I merely wished her a quiet day. Fidel was still asleep, having not made it home till five in the morning and was due back at four in the afternoon. The kids were happy to see her.

Johnny D came over upon seeing us arrive. He thanked us for coming and promised a few minutes later. He didn't look much better than Rebekah! We mingled. Quite a few people I didn't associate with

Johnny's bar came over, being familiar with Agnes as one of Johnny's fronts. It was from them I learned of Rey's past.

"Tough" was a common description of those times and of the man.

"He was captured, tortured, spent many years in prison, but never denied his family, though they denied him." This from a fellow named Ramon. "Yet he held to his convictions, even in exile..." Ramon didn't expand on what those convictions were, but most revolutionaries of that time were communists or socialists.

"It was Johnny who brought Rey along when he came to the states. He had the connections to keep Rey from being deported, and he was family, you know," was the answer to one of my questions about how Rey ended up in West Covina. There were stories of living in the jungle, of raids, of a wife and child lost to a reactionary's bomb. As I listened, I didn't think it strange at all that they were talking about a man I knew only as an octogenarian bartender in a rundown dive.

Johnny came over towards the end and embrace both Agnes and me, surprising, as Johnny was a known hands-off guy. We stood for a moment, observing the crowd. "It warms my heart that you two have found each other; it makes it easier for me to go," he said at last.

"Should I ask why you're going?" I was curious, something he noticed.

"Family. I have responsibilities now that I didn't have before, and the situation in Colombia has changed. I hadn't planned on taking Rey home this way, but..." His eyes misted up. "But maybe it's best this way. I find America is changing, becoming more insular and unhappy. It's too bad."

"You can always return," advised Agnes. Johnny smiled at that, but it was not an engaged smile.

"Perhaps," was his reply. His melancholy echoed the persistent vibe I'd been getting recently.

"Man," I blurted out, "what's with the world these days? Everyone's bummed or worked up? Some even talking like the end is near, and that's people with all kinds of money!"

A more genuine smile came to John Dulcimer.

"The rich are never happy, never content, are they? Some even complain of their easy earlier lives, of simplistic endeavors now seemingly lost..." Both he and Agnes were giving me the eye.

"Yeah, yeah, I might be guilty of that. But I'm not thinking it might be time to do away with democracy in this country." The minute I said that, I worried I'd be considered an alarmist or a crackpot. Agnes shook her head, but Johnny did not.

"Have you been hearing things, Monk, things certain people whisper?" Johnny asked.

"I have, and from people I would never think of believing that kind of talk." I wanted Johnny to laugh it off, but...

"I come from a land where that is never just idle talk, and it concerns me when I hear it here, and I have heard it too. I know it sounds outlandish, certainly nonsense, but like you, I hear it from serious people with serious interests..." He looked down for a second, then took our hands. "But that's just talk. Don't worry. You promise me you'll take care of one another? No more foolishness from either of you?" His grip was firm and his eyes unwavering.

"You know we will, Johnny," Agnes assured him. "We're going to miss you."

A last smile from Johnny D. "And I, you." He turned, took a few steps before turning back towards me. "You once asked me about my part in the Marshan affair, Monk, remember?" I knew he was baiting me.

"No, I had a few questions, but I never asked."

John Dulcimer nodded.

"He was my grandfather." And with that, he walked away.

9

Agnes didn't get it.

We were standing by a table with two pictures of Rey, one recent, the other a black and white from many years before.

"What question did he answer?" she asked.

"The great man, murdered for his hidden money. You remember?"

A crossed looked slowly morphed as she put two and two together. "Johnny set that up?" She seemed surprised.

"He was part of it, yes, as was his uncle and Marsyas Durant, among others."

"Oh..."

Oh, indeed.

.   .   .   .   .

The ride back was quiet. We passed the once and future mall that had housed the bar and the money business, where Agnes had worked for so many years trying to put her life back together. The sign announcing the imminent demise of the property and its new beginnings as a mixed-use apartment complex was affixed to the temporary fencing that had been quickly erected two days before. Agnes sighed.

"Maybe a vacation is in order," I said, basically to move any conversation away from the past, recent as it was.

"Yeah," was all she said.

·   ·   ·   ·   ·

The last task of the day took us to Bernie's to pick up the Benz. I appreciated the offer to deliver it, but it belonged at the big house, and no one was there to let them in, and we had to head that way anyway to meet with Anna for dinner. Wednesdays were her day off and once a month, whether anyone wanted to or not, we got together to eat and argue about whatever happened to be bugging either Agnes or Anna or both. Mikal was a hot topic for a while, but that cooled because Anna refused to discuss it. Period. This exasperated the wife, but there was little she could do about it and I refused to play the intermediary.

Then came Isaac.

"What do you think about Isaac and Anna?" Agnes threw this at me while I was daydreaming about the beach.

"He's busy driving Dunkle nuts," I answered.

"That's not the answer I'm looking for and you know it!"

"No?" I knew better.

"No!" So did she.

I thought long and hard and came up with nothing. "I think that would be up to them," was all I had.

"Is that all you've got?"

"Sorry."

Agnes was unamused. "Sometimes, Buttman, you're no help at all," she huffed.

"I thought that was a given?" sprightly offered, I might add.

She remained unamused. "Your phone is buzzing." Her annoyance shifted to my laissez-faire attitude towards answering my phone.

"It's just a text—"

"BUTTMAN!" she shouted and then smacked my arm.

Some people are never happy.

I pulled the Dart into the parking lot at Bernie's and pulled out the phone; the text was from Jones: *Call!*

"Yes?" was my response when he answered.

Mr. Jones' attitude mirrored the annoyed woman sitting next to me. "Not in the mood, Buttman! I need a favor. I need you to ask that friend of yours, Bernie I think is his name, what he's heard about Jontaveus." I thought the irony rich that he would ask as I sat in front of Bernie's shop.

"Should I ask?"

"I ain't got time for your goofy shit right now, ok! Will you do this for me? We can talk tomorrow." I could hear the worry as he spoke.

"My apologies. As luck would have it, I'm at Bernie's now, picking up the car. I'll ask." Jones mumbled something and hung up. I looked over at Agnes, who was looking back at me.

"Problems?" She arched her eyebrows.

"No problems," I said.

. . . . . .

Jontaveus Montgomery was introduced to me by Jones at the Manifesto a few months back. A large group from his church was there to hear a jazzed-up gospel choir. He was an engaging young man with energy, drive, and that air of confidence that makes you believe he's got it all worked out. Age told me he didn't, but his enthusiasm was infectious, and his calling was politics. Not the sour angry politics eating at everyone I came across, but one of deliberation, of service, of community. He had no time for either party or their tired platforms and endless arguments. No, his focus was right here, right now; a blend of the helping hand and the resilient, creative soul.

"People need opportunity, real opportunity, not the kind that makes others feel better about themselves," he preached. "Wealth generation is the only way we're going to get ourselves of out of these cycles of poverty and government assistance can only do so much. That doesn't mean it can't help, but we can't be reliant on people who don't really know us, who can be capricious or thoughtless, whose priorities can change with the wind, and all their promises blow away like so much fairy dust."

As he spoke, he reminded me of the Moses of my youth. "Governments don't change minds that aren't ready to be changed. Right or wrong, people don't like to be pushed or lied to. We know what must be done, and we know where that help, that support, can come from. But the language can't be the same as it's been because it's caustic and heavy with anger and resentment." His face lit up as he spoke.

"And how is now any different from, say, fifty, sixty years ago?" I asked.

He smiled at that.

"Just look around. How many mixed couples do you see now? How many mixed babies, mixed ethnicities, mixed religions, mixed cultures? That's how. That didn't exist back in the day, but it exists now. The more we interconnect, the more the old ways continue to die out. Blacks are more demanding, sure; maybe some don't like that, but our voices have to be heard. And I believe more of America is receptive to that than you might think, so long as you aren't waving fingers in people's faces, ours, or yours. People don't like that, but they do believe in a sense of fairness. That's how you attack that! And all the people in the closet who are out now, out and proud; you didn't see them sixty years ago, but you see them now. They're not the devils or pariahs people thought they were, and people like me, people my age, don't fear them or castigate them. That's why. Is that true of everyone? No, but there's a wave of acceptance that will continue to wash over us no matter how much some may hate it, that's why."

Orville Riley was clearly taken with Mr. Montgomery, so much so that he was willing to push the idea that I might send a little support Montgomery's way.

"Maybe it's time for new leadership, Monk. You know I don't like asking, but you got the means and I believe Jontaveus has potential," he enthused. I was trying to remember the last time he used the word Monk.

Carson Macklgrew was not so enthusiastic. Politics was a poor substitute for thoughtful market analysis and politicians were always begging for money and support. "And there's no guarantee they'll come through in any way. If you're going to give your money away, at least with your family and friends, you have fewer illusions," he warned.

But, like Jones, I found Montgomery an interesting young man, so despite Macklgrew's misgivings, I put some money in the Jontaveus Montgomery political action kitty.

●   ●   ●   ●   ●

Bernie was in his office staring at what I assumed were papers related to the business of repairing vintage automobiles.

"Hey Bern," Agnes called out. Bernie smiled at that. Only Agnes called him Bern.

"Dart working out?" He directed this to Agnes.

"Yep, Joy-Boy here is even letting me drive it!" she said with an unnecessary level of glee.

"Interesting." He directed that at me.

"Yes," I harrumphed, "it's quite the seismic event. We're here to pick up the Benz and ask a favor. Well, actually, I'm asking for Jones."

Bernie's eyes lit up.

"And what would the esteemed Mr. Jones be asking of me?"

"Whatever you might know about Jontaveus Montgomery..." I let that hang in the air for a moment. Bernie's eyes did not dull.

"Really?"

"Yes, and, to make your day even more interesting, Dunkle asked if I wanted an introduction to Ashley Carmichael and I said I did." A little icing on the cake.

I could see Bernie was intrigued. "What's going on in that head of yours, Monk? Bored, aching for some excitement?"

"Let's just say that with what I've heard lately, maybe I should check it out for myself."

"Really? And what do you think about this, Agnes?" Agnes wasn't paying attention.

"Umm..." She looked at me, but knew by my expression that I would be of no help. This made her frown. "Monk has been his usual forthcoming, so I have no idea what you're talking about."

Bernie laughed.

"It's good to know some things never change!" He sat up and put his hands together. "Ok, I'll see what we have that I can share on Mr. Montgomery, and I want you to get in touch with me before you go out to the desert to talk with Carmichael, assuming he's willing to talk—"

"Why wouldn't he?" I interrupted.

"Maybe the better question is why *would he*?" Bernie got up and walked over to the cabinet holding the keys to all the cars here at the shop. He sorted through a few before handing me the fob. We walked out to where the Benz was. I noticed that the Falcon was gone. "Sorry, Monk, but it's off to be scrapped."

"Yeah..."

He put his hand on my shoulder, "Like I said, get in touch if you're going to see Carmichael. There will be things to do first."

"I wouldn't want it any other way," I said, certain I was making a mistake.

•　　•　　•　　•　　•

"Should I be worried, Sunshine?" Agnes was tapping the door panel of the Dart as I closed the garage door at the big house. Anna was waiting to meet us down the road at a restaurant called the *Lauranne*.

"Any more than usual? Probably not..." I got in the passenger side and set the lapbelt.

"That's not very reassuring," she grumbled.

"No?" I said with a slight lilt to my voice. "Well, at least this time you get to join in the adventure."

"Again, not very reassuring." She put the Dart in Drive and we were off to more familial excitement...

... Which included not only Anna but also Denise. Agnes visibly tightened as we approached them. They both rose as we neared the table.

"I know I should have warned you, but—" Anna started.

"It's my fault," Denise added. "Please don't be mad. I came to apologize for what I said." Agnes simply stared at them. "Agnes, please..."

Agnes Jean looked at me. I shrugged as I pulled out a chair for her. Agnes took her time sitting down. Deep unease permeated the table as a bottle of wine was ordered and menus desultorily reviewed. Anna looked at me, hoping, I assumed, that I had something magical in my pocket to break apart the gloom. I did what I could to convey I had nothing. Denise kept her head down and Agnes simmered near her boiling point. Our waiter, duly noting the gloom as he poured the wine, made several reasonable suggestions based on the few monosyllabic responses he received to his questions. Anna and I were circumspect; Denise and Agnes, weary and angry.

"How would you like to go out with Isaac, Anna?" That brought all eyes to my corner of the table. Agnes groaned, Anna laughed, and Denise didn't know what to say.

"I don't know. Did he ask you to ask me? I mean, he didn't strike me as the shy type like Jacob..." She stopped as she said Jacob. "Sorry, I mean, why do you ask?"

"It came up in a different conversation and this silence is deafening, so I'm just throwing that out there." I looked over at Agnes, who was now mad at me as well as her mother, who couldn't stand being ignored.

"Agnes, I said I was sorry! Can't we not be angry all the time?" Denise was ready to add tears to our already joyful dinner.

Agnes glowered at her mother. "I'm tired of being treated like I'm some horrible person. *I'm* the one he nearly beat to death. *I'm* the one with the reconstructed face and the nightmares, not you. Isn't that enough? Why must you constantly throw it back in my face?" She was shaking. "I don't want to be angry with you, but enough is enough, whether it's you or anybody else. I don't want to hear about it anymore."

"Mom," Anna reached out and took Agnes' hand, "it's ok. I promise, ok?"

"You were right, Monk." Denise was wiping her eyes.

Agnes again turned my way. "What does she mean?"

Denise reached out tentatively for Anna's hand, the one resting on Agnes'.

"It's not like that, dear. It was what he said. It's been ringing in my ears and he's right. I forget how badly you were hurt and how angry Anna and Barron were and, and how I stayed back because I was ashamed, but that was me, not you. Monk's right, we have no right to judge you, and I understand that you meant him, and it was mean of me to bring up Jordan..." Denise pulled her hand back to staunch the tears running down her face. Agnes reached under the table and gripped my hand. I noticed the hint of anger at me had changed. I smiled at her and nodded. Sometimes I get it right.

The waiter had returned and was trying to ignore the blubbering and distemper at the table. He pointed out what we had ordered in case we hadn't actually been paying attention because I had no idea what I had ordered. We thanked him and ate in silence. Since Isaac was a bust, I asked Anna about the Manifesto, even though I already knew everything I needed to know just to hear voices not from the crowd ignorant of the pain at our table.

"We're going tomorrow. Maybe you'd like to go, Denise," I said.

"I'd like to, but…"

"Come along," Agnes told her. "It'll be alright."

"I'll make you a great dinner, Grandma," added Anna.

"I'd like that," she said.

"Ok," I interjected, sensing an opportunity for my fine brand of humor. "Now that that's resolved, are you ready to talk about you and Mikal, Anna?"

Anna smiled at me.

"No!"

It was worth a try.

10

Much like dinner, the drive home was somber and still, with little said. Occasionally, Agnes would look over at me as if there were words to share and then turn back to the ever-pulsing rhythms of the Los Angeles tangle of interstate highways. My neck throbbed, but I too was silenced by my idiotic desire to drive, even though my range of motion was curtailed by a restrictive plastic brace.

"Wouldn't it be better if I drove?" was Agnes' plaintive argument as we approached the car.

"It'll be alright," I assured her without really giving it any thought. Now, my pride and stupidity were on the line should I own up that she was right.

But she was lost in thought.

It was possible that she wanted to know what I thought of her lack of entreaties to her mother, but wouldn't I bring up her daughter's lack of the same not that many years ago? Knowing me answered that question!

She once again turned to me as I pulled the Dart into our carport.

"Maybe a vacation isn't such a bad idea, but the desert?"

"Well, we could always go up to Michigan." Wait for it...

"Michigan?"

"Yeah, I have a house there, on the lake, remember?" My beloved Agnes frowned such that I couldn't help but laugh.

"No, I don't. When did you get a house in Michigan?" I found her umbrage oddly endearing.

"It was part of the Judith package. I figured I should check it out at least once. Might be fun," I teased, well aware that bringing up Judith might not be the smartest move.

"Why didn't you mention this before?" She seemed surprised.

"I thought I did." I couldn't actually remember.

"We'll start with the desert," she said with just enough tartness that I again laughed. "Not in the mood, Monk!" Monk being one of her general signifiers, much as Buttman and Sunshine were: It meant *watch it!*

"Yes dear. As soon as we can free ourselves of babysitting duty, we can take off. And the desert is nice this time of year, not so hot—"

"I said ok!" she harrumphed and headed into the house.

I stifled a laugh.

· · · · ·

The next day followed form with me rising first. Agnes threw a pillow at me as I roused her, and after a few choice profanities, she rose as well. Rebekah, rushed as ever, dumped off the kids and mumbled something as I handed her breakfast. The kids, used to this by now, watched as their mother headed out and then found their places at the table. Zach decided to help his sister into her highchair, and, with a little assistance, declared it a great success.

"Yes," he bellowed after ably maneuvering himself onto the booster in his chair.

Today, it turned out, was Pancake Day with blueberries and whipped cream, demanded by the oldest kid in the room, Agnes. Normally we had oatmeal on Thursdays, but someone was in a mood.

"Bite me," was her rejoinder to my scolding about adding so much sugar to the meal. "Besides, at this point, a little more sugar is the least of my worries."

"My apologies. I'd forgotten how unbearable your life has become. Everyone be nice to our poor, poor Agnes today, ok kids?" I directed this to the two children who were more interested in their fluff breakfast than in my efforts to bug grandma.

"You're a jerk, Buttman," she spat before sticking out her tongue. Zach laughed at that.

"It's important to have a plan for the day." I ignored the childish display on her part.

"Being mean isn't a good plan!" More umbrage from the aggrieved Ms. Duquesne. I chose to ignore that, too.

After breakfast and a few more barbs from both sides, we adjourned to the park at the end of the block. There we joined three other moms and their five kids. I blissed out to the howling and shouts of the kids, and the small talk between the moms of which Agnes was now a part. The topic of their conversation was unknown due to my own disinterest, and theirs in having me be an active participant. If I heard my name, I instinctively knew to nod in agreement, as the one asking was invariably Agnes seeking validation for whatever point she was making. Being the older mom; she disliked Grandmother, she felt the need to dispense, as judiciously as possible, the font of her knowledge on the ups and downs of dealing with children.

The font of *my* knowledge on the ups and downs of dealings with children went unexplored. I was ok with that.

Midway through my reverie, the phone began jangling, and I answered it just as Agnes turned to me, no doubt irked at the exceedingly slow pace with which I am known to answer the phone. It was Bernie.

"I have the information Mr. Jones asked for, and, if you're serious in going out to see Ashley Carmichael, the equipment you'll need for your trip."

"Equipment?" That sounded ominous.

"I'll explain when I see you, which will be...?" So did his serious tone.

"Later today. Thanks." I put the phone away. My bliss had been taken by the wind, which was blowing an odd sense of angst my way. For a moment I worried the glum that was infecting those around me was circling, intent on adding me to the party. Fortunately, my grandson broke that thought, wanting to be propelled on the swing he was in and was bellowing my name.

Just like his mom. I spared the moms this font of wisdom.

"Who was calling?" Agnes asked as we were walking back to the house.

"Bernie, he's ready for us." Zach was swinging my hand in his.

"What does that mean?"

"That our new adventure is about to begin."

Agnes merely rolled her eyes.

· · · · · ·

For once, Rebekah came to claim her children in the early afternoon. I informed her of our impending vacation to the wilds of the California desert and that other arrangements for childcare would have to be made.

"Ok," was her response. She found it cute that I expected her to be more upset. "It's actually a good time because our shooting schedule for the next four weeks doesn't require my being there, and at some point, I'm going to have to slow down, anyway." She pointed to her expanding belly.

"You barely have one out of diapers and another will be here soon!" I felt it important to harp on the subject.

"I guess," she said with a big smile, knowing it bugged me. "On the plus side, with all the work, Fidel is thinking it might be better to go ahead and hire another tech. That way I can take care of the kids, and if I have to do any company stuff, I can do it from home. That way, you won't be so burdened." That got Agnes going, which Rebekah expected.

"It's certainly no burden, right, *Monk*?" Sweet gullible Agnes!

"I don't remember using that word," I smirked.

"Didn't you?" my daughter smirked back.

"No!" I was certain I didn't. My grandkids were a lot of things, but a burden was not one of them.

"Well," she cooed, "thanks for watching the kids. When are you leaving?"

"We'll let you know," I cooed back. Rebekah laughed, which made Zach laugh, which made Lizzy laugh, which made Agnes groan.

"You're something else, Buttman," she said after our guests had left.

"Yes, I am."

"I don't think that's something to be proud of—"

"No?"

"No!" Apparently, that was the end of that.

·   ·   ·   ·   ·

Bernie was waiting as we entered his office, solemnity again infusing the room. He handed me an envelope containing the information Jones had requested. As I opened it, Bernie countered the need. "Mr. Montgomery has been busy meeting and greeting the kinds of people that might normally raise the eyebrows of those who support him in this neck of the woods, but as he has claimed, he sees the world in different terms, through a different lens."

I recognized the subtle dig in reference to Montgomery's common theme of approaching the intractable problems of modern life, certainly for those struggling economically, and those of the wrong color or ethnicity, in a way that was counterintuitive to mainstream practice, whatever that might be.

"People like Delton Manaforte?" For some reason, Xavier's man of mystery popped into my head.

A slight smile came to Bernie Schoor. "As a matter of fact, Mr. Montgomery has been noted in the company of Mr. Manaforte. Do you know him?"

"No. Dunkle brought him up. Apparently, he's a big behind-the-scenes mover and shaker in the tech industry."

Bernie's amusement did not abate. "Among other things, yes. He is also vocal in his belief that our better natures are not being served to our benefit in the present political climate; thinks technology, while providing many positives, certainly to his bottom line, also exposes the fault lines in many Americans inability to absorb information that is progressive in the sense of moving the human condition forward." His smile faded as he said this.

"To each his own, I suppose. Wouldn't it be to Montgomery's advantage to know people like Manaforte? Even if only tangentially? I mean, isn't the whole business of politics in who you know and who can help you?" I was certain that made perfect sense.

"That depends on a belief of equal footing between the parties, and right now, Montgomery is not in Manaforte's league. He may think that he is, but if he does, he's a bigger fool than I thought. I wouldn't express that concern to Mr. Jones." Bernie ran his fingers along the edge of the desk. "I understand the desire to reach out to power beyond or outside your community, especially if that power has expressed ideas that you find compelling, but Delton Manaforte's mirth is not to be underestimated. He does not give without reciprocation. Ever."

"I'll pass that along," I noticed Agnes, who had been drifting off, now tapping the side of my chair. She was tiring of the conversation. "And the prep for the trip?"

"What prep?" she asked, suddenly attuned to what was being discussed.

"A few attachments to the car. That will allow us to keep an eye on you," he said, with the enthusiasm I normally associated with Bernie.

Agnes tapped my shoulder. "Why do you need to keep an eye on us? I don't think I like that, Buttman."

"Come on, where's your sense of adventure?" I teased.

"It's merely precautionary, Agnes. I don't expect that anything will happen," said the man with the plan. Agnes looked at me with an expression that did not indicate she had been properly assured.

"Hey, I've always come back in one piece, haven't I?"

"No," she smacked my arm, "you haven't. That's what worries me."

"Then it's all for the better because Bernie is more level-headed than I am." I was certain that would satisfy her.

"Uh-huh." Apparently not.

As if on cue, Javier came in to say the work was done, just like that. Agnes shot me another quick look of disapproval, but chose not to express herself out loud. She'd save that for later. We said our goodbyes, and I promised to let Bernie know when we were on our way to the lair of Ashley Carmichael.

"Why would you call it a lair, Buttman? What exactly is going on? I thought we were taking a trip to decompress and relax..."

"And we shall, my love. We're just going to gather a little information while relaxing, that's all." I pretended to know what I was talking about.

"I think you're full of shit, Mr. Sunshine."

"Wow," I complained, "I'm not feeling the love right now."

"Good," she said.

·   ·   ·   ·   ·

Jones stood there flipping through the pages pulled from the envelope. Agnes and Coretta were at Anna's "Food Truck" watching and chatting as Anna explained the operation to Denise. Whether or not the freeze had thawed between mother and daughter was hard to discern from my vantage point, and I didn't want Jones to think I didn't care about his concerns for Jontaveus Montgomery. He continued to focus on the papers as the women returned with food in hand and directed us to a table.

"Orville, whatever it says will still be there when you finish, so put it down and eat." Orville looked at his wife, then me, and returned the pages to the envelope and set it on the table. I merely shrugged.

Small talk ensued over children, school, boyfriends/girlfriends, and other consequential issues. Agnes and Denice played nice as Anna joined the party. Mikal made the rounds, glad-handing and the like. He was, as always, solicitous of Agnes, well aware of her dismay that he and Anna might have something going on. Neither ever admitted as much to Agnes, and what I knew was technically a possible maybe and therefore of no help to the situation. This had been made plain to me on many occasions.

"I'm sure you're hiding the truth from me, Buttman," was a common complaint.

"You know I could never hide the truth from you, baby," was my simple reply.

"You are so lucky I love you, Sunshine!" she would harrumph. I would respond with a smile and a kiss.

"Monk," Mikal interrupted my daydream, "guess who called asking if she could come by and maybe sing a song or two?" He knew that I knew.

I smiled and asked, "What did you say?"

Mikal Thorvaldsen laughed at that. "Why not?"

"Yeah, why not." I was surprised, but that's ok, what do I know?

Jones' preoccupation with the contents of the envelope resumed as we found our seats and the bands hit the stage. The first was a Jazz/Gospel outfit, while the other played straight-out Seventies Jazz-rock. I put out my hand as he went through the pages and he reluctantly passed them to me after he went over them. They were quite a group of industry titans our Mr. Montgomery was engaging with, though the industries were mostly tech and finance, but a sprinkling of ideologues were included, as the notes Bernie added made plain. Jones would occasionally shake his head. Coretta elbowed him several times. His restlessness was conflicting with her desire to enjoy the show.

"Orville!" she commanded, and he obliged, requiring me to return what he had given. He remained restless for the last of the concert, but said nothing. That came as we were standing in the lobby waiting for the women to join us after hitting the restroom.

"You seem bothered by Montgomery's forays into the establishment?" I decided not to mention that they were all white guys.

"It's not that," he said, though the disdain was evident. "It's that no one has heard from him in a week or more. That's not like him."

"Maybe he's just busy?"

Jones wasn't fooled by my equivocation.

"Maybe, but how hard is it to call or text? Nobody's heard from him. Family, friends... something's up, I know it. I just don't know what." I noted his repeating himself.

"Like what?" Jones pondered that while putting on his sunglasses, even though the sun was long gone. "Doesn't that hinder your ability to see at night?"

Jones regarded me with the usual contempt he reserved for my obvious questions. "No, it does not."

"So, what's bothering you, really? It can't just be that he isn't in constant contact."

Jones took a minute to decide whether to say anything, pondering, I assumed, what I might think.

"I know people like *these* people," he said at last. "They think we don't hear them or they don't care, but we do, every time we haul them around or protect their arrogant asses. I get that they got the power, and I get that nothing is gonna change without them, and that they believe that. But we got to be mindful of whether they mean what they say, cause more often than not, what they say don't mean shit."

"Bernie said the same thing, in not so many words, that Jontaveus needs to be careful. That may be true, but I don't think he's some babe in the woods."

"Yeah," Jones admitted, "but even if you're a bear in the woods, you still gotta be smart." Agnes and Coretta were coming our way. "You hear anything? You let me know."

"I will." I thought about mentioning Carmichael, but held my tongue. I assumed there'd be time for that later.

11

Agnes stared at the suitcase propped open on the bed. Decisions, decisions. My bag was packed and waiting by the door. She was not amused by my efficacy.

"Nobody likes a showoff, Buttman."

"Now, now, don't take it personal, it's not an indictment of your packing prowess or anything like that. I'm merely more efficient."

"Same thing," she whined.

"Would you like me to pack for you?"

"Nice try, but no."

I took the hint that it was time to move on.

• • • • •

Xavier had called the day before; the letter of introduction was ready. My appraisal was complete, and based on whatever criterion was required, I was in. He was heading north and offered to drop it off.

"Anything I should know before I meet this guy?" I asked as he handed me the letter.

"He's very patrician for a guy living off the grid in the desert. Of course, it's not like he's living in a tent or a yurt. It's a nice place, but all the utilities are on site, no outside ties. The place reminded me of something out of those old spy movies I watched as a kid. You almost expect the desert floor to open up and expose a secret missile silo. Also, he talks very grand and yet is not above petty remarks should you say something he doesn't agree with..."

That made me laugh.

Dunkle smiled, "Yes, I foolishly expressed my belief that he was full of shit, in the nicest of terms, mind you, but he was not amused. Quite frankly, I'm surprised he even accepted my entreaty on your behalf, but money talks and there are members of my family with whom he is held in high regard."

"I imagine so. Anything else?"

Dunkle looked around before answering, which baffled me.

"Keep your eyes open. He has people who watch over his operation and I don't just mean his compound," he said while rubber-necking. This caught Agnes' attention as she came out of the kitchen.

"What does that mean?" she demanded.

"Nothing, nothing at all. Have a pleasant trip. As always, it's lovely to see you, Agnes. Goodbye." And with that, he made his hasty retreat.

"Do you have any normal friends, Buttman?"

I shook my head at that. "I would ask you the same question! Are you ready to talk about what MaryAnn is up to?"

Agnes smiled and patted my ass.

"No."

• • • • • •

Agnes bellowed from the bedroom that she was ready to go. I lugged the suitcases to the car. While in the trunk, I made sure the 45 was ready, willing, and able should the need arise. Memories of the Falcon flooded in as I held the iron. I called Bernie the night before informing him that we were leaving, and the only thing left on the list was to troop down the street to inform my daughter and then hit the road.

"We might go up to the big house this weekend. I assume that's ok?" Rebekah informed me.

I turned to Agnes, who ignored me and instead took Lizzy in her arms. No *have a nice trip* or *be careful!* No, the sentiment was *mind if we trash the house in the hills while you're gone?*

"Oh stop." Agnes wasn't in the mood to hear me whine. "They're not going to trash your precious Beverly Hills home, for Chrissakes."

"You don't know that," I mumbled.

"Oh, brother!"

The day was pleasant enough. It was argued that I would start the trip and then Agnes would take a turn. Well, technically, I argued, and Agnes simply ignored me. Again. We hit the road with the top down and the wind in our hair; the antiquary, his wife, and their things. Given the car and what we were wearing, motoring towards the desert and whatever excitement awaited, we were a 60s automobile advertisement come to life.

After I had taken the wheel, Agnes got out her compact and surveyed her features. There were no mirrors behind the sun visors to use. She didn't seem pleased. She then took what appeared to be an inventory of the rest of her body before making a face of disgust.

"Problems?" I inquired.

Agnes sighed quite loudly.

"I'm getting old, wrinkled, and flabby!" She grabbed a portion of her midsection as a point of emphasis. "You probably haven't even noticed."

"I think you look beautiful!" I wasn't going to get sucked into a conversation I had no chance of enjoying, much less one where encroaching decrepitude was the topic.

"That's your answer whenever I ask…"

"That's because it's true," I assured her.

"Uh-huh, like Judith beautiful?" She poked me in the ribs, my turn to groan.

"Exactly."

"Seriously, Monk!"

"Seriously indeed," I countered. "So, what's bothering you? We all age and lose our youthful luster, but I'm not going to call you old, wrinkled, and fat—"

"I said flabby, it's different," she interrupted.

"Sorry, flabby." I wanted to tilt my head, but the goddamned neck brace wouldn't let me. "I know something's bothering you. You've been moody and grumpy and whiny."

"Maybe you should see if *Monika* is still available?" she sneered.

I groaned, nice and loud. "I rest my case, your honor."

Agnes crossed her arms and tried to act peeved. "Why are you so mean to me?"

"I'm no different that I usually am. What's bothering you? Family, work, kids, mean me, what?"

"Mean you!"

"Really?"

"Really!" She was trying to make that stick and failing as a grin found her lips.

"You know I can see you smile, right?"

"You don't know that," she teased.

"Uh-huh. Well, I offered to talk, so I don't want to hear it later. Besides, what do you have to be bothered about, anyway? You don't have to work or worry about money. The kids are doing about as well as they can. And you've got the super delightful Mr. Buttman to keep you warm at night and grandkids who adore you. I don't think you have any problems at all, my dear."

The delightful Ms. Duquesne smacked me lightly on the arm.

"I suppose," she said.

I let the breeze, as the car plowed through it, do the talking. Agnes looked at me once or twice before turning back to the road in front of us.

"The problem is, I don't know what I'm supposed to do now. I mean I know you're right that I don't have to worry about money or a place to live or even love, but I liked working for Johnny, it was interesting and maybe a little dangerous, and probably illegal, and I certainly met some odd characters, some with silly names," she said this while looking my way.

"Why are you so mean to me?" I harrumphed.

"Don't interrupt!"

"My apologies."

Agnes poked me again, knowing I didn't like that. "Anyway, a lot of my life was centered there, and then there was the bar and Rey. It was my home, and they looked after me and now it's all gone."

"Change is like that. I never thought I'd end up where I am now, but here I am."

"That's not terribly helpful," she grumbled.

"Then what would you like me to do?"

"I don't know..."

"Well, let me know when you do," I advised.

"Who is this guy we're going to see?" she asked after putting the compact back in her purse.

"A philosopher," I told her.

"Philosopher?"

"Yep."

"I'm going to need a drink!" she whined.

•   •   •   •   •

Ashley Carmichael lived on a compound north of Barstow, south of Death Valley, and west of the Mohave, or, as Agnes put it, the middle of nowhere. A lone Joshua tree or a patch of creosote bushes periodically broke up the arid hardscrabble landscape. Hills, crags, and mounds rose here and there, with the tail end of the Sierra Nevada Mountains rising to the northwest. The road was empty save for two joyriders on motorcycles roaring past us.

The gate to Carmichael's compound was locked. A patrician sounding voice told us to wait after I rang the buzzer.

"Hector will be there momentarily, Mr. Buttman."

We watched as Hector approached the gate. He took both the letter of introduction and my license, looked at them, then at me before opening the gate and pointing to a cluster of small buildings surrounding a larger one along the horizon. He handed the papers back and watched as we drove in. The compound was indeed reminiscent, as Dunkle had noted, of the sets used in movies back when suave spies tangled with nefarious super-villains set to take over the world. I wondered if there would be a collection of disinterested hot babes lounging by a pool in vintage 70s bikinis.

Probably not.

A large circle drive with a cactus garden in the middle led us to the front of the main house. The architecture was an odd blend of Spanish adobe and mid-century modern. A slender man, tall, with a tight face, wearing a white shirt buttoned to the neck and white slacks, stood next to a shorter woman wearing a caftan dress, indigo, with zigzagging white vertical stripes. Carmichael sported a trimmed grey beard minus the mustache and close-cropped hair. His wife, Idina, let her equally grey hair flow along her shoulders.

Both carried an air of deep suspicion.

After formal introductions, which included a pro forma comment on the brace occupying my neck, they led us inside where it was made plain that the women would not be a part of the discussion. Agnes was pleased to hear this, just as she was to hear that Idina was a potter. Idina, for her part, seemed pleasantly surprised that someone shared her interest and wanted to know more of her work and art. Tea was served along with a quick tour of the property.

Desert gardens interspersed the house and the out-buildings, which consisted of a potter's studio, garden shed, garage, and utility house where the emergency generator, well pump, and water filters were located. I didn't discern any large open space where rockets might suddenly appear. Carmichael pointed off in the distance, where the faint glint of metal indicated the location of the solar panels powering the compound. Once back in the house, lunch was presented by a woman with the name Bettina, who appeared to be about the same age as Hector, which was slightly younger than Carmichael and his wife, whom I presumed to be in their early seventies.

Carmichael, for his part, said little as Idina, finding Agnes to be clearly interested in her life out here in nowheresville, became more animated. Agnes, while no fan of the desert, listened intently as Idina proselytized the glories of life in isolation. They talked, and we listened, and Idina, sensing that Ashley desired privacy, invited Agnes to her studio. We stood as they left and Bettina cleared the table.

"This way, Mr. Buttman," Carmichael directed, leading to his study.

The study contained a desk and chair near a window looking towards the Sierra Nevada's, a tan leather couch, and two companion chairs. The bookshelves, which lined all the walls, and a table, were stacked with books and papers in no discernable order. I sat in one of the leather chairs as Carmichael sat in the other.

"In what way are you interested in meeting with me, Mr. Buttman?"

"Call me Monk," I said.

Carmichael raised his eyebrows at that.

"I prefer formality, at which one might note the error in being associated with such a, how shall we say it, crude moniker." A faint smile found his lips. "I understand names can be changed."

"True, but it's a conversation starter, if nothing else, and it lends itself to a certain humility, certainly to one's ability, or lack thereof, in making good choices. Either is fine with me, but I've noticed many people's reticence in saying, Buttman."

"Of course." Carmichael leaned back. "However, back to my initial inquiry as to the purpose of your visit..."

I took a moment to decide how blunt to be. I was, after all, a guest in his home. "The nuanced answer lies in the book I was given, your book, the reaction to it and the uneasiness of our times. That includes the suggestion by some that our form of government has reached the end of its usefulness and that your book has the necessary antidote to the problem."

"Have you read the book?"

"I have. First out of obligation, then again just to be sure—"

"Sure of what, Mr. Buttman?" His curiosity seemed genuine.

"Its subtle irony," I answered.

Ashley Carmichael smiled at that.

"What is it you do, Mr. Buttman, and what, if I may ask, is your level of formal instruction?"

That made me smile.

"I am a reluctant philanthropist and a failed nobody. Before that, I was a farmer, and before that a punk. I have very little formal education to rely on. I am, to use the term, an autodidact. Having realized that farming was not intellectually challenging and understanding that wasting what little education I had was counterproductive, I utilized the time I had in those days to read up on what interested me. And you, sir? I noted there was no biographical information in the book."

Ashley Carmichael put his hands together, which he then brought to his lips.

"My education was much more formal and fundamental. My father demanded a high level of intellectual intercourse among his children and was equally demanding in our fidelity to instruction. He valued it to the point that he spent the majority of his income on it. As you may have surmised by the book, philosophy, history, and the classics of what are considered the canon of Western education were the primary focus of our instruction. He also introduced me to the art of procuring patrons for my work, and it is indeed an art. The rest is personal and not germane to our discussion."

"That works for me. My interest is in the book."

"Then we have the parameters of our discussion." He pulled a copy from the table beside him. "I assume you will not be duplicating your sponsor's attempt at sarcasm or drollery?"

I laughed at that.

"No, I'll leave that to Xavier. He finds that much more amusing than I do," I lied.

Carmichael may have picked up on that.

"It's a product of his deep ambivalence to his position and wealth. I've had the good fortune to meet and have a broad range of discussions with members of his family, his father and uncle foremost, and their intelligence is congenital but not necessarily utilized to its best effect. Mr. Dunkle's gifts for sarcasm and irony are undercut by his unwillingness to think first, and far too often what he affects most is self-loathing. The rest of his family... Have you met them?"

"No, I haven't had the pleasure," I said.

"The others are far more serious and content about their wealth, and unlike your friend, unable to perceive the humor in life."

"Yes, he's mentioned that many times." I pointed to the book. "I didn't note a publisher's mark."

"The book is self-published. As a matter of fact, it is a private treatise I wrote mostly for myself in rather florid language, and which I reluctantly agreed to have printed at the behest of several of my patrons." He thumbed through the book.

"Patrons like Delton Manaforte?" Carmichael continued thumbing through the book.

"You know Mr. Manaforte?"

"Only by reputation, but his name came up when I discussed your book with others," I added.

He paused briefly, then closed the book. "I see. And these others, Mr. Dunkle included?" I noted the seriousness of his inquiry.

"No. In Xavier's case, I noticed an extreme reluctance to speak of Mr. Manaforte in other than a whispered reverent tone, which surprised me."

"And yet you are here, nonetheless?" He leaned in.

"It's your book," I answered.

"So it is." He pondered his slender fingers as he said this.

●　　●　　●　　●　　●

I half expected our conversation to end, but my half expectations were in error. Like his wife in the comfort of Agnes' company, Carmichael found comfort in mine and he soon regaled me of his book, its meaning, and what others believed it to mean. It was at this point that he drew close, as if concerned we might be overheard. I too leaned in, ridiculous though it seemed.

"It amazes me to admit this, given the individuals I have given the book to, but you are the first to recognize the subtleties in the book, as well as its omens. That was the point of the language I used. Ambiguity has its place where certain ideas are entertained, but not all entertainment is to be acted upon. Remember that, Mr. Buttman, and remember too that to a select few, it is not entertainment." He turned to the window before turning back. "It is a tired trope, but beware the affable manner of the smiling face. The merry prankster will kill just as surely as the lunatic!"

"I'll keep that in mind," I said, not meaning a word of it.

Carmichael, however, ignored my glib response. "You will, Mr. Buttman, of that I have no doubt."

12

The compound, we were told, had an alternative gate to the north, and as Death Valley was our next stop, Carmichael had Hector open the gate for us. Agnes held a pot that Idina had given her. She seemed fascinated by it, holding it up in various positions and pointing out how the glaze sparkled in the sunlight.

"It's a lovely pot," I admitted.

"Maybe I should take up pottery," she announced.

"Maybe…"

"I know," she said in a way that immediately put me on the defensive. "I could set up a studio at the farm! I'm sure Meri and Moses would love that."

"Uh-huh."

"You should be thrilled," she teased.

"Uh-huh."

Agnes shook her head. "I guess I'll just have to take care of it without you."

"Well," I let that hang in the air, "you let me know how that goes."

Agnes frowned. "You're a jerk, Buttman!"

"It's in the script."

It was during our playful banter that I noticed the two bikers tailing us, the two from earlier in the day. Xavier's admonition began playing in my head, *"He has people who watch over his operation."* The dirt road stretched to the horizon with nothing in sight, save the lonely Mesquite grove to our left. The top was down, leaving me feeling exceedingly vulnerable. The 45 remained tucked away in the trunk. Agnes continued to blather on about pots and the farm. The bikers split from each other at the edge of the road before taking off into the desert, flanking us on either side.

"I think you should put the pot down."

"Why?"

I pointed to the bikers. Agnes put the pot back in its box.

I slowed down, hoping, vainly, that the bikers would pass us by. Instead, one rode up in front of us, while the other fell behind. I slowed further, noting how rocky the road had become. The bikers, now on the road, were right ahead and behind us. The one in front revved his motor.

"I think you should get under the dash," I said as I pushed Agnes down.

"Why?" she asked, alarmed at my pushing her.

There was no need to answer. The biker in front began spinning his rear wheel back and forth, slamming rocks into the car. Agnes screamed and dove under the dashboard as the windshield cracked into a useless mosaic. The biker behind us turned, spinning his rear wheel, sending more rocks and debris at and into the car. I could hear the lenses and lights shattering, the cacophony as the rocks; stones and dirt struck the sheet metal. I stopped the car and huddled over Agnes as we were pelted again and again. The bikers finished their happy dance by racing around the car, sending a billow of dust into the air. One of them shouted something, and they sped off. We waited for the quiet to return before sitting up. I could feel the bits of rock and dirt digging at my neck as I sat back. Blood was running down the side of my head. I put my hand to the spot that suddenly began to ache. Agnes shook her head and took off the scarf she was wearing.

"Jesus, Monk, you're bleeding!"

"Yeah, I think I took a couple of shots to the old noggin." I winced as I moved my head. "I need you to help remove this brace. There are rocks digging into my neck."

As the dust settled, Agnes loosened the Velcro straps and pulled the brace off. The rocks and pebbles rolled down into my shirt. Lovely. She gave me the scarf, which I pressed to the bleeding cut. Once the brace and my neck were brushed off, she put the brace back on, much to my dismay.

"You have to keep wearing it," she demanded.

"I don't like it!"

"I don't care. Just do it."

"I want a divorce," I whined.

"Tough!" She tightened the straps. "You're not getting one!"

"I think *you're* the mean one!"

"Uh-huh." She leaned in and kissed me.

I was surprised. I thought Agnes would be completely freaked out. Instead, she took a moment to check herself before we got out of the car to assess the damage.

"It doesn't look good, Buttman," she said as we surveyed the cracked windshield, broken lenses, lights, and the dents and pockmarks in the grill and paint. On the plus side, the tires still had air, and the motor was running. I popped the hood to see if the radiator was leaking; to my second surprise, I could find no leaks. "What now?" she asked.

"We'll see what our man in the sky says."

"What does that mean?"

I smiled at that. "Bernie." She still didn't get it. "You'll see."

He answered on the second ring. I put the phone on speaker so Agnes could listen in. I told him of our encounter; he didn't seem surprised. Instead, he asked a few questions about whether I thought Carmichael was responsible and was the car drivable. I told him it was, but with the windshield damaged and the lights out, not to mention all the broken mirrors, it would draw attention and night driving was out of the question.

"There's a café about fifteen miles away. Take the car there. I'll have a replacement sent. Stay in touch," he said. Agnes started to speak and then stopped until the call was over.

"He's tracking us, isn't he?"

"Yep."

I swept out the car with the small utility broom I kept in the truck. I also retrieved the 45. Agnes watched. I could tell the wheels were spinning. We got in and carefully motored the five miles to the state road. I was trying to remember the last time I drove with my head out the window.

We made it another five miles towards the diner before the fuzz pulled us over. The cop stared at us periodically as he walked around the Dart. I handed him my license and insurance. He asked a few perfunctory questions before wandering back to his squad car. I could see him on the radio. He returned and stood there.

"This car isn't drivable," he stated.

"It drives just fine," I said.

He didn't care for that. "I'm not going to argue with you. The car doesn't have the *required* working safety features. You're going to have to leave it here."

"And I'm not going to sit here in the middle of nowhere. Don't you think the bigger issue is the two pricks who did this?" I argued. It wasn't working. "There's a café just down the road. I'll take it there." The cop stood there, staring down at me.

"Wait here," he ordered and returned again to his squad car.

"You think it's a good idea to piss off the police?" Agnes was irritated with me, too.

"We'll see," I answered.

"Stay on the shoulder, I'll follow you there," he monotoned.

The café was a long, slow five miles down the road. It sat on one side, along with a gas station, while a few worn wooden buildings that at one time housed a motel sat across the road. As I pulled into the parking lot, the cop took off. It was only after I stopped that I noticed the two motorcycles parked just off the road.

"Our friends are here," I said to Agnes as I pointed to the bikes.

"What do we do?"

I thought about it. "Time for call number two."

Bernie, again, answered on the second ring, "What'd the police have to say?" he inquired. That made Agnes frown and mouth: *how does he know that?*

"Very little other than the car can't be on the road. He didn't ask about my bloody head, and he didn't seem particularly interested in how the car came to be in this condition or the two bikers responsible. Speaking of which, they're here at the café," I said.

"Are they..." We could hear him shuffling over the phone. "How would you like to have a little fun with them?"

"What kind of fun?"

He laughed. "That would spoil the surprise. I'd need you to keep them there for the next ten minutes or so. Think you can do that?"

"We're on it, bucko," blurted Agnes. She grinned at my shocked expression. Bernie kept laughing.

"Careful, Agnes, this work can be addictive. Ten minutes," he warned.

"Hey, you two forget I worked for Johnny D! I'm no babe in the woods. Let's go, Sunshine." Agnes checked the abrasion on my head as Bernie hung up. "It's clotted up, but we'll need to get this cleaned."

We got out of the car and entered the café. It caused a bit of a stir, mainly due to the guy with the neck brace and the dried blood on his jacket and head.

"Accident," Agnes explained.

The two bikers turned for a moment to check us out. One smirked before turning back around. The hostess led us to a table. It afforded us a fine view of the road and the two smirking punks, neither of whom looked out of their twenties. The waitress handed us menus and set down glasses of water. We eyed the smirking punks.

"What's the plan, Buttman?"

"You tell me, dollface, after all, you're the one who worked for Johnny D, remember?"

Agnes laughed at that. "And don't you forget it." She looked at her watch. "I'll give 'em a couple more minutes."

There was food in front of them. I assumed they meant to finish, and they didn't seem terribly concerned to see us. As I looked at the menu, my phone beeped. A text: *two minutes*.

"It's time," I told Agnes. She smiled and got up. I followed her cue, and we approached the punks. They were quite the pair. Both had long ratty hair and thin wispy beards, one a dirty blond and the other brown. The dirty blond looked at us.

"What?"

"It wasn't very nice of you two to treat us that way," she said in the voice she used on Johnny's goons.

"I don't know what you're talking about, bitch!" He laughed at that. His companion was more circumspect as he watched Agnes engage his buddy.

It was then that a loud horn sounded. Everyone in the café turned as the semi roared down the road. It was fitted with a thick protective grill and it smashed into the bikes, sending them flying through the air along with a cloud of dirt and debris. I thought that fitting. The horn continued to sound as the truck sped away.

Agnes turned to the punks.

"You two shitheads got any other smart-assed comments to make?"

Blondie thought about getting tough, but I made sure he noticed the 45 in my pocket. "You won't get away with this," he sneered.

"I don't know what you're talking about, bitch," Agnes sneered back. "And in case you dickheads get any ideas, you might want to remember it's a big desert! Sometimes motherfuckers get lost."

We returned to our table. Once we sat down, the punks ran out to take stock of what was left of their bikes. My phone beeped again. Another text: *car will be there in a few minutes. How was the show?* I assured him the point was made. The shocked waitress stumbled over and we ordered sandwiches. I asked if this sort of thing happened very often? She said no. Agnes suppressed a laugh. I asked if we could get those sandwiches to go.

She said sure.

The sheriff arrived as the Dart was being hoisted onto the tow truck. He talked to the punks who pointed in our direction. I told the tow truck driver to take off. The sheriff came over. He didn't seem to be particularly good-natured.

"Who told you you could haul away that car?" he demanded, as he looked over my license.

"Your deputy." He didn't have an answer for that.

"What do you know about the truck that slammed into those bikes?"

"About as much as those punks do about trashing my car."

"I don't like people coming in here and making malicious allegations, *Buttman!*" The sheriff, a man who must have been slender at one time because his heft didn't match his frame, moved closer to me.

"Does that mean there are lots of riders out there with the same helmets, outerwear, and motorcycles as those two?" I replied.

"Don't fuck with me, Buttman! Did you threaten those boys?"

"Why would I do that, and to anticipate your next question, I have a permit to carry."

The sheriff, glowering, had had enough of Monk Buttman. "Grant," he screamed to the cop who had pulled us over, "put him in the car!" Grant stood there for a moment before coming over as another squad car arrived, lights and sirens blaring. My head throbbed in unison to the noise. The sheriff reached in my pocket and took the 45.

"You can't just haul him off," yelled Agnes.

The sheriff gave her a nasty look. "I can do whatever I want," he yelled before walking away. Grant pulled my arms behind me and applied the handcuffs.

"I don't know that it'll do you any good, but you can follow us to the station," he told her. He then pushed me in the direction of the squad car and shoved me in. In a matter of minutes, we were off, three police cars for a malcontent with an aching head and a smart mouth.

It was a long, painful drive.

Once we got to the sheriff's headquarters, I was hustled in and basically thrown onto a hard wooden bench. A woman wearing a deputy's uniform that was too small for her ample frame called the sheriff to her desk.

"Cordry's on the phone." She held out the receiver.

"What the fuck's he want? Tell him I'll call him back."

"He said now!" The deputy was not amused by the sheriff's profanity. The sheriff grabbed the phone away from the woman.

"It's Dorfman! What's so goddamned important?" the sheriff quickly turned to me. "Why?" he asked, clearly angered by whatever was said. "How the fuck did they even know he was here?" The answer only made him more pissed off. "I don't fucking like this, Gordon! It's bullshit. You hear me, bullshit!" The sheriff slammed down the phone. He came towards me. "Who the fuck are you, Buttman?"

"A nobody," I informed him.

I could tell he really wanted to belt me, maybe break some teeth or my jaw, but everyone was watching, even Agnes, who had just rushed in. The sheriff was stuck.

"Get him out of here," he said as he turned to leave.

"Dorfman," I shouted, "I want my 45 and my license returned."

The sheriff, livid, took the 45 out of his pocket and tossed it on the table. The license went flying across the room. Having complied with my perfectly reasonable request, he stormed into an adjacent office and slammed the door. Grant and the woman, whose name was Rhonda, came over. Grant to uncuff me, and Rhonda to hand me the 45.

"Who's Cordry?" I asked as I rubbed the sore wrists, joining the sore head and neck.

"*Mr.* Cordry is the county prosecutor. If I were you, sir, I'd get while the getting is good!" She was serious, and I wasn't about to argue. I'd had my fill of that.

I picked up my license. "Thanks."

. . . . .

The car was a nondescript white Chevy something, which bummed me out.

"We'll get you another heap when we get back," my less than supportive wife snorted.

"I want one now!"

She ignored me.

Agnes drove to the hotel at the edge of Death Valley National Park in Tecopa. She checked us in, leaving me in the car. No need to raise the suspicions of the people running the place by having a blood caked man at your side. Once we got to our room, she helped clean me up, and unhelpfully remarked on my sad state of affairs. "You're not the man I married, Buttman," she sighed.

I pondered that.

"I love you too, beautiful."

What else could I say?

13

The restaurant, conveniently located to the left of the front desk, was quiet. It was late in the evening, and there were only four or five other tables occupied. Allowed to seat ourselves, we found an isolated booth in a corner, which gave me a clear view of the place. Agnes' earlier angst at her suddenly drifting and uncertain life had morphed into outright excitement. Rather than being upset or worried over the day's events, she was instead metaphorically rubbing her hands together in anticipation of more intrigue to follow.

I didn't know whether to be shocked or concerned.

"Today was kind of fun, huh?" she mused.

"Fun?"

"Well, in a scary way, but interesting, don't you think? I mean we're ok and everything, but I don't know..." She paused. "I know this sounds crazy, but I thought it was thrilling."

"Thrilling?"

"Yes, thrilling," she chided. "I thought you were into this, these kinds of adventures?"

She was serious!

"Sorry, I forgot almost being killed and thrown into jail is always a thrilling adventure," I replied.

Agnes frowned. "Geez, what a grump!"

I chose to ignore that.

She sipped her drink, all the while eyeing me from across the table as her mind was going a mile a minute. "I didn't get the chance to ask, but what did you and Ash talk about?"

"*Ash*?"

More frowning.

"Yes, *Ash*! What do you think Idie calls him? Ashley? That's a girl's name," she snorted.

"Obviously. So, before we get to *Ash*, what did Idie have to say?"

Agnes looked around before leaning in, her face alight in serious conspiracy. "I got the feeling that she wanted to say more, but all is not paradise in the desert, if you know what I mean—"

"No, I don't believe I do."

"Geez, Monk," her frustration at my lack of enthusiasm was palpable. "How can you not be excited by this? There's obviously something going on here. Why else would we be attacked like that, and why would Idie be so certain that her swell little life was closing in on her?"

"You tell me, dollface?"

Agnes looked at me with what can only be described charitably as deep disappointment. "She said it was that stupid book that was causing all their trouble. No, that's not right, she said that *goddamned* book! That's what she said."

"Did she say what kind of trouble?"

Agnes' eyes were sparkling, "The biggest thing was all these people coming round, like you, Buttman, asking about the book. Idie likes her privacy."

"He's a writer, or philosopher. People are going to want to talk to him about what he writes," I said.

Agnes merely shrugged. "I suppose, but that wasn't the problem. The problem was that she was excluded from whatever they were talking about, and a lot of them had, as she put it, thugs with them, security guys. She said they wouldn't even let her into the house while their bosses were there." I smiled, which made Agnes raise her eyebrows. "Yeah, don't even think about it, Buttman!"

"I'm shocked you would think I would do something like that," I teased. "I assume you asked how that affected their relationship?"

Agnes feigned shock. "How long have you known me?" She didn't let me answer. "That was the other problem. Apparently, and I deduced this because she didn't say it outright, but I don't think they had a normal relationship like we do—"

"We have a normal relationship?" I couldn't help myself.

"Shut up! Anyway, unlike us, although things have been pretty thin lately loverboy," she raised her eyebrows again, "sex isn't a part of what keeps them together, and I got the impression that this was a more recent change and that Idie was tiring of having to provide for her own orgasm, as MaryAnn would say—"

"Speaking of MaryAnn…" Again, I couldn't help it.

"One more idiot comment and I'll make your headache worse, got that?" She held up her hand.

"My apologies. Go on." I was almost certain she wouldn't actually smack me!

"Sometimes, Buttman. What was I saying? Oh yeah, the sex thing. While the sex had dried up, they were still, she said, intellectual equals, and it really made her angry that she was shutout of whatever was being discussed. To make things worse, Ash would not talk to her about any of it later. She was a truly frustrated woman! No sex, nothing to talk about. All she had left was her pottery, and Ash was trying to keep her holed up and away from her artist friends. Then there's the whole thing with them even staying there! Apparently, being a philosopher and a potter doesn't pay particularly well."

"I'm shocked! Although I don't know why now that you bring it up, but I assumed they owned the property."

Agnes groaned and sat back.

"Nope, it belongs to some rich guy who bought it from a crazy guy a few years ago." Agnes noted my confusion. "I thought the same thing, but they started out as caretakers for the crazy guy as a way to continue their intellectual thing and still have a place to live, and both of them liked being out in the desert apart, but not really, from the rest of the world."

"Did she say who the rich guy was?"

"No," she leaned back in with a sinister grin, "but the crazy guy was a Dunkle."

"Really? Odd that Xavier didn't mention that..."

Agnes sat back. "Uh-huh. So, what *did* you and Ash talk about?" It was my turn to lean in.

"The goddamned book, of course," I said with as much glee as a neck brace would allow.

"I'm gonna need more, Buttman!"

"That might explain the thinness of late," I laughed.

"Not funny—"

"No?"

"No!" Agnes' patience was apparently wearing thin as well. "Talk, Buttman."

"Ok, the book is the blueprint for the end of democracy in America," I stated blandly.

A look of disbelief overtook my delightful wife. "Seriously?"

I was surprised she doubted me. "Seriously."

The rest of the evening was concluded with a confused explanation, alcohol, and sex, thus sating, for the moment, Agnes' desires. Whether she believed what I described as the contents of the book remained unstated.

• • • •

The next day's wanderings through Death Valley weren't nearly as exciting, at least from Agnes' point of view, as the day before had been. I found it to be quite relaxing. For whatever reason, the crowds were few and far between, which gave us the luxury of solitude in a solitary landscape. I was wearing my beloved sombrero, which I didn't often get to do.

"That's because it makes you look like an idiot." Agnes did not care for the sombrero. "Plus, it's culturally insensitive on your part."

"Nonsense, I'm wearing it exactly as it was intended, and as Mexicans themselves wear it, to shade my precious head from the heat and sun. Besides, it's not an ornamental style sombrero like the

Mariachi's wear, and it's authentic rather than some cheap party hat. So there!"

"Uh-huh. You still look like an idiot."

"How can you say that? It complements the neck brace so well."

"Uh-huh."

"Uh-huh? Is that all you can say?"

Agnes laughed. "Uh-huh."

I tried unsuccessfully to shake my head.

Our good humor, along with the peace and quiet of the day, dissolved as my phone rang and our guy in the sky pressed upon us unwanted news.

"Carmichael and his wife were found dead this morning. Murder-suicide," Bernie informed us. "You might want to head back home since it's possible Sheriff Dorfman is looking for you, and I doubt his mood has improved. It's better if he has to interview you on your lawyer's turf rather than at the county prosecutor's."

"Why would he want to talk to us? Carmichael was alive and well when we left, and his man, Hector, can attest to that," I said, being in no mood to share pleasantries with Dorfman.

"Yes, but Hector was not privy to your conversation, correct?"

"True..."

"They'll still want to find out what you know. Plus, it's possible the feds might want a word with you too," he added.

"The feds? What for?" I didn't like the sound of that.

"I'll leave that to them. Swing by." He hung up. I passed the cheery news along to Agnes.

"Wow!" Her mood improving.

"Yes, wow," I answered.

Not wanting to cross paths with any angry sheriffs, we cut short our plans and headed back to bustling LA. Agnes brimming with anticipation; Monk not so much. While Agnes drove, I rewound the day before and tried to focus on Carmichael's words, words I let idly slide by, never thinking he'd be dead the next day.

"Should I be worried, Monk?" Agnes blurted out while I stared at the vast expanse of desert surrounding us, wondering how many bodies lay out there lost to time.

"Worried about what?"

"I mean, shouldn't I feel bad or something? I just talked to her yesterday and now she's dead, killed by her husband!" She then tapped me on the arm. "You wouldn't do anything like that, would you, Mr. Sunshine?" A wry smile accompanied the question.

"Bernie didn't say he killed her and yes, you should be worried. This isn't a game."

Agnes frowned at that. "I know it's not a game, wiseguy, and you didn't answer the question..."

"I hadn't actually given it any thought, but I'll add it to the list of possibilities if you'd like." This time, she smacked me.

"You're a jerk, Buttman."

"I aim to please."

Agnes glowered at that. "Uh-huh," her voice rising, "so maybe she killed him?" she didn't wait for me to answer. "I can see that." She paused again, the smile returning. "I can see how she could reach a point where she just loses it. Some men are like that..." a final smack for emphasis.

"Right back at ya, Ag!" It was my turn to grin. Ag was not amused.

"We discussed this, Buttman! We do not use the Ag word."

"Sorry, Ag," I smirked. Ag groaned.

"Just sit there and be quiet," she muttered.

"Yes, dear." We laughed at that.

·　　·　　·　　·　　·

Bernie was in his office. We noticed the Dart occupying the same space as the Falcon had. I saw that as a bad omen.

"Stop with the whining, Buttman." Her interest was in what Bernie was thinking of this suddenly more lethal affair. "So, who killed who?"

That made Bernie grin. "I don't know," he answered. "My assumption is that he killed his wife and then himself. That tends to be the predominate pattern in spousal murder. Why? Do you think she killed him?"

"I think it's possible. I know she wasn't happy with their situation." Agnes turned to me. "Did Ash complain about his wife or life out in the desert?"

"It didn't come up, and I didn't ask." I noted Agnes' trenchant disapproval of my unwillingness to ask those sorts of questions.

"That's why you guys are always bouncing off the walls. You don't inquire into the heartache and unhappiness until it kicks you in the shin!" she announced, which got a laugh from Bernie. "What?" she demanded. She was on a roll.

"You are entirely correct. Matters of the heart are almost always at the heart of the matter," he intoned with an insincere gravity. Agnes didn't care for that. "However," Bernie moderated his tone, "Agnes' point is well taken that the possibility exists that this is more about their relationship than anything having to do with his book and its influence on the impressionable. I am, however, skeptical."

"Meaning you seriously believe that someone might try to take over the country?" Agnes asked.

"Someones," he answered. "My hope is that it's just a sad end to an unhappy relationship, but there are other factors that make me think more is going on here, and I don't say that to be cavalier about the deaths of two people."

"Such as the feds wanting to talk to me," I interjected.

"The feds," Agnes nearly shouted, "you didn't say anything about the feds?"

"Sorry."

Agnes turned to Bernie. "Why would the feds care or be interested? Was Ash one of those anti-government types?" The wheels were once again spinning. Bernie and I watched her turn the last day and a half over in her head. "I can see that. I can see him collecting rich pissed-off rubes thinking they could take over... It's that, isn't it?" She was nodding in advance of our agreement.

"Of a kind, yes," Bernie agreed, "but while some may be rubes or fools, some are not and that's the scary part; that they are serious, and they have the means to move forward with their plans." Agnes continued nodding, obviously delighted that she was right and that dangerous intrigue was afoot.

"Ah, you both realize this sounds like a really bad B-Movie, right?" I felt the need to point that out. "I read the book and any serious person, and yes, I know how that sounds, but any serious reader would have noticed both the caution and the subtle humor Carmichael injected into the book—"

"Did Carmichael admit that?" Bernie asked.

"He did."

"Did you consider that he admitted that so if asked, you'd have to accept that the book is merely a fun little exercise in literary exposition on the topic of treason?" he continued.

"No."

Bernie looked at Agnes before turning to me. "The people we're dealing with are well aware of the nature of these ideas and how explosive they are. All the better to couch them in parody and humor in case the wrong people, like the feds, come asking a lot of problematic questions. That's why I'm so concerned with this, because I know the attitudes of these people, of their antipathy towards universal suffrage, of their disdain for the sloppy, haphazard nature of democracy, and how much better, to their minds, a more autocratic society would be."

"Ah, but they would introduce the world to the flowering of Socrates' philosopher-kings, and a benevolent oligarchy rather than corrupt venal kleptocrats," I said. Bernie was not persuaded.

"History is littered with so-called philosopher-kings who were no more than dictators who robbed and oppressed the population," he stated.

"You sound like Moses," I said. I couldn't resist.

"That's because Moses is right."

"So, what do we do now?" asked Agnes. I don't think she was particularly interested in philosopher-kings, oligarchs, or kleptocrats.

"I have the strong feeling that you will be the focus of a lot of inquiry by a lot of people on both sides of this. I recommend that you be very careful with what you say and to whom you say it," was his answer. While Agnes pondered this, Bernie pulled a small phone from his desk. He handed it to me. "This is an encrypted phone. Let me know of who and what you encounter."

"What about the car?" that made Agnes groan and Bernie laugh.

"Unfortunately, the Dart's going to need a lot of bodywork, given all the dents and dings. However, in anticipating your appreciation of less loved convertibles of the 60s, I found a nice '67 Ford Galaxie 500." Bernie gestured that we all get up and follow him.

Agnes sighed. "You have a perfectly good Mercedes that you barely use. Why do you need another old beater?"

"Classic, my love, classic," I admonished.

It was a radiant candy-apple-red with a white top and a white interior. Bernie assured me it was in excellent shape, had low miles, and could be mine for the exceptional price of thirty grand.

"Ah, what the hell," I said. Agnes shook her head, but admitted it wasn't that much money to spend, and it was a nice-looking car.

"Hopefully, it'll last longer than the last one," she snarked.

"Hopefully."

I signed the paperwork, assured Bernie we would keep him apprised of our fun and games, and headed home.

The car handled the road nicely, and I pulled over midway so Agnes could take a turn. She found this amusing given my reluctance to let her drive the Falcon. I ignored her comment that the accident with the Falcon had knocked some sense into me.

"That's hearsay and you know it," I sputtered.

"Uh-huh."

It's the little things, I told myself, that make marriage the joy that it is. I chose not to share this with the woman at the wheel.

14

The tall one spoke first. We found them waiting at our front door. They wore dark clothes and affected an air of menace. Having spent a fair amount of time around men who felt the need to practice such artifice, we were less than impressed. It didn't hurt that the 45 was resting in my hand in my coat pocket.

"What do *you two* want?" Agnes demanded in the voice she perfected working for Johnny D.

The short one grinned.

"We got a message for you," the tall one hissed.

"From whom?" I asked.

"You'll know."

I speculated on whether he had any idea how incomprehensible that statement was.

"The message?" Agnes demanded.

The short one stepped up. "Keep your nose where it belongs, understand?" Apparently, they both went to the same school of nuance. Agnes looked at me before getting out her phone. This prompted the tall one to step towards her, which prompted me to pull out the 45. Both of them noticed it glimmer in the porchlight.

"Anything else before we call the cops?" Agnes had her fingers on the phone.

"Come on," the tall one said, we assumed, to the short one. He patted me on the head as he passed. "Don't shoot yourself, tough guy."

The short one thought that was funny. "Yeah, don't shoot yourself, dick."

They sauntered off the property and got in their car parked across the street.

The car wouldn't start.

The tall guy was cursing the short one. On the fifth or sixth try, the motor belatedly rattled and coughed. The two mugs puttered down the street and out of view.

"There's gotta be a higher quality of goon out there, don't you think?" I asked, as Agnes unlocked the door.

"You'd think, but the truth is they're not the brightest bulbs to begin with, and with the breakdown of the mob, you get what you get. The smart ones rarely stay goons for long; they know to move up, or get out," she replied. We walked the house to make sure nothing was planted or out of place. Agnes intoned it was doubtful that whoever was behind this would leave something that important to those two. I decided if Bernie was that interested, it was time to test the phone. He was neither shocked to hear from me so soon, nor that we were already being threatened.

"It might not be a bad idea to stay at the house in Beverly Hills," he advised. I passed this on to Agnes. She was less enthusiastic.

"It's just two guys," she said.

I wasn't so sure. "Perhaps, but you don't have Johnny's muscle to rely on now."

"True, but we can always get Anton or Josef if we want..."

"Maybe..."

After declaring the house safe and putting away the clothes and toiletries from our aborted trip, we sat on the couch sipping wine and wondering if we'd survive the night.

"Makes you wonder if Ash and Idie's deaths weren't more sinister than people think," I mused.

"Or they know, but are playing dumb to see if anyone shows their hand."

"If that's true, we need to watch what we say..."

"Isn't that what Bernie said?" she teased.

"Maybe."

The wine took the last of our energy and we shuffled off to bed with the not so vague understanding that bad intent might be our unwelcome guest for the foreseeable future. Agnes slept better than I did, dropping off almost as soon as she hit the pillow. I marveled at that. Was a time I considered her far more fragile, that her act as a tough broad while at Johnny's was just a façade to cover the fear and anxiety stemming from her time and terror at the hands of Jordan. But while I was sure that part of her lay under the surface, it no longer seemed to grip her so tight, and for whatever reason the more adventurous and determined aspect of her character was taking charge.

I didn't know if that was good or bad.

Despite my desire for sleep, other complications were keeping my eyes open and my mind alert. I hadn't been entirely honest with either Agnes or Bernie about Carmichael and our little *talk*. Before hearing he was dead, I considered the delusional nature of his quest simply the ravings of someone too long disconnected from society, outside of his patrons, and obsessed with a kind of fantasy existence out in the desolation of a post-apocalyptic American dream. That he was able to finance that fantasy by duping rich pissed-off rubes was, to me, the very essence of the American dream. Ironic that it might have killed him.

Then again, he had assumed that I, too, might be a rich pissed-off rube!

I might be rich, I mused in the dark; I might occasionally be pissed-off, but I liked to think I was a better class of goof than a rube. I recognized the scam, but played along just to hear the pitch. That I *got* the *sarcasm* woven into his short book of verbose prose was as part of the scam, as was the need to separate me from as much of my ill-gotten wealth as possible. I thought, all in all, it was a righteous scam and anyone buying into it got what they deserved.

The only problem was that he was buying into his scam and that killed him, either by his, his wife's, or some other hand. That he, or his wife, were responsible for their deaths was one thing, but the possibility of conspiratorial murder was quite another. That made Bernie's gloom more infectious, and the two goons materializing at our door were not helping to allay my growing anxiety. Added to that was Agnes' new found passion to play detective, or chump, that only brought back bad memories of the Marshan affair with its bloody heads and dead eyes.

I was, I told myself, content to play grandpa rather than Marlowe or Spade, but I could never leave well enough alone. No, I wanted to talk to the prophet, and now the prophet was dead, and I was the last conspirator to bask in his presence.

It was easy to see why I would be popular with quite a few interested parties.

I knew the plan.

I thought...

At some point during the night I drifted off and as the light broke through the window to greet the new day, I awoke to find Agnes Duquesne standing over me, her arms crossed and a look of impatience directed at the stooge still in bed.

"What?" seemed like a perfectly legitimate question.

"Let's go sleepyhead! There's doings a transpiring."

"That's not my problem."

Agnes was unmoved.

"Up, Buttman, I'm hungry." Her demands grew more strident.

"You know how to cook..."

"UP!"

"I want a divorce," I whined as I slowly got out of bed.

"Tough. You have twenty minutes." She turned and walked away. I should have gone back to sleep.

Breakfast was interrupted, twice, by the vile phone yoked about me. As expected, it was the authorities seeking my input, they said, merely to complete the narrative of what was discovered at the compound of the departed author and his wife. The first came from the sheriff's office via the state police. I said I would happily answer any questions at my lawyer's office. I gave them Ms. Lagenfelder's number and assured them that she would take care of the arrangements. The second call came from my dear friend Jackson

Mallory, the LA homicide detective, letting me know I should expect a visit from the Secret Service.

"You're kidding, right?" I noted Agnes raising her eyebrows as I spoke.

"Nope, and this is just a friendly what's up. I'll deny that we discussed anything other than your yearly gift to the Police Officers Guild."

"You know they listen in on everything we say..."

Mallory laughed. "I don't know anything of the sort. Goodbye, Mr. Buttman, and thanks for your donation." He left me to my thoughts.

My beloved wife continued eyeing me as she sipped her coffee.

"What'd you do now, Sunshine?"

"It's a little early for the 'tude, don't you think? And for the record, I don't believe I've done anything that I haven't done before. It's that, as expected, the law would like to have a chat with us, so perhaps the question is, what did you do, beautiful?" I eyed Agnes back.

"Perhaps, but I won't cop to anything," she stated.

"I would expect nothing less." I handed her my dishes. "It's your turn."

Agnes frowned. "For a rich guy, you're something of a disappointment, Buttman."

"Your disappointment is duly noted," I said as I reluctantly called my attorney, Ms. Lagenfelder.

"Mr. Buttman, what can I do for you this fine day?" The woman was far too up beat. I dismissed her undue enthusiasm and explained our situation. "Interesting," was all she said before informing me that she'd take care of it in reassuring tones. Agnes returned to the table after helpfully placing the dishes in the sink.

"Not even the dishwasher?"

"I have my own methods, thank you very much. So, what's going on with all these calls?"

"I already told you—"

"No," she harrumphed, "as usual, you think you've told me, but I'm going to need more—"

"More what?"

"Information, butthead!"

We both laughed at that.

"That unfortunately won't come to light until we find out what the cops and the Secret Service want."

"Secret Service? You didn't mention that!" She seemed shocked.

"Didn't I?"

Agnes groaned. It was going to be that kind of day.

Ms. Lagenfelder called back to tell us the meeting with the sheriff's office would be the next day. As for the Secret Service, there had been no contact, and she suspected that any visit would be unannounced.

Meaning? "Get ready for a knock on the door at any time," she cautioned.

Agnes, already bored, was disinclined to wait around. "I say we get a hold of Dunkle and find out what he's hiding."

"And what might he be hiding?"

Agnes seemed amazed that I'd even question that. "If he had nothing to hide, then why didn't he mention that Ash and Idie lived on Dunkle property?" she said, her arms crossed. "And, knowing that, why would he be so nervous about saying anything? I noticed his little act by the door before we left, you know."

I smiled at that.

"Yes, I know. But, as you also know, the crazy Dunkle had sold the property and so Xavier no longer had any leverage, if that's your implication—"

Agnes was having none of it.

"Uh-huh." She tilted her head just a little as her eyes narrowed. I knew the look; the picture was forming. I had no one to blame but myself. It was divine retribution for my allowing her to spend enough time with me to discern my quirks and deceptions. "You're keeping secrets again, Sunshine. I can see it in your beady little eyes. You already knew that Dunkle's family owned that land, didn't you?"

"It may have come up," I admitted. Agnes leaned over me.

"Spill, Buttman, no more holding out."

"Why, whatever do you mean?" I asked.

"He's in on it, isn't he, your creepy little buddy? Having himself a good laugh hanging with the conspirators. But now the ringleader is dead and if the Secret Service is interested in you, then it makes sense that they'd be interested in him too, right?" Agnes was almost giddy. I found it alarmingly attractive.

"Maybe. He does have a penchant for mischief, but I doubt he'd be serious about something like this, and just for the record, Carmichael was not the ringleader."

"No? Then who?" She leaned in further, exposing the cleavage of her fine breasts. It was hard not to want to caress them, something she picked up on. She glanced down before smiling. "Boobs for answers, loverboy."

"That, my dear, is the question. Ash was coy about reveling names, but I know he's heavy into tech. Good enough?"

She grinned in a way that I knew meant yes. We both got up together. Agnes pressed her marvelous breasts against me and ran her hand along that part of my pants holding back my excitement. Her hand then took mine and pressed it between her legs. We stumbled to the couch, kissing and yanking at each other's clothes. Soon her unfettered breasts were in my hands and my mouth on that warm place further south. I kept up the pressure till she pulled me up and put me inside her. She came almost immediately with me not far behind. We stayed intertwined, our breathing the only sound in the room, until the small of my back began to ache. The couch was not actually designed for spontaneous sexual release and required positioning that did not favor older bodies, particularly one in a neck brace. Once we disentangled, we sat next to one another amid the mess of clothes and semen. Agnes didn't seem too bothered by that.

She ran her finger along my exposed thigh. "Boy, talk about hitting the spot! This sleuthing stuff is a real turn-on."

"Can't argue with that," I said, running my hand along her exposed thigh. Agnes moved her hand to my surprisingly insistent erection. She pushed me back into the couch and then straddled me, making sure the erection was where she wanted it. Slowly and methodically, she pushed her hips up and down.

"You're so nice and hard today. I like that!" She moaned and lowered her breasts into my face. The second orgasm was almost better than the first. Agnes shuddered as she came, then kissed me till her legs cramped.

"Damn couch," she sighed as she carefully lifted herself off me.

We stretched out as best we could, not wanting to move, but the mess required attention and I reluctantly got up. I handed Agnes her clothes while grabbing mine. We shuffled to the bathroom and washed ourselves. It was then that the doorbell rang. Agnes looked at me as if I knew who it was.

I merely shrugged.

With pants on, I went to the front door. Before me stood an Asian man about my height wearing a tan sport coat and a grey turtleneck, not exactly the uniform of a government agent. He had a pleasant smile beneath his jet-black hair, which was lacquered to a distinct shine.

"Mr. Buttman?"

"For the moment," I admitted.

The man pondered that.

"I'm Agent Nakatomi." Agent Nakatomi produced a badge from his coat pocket. He noted I was not completely dressed. "I'd appreciate a few moments of your time."

I pondered that. "Secret Service?"

"For the moment," he answered.

"Then please come in." I directed him to the kitchen table. Given the immediate activities on the couch, I felt it might not be appropriate till I had a chance to clean it. I put on my shirt. Agnes, having dressed herself, entered the kitchen, gave the Agent the once over, arched her eyebrows at me, and joined us at the table.

"I'm Agnes Duquesne, Mister?"

"This is Agent Nakatomi, from the Secret Service. He'd like a few moments of our time," I said.

Agent Nakatomi gestured for Agnes to sit down.

"Is this about the Carmichael's?" she asked.

The agent smiled.

Hard-boiled private dick Agnes Duquesne smiled back.

15

"Why would the Secret Service want to talk to us?" Agnes pressed. I had risen to get a cup of coffee. I frowned at the dishes in the sink; Agnes smiled at that, something the Agent took notice of.

"Your visit with Mr. Ashley Carmichael and his wife," he answered.

"Why would the Secret Service care about them?" she continued.

"At present, I'm not at liberty to discuss that."

"Then what liberty would we be at to discuss it?" Agnes crossed her arms. Sex had obviously emboldened her. Agent Nakatomi didn't appear overly concerned.

"As a matter of good citizenship," he said with a wry smile.

"I went out there to talk to him about his book." I swirled the coffee in the pot. "Agnes, as I'm sure she will tell you, spent time with Idina Carmichael and her pottery. Coffee?"

"Thank you." I put the cup in front of him and poured. Agnes waved me off, keeping her steely gaze on the agent. I sat down. "Were there any others with you while you were there?"

"No. Other than Hector and Bettina, who I assumed worked there, we saw no one else."

"And the substance of your conversation?"

"Oh, this and that. The vernacular of politics, the ahistorical nature of the common man, the end of the American experiment," I monotoned. The coffee was hotter and stronger than I normally preferred, but as the man responsible, I had little recourse to complain.

"Interesting." he took a sip of the hot coffee. "And what do you think of the end of the American experiment, Mr. Buttman?"

"Generally, I try not to, but it depends on the mood of those around me and whether I choose to wade into the body politic or listen to the news. For the most part, I see it for what it is, a sometimes glorious, sometimes maddening exercise in trying to, or trying not to, live up to a creed that's impossible to achieve." I felt a certain smugness at my clever reply.

Agnes rolled her eyes. "What a load of bull."

"Au contraire, my love, it is as I see it." I peered at our guest. "So, what exactly does the Secret Service hope to glean from overly academic polemics on the perceived failures of universal suffrage?" Agnes continued to frown at my choice of words, but it was rare that I got a chance to throw them out and I was feeling frisky. "Did you have a chance to talk to Mr. Carmichael before his death?"

Agent Nakatomi didn't answer.

"But you are, I assume, acquainted with the substance of his book, which is that all democracies fail, and if ours is at that point, are there those who wish to give it that little extra push? And since you're here, am I one of those looking to push?"

The agent smiled. "Are you?"

"Fortunately, I'm too pessimistic to believe such a push would produce anything other than misery, and if I may anticipate your next question, Carmichael intimated that there might be those moving in that direction if I were so inclined. But he didn't give any names, and couched his words such that if I became shocked or angry, he could reasonably say that he was merely speaking in hypotheticals, nothing more. It was, I believe, a feeling out process for the both of us."

"Do you believe, if you had been so inclined, he would have taken you into his confidence about any adventures that he knew of?"

I thought about that.

"He gave the impression he would, but that he needed to confer with unnamed others before he could be expected to take me into their confidences." I stared at the cup in front of me. "I have to say that I thought the whole thing was a ruse. A con or scam he, and maybe others, ran on fools with more money than sense. I didn't consider it legit, and I don't know that I consider it any differently now that he's dead. I mean, it could be a simple matter of domestic violence rather than anything more sinister."

Agent Nakatomi took this in before asking Agnes about her time with Idina. Agnes reiterated Idina's unhappiness about Carmichael's not allowing her to participate with his circle of friends, as well as the mood of unease she felt while talking with Idina. Nakatomi wrote a few notes on a pad he pulled from his pocket. He thanked us for our time and we walked him to the door.

I had one more question for him.

"Are you familiar with a Detective Mallory of the LAPD?"

Nakatomi pulled a pair of sunglasses from the other pocket in his coat. "I got my start with the LAPD. Detective Mallory was a mentor."

We watched as he left.

Agnes was staring at me.

"What?"

"Oh, I was wondering if you were ok," she ran her finger along the brace. "I was so in the moment earlier that I forgot about your neck when you went down on me and now I feel kinda bad about it."

"I'm fine," I assured her.

"Really?" She tapped the brace again.

"Really. Other than the angle, and I compensated for that by raising your ass. I didn't notice the brace either and since I can't move my neck because of this stupid thing, it didn't hurt."

Agnes smiled and kissed me. "Did I mention how much I love you, Sunshine?"

I kissed her back. "Yes, you mentioned it this morning while you were rousting me out of bed."

"Do you still love me?" she whispered in my ear.

I put my arm around her waist. "With all my heart, beautiful." There was more kissing.

"You've got great lips, Sunshine."

"Thanks." I noticed the gleam in her eyes. "What's on your mind, beautiful?"

She leaned back and grinned. "I think we need to find out what Dunkle is up to."

"You think so?"

"I do."

Agnes was on the prowl for more than great lips!

• • • • •

Dunkle didn't answer. I wasn't surprised. Call, I messaged, not expecting him to. Agnes was unimpressed. She had other ideas.

"There's always Natalya," she winked.

I nodded. "We'll keep that in our back pocket for now." I pressed another icon on the phone. Jones answered on the fourth ring.

"What?" he groaned.

"Any word from Jontaveus?" I asked, ignoring the slight.

"Yeah, he's back." Jones did not sound happy.

"I'd like to talk to him."

"Anything else?" He was also unusually brisk today.

"I might need Josef or Anton to hang with me and Agnes."

That perked him up. "Why?"

"Couple of toughs making threats," I answered.

Finally, a laugh from the perturbed Mr. Jones. "Do we need to talk, Buttman?"

"Lunch, noon-ish, at the Manifesto. Does that work?"

"It's a good thing I tolerate you, Buttman," he groaned.

"I love you too, man."

Mr. Jones hung up.

I considered our position. Once again, I was in the middle of something that didn't make sense, only this time I had the eager beaver Agnes along for the ride. Two words repeatedly popped in and out of my head: *chump* and *con*. I had no interest in either. Unfortunately, the eager beaver did. She was anxious to get moving, to interrogate, to get to the bottom of whatever this was. I retrieved the book from the shelf in the living room and handed it to her.

"This is part of the answer," I told her.

She sat down at the table while I rinsed the dishes and put them in the dishwasher. "I was going to do that, you know..."

"I don't know that!"

"Suit yourself." Her cheer in my debasement was manifest. "It's not my problem if you can't wait a few minutes."

I didn't have an answer for that. "Yeah, yeah, yeah" was all I could think of.

I sat down across from her after the kitchen was clean. We had an hour before it was time to join Mr. Jones. Agnes periodically looked up at me as she made faces trying to understand Carmichael's gobbledygook. My plan was to watch and wait.

After ten minutes, she tossed the book on the table. "This *book* is unreadable," she exclaimed.

"No, it's quite readable once you get used to the vernacular, which I'll admit takes a little time, like Shakespeare." My cheer at her befuddlement was manifest.

"Don't be a jerk, Buttman." She picked up the book and sarcastically read one of the numbered paragraphs to me.

"*Recognition of ignorance, of ahistorical mindsets within the commonality, are to the benefit of those so inclined by position or station to exert a fundamental narrative upon the needs of the commonality...*"

Agnes peered at me over the top of the book. "What the fuck does that mean?" she demanded.

"It basically states that most people, the commonality is his term, are ahistorical, meaning they're ignorant shlubs, and any historical education they receive is inevitably fable and myth because they did not experience it and therefore are easily manipulated by the myths fed to them by the ruling class or elite of society."

"Again, what the fuck does that mean?"

"It means the common man is easily taken advantage of because he doesn't care about history as fact, or as nuanced, only as myth. Myths that are then used to control and manipulate him," I said.

Agnes continued to frown. "What does that have to do with anything?" she huffed.

"Don't get mad. Carmichael's book is basically three sections dealing with history as myth, the inevitable failure of universal suffrage, and the means to use the ignorance of the masses against them to set up a more structured society where the decisions are made, not by politicians, but by learned men and women who are selected and educated for just such a position in society."

"That doesn't make any goddamned sense!" She handed the book to me.

"Perhaps, but that doesn't mean there isn't a segment of society that wouldn't love to see something like that come to pass," I said.

"Like Dunkle?"

"Perhaps. The big question is to figure out whether this is a serious situation, which would legitimately involve the government, or a con gone bad, both of which might explain the recent deaths of Carmichael and his wife." I watched as Agnes mulled this over.

"What about this Montgomery kid, the one Bernie is suspicious of?"

"He, my love, might be the wildcard in our little mystery."

"Then why are we just sitting here? Let's get to it!" The eager beaver stood up.

"Yes, dear."

I put the book back in my valise and into the trunk of the car. I assured myself it would all be ok. After all, the sun was out.

·   ·   ·   ·   ·

Jones was waiting at the Manifesto. He pointed to his watch as we sauntered in. "Time is money, Buttman!" He turned to Agnes. "I hope you're keeping him in line?"

I laughed at that. "It's the other way around this time," I said.

Agnes shook her head. "Ignore him," she told Jones.

It was his turn to laugh. "I try, lord knows I try."

I looked over to see if Anna was around, worried that she was with Mikal, assuming we were still off in the California desert. Jones must have picked up on that. "She's not here." He then tilted his head in the direction of Mikal's small office. "Or there."

"Just curious," I mumbled. Agnes shook her head.

"Of course," he said, sounding both incredulous and disinterested in my response. "I ordered us something to eat when I came in, so have a seat and explain to me why you might need protection from, as you put it, a couple of toughs." He smiled at the thought of that.

"It might involve Mr. Montgomery, which is why I asked to talk to him—"

"Meaning?" Jones inquired.

"Meaning something's up. When Bernie Schoor brings up his name and associates it with powerful people with crazy schemes, and then one of those crazy schemers ends up dead and the Secret Service comes a knocking, I worry. That's what it means. So, I'd like a few words with him."

"Secret Service?" Mr. Jones was now worried, too.

"Yes."

A kid, whose name I thought was Marco, brought over our food. We thanked him and sat down. Agnes was unusually quiet. No questions about Anna or comments about Mikal, just those bright blue eyes watching me and Jones. Jones waited for Marco to depart, taking off his sunglasses, before asking the obvious.

"Alright, out with it. What's going on that might have Jontaveus in a bind?"

Agnes chimed in, "Yeah, Buttman, out with it!" So much for the quiet!

"Nice," was my response to her. To Jones, "That's the million-dollar question." Neither cared for that as an answer.

"Buttman!" they cried nearly in unison.

"Alright, alright, but this is only a supposition at this point since no one has said anything out loud to me; it's only an inference—"

"We get that, Monk."

I smiled at my wife's exasperation; it's the little things.

"First, we start with the book..." I began.

"What book?" Jones interrupted.

"It's unreadable," Agnes added.

"To some. May I continue?" Agnes merely frowned. "Thank you. Yes, the book is hard to read, but I think that's part of its allure. If you can get into it, it's basically a way to bring about a new, or if you're into old Greek philosophy, an old proposed form of government that isn't the mess we endure today."

The two of them stared at me.

"In English," Agnes pleaded.

"You're talking about overthrowing the government," Jones said at last.

"In so many words..." I waited.

"Now how hard is it to just say that, Buttman?" And was rewarded.

"That's what I did say."

Agnes was not amused, and Jones was not interested in our delightful repartee.

"So some guy writes a book about overthrowing the government. Lots of people do. It's called fiction; it keeps them out of jail. What makes this guy so different?"

"It's not the book itself, and you're right, it's written in a way that allows it to be viewed as fiction if pressed. But for a select few, it's a roadmap to how you can get rid of our pesky and unreliable democracy, and replace it with something that works more the way they think it ought to—"

"The Greek thing," he interrupted.

"Yeah."

That made the big man laugh. "You can't be talking about that philosopher-king shit they made me read as a kid, are you?"

That made me laugh. "I know how it sounds, but yeah, I'm talking about that philosopher-king shit they made you read as a kid."

"And how the hell would some bullshit like that even happen? And more importantly, how would Jontaveus have anything to do with it?" He sat back and crossed his arms.

Agnes, clearly perturbed that she wasn't getting any of this but that Jones was, mimicked Jones. "Yeah, Buttman, how?" she demanded.

I gave it a minute before answering, while the smirks were still plastered across their knowing faces.

"You start by killing the president," I said.

16

There are moments, brief, fleeting, rare, such that when they find you, they must be taken in fully, like a beautiful woman or a fine wine. More prosaically, they can be like finding a wad of gum stuck to your very expensive shoes on that first step out the door. Such was this moment.

"Kill the president?" Jones asked uncomprehendingly.

"Maybe the vice president too," I added.

Agnes simply stared at me. "That's what you think this is about?"

"I know it is."

Their expressions of disbelief made my day.

Jones wasn't having it. "Do you have any idea how well protected the president is these days? How hard it would be for anyone to try to assassinate the guy? Even if you did, how would that end democracy? It didn't end after Kennedy was killed! And even if the vice president was assassinated too, there's always someone else to take his place, right?"

"I know. I didn't say I knew exactly how it might happen, only that it's considered the linchpin of the plan. That for the rest of it to be put in play, something big, something shocking, has to happen, and the president being assassinated would be big."

"Is that what Carmichael told you during your *secret* talk?" I could tell Agnes was feeling left out of the conversation.

"That was part of it, yes."

"Who's this Carmichael?" Jones asked mockingly.

"The dead schemer in the desert. We were the last visitors he and his wife had, so they say, before they were killed." I reached for my sandwich. I noticed neither Jones nor Agnes had taken a bite. Agnes relented, digging into her salad, but Jones continued staring at the clod in the neck brace.

"How do I know this isn't some goofy shit caused by your being hit in the head? I know you got a brace for your neck, but they don't make one for your head."

"Nice try," I sighed, "but this isn't just one of my more florid hallucinations—"

"But you do have them?"

"Merely a figure of speech," I allowed. "You don't have to believe a word I'm saying. It could be simple coincidence, government sensitivity, Agnes being bored—"

"Hey!" she huffed.

"She very sensitive, you know," I said to a less than amused Jones.

"I'm not here for an episode of the Monk and Agnes show, Buttman!" Everyone's a critic.

"My apologies, but you asked."

Jones, still annoyed, uncrossed his arms and leaned in. "What does this have to do with Jontaveus?"

"Maybe nothing. Maybe it's just that he's an odd duck in the mix. I mean, he's not a wealthy techie; he's not an entrenched politician or crony; he not an entrepreneur in the obvious sense, but you and I both know that sometimes, no matter how noble their intentions or their smarts, people like Montgomery can be played for suckers."

"What do you mean by 'people like that'?"

I got his inference.

"I don't mean it as a black thing, but to others it could be. I don't know. I know he stands out. I don't like saying it that way, but it's true. He knows it, and you know it, too. We talked about that." I could see Orville grousing behind the sunglasses.

"So, we did."

"Another reason to be concerned," I said.

"Yeah."

Color and racism didn't come up too often between us, and I knew there were times when my casual glibness and smart-assed remarks were not welcome, however well intentioned. Orville Riley was, as the saying goes, a prideful man and I did my best to respect that.

He got that Jontaveus Montgomery wanted to step outside expectations and beyond the usual regimented brackets that held in black politicians or aspirants to the cause; understood that it was important. But history and historical harm passed down through generations are not easily cast off, even by the enlightened young. People like Delton Manaforte may be equally enlightened, maybe, but they can also be enlightened only so far as it aids and comforts them.

Orville wanted the best for Montgomery, but like me, was more wary, concerned for the way that talk is cheap in the black community when uttered by whites, however well meaning.

Agnes finished the last of her salad. "Anything else, Sunshine?"

As if on cue, Anna walked in with, of all people, her grandfather Jerry. Agnes visibly stiffed. So did Anna. Jerr stood there giving Agnes Jean the once over before heading, on his own, towards the faux food trucks populating the west end of the dining room. Anna pointed to the other side of the room, and Agnes joined her there. Jones and I kept our mouths shut, other than to eat, and our eyes on the proceedings; mine on the women, Jones on the Jerr. While it was whispered, the conversation was not convivial. Agnes was clearly upset, and Anna measured in response to her mother. After a few tense minutes, they parted, returning to their respective corners. I was about to foolishly open my mouth when Jones, not so subtly, set his drink down and raised his eyebrows. I got the message; when Agnes wanted to talk, she'd start. The family rope-a-dope king smiled and wiped his chin.

"Much as I dig my time with you, Buttman, I got work to do. As always, it's a pleasure to see you, Agnes." Agnes did her best to smile back. Jones got up and returned the sunglasses to their rightful place. "I'll find out if Jontaveus wants to talk. He's been less communicative lately..." His voice trailed off. "You'll keep me informed?"

"I will."

"Alright then." He looked over towards Anna and the Jerr. "Well, good luck," and was on his way.

I finished my lunch as Agnes sat watching. Mikal came out of his office, took one step in our direction before stopping. I watched his eyes dart between us and Anna and her grandfather. He wisely waved and headed off towards the rehearsal rooms.

"Maybe it's a positive sign," I said. The silence was getting to me.

"Monk, not now," she growled. Jones did warn me.

"Sorry."

Jerry started our way, clearly wanting to say something to his daughter, but Anna steered him to the door. "I hope you're right," we heard him whine as he was leaving. "I'm still her father, you know. That should count for something!"

"Thanks for coming, bye," was Anna's reply. She came to the table once Jerry was out of sight. "May I sit down?"

"Of course," I told her, pulling out a chair.

"Mom?"

Agnes slumped, well aware that it wasn't that long ago when Anna would have nothing to do with her. "It's ok, you know that."

"Do I?" her daughter shot back.

"Anna please," Agnes implored, the anger abating quickly. "I'm not angry at you—"

Anna cut her off as she sat down. "Bullshit!"

An interminable few moments of silence followed.

Agnes' slouch grew as Anna waited for her mother to crack. "Alright, I'm angry with you," Agnes muttered.

"Was that so hard?" Anna pressed.

"You know it is. I don't like being angry with you, and you know how fearful I am that you'll stop talking to me like the last time," Agnes cried, wiping her eyes.

Anna, while still sitting erect, allowed her expression to soften. "This isn't like the last time and you know it." Anna hesitated. "I mean, I understand that you worry, but I'm not so... I don't know, easily offended that I can't tell one situation from another. Besides, the whole point of this is to talk about it."

"Talk about what? What a failure I am?" Agnes was devolving into her pitiable alter ego, the exact opposite of the woman so excited to play detective. I stifled a groan as Anna rolled her eyes.

"Stop with the crying and whining," Anna demanded, rather stridently. "This isn't about what a *failure* you are. This is about me trying to help grandma. You weren't even supposed to be here."

"See," I offered, knowing it would make me the bad guy.

"Shut up, Monk!" she hissed.

"Why are you here?" Anna continued, less stridently, hopefully to calm the situation.

"Buttman..." Agnes was punting the ball to me.

"We were supposed to be out on our little vacation, but we ran into some problems and decided to shorten the trip," I explained, knowing it would exasperate the daughter just as it would her mother.

"Uh-huh." Anna looked over at Agnes. I wondered if she knew how much she sounded like her mother when she said that. No matter. "You realize you have this habit of offering no specifics whenever anyone asks you a question?"

"See!" Agnes sneered. I merely shrugged.

"It's what makes me so delightful," I said. "But if you must have specifics, then here you go. We stopped to talk to a guy, well I did; Agnes talked to his wife. Then a couple of punks on motorcycles attacked us, and then we heard that the people we'd just talked to were dead, and the cops and the feds wanted to talk to us, so we came back. We're *here* because I wanted to have a few words with Mr. Jones. It's as simple as that."

"Simple as that," Anna mimicked.

"Simple as that," Agnes sarcastically mumbled, impugning the good character of her husband.

The good husband chose to take the high road and withhold comment. That forced Agnes back onto the Anna track and what was going on with the Jerr. "So, if it's ok to ask, how are you trying to help?"

"Grandma thinks a lot of our recent problems are because we're not including them, and as you know, grandpa gets a little sensitive sometimes, and lashing out at you is how he responds." Agnes tried to say something, but Anna cut her off, "Yes, I know, he can be a jerk—"

"Hey," I whined.

"Not your kind of jerk, Buttman," Agnes kindly said.

"Thank you!"

Anna wasn't any more interested in our repartee than Jones.

"Are you two done?" We both nodded. "Good! So, I was just showing him around, that's all. I took him down to my condo and then here. Simple as that."

"Simple as that," I said, smiling. Agnes groaned and shook her head.

"You're a jerk, Buttman!"

"It's in the script, remember?"

It was Anna's turn to groan.

"You two are something else," she said. That made me wink at Agnes, who laughed. Anna got up, none too pleased, but not too peeved. "I have things to do."

"Can I call you later?" Agnes asked in her insecure voice. Anna shook her head but smiled, anyway.

"Yes, Mom," and off she went.

Now that the coast was clear, Mikal came over to say hello. Agnes, too emotional to heckle him, merely said hi. I asked how things were going and he chatted on about the concerts, the kids, and the fact that the place was humming with activity. He neglected to mention the place wasn't making any real money, but I knew that already and it wasn't a problem. We'd have to raise the rates if we wanted to be anywhere near profitability and I didn't want to do that. As long as the place wasn't sucking the former estate of Judith Delashay dry, I was good with it. Plus, I knew it annoyed Macklgrew, which made me happy.

"If you're in town this Tuesday, come on down. Joanie's going to sing with us." He saved that for last. I stared at him for an unknown amount of time. He laughed at that. "She said it was your suggestion."

"Yeah, sounds like something I'd say." I looked at Agnes, who showed no interest whatsoever. "I'll try," was the best I could come up with.

"Great!" And he bounded off.

"Take me home, Sunshine." Agnes was visibly exhausted.

"Yeah, I need a break, too."

It had been a long day.

·   ·   ·   ·   ·

It got longer! We'd had visitors while we were gone, the kind who weren't terribly careful as they rummaged through our stuff. Books were off the shelves, drawers opened, and the contents spilled. I worried for a moment that Agnes would crack after the events at the Manifesto, but I'd forgotten about the new Jeckle and Hyde I was married to. Sullen Agnes was gone and the hard-boiled private dick Duquesne was on the job. She had her hands on her hips and her lips pursed as she surveyed the house.

"I don't see anything missing, do you?" I never had a chance to answer. "Makes you wonder," she mused, putting a string of fake pearls back in their tray on the dresser. We inventoried the house just to be sure. It didn't take long; it wasn't large or overly stuffed with the detritus of our years together.

"It seems to all be here," I said as we finished. "Nothing seems to be missing." The items of any value to thieves were where they should be, the TV, the stereo, jewelry. Methodically, I began to clean up. Agnes stood there, deep in thought.

"Doesn't make any sense, does it?" she announced at last.

"Depends on how you look at it."

"Meaning?"

"Meaning—"

"Meaning what they were looking for they didn't find," she interrupted with self-evident glee. "They weren't here just to steal stuff." She picked a book up off the floor. "Now the question is what?"

"That's the question." We continued putting the place back together. All the while, I watched the wheels spinning in Agnes' head. She didn't seem at all concerned that someone had broken in, that our little sanctum had been violated. I, on the other hand, was. The only other things they might have been after were the firearms. The 45 was still in my pocket and I found the shotgun where it always was, behind the seat in the truck. Agnes continued milling about, thinking, tapping her foot as I returned from the carport.

"Any answers?" I queried the budding sleuth.

"No," she said, vexed.

"Maybe, like the visit yesterday, it was more a warning than anything else."

She thought about that. "Warning about what? That we talked to two people, who—"

"Who are now dead," I said, finishing the thought.

"What do we do now?"

It was then that I realized I hadn't discussed having Anton or Josef tag along with us during our chat with Jones. "I think we take Bernie's advice and hide out at the big house."

Agnes frowned at that. "Yeah, I guess," but didn't shoot the idea down.

I reached in the small drawer of one of the small accent tables by the couch, taking out the sap. I handed it to Agnes.

"What do I do with this?"

"It's for whacking guys. Tough babes like you might need it for protection. Would you prefer a gun?" I knew the answer.

"You know I don't like guns." Agnes swung the sap in a small figure eight. "The thing's heavy," she said.

"Yeah, you smack 'em at the back of the neck, knocks 'em out." I pointed to the back of my neck. Agnes playfully tapped the brace with the sap.

"Like that?"

"Like that."

With a reluctance we both shared, we dolefully locked up the small house in West Covina before heading to the big house in Beverly Hills. Agnes recommended calling Rebekah. We'd already surprised one daughter. Was it wise to risk surprising another?

"They might be running around naked for all we know," she said blithely. All I could think of was me and Judith running around naked. It was, however, something I wouldn't put past my adventurous daughter.

"Maybe." I sent a text: *we're coming over, details to follow*. I didn't include any details.

Rebekah's return text was: *ok*. There was no follow up asking for details.

They were, as expected, lounging around the pool. Zach and Lizzy shouted upon seeing us and ran to the threshold of the sliding door, knowing that house rules prohibited them from running around the house all wet and everything!

It felt like old times.

17

"What'd you do this time" was how my grateful daughter chose to greet me.

"I killed a guy just to watch him die, so I'm hiding out here," I smirked.

"Nice."

The kids waited patiently by the pool while grandpa put on his suit. Agnes demurred, preferring instead to pour herself a drink and fall asleep in the cabana. Once I emerged from the changing room, each kid grabbed a leg and we stick-walked to the shallow end. I advised them to not be too loud or the grumpy woman would complain.

"I heard that, Buttman!"

Laughter followed.

Later, we ordered pizza and ate too much. The kids were put to bed, and the evening ended in quiet reflection, or what passed for it, with us sheltering our own thoughts as the city rumbled below.

The next morning, like the evening before, brought back a flood of memories as I rose early to make breakfast. Fidel, ever mindful, ever diligent, was up not long after me, prepared to face his day with a steadfast combination of drive and good humor. Consequently, it was important to me that he start his day well fed. It also gave us a few minutes without the distraction of wives and kids.

The state of things was best examined at this time.

After seeing him off, and ruefully noting how easily Rebekah assumed my taking care of her husband while she slept, I waited for the others while nursing a cup of coffee. The kids were next, expecting pancakes or some other exotica from Gamps. They were not disappointed, for they were greeted with waffles and a bounty of sugar to either pour or sprinkle upon them. They dug right in. There were strawberries and blueberries as well, mainly to ease my troubled mind. I thought, as I watched them, that there was no greater pleasure on earth than feeding delighted children and allowing them to share their interests and laments.

Zach, now three, had become quite opinionated in his likes and dislikes, and was keen to discuss them. These activities of late concentrated on anything requiring precise hand-eye coordination. His passion, at the moment, revolved around constructing things, understood only by him, using the impressive pile of used Legos I bought on impulse at a garage sale down the street from the little house, and which accompanied him wherever he went. His other great love was water and between the kiddie pool in West Covina, the infinity pool here on the hill, and the ocean not far away, he was always close to his native state. He talked of that as well.

Lizzy, nearly two, was ever eager to join her brother in our conversations. Her vocabulary and ability to speak clearly were still works in progress, but that did not stop her trying and by and large it did not annoy Zach as she babbled alongside him. They were a joyous cacophony to my ears, and I took seriously the substance and topics of our many talks. We were in the midst of one such conversation, with Zach demonstrating, using hand gestures, the value of the little round red connectors, while Lizzy played along verbally, when Rebekah and Agnes finally came out of their rooms, no doubt enlivened by the volume of our fierce debate.

"You know I can hear you guys all the way down the hall," their grouchy mother informed them. We stopped only long enough to show we didn't care.

"Hungry?" I asked, knowing it was a stupid question to ask this particular pregnant woman whose appetite did not suffer through gestation.

"I'm on a diet, you know!" I smiled as she piled the waffles on her plate. Having observed her through her two previous pregnancies, I decided not to comment.

Instead, I handed Agnes her cup of coffee. I watched in satisfaction as they scarfed down their confectionary breakfast. There were complaints that there wasn't enough, but I like to leave them wanting more. Zach and Lizzy kept up the conversation while I cleaned the kitchen. Agnes and Rebekah retreated to their rooms, presumably to make themselves presentable to the outside world. I made a comment about that once but was told, as a man, I wouldn't understand, and they were right.

"What are you two up to today?" my daughter asked as I helped put Lizzy in her car seat. It was time for them to return to their home in the burbs.

"We have an appointment to see the fuzz down at my lawyer's office."

"Why do you need to talk to the fuzz?" Rebekah laughed as she said the word, fuzz.

"It's about two people that died not too long after we talked to them." I kissed Lizzy on the forehead. Zach frowned, so I kissed his forehead, which made him laugh. The world was right again.

"So, you weren't joking about killing a guy just to watch die, eh?"

I just shook my head. "Nice."

Agnes slipped her hand in mine as they drove off.

"It's time to go, Felonious Monk." She starting laughing at her joke.

"Very funny." My attempt at solemnity only made her laugh harder. I sighed and pushed the comedian towards the car.

•   •   •   •   •

Taylor Lagenfelder was delighted to see us. I saw no reason for this, but she persisted. She and Agnes made pleasantries while I looked for signs of the fuzz. The state police, she said, were waiting, but not expecting us for another ten minutes. Was there anything she should know before we went in? I told her what I knew, as did Agnes. I passed on what Nakatomi had asked us, then asked for her thoughts on the matter.

"I'll have to think on it," but I could see lights coming on. I wondered if Agnes saw it, too. "I wouldn't bring up Agent Nakatomi unless asked. They can talk to each other if need be."

That was good enough for me. Agnes, new to this game, took mental notes.

The state police, gathering information for the county, were waiting in one of the meeting rooms at the end of the hall. They were dry as toast, matter-of-fact, and perfunctory. The questions rote: When were you there? What were you there for? How long? Did you notice anything odd? What was the context of your conversations? Thanks for your time.

As we stood up, I asked my question, "Was it murder or murder-suicide?"

"She shot him," the investigator replied, "then hung herself." They thanked us and that was that.

Agnes grimaced as they left.

"Shocked?"

"I don't believe it," she replied. "I mean, she was upset, but I didn't get the impression she was *that* upset."

"Not enough to kill?"

"Not enough to kill herself!"

"But enough to kill him?" I smiled.

"Maybe," she smiled back.

Ms. Lagenfelder greeted us at the door, asked what we thought, if there were any problems. We passed on that we thought it odd that Idina Carmichael killed herself. Taylor Lagenfelder nodded.

"Mr. Durant asked if you had a moment to talk with him." Durant? I hadn't spoken to Marsyas Durant since he came to the big house after Judith died. "I got the impression it's important," she added.

"I'm in on this too, right?" Agnes had her arms crossed and a serious look on her face.

"It's ok with me," I assured her.

"I'm sure it is, Agnes, but let me check." We stood there as she called, asked, nodded to us, and then thanked Durant. "I'll take you up."

I noted the look of satisfaction on my beloved's face.

That look changed to awe as she took in the splendor of Durant's penthouse office. The day was unusually clear, which only magnified the breadth of the vista beyond the windows. We watched as she wandered along the expanse of glass, taking in the cityscapes below and the Pacific in the distance.

"Impressed?" Durant stood to her left as I stood to her right.

"And then some. Wow!" she exclaimed.

"I assume that Agnes is to be privy to our discussions?" Durant asked as we moved from one large window to the next. I was surprised by the almost deferential tone in Durant's voice. Perhaps it was my change in status. Things *had* changed since we last met. Before that I was just a shlub, a former employee. Now, because of Judith's wealth, I guess I was more important.

"No need to keep secrets," I answered.

"Good call, Buttman."

"Excellent." Durant seemed amused by Agnes' tone. "Then perhaps as we enjoy the view, I'll explain why I asked to see you."

"Works for me. Agnes?"

Agnes, dazzled by the opulence of her surroundings, merely nodded.

"Ever heard of a man named Loran Tasabian?"

"Vaguely." An image from the newspaper came to mind.

Durant must have noticed the change in my expression. A wry smile came to him. "He's a peculiar character. In days past he'd be labeled an attack dog or shyster by certain elements of the press, but for our discussions we'll say he's often the implacable front for those businesses and individuals who want a determined, if not defiant, presence in their stead when pursuing less than, how shall I put this, popular agendas?"

I was about to answer when Agnes cut in. "So how does the Tool have anything to do with us?" She smiled wide at the shock on our faces, mine lasting longer than Durant's. Apparently, Agnes was toying with us.

"He had dealings with Johnny D?" I blurted out.

"Yes, he did," she answered, "but not necessarily to his liking, or, as you say, his client's liking. Although, now that I think about it, Johnny once said that Tasabian liked people to think he was more important than he was, that you had to make certain he wasn't trying to game you in somebody else's name. That's why they call him the Tool. He's a sneak and a liar and you can never be sure if what he's telling you is on the up and up."

"Indeed," Durant added. "He can be more trouble than he's worth, and I don't know exactly why he chose to go through me, but, as it's his calling card, he intimated that you, Monk, are in possession of something belonging to one of his clients and the client wants it back."

"What something is that?"

"He didn't say, only that you would know what he was referring to. He also intimated that there could be trouble if that something is not returned."

"Trouble?"

Durant laughed at my supposed indignation. "His modus operandi, for himself or his clients, is to tie up your time and assets in court proceedings to the point where you have to seek relief or a settlement." Durant seemed amused as he said this.

"But I have Aeschylus and Associates on my side," I countered.

"Yes," he said as the smile disappeared, "but your family might not, and the other intimation was that they were fair game in an industry where his client carried a lot of weight."

"Like Delton Manaforte might?" I inquired.

"Is that true?" Agnes added. She seemed genuinely alarmed at the idea that our kids would be targets of reprisals.

"It's possible. Mr. Manaforte has quite a bit of influence in the entertainment industry, and while he presents himself as a cheery optimist, stories of his dark side have made the rounds, though in hushed tones. My concern is what's in play here..."

"It doesn't add up, does it?" I said.

"No, it does not." Durant directed us to the chairs by the south-facing windows. "Let's start with the something. Do you know what he's referring to?"

"I assume Carmichael's book, *The Court Jester*, but as far as I know, it belongs to Xavier Dunkle. He gave it to me."

Durant leaned forward. "You have an *actual* copy of the book?"

That surprised me. "Yeah, is that a big deal?"

"And Xavier Dunkle *physically* gave you the book?"

"Yeah. I don't get the problem, it's just a book."

Durant looked over at Agnes. "Have you read the book?"

Agnes looked at me. "Buttman's read it. I tried, but..."

"Where is the book now?" he asked.

"It's here." I reached into the small valise I brought from the car and removed the book. I handed it to Durant. I thought he'd be amused by it. Instead, he took the book and examined it with an unusual amount of intent, carefully examined the binding, then the index before turning the pages. Occasionally, he'd look up, but only briefly, before returning to whatever page he was on. I watched his eyes roll across the words on the page. Agnes was just as focused on Durant. Her fascination with his surroundings had faded. The thing now was this book and its gobbledygook.

"Do you understand it?" she asked.

"For the most part," he answered, not taking his eyes off the book. "What did you think of it, Monk?"

"I thought some of it had value, but mostly I considered it a rich guy's pipe dream. And to be honest, I think the whole thing's a scam, but now that Carmichael is dead and we've had visits from both goons and the Secret Service, I could be wrong."

"You told Jones it's about killing the president," Agnes harrumphed.

"I got that from Carmichael, or that's what he used as an example," I harrumphed back. Durant put the book down.

"You spoke to Carmichael?" I noted the surprise from Durant.

"Yes, apparently just before his wife killed him, after which she hung herself—"

"Which I don't believe," Agnes interjected.

"Did he know you had the book?" I began to understand that he wasn't completely in the loop as far as our visit here was concerned.

"Yes. He liked, or maybe appreciated is a better term, that I had read it and had picked up on the satire, something he said that the others didn't get."

"Did he say who the others were?"

"Not by name, but by inference. I'm sure that some of Dunkle's relatives have read it, as has Mr. Manaforte. So, what am I missing here, Mr. Durant? What do you know about all this?"

Durant was a smart, connected guy who knew just about every important player in Southern California and beyond. If there were legitimate kooks out there, he'd have heard about it.

That was my hope.

Durant continued skimming the book. "I've only ever heard rumors of this book, probably because I'm less inclined to fanciful ideas concerning philosophical utopias, and deeply suspicious of people who believe they can pull it off. Some ideas, I believe, are best left alone. There are always complaints about our political system; there always will be, that's by design." He closed the book and handed it to me. "It might not be a bad idea to lock this up until its true ownership is determined." Durant sat back as I pondered the small leather-bound volume in my hand. "You mentioned goons and the Secret Service. Do you think their visits are related?"

"It's possible. The goons made an implied threat, but didn't actually demand anything outright—"

"They told us to mind our own business," Agnes blurted out.

"But they didn't say what business," Durant mused.

"No," she answered.

"Makes you wonder if they know, doesn't it?"

I noted the gleam in his eyes. So did Agnes.

"Do you think it's really possible that there's a group out there that wants to kill the president and somehow take over? And how can this silly book have anything, really, to do with that?" she demanded. I assumed she was asking me, but I wasn't sure. Durant caught her drift.

"Anything is possible, Agnes. Hubris has not diminished in the human spirit and we've allowed those with more money than brains to believe themselves superior. The more prosaic concern is who actually owns the book and who the goons are working for." Durant stood up. "Unfortunately, less interesting business requires my attention, so we'll have to talk about this another time. Meanwhile, I think it might be wise to be mindful of others."

We rose, and he escorted us to the elevator. We thanked him for his time. As we rode down the elevator, a devious notion came to me.

"Interested in having a little fun?" I asked my partner.

"What kind of fun are we talking about, loverboy?" Agnes put her arm around me and squeezed in tight. I laughed and kissed her.

"We'll ask MaryAnn about that kind of fun. I was thinking about using this book as bait. What do you think?"

She had frowned when I mentioned MaryAnn, but smiled at the second suggestion. "Might be interesting. As for MaryAnn, we'll save that for another time." I feigned a pout, which she ignored. "What's the plan?"

"You'll see," and I left it at that.

18

Well, sort of.

I asked Ms. Lagenfelder if there was someone around, an assistant maybe, who could make a copy of the book. She didn't think that was a problem, and soon enough, an earnest young man appeared and dutifully took the book. As we waited, we plotted our strategy in the event Tasabian and his unknown client went after us, or our kids. Since Durant was in the loop, and was as well known in the entertainment community as was Manaforte, assuming he was the client, we decided that for now that threat was a push.

I wasn't terribly worried if they came after me. It was whether they would try to hurt Fidel and Rebekah's business. As for the plan, I wanted a copy of the book just in case I needed to reference it, otherwise we'd keep the original locked up here at A and A. Given the size of the book, in case we were being watched, I'd find a book of similar size and color and make a show of having it with us. Agnes and Taylor were dubious, but made no overt objections. The young man returned with both the book and the copy. The book was placed in the safe.

"If there are individuals, goons, as you like to say, watching," Ms. Lagenfelder smiled at that, "or following you, does it make sense to have some protection?"

"Not to worry," I blithely responded, "I have my trusty 45."

Neither woman seemed comforted by that.

"She's intimating that we get Josef or Anton for protection, you doofus."

"Doofus?" I acted shocked.

"You heard me." Agnes had her arms crossed for emphasis.

"That might not be a bad idea," Taylor added in a more measured tone.

"Fine, I'll call Jones. Are we good?"

"I think so. If you need any assistance, please call." Taylor Lagenfelder walked us to the lobby. "Good luck," were her parting words of wisdom.

• • • • • •

A second call to Dunkle went unanswered. The feeling that he was avoiding me was gaining momentum. At some point, I'd need to talk to him. That brought to mind Natalya, his obvious weakness. Agnes eyed me as I called her.

"It's business, baby, business," I assured her.

"So you say..." I could tell she was mocking me.

"Yes, Mr. Monk, what can I do you for?" Natalya inquired in her almost perfected business voice. I held my tongue at her odd turn of phrase, one of the few hints you'd get that she did not start her life here. The last couple of years, she had worked hard to eliminate her eastern European accent, which oddly bummed me out. Still, though barely noticeable, the lilt was there if you listened for it. I didn't care for Mr. Monk either, but she hated saying Buttman and I refused to have her call me Sunshine, something Agnes, on the sly, had tried to talk her into.

"Have you heard from Xavier lately?" I asked. She hesitated.

"Not lately, no..." I got an odd rush knowing that she was lying to me. "Why do you ask?"

"Because I need to talk to him, and I'm pretty sure he's avoiding me." I could hear her thinking through the phone. "It's important, and he knows it, really important, Natalya. Please have him call me. How's business?" I threw that in to gage her distraction. If all was normal or well, there would be no hesitation. Instead, I got a hem and a haw as she reoriented herself to the blandness that was Sunshine Enterprises.

"Oh, a man called, I mean his rep called," she said at last, adding no other details.

"Does this man have a name?"

"Oh, wait…" The phone echoed her shuffling of notes. "Here it is, a Mr. Manaforte. He would like to meet with you to discuss our organization's work."

"And?"

Silence. Natalya seemed perplexed by the question. "And what?"

"And when did he, or his rep, say they'd like to meet?" This, too, was met with silence.

"He didn't say. I can call. I have their number."

"Please do," I said.

"Ok, bye." She ended the call. No questions for me about recent events, or upcoming meetings, or business, or art, for that matter.

I noticed Agnes smirking.

"What?"

"I didn't say anything." The smirk continued.

"Yes," I dryly noted.

•   •   •   •   •

Jones was businesslike as I made my request, "When do you want him to start?" he asked.

"Probably tomorrow."

"Probably?" He didn't care for my indecisiveness.

"I don't know exactly…"

I could hear him sigh through the phone. "You're killing me, Buttman, you really are," he whined.

"Fine," I whined back. "Tomorrow, at the big house. Anything on Jontaveus?" It was Jones' turn to equivocate and my turn to sigh. Mr. Jones didn't care for that, either.

"I don't need the bullshit, Buttman!"

"Nobody does, but there you are. Any word?"

"I don't think it's gonna happen. He said he needed to take a break from you white middle-aged know-it-alls. I got the impression his trip to Washington was a bust. Sorry, man, I did what I could." Middle-aged?

"That's too bad, but if you would be so kind, would you let him know I'll be at the Manifesto tomorrow night if he changes his mind?"

"Why tomorrow?" he asked, intrigued.

"Mikal said Joanie was going to sing with them, so I figured, what the hell."

He laughed at that. "Alright, I'll pass it along. Anton'll be over in the morning. Any specific time?"

"Ten works," I said.

He hung up, half-laughing, half-muttering.

· · · · · ·

The next stop was a stationery store that had the kind of bound notebooks that resembled Carmichael's book.

Agnes shook her head as I made a show of carrying the briefcase out of A and A.

"Maybe you should just hold up the fake book so whoever you think is watching can see it," she mocked as we left the stationery store.

"Maybe I will, Ms. Smarty-pants, maybe I will," I huffed.

"Do you honestly believe this will fool anyone?"

"Do you honestly believe we will encounter anyone more erudite than the two goons we encountered at the house?"

Agnes frowned at me. "I don't know what that means, *Mr.* Smarty-pants."

I smiled at that. "It means at this level we're not dealing with the brains of the operation, and as such, we can be more theatrical, if you will, in our approach. You have to be smart enough not to be fooled, and I doubt whoever is being tasked to keep an eye on us is up to that."

"We'll see, won't we?" she countered.

"We will indeed." I placed the notebook in the briefcase, which I put it in the trunk.

"Now what?" she asked as I started up the 500.

"Lunch." I was hungry.

•   •   •   •   •   •

Natalya called. Mr. Delton Manaforte has time tomorrow around lunch. Would it be convenient to meet? I said sure, we could meet at the big house for lunch. I asked her to find out if he had any food preferences or dietary restrictions.

"Should I be there? It is about the foundation, no?" she asked.

"Ostensibly, so yes," I don't think she knew what ostensibly meant, but it was new word day with all the women in my life. I noticed Agnes scowl at the word. I simply smiled at her. "Let me know." Natalya assured me she would. No mention of her paramour, although she might object to that term being applied to Dunkle.

Agnes directed me to In-N-Out burgers for lunch. I muttered something about eating right, which she ignored. As we sat waiting for our order, with the bustle of the restaurant adding its own brand of ambiance, Agnes leaned in and motioned that I do as well.

"Yes?" I asked.

"MaryAnn texted me and..." She let that hang in the air. I knew what she was up to. The question was whether to play along.

"And?"

A sly smile followed. "And—" Our number was called. I shrugged and left my bemused wife for the counter and our singles with everything, fried onions included. I handed Agnes her burger upon my return and watched as she carefully adjusted the wrapping so as not to spill any of the burger's contents upon her person. I did the same. As she took her first bite, I made the next move in our MaryAnn chess match.

"I think it might be best if we get the fact that you slept with MaryAnn out in the open as a pretext to whether it's a good idea for us to have a three way with her."

Agnes nearly gagged.

"Monk!" was all that came out after she stopped choking. She then did a quick survey of those around us to see if my query had drawn any unwanted attention from the other diners.

"It's important to completely chew your food before swallowing," I advised with a wink.

"I don't want to talk about it now," she bristled, ignoring my helpful hint.

"Sorry, babe, but you brought it up, and I'm tired of the tease. It's true, isn't it?" I took a righteous bite of my burger, remembering to chew thoroughly.

Agnes pondered her options while munching on a handful of fries. I knew what the sheer number she was trying to digest in one bite meant: her ploy had backfired. I sensed she wanted to come clean about MaryAnn and whatever they had done, but she was also, bizarrely to my mind, worried I might be outraged and that our happy little life would somehow be tragically undone because she had committed an act of lesbianism. Thus, the now tedious tease about something she seemed loath to participate in.

I wasn't particularly interested in a three way with MaryAnn, but that declaration wasn't yet needed.

"Maybe" was her answer.

I snorted at that.

"Just be honest before you choke on the fries too!"

"You probably had your moments too, Buttman," she harrumphed.

"Yes, it's true, I'm a brazen homosexual," I countered.

"I don't need the snark, Sunshine!"

"Neither do I, now talk," I demanded. Agnes again surveyed the crowd to see how many were waiting on our every word. Sadly, none were.

"It was only two or three times," she sheepishly admitted in her little girl voice, which she knew I found erotic.

"You don't remember how many?" I goaded. She frowned at that.

"I don't know," she stammered, her head tucked into her shoulders. "I'd been drinking. I mean, it wasn't drunk sex, but you know me, I like to prime the pump sometimes..." She looked me in the eye to gage my disapproval. "Anyway, so maybe I was a little curious, and... sometimes it's nice to have someone pay you a little attention down there, and I didn't know you then," —as if that were important. "That's all, that's it."

"So, what's the big deal, then? Why the games?"

Agnes grinned at that. "I like to play games with you, you know that. As for the other, well, I haven't been shy about how I feel about Simon and Eric and what they do, and I didn't want to be a hypocrite even though its not like I wanted to marry MaryAnn or anything like that," she argued.

"No, nothing like that," I added. Agnes curled her lips but held her tongue.

The next few minutes were occupied with our burgers, which were threatening to spill out of their wrappers and onto our laps. I sucked down a portion of my Neapolitan shake before asking the big question.

"So why all the subterfuge about the three of us getting together? Why not be honest about what happened and either yeah or nay the proposition?"

She seemed shocked, as if I hadn't given it any thought.

"How long have you known me, Buttman?"

"I don't know, couple of months?"

"Ha, ha," she groused, "very funny. You know me well enough to know all about my insecurities and MaryAnn isn't an unattractive woman—"

"No," I interrupted, "she's a quite attractive woman." I smiled broadly as I said this.

"You're a jerk, Buttman!"

"It a part I was meant to play, but seriously—"

"Seriously," she interrupted, "the last thing I need is for you to run away with my best friend because you like her blowjobs better than mine! I won't go through that again." Agnes leaned in further. "You're thinking about that right now, aren't you?"

"I wasn't, but I am now." Which was both true and disorienting. "So just say no."

"I did."

"Yet you then teased me about it, which means that you've at least thought about whether you might like to give it a whirl, no?"

"No." She leaned back and took a drink from her diet Coke. "Well, maybe, but that doesn't mean we're going to!"

I simply shook my head. "I'm glad we got that worked out. Feel better?"

"Maybe." Her little girl voice was back. I rolled my eyes and finished my lunch. Thankfully, Agnes did the same.

• • • • • •

The two goons were across the street. I pointed them out to Agnes, who waved. I drove us back to the big house, weaving around and about the streets of Hollywood and Beverly Hills. Along the way, Agnes pulled the sap from her purse and slapped it against her palm, no doubt imagining the effect if used on the two goons behind us. I debated whether it was a good idea to try to lose them by running lights or making quick turns, but decided with my sore braced neck and my recent car troubles that this was not the time. Agnes must have been having the same thoughts.

"Don't even think about it, Monk."

"What?"

"Driving like an idiot, of course." The drollery was evident in her voice.

"I'm shocked you would think so little of me!"

"Uh-huh." She again slapped the sap against her palm. "Don't make me use this, because I will."

"And here I thought you loved me? For shame, for shame..."

"Oh, stop," she snickered. As she did, a thought came to me.

"Take Bernie's phone out of my pocket, will ya?" I tried to angle my head to the right to indicate which coat pocket it was in.

"What else would you like while I'm in your pockets?" she cooed. Her free hand was now on my thigh. That produced an erection which I probably didn't need while driving.

"What would MaryAnn do?" I asked, innocently. Agnes smacked me with the sap. "Hey?" I whined.

"I warned you, so play nice."

"Fine, we'll save that for when we get home. For now, call Bernie." Agnes shrugged, but not before running her hand along my erection.

"Promise?"

"Yes, I promise, now call."

Agnes laughed at my poor attempt to keep a straight face. Bernie answered on the third ring. As I was driving, Agnes explained the situation, then asked me what else. "I just wanted you to know we have company now," I said out loud, hoping he could hear me over the sound of the road and the car. "I don't know who they're working for, might be Manaforte, or a guy named Loran Tasabian."

"Tasabian? Interesting! Keep in touch, Monk."

"Yeah." Agnes put the phone back after Bernie hung up. Her hand returned to my thigh. I nonchalantly pulled up to the gate and then the garage. We listened as the garage door closed, leaving us alone in the semi-darkness. Agnes' hand began exploring the contours of my trousers. "There's a nice bench seat in back if you're interested?" I pointed to the back of the car.

"If I go down, will you go down?" The little girl voice was back.

Like I'm going to say no!

19

We had the house to ourselves. I tried to remember the last time it was just the two of us. I couldn't remember. The situation, coupled with our debauchery in the garage, led me to remove the rest of my clothes and jump in the pool. Agnes was aghast.

"What in the world are you doing?"

I was surprised by the question. "I'm swimming." It was all very obvious, I thought.

"You know what I mean!" This from a woman wearing little from the waist down.

"Look who's talking," I replied.

Agnes looked around, just as she had at the burger joint. "Someone might see you!"

"Who?"

It was then that the lights went off in her pretty little head. "This is a Judith thing, isn't it?" she demanded.

It was my turn to look around. "What?"

"Don't play dumb with me, you know what I mean!"

I did, but had no interest in admitting that.

"I don't think I do, beautiful." A languid smile illustrated my point. Agnes continued looking around before tossing her pants and underwear on the chaise lounge next to her. She then removed her disheveled blouse and bra, placing them with the other pieces of discarded clothing, and carefully stepped into the pool.

"If she can do it, so can I," she grumbled. "It's a good thing I'm an understanding woman, Monk Buttman!"

"I suppose it is."

Agnes continued looking around, certain we would soon both be covered and shamed by our nudity here in so public a place. On the plus side, the pool was nice and warm and she was soon covered by the sparkling blue water.

"Did you do this often with her?"

"Swim?" I feigned confusion. "All the time, it's what the pool is for."

Agnes grabbed one of Zach's beach balls and threw it at me. Her aim was still off.

"Swim naked, skinny-dip, you turd. That!"

"Swim naked? I'm shocked you would suggest such a thing."

"I thought you told me she liked to walk around naked," Agnes protested.

"She did."

Agnes stood up, naked and wet, the water lapping at her waist, trying desperately to be mad at my insolent behavior. I, on the other hand, continued to ogle her magnificent breasts, which she noticed. She smiled and splashed me before sinking back into the water to cover her shame. I swam over to her side of the pool.

"Seriously, Monk..."

I thought about it. "She refused to wear a bathing suit in her own pool. I hope that answers your question."

"That wasn't the question and you know it."

"No?" Agnes shook her head. "Well, if you must know, I did, on several occasions, swim butt-assed naked." I didn't mention Jones and that particular incident.

"Did you like it?"

I shook my head. "No, it was quite traumatizing," I confessed.

"I can see that," she motioned to the erection just under the surface. "Did you have sex in the pool, too?"

"I think the more pertinent question is, do you want to?" Agnes looked around one last time.

"No," she pointed to the lounge chair under the cabana, "but I will there."

A warm shower and dinner followed round two under the cabana. As the sun faded, I poured us both a second glass of wine and we watched the natural light disappear.

"Do you miss her?" Agnes asked out of the blue.

"Miss who?"

"Oh, for chrissakes, why do I bother?" she groaned.

"Why does anybody?" I helpfully added.

Agnes slumped into her chair, "Why can't you just talk to me?" Apparently, I'd played out my moment.

"Sometimes I do." How could I not? She was still here, roaming the rooms of her beautiful Beverly Hills home. "It's one of the reasons I prefer to live at *our* house. But to answer your inevitable next question, I don't think about her that often anymore. There's plenty going on to keep me occupied."

"Uh-huh, but thinking about someone and missing them is different. Do you miss her?" I looked over at Agnes. She tilted her head down just enough, while her eyes stayed serious, to signal that she wanted the unvarnished truth.

"Yes, there are times when I miss her, but if I don't think about her, then those feelings don't come up as often. And in truth, I didn't really know her that long to begin with, so I have to be careful that I'm not simply projecting some kind of indefinable personal loss onto her memory."

Agnes curled her lips. "In English, Buttman, not your brand of gobbledygook!"

"Oh, brother! I admitted I sometimes miss her. It does not mean I wish she was still alive because she was better than you or any of that nonsense."

"But that's only because she's dead. If she *was* alive, that would be different and maybe you would be up here running around naked and living the good life with your gorgeous girlfriend!" She turned back to the sunset.

"Yes, you're probably right, but she's not alive and I have a gorgeous wife to run around naked with, so it works out," I reasoned in my brand of gobbledygook.

"Nice try," she admonished while smiling.

"It's true whether you accept it or not." She didn't object, which I took as a good sign.

The night went quietly to sleep with us.

·   ·   ·   ·   ·

When meeting someone for the first time, in this case Delton Manaforte, there comes the internal reverberations and cartoon images of the comments and cautions you heard prior to. I was both intrigued and alarmed by the possibility that dark ambitions were afoot and that I might be amenable to join or participate. The fact that I was even entertaining the idea was upsetting. Better to not get ahead of myself, I reasoned.

As if I knew what I was doing?

Which didn't help.

The morning was uneventful, with my faithful, if that's even the right word, assistant arriving promptly at ten with the amused Anton in tow, to prep for our talk with Manaforte. He was scheduled to appear at noon, with the caterers following at twelve-thirty. Natalya set out the facts and figures brochure she had created detailing the work of the Jacob Bohrman Veterans Foundation, along with glasses for water and coffee in the library. She had procured the brand that Manaforte preferred and set about brewing a pot as a test. At ten-thirty, Theresa arrived with flowers. Natalya liked having fresh-cut flowers at these presentations. I worried about Theresa and her flower shop, but I had heard no murmuring, so told myself everything was as it should be. She seemed happy enough, trading pleasantries before rushing off. Natalya continued to survey the house as I stood there. The house had been cleaned the previous morning.

"Is there anything I can do?" I asked her. She shook her head no.

"Is Agnes joining us?" She cocked her towards Agnes, who was sitting on the couch with her phone.

"Yes, she is," Agnes blurted out.

"Did Mr. Manaforte say if he was bringing anyone with him?" I felt I should act somewhat in charge, even if I wasn't.

"Just him, although he might have a security detail," Natalya replied in her crisp, working voice. She still favored matching the color in her hair; today's color was copper, with that around her eyes, and her clothing, which was business chic and expensive. I was probably paying her too much, but she genuinely liked the job, appeared more than capable, and I was an easy touch. That she was stylish, prone to bold colors and fabrics, did not diminish the beautiful young woman she had become, and did not distract from her business-like manner.

Agnes, being Agnes, continued to be weary around Natalya for no good reason, always thinking something might be up. Thank God for Isaac and Dunkle, otherwise I'd never hear the end of it.

"Why isn't Isaac here?" Agnes asked, again reading my mind.

"He wanted to meet Mr. Manaforte, but had to go up north to see his father," Natalya answered.

"Did he say why?"

She seemed surprised I asked. "Something about his older brother, not you. He didn't tell you?"

"No, but I'm not offended." Yeah, better him than me. I wasn't particularly interested in what Sterling was up to now. I had my own mid-life crises to deal with. Natalya's surprised expression morphed into disbelief at my casual disdain for the peculiars of the Bohrman clan. After making sure I picked up on that disdain, she moved on.

"Also, Mr. Macklgrew will be here at three to go over your accounts."

"Lovely," I sighed. Natalya Constantinescu smiled at that.

"You're lucky he isn't ripping you off, Monk," Agnes barked, "so be nice!" Natalya smiled at that too. And she wonders if I miss Judith. Then again, she'd probably bark at me just as Agnes does.

. . . . .

Delton Manaforte arrived at the proscribed time, a broad smile on his face and a hand outstretched. He was not into suits, unlike yours truly, preferring a more casual appearance, but I doubt it was inexpensive. He was tall and lean, blond, reminding me of Martin Delashay. I assumed he was more informed than Martin. We welcomed him in, gave him the tour. He was fascinated that *I* had come to end up with Judith Delashay's well regarded and wondered about home.

"Happenstance" was my cogent response.

"Good lord, Buttman! He and Judith Delashay were lovers, that's how," Agnes nastily added. Natalya smiled but made no comment of her own.

"I'd heard something to that effect, but you never know, given how rumors are spread." He seemed amused by that.

"Yes," I said, lightly elbowing my wife in the ribs. She responded with a pinch.

With that out of the way, we adjourned to the library where Natalya gave her presentation, helpfully pointing out the obvious as we went along. Manaforte asked about Jacob, which prompted a certain amount of censoring on my part concerning the events of his death. If he was that curious, then he already knew. He didn't strike me as someone who came unprepared.

"So, nominally, this is a funding vehicle for various services and charities," he said, stating the obvious.

"Yes, I saw no reason to create more bureaucracy. We found that there were plenty of organizations out there with the aim and ability to help veterans, particularly those who fall between the cracks due to discharge status or homelessness. What they lacked was money. That's where we come in. My brother Isaac is responsible for vetting the organizations."

Manaforte nodded at that. "You prefer to keep it within the family?"

"Only because his mother prodded me to. If you're concerned as to his ability, he has to answer to our moneyman, Mr. Carson Macklgrew, rather than to me. I'm simply a figurehead." That caused Agnes to snort, which I ignored.

"I know of Mr. Macklgrew's reputation," he laughed. "Do you object to Mr. Macklgrew, Agnes?"

"It's not Macklgrew, it's the figurehead." It was her turn to laugh.

"You're aware I'm injured, right?" I protested while tapping on the brace.

"My apologies. Monk can be a little sensitive," she continued, much to her own personal amusement.

"Be that as it may, perhaps we shouldn't be wasting Mr. Manaforte's time with my perceived peccadilloes."

Fortunately, the caterers had arrived. Lunch was served out by the pool. Natalya took the opportunity to pepper Manaforte about his thoughts on business, while Agnes was curious about his liaisons, as he was rumored to have bedded many beautiful actresses. I did my best not to look uncoordinated as I ate. The brace occasionally caused me problems with the delivery process.

Manaforte didn't mind talking about his relationships. He was, surprisingly, rather chatty. "Actors are interesting people. You have the ones who avoid relationships with other actors because they know what actors are like, and then there are those who prefer relationships with actors because they know what actors are like."

"Because of the business?" Agnes asked.

"In part, but surviving in Hollywood requires that you be focused on yourself and your career, to the exclusion of nearly everything else. You, therefore, tend to be very self-centered and narcissistic. You have to be, unless you're an A-list talent with a string of successes to your credit. Otherwise, you can easily be replaced. You might find this strange, but I enjoy not being the center of attention. I get enough of that with business, and if I'm honest, I'm not looking for a life partner at this point, so it works to the benefit of both of us."

"You don't worry that they're trying to use you?" I asked, feeling as if I should be somewhat interested. Agnes frowned at that. Manaforte simply shrugged.

"No more than the belief that I might be trolling them. People talk in this town, so you quickly learn who is looking for what. As long as the search for advantage is mutual, it isn't a problem. For those in my position, you have to be smart, otherwise you end up dealing with the kind of blowback no amount of charm can stop. And there are always NDAs if necessary."

"Yes, my son-in-law works in the business and he's noticed, as he put it, a certain carefulness on the part of those in positions of authority these days."

"As it should be. He and your daughter own a company, correct?"

"Yes," I noticed Agnes stiffen, "technical support."

"So I've heard."

There were more questions, mostly from Natalya, about the personal business of Hollywood, of relationships and contacts, rather than funding or investment. Manaforte answered her questions with a smile and, as far as I could tell, some useful information.

With lunch finished and the conversation waning, I assumed the meeting was coming to a close. Manaforte had complimentary things to say about the foundation and pledged a contribution. His people would get in touch with Natalya, he promised. We wandered to the edge of the pool overlooking the city of Angels and took in the view; it never failed to amaze.

"It's quite a panorama," he remarked.

"That it is." What else could I say? "Is there anything else, Mr. Manaforte?"

"Yes, if you have a moment."

Yes, there was that.

He turned to Agnes and Natalya. "Would you ladies be so kind as to give us a few minutes alone?" Natalya smiled and headed towards the house. Agnes was more ambivalent before relenting.

"Remember what happened to Carmichael, Buttman," she huffed as she walked away. I noticed a sly smile on Manaforte.

"We can talk in the library," I motioned.

Once inside, I made sure the doors were closed to protect our privacy. Manaforte sat in one of the chairs looking out towards the pool and the cityscape beyond. LA's famed smog was thin enough to add just the perfect filter to the sunlight, hazy but not obscured. I wondered if our conversation would follow that tact. I sat in the chair opposite.

"Do you believe she killed him?" I thought it an interesting way to broach the subject.

20

Delton Manaforte was amused by the question, but he seemed amused by all the proceedings so far.

"I can see you're new at this," he said after allowing his bemusement to stretch out.

"At what?"

"All of it, I suppose." Manaforte's green eyes darkened. "I don't just wander into situations, Monk, that's not how I succeed. I do my research. I like to know how firm the ground is under my feet and the ground here is soft. There isn't much out there on you, and Mr. Macklgrew has done a marvelous job of obscuring the length of your fingers, which suggests a desire to preserve your anonymity. Maybe that comes from being uneasy with your newfound wealth. I've come to find that not everyone has a love of money." He shook his head at that. "Even if you're insecure about coming into Judith Delashay's estate, you've continued her philanthropy in the arts. And then there's this foray into veteran's services, but I don't sense a lot of desire or direction, it's just something for you to do. Generally, when I come across people like that, I walk the other way..."

"And yet?"

A smile came to my guest as his brows tightened above his eyes.

"I also find that I'm good at taking the stock of a man, and despite or perhaps because of your lurking in the shadows, I'm aware of your connections to some rather disturbing incidents, killings, be it those associated with Martin Delashay, or the preacher in Oklahoma. Even the death of your brother and the quiet tidying up of the other murders connected to that. You have a rather nasty history. And now we have Mr. Carmichael and his wife, who you just happened to talk to prior to their deaths. You're either very fortunate in your travels or very lucky having survived, and yet you seem to be composed and outwardly unaffected; few others would be. That intrigues me."

Manaforte was quite pleased at having the goods on me.

"I would think that intrigue would have more to do with what Carmichael had to say to me about you and about his book," I countered.

Manaforte laughed at that.

"That's what I mean, the darker face behind the failed nobody. You're more clever than you pretend to be, and far more observant. That makes me wonder if Carmichael was paying attention during your talk."

"He seemed to be. Now that he's dead, it probably doesn't matter, but I think he had a fair amount of contempt for some of his benefactors—"

"Me, for instance?" Manaforte was tapping his finger on the armrest.

"No, he was more cautious where you were concerned, but the others not so much. He also felt that too much was read into his book, or that its humor and sarcasm was not picked up on."

"And you shared that, or did he?" Manaforte's tapping continued.

"It was my observation. Have you read the book? Do you have a copy?" I was watching his fingers, noting the rhythm.

"I have and I do. Why do you ask?"

"The word's gone out that the copy I have is not mine to have and it needs to be returned. But the person who gave it to me has become disinterested in answering his phone. And when this information is given to me by Marsyas Durant, it piques my interest. Why would they contact Durant? While I may be, as you put it, lurking in the shadows, I'm not invisible. Why the play?"

"What do you think?" The meter on the tapping had picked up.

"The conspiracist is me wonders if something is now in motion. Carmichael was dismissive, but he had to be. You're not going to announce plans to murder the president and send the country into chaos to a stranger, whether you're a joker or not. Then again, if you're sniffing out possible confederates and allies, reaction is everything."

The tapping slowed.

"Then there's the matter of the convoluted syntax used in the book," I continued. "Assuming you're reading it right, it displays a barely concealed contempt for much of the country, certainly its intellect, and proposes using the atomization of modern technology to shock and awe them, while at the same time dismantling the democratic structures supporting them all in the service of a new more, how did he put it, enlightened elite. It doesn't help that he aped a French Situationalist's manifesto from the Sixties, whether by design or not, but then I doubt many know of *that* book either."

Whether Manaforte knew of the French book wasn't important; the only reason I knew about it was I was a bored farmer with time to listen to a disaffected communist stranded after wandering in the wilds of rural Virginia.

Manaforte stood up and moved to the glass doors separating us from the great outdoors.

"Yes," he said at last, "Carmichael's little book has its virtues, and it's no secret that some of us share its disdain for the supposed wisdom of the average person. However, the idea of it being the template for change is misplaced." He turned towards me, the afternoon light flowing around him, obscuring his face. "Are you a man of the people, Monk?"

"That depends on how you choose to construct a man of the people." I decided to make use of what little history I knew.

"Meaning?"

"Meaning a man of the people has to have the education and enlightenment to recognize the best direction forward. I think that's why the original version of the U.S. Constitution limited who had a say and a vote. The founders were well aware, or at least some of them were, that uneducated men were easy prey for charlatans and demagogues," I offered.

"Yes, some believe we're in the midst of that foolishness now. We've devalued the idea of leadership as a noble pursuit. It's now so tied to money and fame that it means little in the larger sense, and we are diminished because of it. Carmichael may be correct that the average man and woman are easily manipulated today. I should know." Manaforte smiled at that. "I have holdings in every business whose focus is the attention span of an average American, not to mention every other being on this planet, and manipulation is a prime component. They want leaders, they say, but what they really want is to be taken care of." Manaforte's smile faded. "The world is too complex, too distracting and disorienting, hence this stupid desire to turn back the clock to a 'simpler' time, nevermind that it didn't exist in the first place."

"And the answer?"

Delton Manaforte moved over to the bookshelves, out of the light, out of view, save for me. "The world is changing relentlessly, Monk, moving to a new dynamic. A new paradigm; a new order. The age of superpower nations is long over, as is the nation-state itself. Commerce is worldwide, has been for some time, but even more so today, affecting all markets. Money flows where it wants to regardless of, or because of, government graft." The smile returned. "They all want their cut, don't they?"

That made me think of Moses and his bromides. "It's part of the deal."

"Yes," he answered, "but the world is in flux. Borders are losing their standing in many places, nothing more than lines on an obsolete paper map."

"There are still armies defending those borders," I said.

"And for what? Who is going to attack them in this day and age? Military imperialism is long dead. People don't have the stomach for it. Besides, there's no benefit to it. The same objectives can be accomplished through commerce."

He returned to his seat.

"Then where do the answers and the changes come from?" I was tempted to offer Carmichael's, but he knew those already.

"Those changes require a different kind of leadership, one that is versed and educated in where the world is going. Our present leaders are politicians, facile tacticians, moneygrubbers funded to prop up a crumbling institution. That decay does not inspire confidence. Instead, it breeds division and dysfunction."

"You don't think we have anyone capable?"

Manaforte perked up at that. His eyes brightening.

"We do. The world is teeming with bright young people ready to challenge the status quo. It's the means, the mechanisms, the parties, and their slide into petty populism and pointless tit-for-tats that prevent those with the best minds from bringing their talents to the service of the people. We need a new articulation and respect for the work it takes to educate and support those who can lead us in the future."

"If we have the money, why not just buy better people?"

"Perhaps, but money isn't knowledge, and the process doesn't help." Manaforte got up, stepping back into the light. I got up.

"Well, good luck changing the process. It seems to be a big deal just to get any kind of budget passed," I noted.

"Yes," he said, shaking his head.

"Maybe Carmichael is right. Maybe it is the time to act?"

"Maybe is never, Mr. Buttman. To act requires something stronger than maybe." The smile returned. "Don't let Carmichael's rather grim tidings be a distraction. Instead, use the means you possess to encourage those with the drive and the vision to change the world for the better. Angry old men aren't the answer."

"Don't tell them that," I joked, for the most part.

Manaforte did his part and laughed.

Our talk was over.

He thanked us for our time and for lunch. He again promised Natalya that he would have his people get in touch with her. Anton stood just outside the door as he left. I noticed the sandwich in his hand.

"Second or third?"

He laughed. "Maybe third," he admitted.

"I don't think we'll need you tomorrow. Besides, you're probably bored." An odd thought occurred to me. "Wasn't Josef supposed to be here?"

Anton shrugged, smiled, and took another bite.

Agnes, who had been quiet as Manaforte said his goodbyes, saddled up beside me.

"Well?"

"Well, what?" I got a shot to the ribs for that. "Now, now, no need for violence. As for Mr. Manaforte, we'll have to see."

"That's it?" She seemed surprised. "No talk of taking over the country, Mr. Smartguy?"

"Not yet. I assume there's time for that later. Besides, we have more mundane things to do, like humor Mr. Macklgrew..."

I pointed to the man pulling up the drive.

. . . . .

The afternoon meeting with Macklgrew was long on brevity and short on anything terribly interesting or fun, unless the accumulation of money got you off. Agnes, deciding she needed to know more about the extent of my, or our, as she huffed when I goaded her, wealth, did her best to keep up. Natalya brought in refreshments and stayed for that part of the conversation dedicated to the foundation. Her evident energy and fascination in the operations of our now rather large philanthropic organization perked up the lagging spirits of Mr. Macklgrew. Sadly, Agnes, or maybe it was just me, wasn't as fascinated as Natalya in the minutia of the financial world.

"Have I sufficiently bored you, Monk?" He often ended our meetings with that particular comment.

"No more than usual," I answered.

Agnes shook her head. "You are so fortunate, Buttman."

"What do you mean?" I had an idea.

She turned and smiled at Mr. Macklgrew. "So long as I get my cut, you are hereby free to embezzle as much of Buttman's money as you want. He certainly doesn't seem to care."

Macklgrew laughed as I feigned indignance.

"I care enough," I protested.

"I could tell." She crossed her arms and tilted her head slightly.

"Uh-huh." I crossed mine but couldn't get my head to move. "Stupid brace!"

Natalya, unamused as always with the Agnes and Monk show, gathered up the presentation material and foundation statements Macklgrew had given us. "Will you be coming to the office, Mr. Monk? Isaac sent a text that he'd like to talk with you when he gets back."

"And when might he get back?"

"Day after tomorrow." She gave Agnes and me her coquettish smile, which I adored and which Agnes did not.

"I'll see you then," I assured her.

"Goodbye, Mr. Monk."

"Goodbye."

Agnes elbowed me as I watched her leave, but I didn't care; it was worth it!

"How was your talk with Mr. Manaforte?" Macklgrew asked as Natalya closed the front door behind her.

"Yeah, Buttman, how was it?" Agnes still had her arms crossed.

"It was as I expected it to be. Long on talk covering what we both already knew." I noted both Carson's smile and Agnes' frown.

"What's that supposed to mean, Sunshine?"

"That, my lovely bride, will depend on what happens next. What do you think, Mr. Macklgrew?"

"Unless it pertains to your finances, I think it best if I leave the conversation to the two of you. Good day." Still smiling, he left as Natalya had only moments before.

"Are you going to tell me or not?"

I leaned over and kissed her. "Unless I completely misread him, he was gauging my understanding and possible interest in what Carmichael was suggesting in the book. Where that might go, I don't know. Maybe he thinks I might be a potential ally or a possible threat. We'll have to see what his next move is."

"So, we just wait?"

I put my arms around her. "As far as he's concerned, yes. Why? What do you have in mind?" I looked into her beautiful blue eyes.

"I still think we need to find out what that weasel Xavier Dunkle is up to."

"Yes, that weasel Xavier..." I slid my hands down the back of her slacks, running my fingers along her delightful rump. My exploring did not go unnoticed.

"What's on your mind, Sunshine?" She put her hands in my back pockets, fondling my ass as I fondled hers.

"What exactly do you have in mind for the three of us, beautiful?"

"Well, if we do, and I'm not saying we are, MaryAnn likes to take the lead, so you might find yourself taking it up the ass because she tells me pegging is the new thing, and you know how MaryAnn likes to indulge in new things." She had a knowing grin and pinched my ass as she said this.

"Yes, you've filled me in on MaryAnn's interest in the latest thing. I might add that if you get to enjoy her doing me, I then get to enjoy her doing you. We both have asses she can peg. Then there are the many other configurations she might want us to try. I guess we'll have to see." I gave her my knowing grin and pinched her ass.

"I guess..."

I kissed her again as we fondled each other.

"Too bad you won't find out," she said between kisses.

"Yes, it's too bad..."

21

There was a time when I hated my life. Every day was more of the same. The routine, the monotony, the isolation. Farming is like that. No time for the weary. Throw in an unhappy wife and a moody daughter; the nature of small communities and seeing the same faces everywhere you went, and life feels like an endless, pointless grind. If it hadn't been for Carlton and Duane, I'd have lost my mind. I couldn't wait to leave.

Now I wonder.

•　　•　　•　　•　　•

Foolishly, I pictured having a nice, quiet day out by the pool. I didn't have anywhere to go till the next day, having agreed to meet Isaac at the foundation's office, and there was Joanie's singing with Mikal later that night, but that was tomorrow. Today was mine. No need to even get up early. Agnes loved to sleep in, and the kids were with their mother. I luxuriated beneath the sheets, avoiding the light of a new day.

"Up and at 'em, Sunshine," bellowed Agnes.

I reluctantly lowered the sheet to see her standing over me. I looked over at the clock. It was eight AM.

"No!" I answered and again covered my head.

I heard Agnes groan. "You have a doctor's appointment in an hour and a half and I'm hungry. Let's go, Buttman!"

Doctor's appointment? "I don't remember agreeing to that. And you can feed yourself."

Agnes tore the sheets away from me and threw open the blinds, flooding the room with warmth and light. "You know the rules, you cook! And I don't want to hear any whining about going to the doctor. Let's go, let's go, let's go!"

She offered her hand to help me up.

"I'm not very fond of you right now," I muttered.

"Don't care. In the shower, Monk." She stood there in her robe, between me and the nice warm bed.

"Are you joining me?"

Agnes smiled and pushed me towards the bathroom. "If it gets you moving, then yes."

The morning routine went quickly, and before I could protest further, I was in the doctor's office waiting. I did, however, continue to mutter under my breath, which Agnes continued to ignore. The exam was without incident and I was found to be progressing nicely. The bruises along my back were gone, and the broken neck bones were healing.

"I can take this thing off?" I tapped on the brace as the doctor placed it back around my neck. It was worth a try.

"We'll see, Mr. Buttman, but it needs to stay on for at least another four weeks."

"You got that, Monk?" added my always supportive wife.

"Yes, dear."

Damn!

If nothing else, I was healing, and I still had a glorious afternoon in which to do nothing. I passed this along to Agnes, who shook her head.

"What about Dunkle?" Agnes Duquesne was still on the case.

"What about him?"

Before she could answer, the phone Bernie had given us began ringing. Agnes picked it up.

"Buttman and Duquesne, how may I direct your call?" She smiled as she said this. Bernie, no doubt, was smiling on his end. I simply shook my head or tried to. She put the phone on speaker.

"I need to talk to the two of you, assuming Ms. Duquesne is still interested in this particular affair," he said.

"She is, Mr. Schoor. What's up?"

"Are you able to come over as soon as possible?" His voice had grown more serious.

"It's like that?" I asked.

"It is."

"We're on our way, Bern." My able assistant was visibly giddy.

"We'll talk then," Bern said before ending the call.

•   •   •   •   •

Agnes' delight did not abate even as she noticed the two goons behind us. "What about those guys?" She flicked her thumb in their direction.

"It might not be a bad idea to try to lose them. I don't know if we want them following us to Bernie's, even though I'm pretty sure he can take care of himself."

Agnes nodded. "Maybe we should call him. He might have another semi ready to roll those two!" She cackled at that.

"Maybe, but let's try to lose them before we call in the big boys."

"Gotcha!"

And with that, she roared across three lanes of traffic, producing a lot of middle fingers and honking horns. She then jumped on I-5 and hit the gas, while I, neck brace and all, tried to see if we'd lost the two goons. Before I could say yay or nay, Agnes again raced across three lanes of traffic before jumping off the freeway. Once off, she drove around a block of buildings and stopped. We sat there, engine idling, waiting to see if we'd lost the goons.

"Pretty exciting, huh?" She was breathing hard, her face flush, looking much like she did when she orgasmed.

"Well, other than that being how my recent accident occurred, and that racing around like that isn't particularly good for my injured neck, yeah, it was pretty exciting," I said.

"Geez, Monk."

Geez, indeed.

We waited ten minutes before slowly working our way through the warehouses and back towards Bernie's. The goons were nowhere to be seen.

· · · · · ·

Bernie was waiting in his office.

Agnes, chomping at the bit, jumped right in with the questions. "What have we got here, Bern?"

Bern laughed as the erstwhile detective, and her less than enthusiastic partner, sat down.

"It's the buzz your meeting with Delton Manaforte caused among his merry band," he said with a touch more seriousness. "They've been fairly quiet of late, but with Carmichael's death and now word that Manaforte is again actively seeking recruits, it appears as if whatever they have planned is now in the works."

"I don't suppose you know what the plan is?" I asked.

Bernie smiled. "It's my understanding that you're already in the know about their plans."

"Yeah," Detective Duquesne added, without subtlety, "Buttman's going to help them bump off the president!"

"Carmichael merely intimated that. He never said it directly..." I stammered, trying hard not to picture myself as a latter-day John Wilkes Booth.

"What did he say, then?" Bernie was trying hard not to get caught up in Agnes' enthusiasm.

"He said that chaos always ends in a period of reformation, usually one of conservatism and retrenchment. 'Therefore,' if I may quote him directly, 'chaos is the methodology by which change is most affected, and I can think of no better way to initiate that change than with politic turmoil, of which the most effective measure is assassination; the higher up, the better.' When I asked if that meant the president, he simply said he couldn't imagine anyone higher." I noticed Bernie rubbing his chin. "Do you think that's possible? Jones thought it was crazy. The president's too well protected today."

"Anything is *possible*," he said as he pondered my question, "but Mr. Jones is correct, getting to the president for the purposes of killing him is incredibly difficult, and the Secret Service has contingencies for every conceivable attempt. So, while possible in the abstract, it's also... unless..." He stopped rubbing his chin, and looked over at me. "Unless you have an inside man, or person," he looked at Agnes, "sorry Agnes, I don't want to be a sexist here. That to me would be the only plausible way, but again, the Secret Service would be aware of that possibility as well."

"So, what do we do?" Agnes asked.

"We play along," I said, "and wait for them to make a move. In the meantime, you and I can find what that weasel Xavier Dunkle is up to!"

"Yeah," Agnes agreed.

"Why the concern for Xavier Dunkle?" Bernie, apparently, was unaware of what the nefarious Xavier Dunkle II was up to. We were too, but Agnes was ready to find him out, regardless of his possible guilt or innocence.

"He's been acting very odd, even for him. And after giving me the book and a cryptic *be careful* before I went out to see Carmichael, he's disappeared. Won't answer his calls or texts," I said.

"I know how to flush him out!" Agnes declared.

"Yeah?"

"Yes, Agnes, do tell." Bern's smile had returned.

Agnes frowned at our lightheartedness. "I'm serious, you two."

"Sorry, Agnes." Bernie stifled his grin.

"Monk!" I put my hands up as a sign of deference. "That's better," she said. "Now, what's his Achilles heel?" She went on before we could guess, though I already knew. "Your little Romanian girlfriend, Buttman! And what gets his panties in bunch faster than anything?"

"Isaac Bohrman," I answered.

"Isaac Bohrman, who, as it happens, will be in town tomorrow to talk to you and your little Romanian girlfriend—"

"Stop with the girlfriend stuff or I *will* make her my girlfriend!" I huffed.

Bernie found this amusing. "That's not a bad idea, if as you intimate, Mr. Dunkle is jealous of your younger brother. It might draw him out. And I agree that for now we have no other choice but to wait and see what other moves Mr. Manaforte and his allies make. On my side, I'll keep an eye on whatever traffic his group is trading in, and I'll keep tabs on you two, just in case any other bikers or goons hassle you."

Agnes got up and kissed Bernie on the forehead. "Thanks, Bern!"

"Agnes," I said, shocked, "hard-boiled private dicks don't kiss their..." I tried to think of a term for Bernie that wasn't demeaning. "... Their guys on the forehead!"

Bernie burst out laughing, as did Javier, who was waiting by the door.

Agnes shook her head. "Oh, for chrissakes, Monk, man up!"

"No!"

We left them laughing.

·   ·   ·   ·   ·

"Well, that was fun," I said, still nursing my bruised ego.

"With you, it always is," my smiling wife insisted.

"Yes. Anyway, it'll be nice to get home and take it easy, have a beer and hang out in the pool."

"First you have to set up Dunkle." Dunkle?

"That can wait till tomorrow." I had no interest in talking about Xavier Dunkle.

"No, it can't."

"Why not?"

Agnes shook her head. "We have to give him time to get worked up."

I groaned. "No, if we call now, he'll try to finagle Natalya into helping him, and I noticed when I talked to her earlier, she acted like she hadn't heard from him, but I got the distinct impression she was lying, and of all of us, he'd be staying in touch with her. We'll make our push in the morning after I have a few words with my little Romanian girlfriend. I'll make sure he understands that if he doesn't show, Isaac is free to make a play for Natalya."

"Will your little Romanian girlfriend play along?"

"If she wants to stay my girlfriend, she will." I made sure Agnes noticed as I raised my eyebrows for effect.

"So long as she's not sucking your cock, Buttman."

"No, I'm looking forward to that from MaryAnn." I braced myself. I didn't have to wait long.

"You're a jerk, Buttman!" she smacked me as she said that.

"It's the role I was born to play. Oh, and just so you know, I'm serious about the Natalya talk, no more!"

Agnes groaned, but held her tongue.

· · · · ·

My nice quiet evening did not come to pass. Barron called Agnes asking if they could spend the night at the big house. Jürgen and Eva's flight home was early in the morning and we were closer to LAX. Agnes, spooked by my demand that she actually cool the snarky talk about Natalya, played nice and asked me if it was alright if they stayed with us.

"Of course, it's ok," I assured her.

The evening was a chatter-fest, particularly between Agnes, Gerta, and Eva, with Gerta translating. Jürgen bounced in and out of the conversation while continuing his exploration of the house, which now including the mechanical systems. Barron, quiet as always, tailed me as I tailed Jürgen as he admired the layout of the hydronic system, the A/C units, and the instantaneous water heater, circ pump and all.

"Much like we have in Germany," he noted with a smile.

"Yes, Judith liked that it could all be programmed and monitored at a single point. I thought she would prefer that."

"You helped her with this?" He seemed surprised.

"Yes, it was one of the few things she asked my opinion on. Usually, when it came to the house, it was her way or out you go." I smiled as I thought of her frowning at my infrequent suggestions.

"Just because I have a liking for you, doesn't mean you get a say, Monk!" she would remind me.

"Yes, dear."

She always laughed when I said that.

Later, as Agnes, Gerta, and Eva continued their conversations of God knows what, Barron, Jürgen, and I retired to the pool, the big TV, and the beers. Barron had taken a liking to the Dodgers, so we watched as they played the Cardinals.

"I want to thank you for being there for Anna and my mom," he said, out of the blue. "Being away much of the time, I sometimes worry that I should be helping..."

"You have important things to do, and it's my pleasure to help. I'm the one who's thankful for having your mother in my life. Just don't tell her that because I'll never hear the end of it. Not that she doesn't know it, but you know your mother."

He laughed at that. "Yes, I know her well."

"As for Anna, she tolerates me, which I'm grateful for, and I like to think I played a small part in helping her and your mother work out some of the distance and anger between them."

"Yes..." He was staring intently at his glass of beer.

I wondered how much anger he still harbored.

Jürgen, probably knowing more of Barron's feelings on the matter, added his two cents. "Family can be a challenge, often, but who else do we have? Time and perspective come to us all, just as we all come to terms with who we are. Family is where we come from and what we leave behind to remind the world we were even here." He raised his glass. "I would like to say how happy I am to be a part of yours and for you to be a part of mine."

"Amen to that," I said.

"Yes," was all Barron said, but a smile had come to him.

"And," I added, "as we helped Anna, we are just as willing to help you."

He nodded and softly said, "Thanks."

The Cardinals were taking it to the Dodgers, and an early morning awaited our guests, so we retired to our rooms and our slumbers. Agnes watched me as I flopped around the bed, making myself as comfortable as I could with the goddamned brace on my neck.

"I heard what you said to Barron."

"Did you now?" I couldn't help noticing there was both a tear and a smile on her face.

"You're the best thing that ever happened to me, Sunshine." She leaned in and kissed me.

"Right back at you, beautiful."

22

We rose early to see them off.

There were hugs and thank you's and plans were made to get together soon, nevermind that Germany was half-a-world away, much less the short drive up to San Luis Obispo, where Barron and Gerta now resided, and to where Agnes and I had only been once.

Soon, we agreed.

Still bleary-eyed, Agnes and I quickly returned to bed once the gate closed. We still had an hour or so before the sun would make its appearance in the east.

• • • •

My executive assistant, as was her wont, called promptly at 9am to remind me of my meeting with Isaac at 11. She liked to be organized and decided I needed to be as well.

"I'll be there," I assured her. "Is Xavier aware that you'll be meeting with Isaac?"

"Why should he be?" The tenor in her voice picked up.

"You know why, my dear Ms. Constantinescu. I need to talk to him. As my executive assistant, I expect you to assist me in my devious plans," I said in my most authoritative voice.

Agnes, standing to my left, rolled her eyes.

"What can *I* do, Mr. Monk?" I could see her smiling coyly at me.

"I know he's been staying in touch with you. And we both know he's very concerned you might find Isaac more *interesting*. I'm not asking you to do anything more than to get him to meet me, however you think you can."

"You want me to manipulate his affections for me, Mr. Monk?"

I laughed. "Yes, I do. All is fair, my dear."

Natalya Constantinescu laughed. "Am I like that?" She didn't let me answer. "As long as I can do it my way, I'll do what I can."

"Works for me. See you soon."

"Bye, Mr. Monk."

On the way out, I looked for the two goons, but the street was empty. Maybe they lost their way, I chuckled to myself.

No need for protection today.

"Barron is thinking of leaving the Army," Agnes blurted out midway to the new offices of the Jacob Bohrman Foundation.

"Is he?"

"That's what I just said! Sometimes, Buttman," she huffed.

"A little early for the 'tude, don't you think?"

She smiled and patted my leg. "No."

I didn't press for the reason and Agnes didn't offer. I knew it would come out at some point.

The offices where the foundation was now located were on the fifteenth floor of a modern skyscraper in downtown LA. In keeping with my overindulging the women in my life, I gave Natalya carte blanche in decorating the offices, with the understanding that it not be over the top. We were a philanthropic endeavor, after all.

Natalya didn't care for my patronizing tone.

"I know all about image, Mr. Monk," she admonished in her own patronizing tone.

Technically, the offices were home to The Judith Delashay Philanthropic Group, of which the foundation was a part. Natalya continued to oversee the grants Judith had started in the local art scene.

There was a foyer, a large meeting room, Natalya's office, and my office, which I didn't want, but was thrust upon by Natalya, Macklgrew, even Agnes.

"You're a big shot now, Monk. No more whining."

Natalya liked sleek modern lines and color. It was a smaller, less expensive version of Durant's office. Local art festooned the walls and horizontal surfaces while jazz and classical music, kept low, wandered the spaces. Natalya had no interest in the thump, thump, thump of modern pop music.

"That's for dancing and sex, not for work," she said.

The view out the large picture windows was of the megalopolis stretching to the east, with the mountains visible on a clear day. Natalya loved the place and was very protective of it.

My dear brother was, as was *his* wont, talking up the smiling Natalya when we arrived. He was perched strategically on the corner of her desk, while she was leaning back in her chair, ever mindful of whatever Isaac, or me, or any of us, for that matter, were up to.

Isaac, upon seeing me, rose and offered his hand. "Monk."

"Isaac." We shook hands. He wasn't quite the hugger Moses was.

"Good to see you, Agnes." He was, however, more than willing to hug my wife.

"Isaac. How's everyone up north?" Agnes asked, knowing I wouldn't.

He looked at me before answering. "It's a bit of a mess right now..." He inclined his head towards my office.

"I see." I gestured towards the door. Agnes looked at me and Natalya before going into my office. Isaac, too, looked at the two of us before following Agnes. I just smiled before turning to Natalya. "Is our dear friend aware of the situation?"

"He is," she said, still smiling, still leaning back in her chair.

I wondered what I'd gotten myself into with the delightful Ms. Constantinescu.

"What did you want to see me about?" I said to Isaac after sitting down. Isaac was in the chair across from me while Agnes sat on the couch by the window.

He turned his head in the direction of the door, which I left partly open. I didn't mind Natalya hearing. She liked being informed whether she showed it or not. "Actually, I just needed to get away from the farm." He stopped for a moment; his eyes focused on me. "Not that I don't have details of the trip to DC, it's just…"

"Is it the usual or something new?" I asked.

He laughed at that. "Well, he always wants me to come back, and there was that, but no, something's up with Sterling. He's been disappearing, or not staying in touch when he goes to San Francisco. Something. I don't know. And inevitably with Moses, it always devolves into what happened to Jacob and me staying, so I told them I had to see you." A sheepish look came over him. "Now that I say it out loud, I don't sound very caring, do I?"

"No, but having been there, I can't cast any stones…"

"No, you can't, Sunshine," added Agnes, a knowing smirk on her face.

"Anyway," I went on, ignoring the slight, "how was DC since you're here?"

"It went well, I thought. Met a lot of people, made, I think, some good connections." He smiled at that. "It's funny. At first it was, 'you're who?' But once they found out there was some serious money behind me, I didn't have any problem, at least getting in the door."

"I imagine so."

"That and I met a lot of people who know you. I was surprised by that."

Agnes laughed, catching Isaac off-guard.

"Like who?" she asked.

"Well, there was a Coronel Jaron at the Pentagon. Actually, there were a lot of officials at the Pentagon who knew of you and a man named…" He snapped his fingers. "Now I can't remember, but they said he used to work at the CIA. And there was a guy from here, Jontaveus Montgomery, though he first introduced himself as Jon."

"The man from the CIA is named Art Devaney. He grows tobacco in Virginia," I said. "What did you think of Jontaveus?"

Isaac seemed mildly surprised at my interest. "I liked him. He was different from a lot of the other people my age I ran into in DC. Not that any of us aren't trying to get ahead in this world, but most of them haven't really seen the world. You know, been somewhere that isn't America or Europe, or maybe China."

"Yes," I agreed.

"And he was interested in the foundation. I hope you don't mind, but he went with me to the VA administration and to the Pentagon, and I tagged along to a few of his meet and greets. He likes to play up the image of the black guy from LA who isn't aligned with the usual organizations. Conservatives ate it up, and the liberals were alarmed and anxious to dissuade him from believing too much of the other side's rhetoric."

"I've spoken with Mr. Montgomery on many occasions," I said, his spiel playing in my head. "I assume you told him you were my brother?"

"He figured that out," Isaac said with a laugh.

"Anything else?"

He started to shake his head, then stopped. "There was this kind of odd moment at a dinner he took me to. Ever heard of a man named Delton Manaforte?"

I looked at Agnes, who merely raised her eyebrows. "As a matter of fact, I spoke with Mr. Manaforte just two days ago."

"Interesting..." Isaac's eyes went out of focus.

"Interesting how, Isaac?" Agnes was leaning back just as Natalya had.

"The dinner was in honor of Mr. Manaforte, and a lot of business heavyweights were there. When I could, I spent most of the night pitching the foundation, got quite a few maybes and made a lot of introductions." He seemed quite proud of that. "Anyway, we were in the back, really just taking it all in, when Mr. Manaforte came over and asked to speak with Jon in private. I watched and noticed how serious the discussion was. When Jon came back, I said something like, 'wow, pretty intense' and he said 'you don't know the half of it, Ike.'" Ike went quiet again.

"What do you think he meant?" Agnes had leaned in.

"I don't know. I didn't get a chance to ask. He flew back to LA the next day, and I still had a couple of appointments to keep in DC. Then Moses called and... well, you know that part."

"We know that part," I commiserated.

Agnes shook her head. "You boys are something else."

"Yes, we are," I agreed. Isaac stifled a laugh.

Natalya came in with a delightfully devious smile and asked if we were interested in getting lunch. She knew of a great place close by. Something was up.

I said, "Sure."

Isaac excused himself. He returned with a raft of papers and a small gift. He handed it to Natalya just as Xavier Dunkle II entered the office.

We all said hello and invited him to have lunch with us.

· · · · · ·

For me, and Agnes no doubt, lunch was great fun. Natalya, while interested, feigned not to care if there was tension between her two suitors. Isaac was more relaxed, even playful, while Xavier tried very hard to be polite and not glower at the interloper seeking the affections of his beloved Natalya. Most of the talk centered on the foundation and the upcoming gallery exhibits I was being roped into seeing.

"Are you sure I have time for these?" I asked, knowing full well I did.

"Quite sure, Mr. Monk."

Agnes enjoyed it all until informed that, as Mrs. Monk, she too was being roped in. "There's more?" she whined.

It was the only time Xavier Dunkle II laughed.

At the conclusion of lunch, Isaac escorted Natalya back to work; they had things to do, contacts to enter into the database, and calls to make. Dunkle seethed as he watched them leave, but I made it plain that we needed to talk. He had to stay.

"Alright, I'm here. What?"

Agnes frowned. "Be nice, Xavier. I'd hate to have to tell Ms. Constantinescu you're a jerk."

"We wouldn't want that," I added. He fumed, but held his tongue. "Why have you been hiding? And why the sudden wariness?" I asked. "Of course, two people are dead now—"

"Three," he interrupted.

"Who?" asked Agnes.

"My uncle, Seymour."

"Is he the crazy guy who used to own the property the Carmichaels lived on?" she continued.

Xavier's eyes tightened. "Yes."

"Did his wife shoot him before hanging herself?" Agnes was having way too much fun at Xavier's expense.

"No!" Xavier crossed his arms, a deep frown plastered across his face. "Food poisoning."

"I see." Agnes had crossed her arms.

I tapped on the table. "Alright, you two…"

"He's too old," she muttered.

"Yes, well, we're not here to argue about that. How old was Seymour?" I wanted to talk about something important, not older men and younger women, whether daughter or not.

"Seventy-four, and before you say he was old, he was strong as a horse. And he was always careful with what he would eat." He stared at Agnes. "It was one of the reasons people thought him crazy," he added.

"Like you?"

Xavier tried to glower at me, but failed because he had regaled me with how his uncle was crazy many times. "It's not like that."

"Then what?"

"The book," he said. "You still have it?" I shook my head. "What'd you do with it?"

"It was Seymour's copy, yes?" I asked.

"Yes."

"And suddenly people are interested in it, want it, maybe even demanding it. And some of the people associated with it are dying..."

"Yes."

"We put the book where it's safe," Agnes told him. "Monk here is pretending to have it with him. Does that worry you, Mr. Dunkle?"

Mr. Dunkle uncrossed his arms and looked between the two of us. "I think it should worry you. I've known these people all my life. I've heard them whine and cry and wail against all the injustices that the poor rich have to endure, and I've found it to be a source of good fun, but all of those people are acting odd now. Some are scared, but some aren't. Maybe it's the times, maybe it's that idiot in the White House, but for the first time in my life, I'm scared. These people have a lot of pull, Monk, and having someone killed isn't beyond them." He looked around the restaurant as he said this.

"Yes, we've already been warned. Do you want the book back?" I was curious.

"No. I want nothing to do with that book. Burn it." He pulled out his wallet and put two hundred-dollar bills on the table. "And I'm not too old," he said to Agnes as he got up.

"Don't be a stranger," I advised him.

"Just be careful," was his answer as he left.

"What do you think, beautiful?"

Agnes smiled at that. "I think things are getting interesting."

In fact, they were just starting.

23

We were expected at the Manifesto at six. Agnes, having not seen Anna since the last time we were there and her seeing the Jerr, wanted to make amends.

"You're going to behave, right?" I couldn't help myself.

"You're a jerk, Buttman!"

"I love you too."

We found a table in the dining room.

I was mostly curious how Joanie, assuming she showed, would react to being around Mikal and whether she'd bring along her hubby, Mr. Brian Whelan. What I was not expecting was the presence of a tall, gaunt looking man asking a lot of questions.

Loran Tasabian.

The Tool eyed Agnes, who eyed him back. After a moment, a languid smile arose around his thin lips.

"I hear that Mr. Dulcimer has returned to his native lands," he said to her.

Agnes, in tough, broad mode, merely nodded.

"I'd like to speak to you in private, Mr. Buttman. If you don't mind, Ms. Duquesne," he continued.

"Ms. Duquesne is privy to all my conversations," I informed him. "If you still wish to speak to me, please have a seat." I held my hand out to the empty seat next to me.

Tasabian sat down.

"What can I do for you, Mr. Tasabian?"

The Tool looked at Agnes before turning his eyes to me. They were dark and set deep in his skull. He had the part of shyster down. "I want the book, Mr. Buttman. I know you have it in your possession."

"Yes, you made that plain to Mr. Durant, of all people." I noted that Tasabian winced at the mention of Marsyas Durant. "I'm curious, what's makes you think I have the book? That it's even in my possession? And why go through Durant?"

"I'm not here to play games, Mr. Buttman. Coy denials and superfluous questions are a waste of time. That book is important and I want it." His tone was terse and his manner grave.

"Why?"

His eyes tightened, which I didn't think was possible. "You know why," he said, looking again at Agnes, who had her arms crossed. "This isn't fun and games anymore, Mr. Buttman. People are dying. People are scared. Xavier Dunkle, for instance, seems to have fallen off the face of the Earth. Maybe it was his uncle's untimely death or the murder-suicide out in the desert. Who knows?" Loran Tasabian cracked an odd, tight smile. "I think you might, Mr. Buttman, and I think you, too, are becoming aware of the book's importance."

"And you'll do what with it, Tasabian?" Agnes was tired of listening. "Play your own games? A little blackmail? A push here and there?"

"Very clever, Ms. Duquesne, and not beyond the realm of possibilities, but for the moment, much more is at stake."

"Then perhaps the best thing is to turn it over to the authorities," I said.

"The *authorities* are well aware of the book, Mr. Buttman, and would bury it—"

"And you wouldn't?" Agnes interrupted.

Tasabian pondered my partner with less than admiration. "I know my reputation, Ms. Duquesne, and I don't shy away from it, but some things are more important. Believe it or not, I am a patriotic man and I care deeply about the fate of this country, and the idea that it is being subverted for the ends of self-deluded plutocrats offends me deeply." He struck the table with his fist for emphasis and pointed at me. "The time is coming, Mr. Buttman, you know it as well as I. And I might add that you should take a moment to reflect on just where you sit in all of this and what that actually means." He reached in his pocket and produced a card. "Don't be fooled by what you think you can handle. I know these people; I know them well and what they're capable of. Better to give me the book."

"It's not my book to give, Mr. Tasabian."

"We both know that's not true, Mr. Buttman." He stood up.

"I'll give it due consideration," I said.

"Soon, Mr. Buttman."

"Goodbye, Mr. Tasabian." Agnes smiled.

"Soon."

"What do you think, beautiful?" I asked after Tasabian had left the building.

"I think his name says it all: Tool. I don't buy any of that patriotic BS. I think he wants the book for blackmail and to push people." Agnes was lightly tapping the lipstick case she had absentmindedly taken out of her purse. "I wonder..."

"Wonder what?"

"If Mr. Tasabian is hurting, if you know what I mean?"

"Money?"

Agnes grinned. "Yeah. I remember hearing he was trying to drum up business. Apparently, his recent divorce was a little too costly. I think A and A represented his ex," she said, laughing. "Anyway, I know a guy who might know."

"So long as you know a guy."

"Yes, Mr. Sunshine, I do." She kept laughing as I rolled my eyes.

•   •   •   •   •

The evening's festivities just kept coming. Joanie, to my mild surprise, made good on her promise to show and brought along her husband, who was delighted to see me, and why not? He made a pretty penny on the sale of the Moonlight Arms, the retirement bungalows I used to own. Joanie made a pretty penny, too. Agnes, who at the time wasn't particularly interested in my pressing affairs, now peppered Brian Whelan on the details.

"Did I know about this, Buttman?" she asked in mock horror.

"It was mentioned a couple of times, yes," I reminded her.

"Was it? Sometimes you think you say more than you do." She raised her eyebrows. I feigned ignorance.

"It's nice to know I wasn't the only one you pulled that stunt with." Joanie, smiling, felt the need to pile on.

"I think the two of you exaggerate." I answered.

Having had a measure of fun at my expense, the talk turned to the marriage of Brian and Joanie, with Agnes asking many questions and me asking none. Everything, they assure us, was going well. I didn't particularly care. Joanie was unusually chatty; in the past, such conversations would not happen, but she was mostly miserable and defensive back then. Whelan, for his part, smiled and nodded, but mostly worked his phone.

Mikal hailed his former lover and performing partner from across the room. He was his usual ebullient self, showing no signs of jealousy or contempt for the man who stole his woman, although that's not technically accurate. *That* was how I chose to think of it. As Joanie excused herself to join Mikal and the band for a quick sound check, Mr. Jones appeared with a dour Jontaveus Montgomery in tow.

Mr. Montgomery's spirits rapidly improved upon seeing Isaac and Natalya stroll in. Natalya looked gorgeous in a tight-fitting blue dress with the requisite matching blue highlights in her hair. Isaac, smartly, was wearing a light grey suit that shimmered in the light. I wondered if Xavier was aware of this night out. Agnes must have been thinking the same thing, because she smiled broadly at me as they came to our table. Anna came over and pulled Agnes away. I half expected Jerry and Denise to be the next to join us based on the sour look that crossed Agnes' face as her daughter spoke to her.

Fortunately, they did not.

Jontaveus introduced Isaac to Mr. Jones and explained their connection. Jones and I were mostly interlopers in their conversations, which revolved around their adventures in DC. As was her wont, Natalya asked them questions about how DC worked and who was worth remembering. Agnes returned, glum. Anna brought food and ignored her mother's glumness. The food was tasty, and having been sated, we made our way to the theater.

"Why so glum, chum?" I asked.

Agnes frowned. "*They* want to talk to me."

"And?"

Agnes continued to frown. "I said I'd think about it."

I decided not to pursue it further.

Joanie sounded great. Her voice, low and soft, danced with the piano and bass; the drums adding just enough beat to drive the songs. The chemistry between Joanie and Mikal was as clear as the notes cascading about us. Jones frowned as Whelan continued working his phone; it was one of his things you don't do when someone is performing. I merely shrugged when he nudged me in exasperation.

"He's not my headache," I whispered.

"It just ain't right," he murmured, shaking his head. "She's his wife, right?" I nodded. "That ain't good." I nodded again.

They played for a glorious hour and a half before taking a break. I used that time to ask Jontaveus for a moment after the show.

"Is this about Mr. Manaforte?" I noted the reserve in his reply.

"It is."

"He said you might ask."

Isaac, standing just off from us, moved in. "Mind if I join the talk?"

"That's up to Mr. Montgomery here," I said.

"It's ok."

The two of them rejoined Natalya, who was chatting up the drummer, a hep-looking dude with long flowing bleached-out hair wearing a Hawaiian shirt. Jones, who was commiserating with Agnes, wanted to know about Montgomery.

"We'll see," I told him.

"Do you ever talk normal, Buttman?"

Agnes thought that was funny. "It's true and you know it, Sunshine," was her response when I scowled at her.

To close the evening, Mikal and Joanie performed a few more songs without the bass and drums. Intimate hardly does justice to their performance. Agnes pulled me in as Joanie sang, and I swear I saw Jones dab his eyes several times. The only person not terribly drawn in was Whelan, which again drew a disapproving comment from Jones.

"That ain't good."

Once the performance was over, we gathered for a few moments to lavish praise on the performers. Joanie was on an endorphin high even as she was exhausted from singing so much.

"It's been a long time!" she exclaimed, smiling broadly.

Whelan, finally ready to acknowledge the obvious, wanted to go. He had a big day the next day. Mikal thanked her for dropping by, telling her the door was always open and I promised to meet her for coffee soon. We walked them to the door. Jones continued shaking his head as they walked away.

"Motherfucker needs to be more attentive, more supportive," he grumbled. Agnes nodded in agreement, but for reasons that probably didn't align with Jones'.

Isaac said he'd like to talk later. He and Natalya had further plans and bid us goodnight. I directed Agnes, Jones, and Montgomery to a table.

"You wanted to talk about Mr. Manaforte?" Montgomery asked. The lightness from the performance was fading.

"Yes. I was curious about your impressions of the man," I said.

Jontaveus Montgomery crossed his arms and pondered the three of us. "This might surprise you, but I'm no babe in the woods. I get why I have access to Mr. Manaforte and his people, and maybe they're thinking that I might be a useful pawn in some bigger game, but I got my own ideas and if it gets me more access with them thinking I can be maneuvered this way and that, so be it." I started to say something, but he cut me off. "And I've heard the stories going round about him, so spare me that."

"And what stories might those be?" Jones asked.

Montgomery cracked a half-smile. "That he's up to something."

Jones frowned. "Is this that killing the president bullshit you threw at me before, Buttman?"

"That was Carmichael's reply to a question I asked hypothetically. Manaforte did say, when I talked to him, that change is happening and young people will be the engine of that change." I didn't actually remember him saying that, but it sounded good. "He made no mention of planning on assassinating the president," I said, smiling.

"Did you hear anything like that in DC?" Agnes asked our young activist.

"I heard a lot of things about the president, most of it bad. But that's how they do things there; smile and say one thing for the press and the people back home, but another to your cronies and pals. I didn't hear about any plans to assassinate anyone, though there were a few I met who wouldn't mind that. Who knows, maybe it'll be me? Mr. Manaforte has invited me to tag along when he meets the president next month."

Jontaveus Montgomery took obvious joy in our shock.

"Maybe that's why there's concern about you," I said after the notion of Montgomery in the Oval Office sank in.

"And who might be concerned?" Montgomery's grin had not abated.

"People whose job it is to take things like that seriously."

Jones, still working his head around Jontaveus meeting the president, slammed his fist on the table, much as Tasabian had done earlier. "I don't want to hear anything about assassinations even as a joke! I didn't go to war to sit by and listen to that kinda talk!"

"You're right, we shouldn't be so cavalier in what we say," I said.

"I didn't mean to piss you off, Mr. Riley. I just think it's a sign of the times that people are taking that kind of talk seriously. I'm not going to do anything to the president other than maybe shake his

hand. Mr. Manaforte invited several of us young people to join him."
Montgomery looked at me as he said young people.

"It's getting late, Monk," Agnes pointed to her watch. "We can talk about some of this another time."

Jones looked at his watch. "Yeah, we need to get going."

We got up and walked them to the door.

Anna came over. "Have you calmed down?"

"Yes," Agnes replied in a voice that was less that convincing.

"Good. How about lunch the day after tomorrow?"

Agnes looked at me as if I could save her. I shrugged. Agnes sighed. "Alright, we'll be here, but I'd rather do dinner... someplace nice."

Anna hugged her mother. "That's the spirit. I have to clean up. See you then. Oh, and I'll make the arrangements. I know just the place."

"I need a drink," Agnes said after wrapping herself around me.

"Big house? Little house?"

She thought for a moment. "Big house. The liquor is better."

•   •   •   •   •

We sat next to the pool, drinks in hand. The city sparkled in the distance.

"Should I worry about Mr. Montgomery?" I was curious what Agnes thought and wanted her to think about something other than dealing with her mother and father.

The phone rang before she could answer.

It was Detective Jackson Mallory.

"I already gave." I told him.

"Save the laughs for another time, Mr. Buttman. I'd like to talk to you tomorrow, police business."

"Concerning?"

Agnes, her interest peaked by something not involving the Jerr, leaned in.

"We found two guys in a car at the bottom of a ravine in Malibu—"

"And?"

"One of them had your name in his coat pocket," he answered.

"The tall one or the short one?"

"We'll talk tomorrow. Ten. Beverly Hills. Goodnight, Mr. Buttman."

"Goodnight, Detective."

"I think we should be worried about Jontaveus," Agnes said at long last.

The city below continued to sparkle.

24

Detective Mallory arrived promptly at ten. He perked up noticeably upon seeing the brace around my neck.

"I got rear-ended on the Santa Monica freeway," I said to ward off any smart-assed remarks.

"Did your beater survive?" he laughed, foiling my plans.

"Sadly, no, and it wasn't a beater."

He continued laughing at my defensive tone.

"It was a very nice heap, dear," Agnes unhelpfully added while handing Mallory a cup of coffee. "Please come in, Detective."

We sat at the counter in the kitchen. "What's on your mind?" I asked, knowing full well.

Detective Mallory stared at me dead-eyed. "Other than the fact that I keep having to ask you about the dead men I come across?"

"Other than, yes."

Mallory took out a folded piece of paper from his jacket and handed it to me. Agnes, who was sitting next to me, leaned in to see.

"It's the two goons," she observed.

"Yeah, that's them," I agreed. "Apparently, *their* heap didn't fare much better than mine, although mine was in better condition and I never had problems starting it."

"Never, Buttman?" Agnes acted surprised.

"Never," I lied. "Since you're here, Detective, I'm assuming the plummet down the hill wasn't just their driving a beater?"

"The brake line was cut. Rather obviously."

"Interesting," I mused, handing him back the paper.

"How so?"

"Well, either whoever did it was an idiot, which I'm not discounting, or was unconcerned that you, the constabulary," Agnes groaned as I used the term, "would recognize it upon inspection."

"Meaning, Buttman?"

"Meaning it's a message," Mallory answered to Agnes' question. "Is it, Mr. Buttman? And, while I'm asking, can you explain why I found your name on the tall one, as you put it?"

I smiled at that. "They were tailing us, and had been on and off since we got back from the desert."

"Why would they do that?"

"The easy answer was to intimidate us, but now that they're dead... who knows? Nor, to anticipate your next question, do I know who had them follow us. The only time they spoke to us, they were rather vague in that regard, making a few threats before driving off. That is, after they finally got *their* beater started."

"Yeah, they didn't appear too bright," added Agnes.

Mallory looked at the two of us, a smile upon his face. "I see. So, if I may," he made a slight motion with his hand. "Let me see if I have this straight. You leave for the desert, and yes, I know about that, to visit Ashley Carmichael and his wife, after which she shoots her husband before hanging herself. Then there's the incident with the two bikers at the diner and your brief arrest. When you return, you're vaguely threatened by two guys who we later find at the bottom of a ravine. Am I missing something?"

"Did they tell you the two bikers attacked us in the desert before we got to the diner?" Agnes asked.

"Didn't come up when I talked to Sheriff Dorfman," he said.

"I'm shocked," I said, just to be part of the conversation.

"As usual with you, Mr. Buttman, all this simply begs more questions." Mallory's smile had faded.

"Yes, it does."

"Any answers this time around versus the usual nada?" He crossed his arms.

"Well, Buttman, are you going to mention the president?" Agnes had crossed her arms, too.

"No, because I consider that, as I've repeated many times, Carmichael's attempt at being clever. But to answer the detective's question, if anyone is to be believed in this idiotic, and now deadly farce, then we must first believe that there is a sincere desire among certain elements—"

"Buttman," Agnes whined, "the point?"

"If I'm explaining, I can take my own circuitous route." Both Mallory and Agnes glowered, exhibiting Monk fatigue. "Alright, alright, believe it or not, it's possible there's a plot to overthrow the government and Agnes and I have sorta been sucked into it." I crossed my arms. "Happy?"

"Seriously?" the detective asked.

"That is the multi-million-dollar question." I noted the skepticism on the detective's face. "If it isn't serious, then why the visit from your friend Nakatomi of the Secret Service? And why are people associated with Carmichael, including Carmichael and his wife, dropping dead? Why when I mention any of this to people in power—"

"Durant, for instance?" Mallory interrupted.

"Exactly, although Durant was more amused by the idea. But he was not quite willing to pass it off as the idle whispering of unhappy rich guys. I don't know what exactly is going on, but I am willing to say that something is. I just don't know what."

"Tell him about the book, Monk." Agnes tapped my shoulder.

Mallory looked between us. "Book?"

I nodded. "Carmichael's book, *The Court Jester*. For some reason, it's at the center of this—"

"Loran Tasabian demanded we give it to him yesterday." Agnes was growing more animated. "What does that tell you?"

"You tell me, Ms. Duquesne?" The detective's smile had returned.

"You know him as well as I do, Detective Mallory, and when the Tool comes around demanding you do this or that, something *is* up. I don't know that I agree with Monk here that this is some kind of conspiracy, but I do think something weird is going on, and I wouldn't be surprised if more weird stuff keeps happening."

Mallory eyed me. "Why did Mr. Tasabian want the book?"

"He believes the conspiracy stuff, or so he said. Agnes—"

"*Agnes* thinks he's looking to use it to blackmail and push anyone associated with the book," Agnes added. "He also said *you guys* know all about it, and would bury it and whatever it means."

"Venality and corruption are our mottos, you know," he said.

Agnes laughed. "So I've heard."

"I heard Johnny D went back to Colombia. True?" Mallory arched his eyebrows.

"Yep," she answered, "he's had enough of the American way."

"I don't know why; he was very good at it. We couldn't get anything on him." Detective Mallory rose from his chair. "When did Agent Nakatomi speak to you?"

"The day after our visit from the recently deceased goons. You did mention that we should be on the lookout for him, remember?"

"Doesn't ring a bell, Mr. Buttman," he said with a straight face. "I'll leave you two to the rest of your day."

We walked him to the door.

"Do you know who the two goons were working for?" I asked, as Agnes opened the door.

"Loran Tasabian," he said.

We bid him a good day.

·   ·   ·   ·   ·

Our plans to return peacefully to the house in West Covina were circumvented by a tired, harried woman named Rebekah and her two restless children. Her husband, it seems, had been required to work more than he had planned, and was therefore unable to assist her in managing their overly exuberant children. Agnes invited them over without my consent.

"This is just so you can order pizza, isn't it?" I harrumphed.

Agnes was well aware the Covina house was much better stocked with healthy food than the house here in Beverly Hills.

"I don't know what you're talking about, Sunshine," she said with a suspicious lilt to her voice.

Rebekah had just enough energy to get her kids here before she dumped them in our laps and made a quick escape to the bedrooms on the other side of the house.

"I want quiet you two, understand?" she bellowed at the two small faces looking at her before lumbering off.

The kids nodded in silence, waiting for their mother to disappear from view. Once she was out of sight, they made a beeline for the pool.

"Lunch!" I said.

Zach slumped his shoulders and dragged his sorry butt back to the kitchen. "I don't wanna wait till after lunch, Gamps," he whined.

"Tough. You know the rules."

Lizzie laughed at her brother as Agnes put her in her highchair. Zach stuck his tongue out at her, which only made her laugh more.

I opened up the fridge. "Uh-oh, no good food here. Looks like we have to go back to the little house for lunch," I teased.

Zach's face fell even further and tears began to well up in his eyes. Agnes frowned at me as he started blubbering.

"You're such a jerk, Gamps," she chided.

"Hey, you invited them knowing full well there was very little food here. It's not my fault."

"There are leftover sandwiches," she huffed.

"How do you know Anton didn't eat them all?"

"Monk!"

"What?" I asked innocently. Lizzie was enjoying the show, even if Zach and Agnes were not. "Fine, here you go." I pulled out four sandwiches. "Zach, stop crying. It's undignified."

Zach wiped his eyes and unwrapped his sandwich.

"After lunch, Grammy Agnes has to go grocery shopping so we can have some healthy fish for dinner. No pizza."

Both Agnes and Zach continued to frown. It was turning into a great day.

• • • • • •

The day got better when an aggrieved Xavier Dunkle II came calling, angered that my nefarious brother was showing the delightful Ms. Constantinescu the town, that I knew about it, and had done nothing to stop it.

"Please come in," I said as I greeted him at the door. "However, we have an exhausted, pregnant woman staying with us, so I must ask you to keep your voice down."

He was no more humored than the two grumps out by the pool, even though I said they could swim quietly for a short time before heading off to the grocery store.

I led him to the library. It was enough that he was pissed. I didn't need the grump Agnes throwing barbs at the man who was too old.

Xavier stared at me from across the large table at the center of the library. It was mahogany with rose and satinwood inlays, set in the French art deco style. Eight matching chairs, two of them occupied, surrounded the table. I could tell he was trying hard to be angry with me, but we'd had the talk many times before; if he wanted Natalya so badly, he should say so and be ready for her answer, good or bad. Unfortunately, he was a coward and therefore not ready.

"How can I help you, Xavier?" I asked with a smile.

"I don't need the sarcasm today, Monk," he grumbled. I took great pride in the fact that I'd caused so many to groan and grumble this day. Including Dunkle, I'd made it to five, probably a personal record.

"I imagine not, but if this is in regards to Ms. Constantinescu, then I don't know what more I can say or do."

"Yeah, yeah, yeah..." He slumped into his chair.

"If this is about being murdered because you know about Carmichael, I don't know if I can help you there either," I said, to see if he was paying attention to what I was saying.

"Doesn't matter…" Apparently not.

His face was turned to the large window facing the city below. I watched as he absent-mindedly played with the keys in his hand.

"Why can't I just tell her how I feel, Monk?" he said at last, still staring out the window.

"Because you're a coward, because you don't want to hear that she doesn't love you. It's pretty simple."

"Yeah. And just for the record, I don't want to be murdered either, but if I hide…" He put the keys in his pocket.

"Xavier…"

"What?"

"You're a lot more fun when you're a jerk and a smartass. Snap out of it. Natalya can handle smartasses, believe me, and if you're worried about being murdered, then get mad and be a little more proactive. Self-pity doesn't suit you; you come off like a sad-assed loser. That's hardly attractive."

"Yeah, you've had lots of success with women. What do you know?" he mumbled.

I smiled at that. "Yes, my recent successes may give some heft to that idea, but I basically stumbled into it."

"Like all this wealth?" He grinned.

"Exactly."

He turned to face me. "Maybe you're right. It's time to find out one way or the other. If she doesn't… well, there are plenty of other fish in the sea."

"I'd still stick with women."

"Ha-ha," he smirked.

"That's better. Now, have you heard anything new concerning the other members of the Ashley Carmichael gang?"

"Yes, as a matter of fact, I have. It turns out a number of them have died recently from a variety of accidents and ailments; four that I've heard of. The rest are frightened. Manaforte is trying to calm them, saying it could simply be coincidence."

"Is he scared?"

Dunkle shook his head. "Hard to say. There's supposed to be a meeting, but I don't know that for sure."

"I have a place in Michigan," I said, not thinking it through, being cute.

A puzzled look came to him. "Do you? Interesting."

Agnes barged into the room, a scowl on her face. "We're getting pizza, Buttman, and that's that! Got it?"

"Yes, dear." I noticed Zach just beyond Agnes, staring in at us. "I see you, Zach!" He laughed and ran off. "Anything else, my love?"

"Not at the moment." Her scowl had magically disappeared.

Xavier Dunkle II took that moment to stand and declare himself. "Just for the record, Agnes, I'm not too old. Got that?"

Agnes smiled and shook her head. "Yes, Xavier, I got it. Now, if you two old men will excuse me, I have a pizza to order."

We watched her triumphantly depart.

"Maybe fish are better," I said.

"I still think you should stick with women," was his response.

"Ha-ha."

I invited him to stay for pizza, but the suddenly emboldened Xavier Dunkle had places to go. I wished him the best.

Rebekah came out of hibernation as the smell of Tomassa's pizza filled the house. She was groggy, but far more amenable to the rest of us than she had been earlier. Smartly, Agnes had ordered multiple pizzas, so when a frazzled and overworked Fidel stumbled in, there was plenty for everyone. Zach gave me the stink-eye for jobbing him at lunch, but it had no effect, and chances were good I'd repeat the performance at some point in the future. Besides, I was feeling proud of myself for not rubbing in the obvious at the exhausted parents scarfing down pizza.

Like I said, it was a good day.

25

Agent Nakatomi was waiting when we returned to the house in West Covina. The morning had been a cavalcade of people going this way and that. Fidel to anther shoot; Rebekah rounding up her children who didn't want to go home; Agnes assisting, and me enjoying the theatrics. Once rounded up and fed, we were off to our own little sanctuaries out east.

Agent Nakatomi was, again, rather elegantly dressed for modern-day LA, wearing a silver suit that shone in the light with a silver tie set against a light pink shirt and two-tone light brown oxfords. I was curious where he bought them.

"What brings you back our way, Agent Nakatomi?" Agnes had arched her brows and cocked her head. She was in full PI mode.

The agent smiled at Agnes. I think he was as taken by Agnes' gruff posturing as I was. "I wanted to talk to you about your recent involvements with Mr. Manaforte."

"He spoke mostly with Buttman," Agnes said as we moved into the kitchen.

"Mr. Buttman didn't share the content of those conversations with you, Ms. Duquesne?"

Agnes looked my way before answering. "He did, but Monk has a bad habit of taking long-winded journeys and using big words when I ask, so while he may talk to me, he doesn't necessarily inform me."

"I see." He seemed to find that humorous.

"Is the Secret Service concerned that Mr. Manaforte is up to no good?" I was curious.

The agent took his time in answering. "The Service is always concerned when it hears that individuals may have... convictions that might lead them to consider harming the President or Vice-President—"

"Or to events that might destabilize the country?"

"As involves fraud or currency manipulation, but other acts would fall under the direction of the FBI if they didn't directly target the President." Agent Nakatomi took the pen from his pocket, then the notebook.

"Does the Secret Service believe Mr. Manaforte may want to harm the President? I'm going to assume if it did, it would have interviewed him by now." I was still curious.

"Any contact between the Service and Mr. Manaforte would be confidential."

"But you're here," Agnes said, stating the obvious, "so you must suspect something, either from Manaforte or from us."

"True, and it's possible word got out, however erroneously, concerning Carmichael's comment to me," I added.

The agent continued to stare at us as we continued to stare back. "Anytime the word assassination comes to our ears, they perk up. It's our primary focus."

"I would expect nothing less. So, if we're willing to extrapolate relationships: if Carmichael said it to me, even as a hypothetical, there's reason to assume he said it to Manaforte, who was one of his benefactors and a member of a group that has historically been disdainful of the extent of suffrage and government expansion over the last hundred years, or so."

"English, Buttman!" Agnes groaned.

I shrugged. "If he said it to me, he probably said it to Manaforte, except to him, he might have meant it. Better?"

"You couldn't just say that?" she fumed.

"I did."

"Are you two always like this?" Agent Nakatomi wasn't as taken by our banter as we were.

"Only when the situation demands it," I said. "What's on your mind?"

"The government is always interested in having an ear present when people talk. I'm here to find out if you're willing to be those ears, to assist me in determining if any action might be warranted in this matter."

Agnes smiled broadly. "You want us to inform on Mr. Manaforte?"

"Yes." Agent Nakatomi did not smile broadly. "It's my understanding that a meeting is being considered, and that you will be invited to take part. I'd like to know what will be discussed. Are you willing to assist me?"

"As concerned citizens?" I asked.

"Yes."

I looked at Agnes, who looked at me. "If I am invited, then I'll contact you and we can go from there."

Agent Nakatomi rose from his chair and pulled a card from the case holding his badge. He handed it to me. "Let me know as soon as you find out, Mr. Buttman." He returned the case, pen, and notebook to his pocket.

"I'll do that." I put the card in my pocket.

Agnes, standing beside me as the Secret Service man drove off, ran her hand along the back of my slacks. Being private dicks, or possible accessories to people open to the temptation of bumping off the president, still turned her on.

"What's on your mind, beautiful?" I was curious.

"Your cute ass."

I checked my watch. We still had four hours before we were to meet with Anna, Denise, and the Jerr. "There's time." I put my arm around her waist.

"Yes, there is."

I saw no reason to bring up the evening's event. Might kill the moment.

·　　·　　·　　·　　·

I mentally watched Agnes run her fingers along the hair on my chest. The brace prevented me from actually looking down. I returned the favor by running my fingers along the contours of her nipples.

"We're getting pretty good at sex with your brace on," she said absentmindedly.

"That's because we're unwilling to go eight to ten weeks without sex."

"You got that right," she said, laughing. "I have a hard time going without for more than a week. I couldn't do ten."

"There's always MaryAnn if I'm not available," I teased, looking for a reaction.

"Maybe, but believe it or not, you're better down there. I like it when you get all excited. It's a real rush."

"I've noticed."

"Are you still interested in having her join us?" She was carelessly pulling the chest hairs.

"Maybe a little. Are you?"

"Maybe a little..." She reached down and took a hold of me. "Anything left in the tank?"

"I think that's obvious..." I closed my eyes and tried to relax as her hand did its magic. Soon she was on top of me and I was inside her. She rocked her hips slowly, pressing those wonderful breasts to my face. Fantasies of her and MaryAnn were dancing in my head, and before long I was in ecstasy, as was Agnes. as she continued to rise and fall to her own rhythms. After a few long kisses, she reluctantly returned to my side, my arm once again around her shoulder.

"I can't imagine how sex with MaryAnn can be any better," she said before falling asleep.

I saw no reason to argue.

The bliss of great afternoon sex and a refreshing nap was harshed by the impending appointment with Agnes' family.

"Do I have to go?" was followed by, "I don't want to go."

"Sorry, baby, but you're doomed," I said.

"You're a jerk, Buttman," she huffed.

"You're still doomed."

"That doesn't help, you know!"

"I'm not here to help," I said, standing over her as she flopped around on the bed. "You have an hour to get ready unless you plan to go naked and disheveled. Not that I mind. I find your being naked quite exciting, but…"

"Yeah, yeah, yeah." With as much melodrama as she could muster, Agnes made her way to the bathroom and made her preparations for the evening's frivolities.

• • • • •

The place was a restaurant called *Du Malle* in Anaheim, not far from where Denise and Jerry Fannis lived. It was a small, intimate French restaurant that Anna had heard about and wanted to try. We picked her up at her condo and made our way south along I-5. Little was said. Jerry and Denise were waiting at a table towards the back of the restaurant. Agnes Jean scowled at Jerry as he scowled back. Anna and Denise traded pleasantries while I smartly kept my mouth shut other than to tell Denise she looked nice.

We ordered a bottle of wine, while Jerry ordered a beer.

"You don't like beer?" Every time I had a glass of wine around him, he asked me the same thing.

"I like beer just fine," I said, as I had all the times before. I don't think he believed me anymore this time than the last. I considered reminding him of the time I drank beer with him and Barron out by the pool, but saw no point in doing so.

Anna tried to lighten the mood with small talk about her kitchen at the Manifesto and how she liked her new home, which she thanked me for once again.

"It was my pleasure," I assured her. A sly grin from Agnes reminded me that it was her idea first. I don't dispute that.

Jerry said nothing other than to order what Anna advised, as his knowledge of French food was non-existent. "If you're sure I'll like it," he grumbled.

As we waited for dinner, Denise found her courage as she took a drink of wine. "Don't you have something to say to Agnes, dear?"

"Only if she has something to say to me," he groused.

"Jerry Fannis, you promised," she chided him.

Jerry Fannis scowled at his wife before turning to his daughter. "Your mother's right, I did promise..." He took a deep breath and then a swig of beer from the bottle in front of you. "I want to apologize for the things I said the other day," he said, staring at the bottle of beer.

"I want to know what you're apologizing for?" Agnes' voice was clear, but not angry. "Dad?"

Jerry looked at his daughter for the longest time. "Will you allow me to speak freely without yelling or interrupting me?"

I noticed the fear in Denise's eyes. Anna's were neutral, and Agnes simply kept her eyes on her father.

"Yes. You can say whatever you want."

Jerry took another swig of beer, set the bottle down, and then spun it twice round before looking across at Agnes. "It's no secret that I don't care much for you. I know that's not what a father's supposed to say, but I promised to be truthful and that's how I feel. I thought we raised you better, but..." He scrunched his forehead and took the beer bottle in his hand. "But that doesn't excuse what I said to you. Your mother's right. I don't know much about you or what happened to you after Simon left. And I'll say I don't understand what happened with Simon, but I don't understand any of that anyway..."

"Why are we here, Dad? If you're just going to tell me you don't like me, I've known that since I was twelve. Talk to Simon if you don't understand what he did, but I'm done dealing with that."

"I know, but we don't have to like each other to get along..." Jerry looked at Agnes. "Do you like me, Agnes Jean?"

"No."

"Then we're even, but that doesn't mean we can't try to be decent or civil to one another." Jerry took another drink, draining the bottle.

"Do you even care about what I went through?" Agnes' voice was steady, but her hands were shaking. I reached out and took one.

"Did you?" Agnes opened her mouth, but Jerry cut her off. "You think I don't care, but did you? I heard what happened, and how you kept going back, time and time again, driving Anna and Barron away,

away from all of us. What was I supposed to do? Congratulate you that somehow you weren't beaten to death after you kept going back to a man like that?" Jerry was shaking, too. Tears began streaming down his face. "What am I supposed to say when you said absolutely nothing to us about it?"

Denise was sobbing quietly in her napkin. Anna, no stranger to any of this talk, was looking off in the distance, her eyes wet. Agnes continued to stare at her father. Jerry, embarrassed, began wiping his eyes.

Agnes sat back. "You're right, I didn't say anything because I was ashamed and embarrassed and I hated myself and everything that had happened to me." She let go of my hand and sat up. The server had our food.

We quietly watched as she put the plates in front of us.

Agnes looked at Anna before turning to her parents. "I'm not interested anymore in whether you love me or care about me or if you ever see me again, but I'm tired of being angry and tired of feeling worthless every time I see you—"

"We don't think you're worthless, dear," Denise said quietly.

Agnes looked at Jerry. "Dad?"

Jerry looked up from his meal. "Your mother's right, we don't think that. There's a difference between not liking what happened and thinking you're worthless. I don't think that." Jerry returned to his dinner.

The rest of us continued eating. Agnes sat quietly, looking at her parents, her daughter, and me.

I motioned she should eat. "It's good."

"Alright," Agnes relented. "No more talk about this. So how's work, Dad?"

"It's all right," Jerry said, not missing a beat. "I thought I'd be retired by now, but they're having a tough time finding any kids to do my job and I don't know what I'd do if I did retire, so it's ok."

"Glad to hear it."

The rest of the meal was without incident, though Jerry did concede the dish Anna had suggested for him was pretty good.

On the drive back to her condo, Anna remarked on the Ford Galaxie 500, my new heap. "I kinda like this one better than the Falcon, sorry."

"No need. It has its charms, like me." Agnes smiled at that.

"Are you ok, mom?"

Agnes had said little after we bid her parents goodnight. "No, but it's my problem."

"I know you don't believe this, but I think grandpa loves you, he just..."

"Just what?" Agnes turned to face Anna, who was in the backseat.

"Well, when I talked to him before, he admitted that he was shocked and angry when he found out dad was gay and leaving you and he also admitted that he took it out on you, but he loved dad and I think he struggled with it being something he didn't understand and it was easier to take it out on you, and the whole thing with Jordan..."

Agnes shook her head. "We don't need to go there."

"I don't mean it like that."

"It's ok, even if you do. We don't need to talk it about it anymore, ok?"

I looked at Anna in the rearview mirror as she considered her mother.

"Ok," she said as we pulled into her condo's parking garage.

26

"What do you think, Sunshine?" We were sitting in the kitchen, sharing a glass of leftover Riesling.

"I think it was good that you finally let it out," I said. "As to your father, I don't know. Before tonight, if I may be honest, I didn't think too much of him, and a part of me still doesn't, but I think he does care in his own way. His problem, as Anna said, isn't with you, but with Simon."

"Then why does he always yell at *me*?" she huffed.

"Because you always let him, you know that. Now it's different. For the first time, you fought back."

She stared at the glass, watching the last of the wine swirl as she played with it. "I guess."

I was ready to call it a day when a loud banging came from the front door. Agnes instantly perked up, downed the last of the wine, and slowly got up. I nearly burst out laughing; it was so out of place with the last five hours.

Agnes simply smiled at me. "Because it's exciting!"

The banging on the door continued.

"Do you have the 45?" she asked as she reached in her purse for the sap.

"Seriously?"

"This is serious business, Buttman," she said without a trace of irony.

"Yes, dear."

I retrieved the 45 from my coat pocket.

Loren Tasabian was about to strike the door again as I open it. He stared at the 45 gleaming in the porchlight. He was disheveled and looked as if sleep had eluded him since the last time we spoke.

"Little late, don't ya think, Tool?" Agnes was back in character. The Tool bristled at his nickname and the shamus beside me.

"I need that book, Mr. Buttman."

"It's not here, Mr. Tasabian. I have it locked up safe."

"This isn't a joke."

"No one's laughing," I said. Agnes continued to smirk.

"The book!" He was very insistent.

"It's late and the book's not here, nor is it close or easily accessible. We can talk about this at a civilized hour, someplace more convivial than our front porch."

He turned, as if spooked, peering down the street. I didn't notice anything out of place. "People are dying, Mr. Buttman, and I don't intend to join them..." He pulled his shaking hands into fists.

"Yes, we heard about the two you put on our tail," Agnes goaded him.

Tasabian's eyes tightened. "That's right, Ms. Duquesne, though I wouldn't be too cute about it. You two are in as much danger as any of the rest of us."

"And yet you still want the book?" I asked, amused.

"Yes."

I turned my eyes towards Agnes, while wanting to turn my neck and silently cursing the stupid brace. "Go home, Mr. Tasabian. I'll call you tomorrow and maybe then we'll see if there's an arrangement we can come to."

Our unwanted guest considered his options. He had none. "Tomorrow, Mr. Buttman, tomorrow."

The Tool carefully made his way to his car, mindful of any noise or disturbance along our quiet suburban street. On the plus side, his car started on the first try. We watched as he stared at us while driving away.

"What a tool," Agnes said, stating the obvious.

The morning came, as it often did, with an ever brightening of the room by a sun completely unconcerned for hard-boiled private dicks and freaked-out shysters. Agnes, invigorated by the opportunity to get in her digs on the Tool, was up with the light and dogging her less than invigorated husband.

"What's the rush, beautiful?"

Agnes, hands on her hips, shook her head. "We're burning daylight, Sunshine. Let's go!"

"Yes, dear."

"I think we should call Bernie. Think he's still watching us?" She was tapping the kitchen table as I poured her coffee.

I wanted to go back to bed. "Probably."

"That gives us the upper hand, don't you think?"

"I try not to," I answered.

Agnes frowned at me. "Sometimes, Buttman." She took out the phone Bernie had given us and called him up. He was surprisingly upbeat and humored that it was Agnes who was calling.

"Has Monk taken off yet?" he asked mockingly.

Agnes laughed. "No, I won't let him."

"Excellent. Time for a conference? I noticed you had a visitor late last night."

"We did, Loran Tasabian. He wants the *book*," Agnes replied.

"I imagine he does. How's one o'clock?"

"We'll be there," she said, winking at me.

I rolled my eyes.

"What do you think, beautiful?" I let Agnes drive us to Bernie's. Traffic was to my evident delight moving along nicely. It wasn't the weekend, but they were no better than a weekday. Maybe it was a holiday I didn't know about. I should go back to reading the paper. Then again, if I did that, I'd be all worked up like everyone around me.

Ignorance is bliss.

"About what?" Agnes was in her own little world, as was I in mine.

"Whether we're in danger," I said.

"Probably. That's why we need to get the upper hand. Johnny always liked to be in front. That way, you have time to turn and shoot whoever's on your ass."

"I don't know if I want to be shooting people?"

"Turn of phrase, Monk, but yes, if we have to shoot, we shoot." She glanced at me in all seriousness.

"Good to know. Any other thoughts about why any of this is even happening?" I held onto the door handle as Agnes weaved in and out of traffic. "Are we in a rush?"

"Oh, lighten up. You're the one who gets into car crashes, not me!"

"Uh-huh. That may change soon!" I harrumphed.

"I know what I'm doing!" she harrumphed back. It took another few weaves and bobs before she answered my initial question. "It does seem a little odd, doesn't it? I mean, for a group set on overthrowing the government or killing the president, they don't seem very organized. In fact, it appears they're the ones being targeted for assassination, rather than the other way round, huh?"

"It does. Which one might think has to do with their so-called plans, but if it was real and people like Bernie were convinced it was real, don't you think the FBI and the Secret Service would be not only aware but ready to move in?"

"You would think, but we're not talking about moron would-be terrorists trying to buy bombs from undercover agents. If Manaforte is the leader of this bunch, you'd think he'd be a lot more careful both in his planning and in what he says, especially in this day and age of surveillance. Maybe it's because they're not your run-of-the-mill losers; they are pretty influential and wealthy. Maybe the government is using its special ultra-secret hit squad to take them out one by one?"

Agnes raised her eyebrows at that, after she zipped around a semi that wasn't going fast enough.

"We have plenty of time, you know?"

"Do we? You heard Tasabian; we could be next."

"With how you're driving, they won't need to send out the ultra-secret hit squad..." Along with the door handle, I was also holding tight to the seat cushion.

"Geez, what a wuss."

"Be that as it may, please slow down!"

"Fine!" she grumbled.

"And for the record, I'm not yet willing to go into crazy-land and start bellowing about government hit squads. Even Moses didn't go there." I let go of the seat and door as she slowed down.

"That's what they all say, Buttman."

We'd reached our exit.

Bernie was standing at the door. Agnes bounded out of the car while I checked to make sure all of the necessary pieces were still a part of me.

"Geez, Buttman, enough of the whining. We got things to do!"

It was at that point that Bernie Schoor burst out laughing.

"Well," I grumbled, "it's good to see you're returning to more of the Bernie I know and love. She's a scary driver." I pointed at Agnes as I shakily made it to the door.

Agnes shook her head. "What a princess."

"Be nice, Duquesne, or I'm taking your keys," I told her.

Agnes ignored me as Bernie kept laughing.

"Speaking of keys," Bernie put out his hand as we entered the office, "we'd like to scan the 500."

"Why?" Agnes handed him the keys.

"Uninvited guests," he said, his term for bugs and tracking devices. Javier, as if on cue, came in and took the keys from Bernie. He was smiling, too.

"Everyone seems so much more upbeat. Are you two also hepped up like the hard-boiled private dick here?" I motioned towards Agnes.

The hard-boiled private dick stuck out her tongue.

"Let's just say that some of our worries have eased, but we're not at the end by any means," Bernie said. Javier left for the car.

We moved to the conference room with all the computers and the operators oblivious to our presence. After grabbing a cup of coffee, we sat at a table on the other side of the room.

"So, Mr. Tasabian wants your copy of Carmichael's book?" Bernie filled his cup with sugar.

"It's not my book," I said.

"Does Xavier Dunkle want it back?"

"Well, no..."

Bernie smiled at my reticence. "Then, my good friend, it's yours. Can I ask where it is?"

"The original in locked up at A and A," Agnes told him. "Buttman has a copy in the trunk of the car."

"Does Durant know?"

"It was his idea to store it there. Tasabian went to him first," I said.

"Interesting. And Tasabian has contacted you twice about the book, correct?" Bernie eyed Agnes, who eyed me.

"You know he has," she said. "The Tool is scared. He thinks the book is his ticket out of this mess."

"And what mess would that be, Ms. Duquesne?" I asked.

"I think it's why Mr. Schoor here is more upbeat. His little gang of conspirators are being taken out one by one, right?" Agnes asked Bernie.

"It would appear that way. Of course, it could be just as it seems; accidents, natural events, and in the case of the Carmichaels, domestic violence. *If* someone is taking them out, as you say, they are very good, much better than the two who were working for Tasabian."

"Another reason for Tasabian to be on edge," I said.

Javier came in, a fair amount of concern on his face. "It's more complicated than we thought," he said.

"How so?" asked Bernie.

"Aaron," Javier answered.

"Aaron Alan?" Javier nodded. Bernie's face tightened. "Is it safe?"

Javier raised his eyebrows just a touch. "It is now. I put a blocker on it."

"Then let's see what the little prick is up to now."

We got up and followed Bernie and Javier into the garage. Along with the 500, there was a '68 Dodge Challenger and a '72 Olds Cutlass Supreme.

"Gotta keep the shop going, Monk." Bernie laughed as I eyed the two beauties.

"You have enough heaps already, Buttman," Agnes groused.

"A man can never have enough heaps, my love." I still had two spaces open at the house on the hill.

Javier took a laser pointer out of his pocket and pointed it at a small object up inside the rear wheel well. "There's the tail, a simple passive responder. If it's our friend, he knows you're here." He then moved the pointer to the gas tank. At the front end, up by the frame, was a small device. "It's a small charge detonator. Light plastic that would be almost untraceable after the tank explodes. Very clever. Just enough to detonate; the gas would do the rest." He took a fob out of his pocket. "It uses a simple frequency signal. This will block it for the time being. It can be reset remotely if he finds out, but for now this will keep it from going boom." Javier smiled at that. He handed the fob to Bernie.

"He'll know if we pull it, correct?" Bernie asked, while fondling the fob.

"He'll know. It's tied into the tail. Nifty little setup." It was as if Bernie and Javier were having their own private discussion.

"Who are we talking about, gentlemen?" Agnes was tired of being a bystander.

"A clever little man named Aaron Alan Sobeski. There were rumors he had died in Asia some years back, but this is much like his work, and it would answer our questions over the visuals we picked up the other day while surveilling the 500. A shadowy character, someone far more adept at this game than Tasabian's two goofs or the two punks you ran into out east." Bernie continued to fondle the fob. "The question is who he's working for?"

"Manaforte?" I suggested.

"Manaforte? Why would he be bumping off his own people?" Agnes asked.

"Could be anyone with the money someone like Aaron would command," Bernie answered. "Manaforte has connections all over the world, and he's made a fair number of enemies through his dealings. Maybe they got wind of his plans and are getting a little revenge?" He handed the fob to me. "What do you want to do, Monk? We can pull the trigger, but more than likely, he'll simply try it again."

"If he has to do that, and you see him, maybe we, or I should say you, can keep tabs on him or take him out," I offered.

"Maybe. We're dealing with a very sophisticated individual who enjoys games of cat and mouse, and you and Agnes would be right in the middle. The dangerous middle of it."

"I can rig the fob to light up if the frequency is reset," Javier interjected.

"Yes, but that might only give them time to ask God for forgiveness," Bernie countered.

"How long has this trigger been on the car?" Agnes asked.

"Two days. Makes you wonder what is he waiting for?" Bernie's eyes lit up. "That's your next question, Agnes?"

"If he simply wanted to get me and Sunshine, why the wait? Or the four of us, if, as I suspect, he knows you two and wanted to clear a few things out? What if it's the car rather than the passengers?" Agnes was being clever.

"You think the book, or I should say the copy of the book, is the target or the bait? Is that your idea?" Bernie was enjoying the clever Agnes. Javier and I were merely watching the show.

"It's in the middle of all this. Seems like the recent rash of deaths have been members of the 'book club,' right?"

"You're talking a very dangerous game, Ms. Duquesne. It puts you and Monk on top of a rolling explosion. You get that right?" Bernie raised his eyebrows above the top of his wire-rimmed glasses.

"Gives it an extra element of danger," she said, smiling.

"You're a lucky man, Monk," Bernie laughed.

"No," I said, "I'm a dead man."

They still kept laughing.

"Did I mention that Manaforte and Jontaveus Montgomery will be meeting the President soon?" I raised my eyebrows. The laughter subsided.

"All the more reason to be careful," Bernie said.

All the more reason to take off for the hills!

27

It was all very simple, they decided. I was more ambivalent. Javier went to work on a fob that would simultaneously alert us and block the trigger being reset. That way, we'd have time to get away from the car before it might possibly be blown up. To allay my fears, Javier said he could add a dump that would disable the trigger, but that would let this Aaron Alan Sobeski know he was being had, assuming he didn't know that already. That and it may not work.

"We're taking a big risk here, beautiful," I told her as we drove off.

"You're already taking a risk with me driving," she laughed. I couldn't argue with that. "Besides, we're not the intended targets—"

"You don't know that. Maybe this Sobeski guy is toying with Bernie and we're merely collateral damage." I didn't like this. I just wanted to be at the beach watching the kids run in and out of the surf. Every bump in the road made me think of the detonator next to the gas tank. I wanted to think of something else. "What do we do with Tasabian? Give him the book? There's still the copy in the trunk. It's just taking up space."

"Maybe." She gunned the motor as we hit the on-ramp. My hands were back on the door handle and the seat. "If we do, do we let Manaforte and Durant know he has it?"

"Can't hurt to spread the word."

"Can't hurt," she replied while weaving through traffic.

Once home, I made a B-line for the fridge. I needed ice for a large stiff drink. Agnes sat at the table, amused at my skittishness for both the bomb and her driving. It still bothered me how quickly she flip-flopped from depressed daughter/mother to hard living private dick.

Maybe she should talk to somebody. The phone went off, disturbing my mental wanderings.

It was Jones.

"Got some news for you and your detective pal," he said, not actually giving me the news.

"I'm all ears, Mr. Jones."

"Couple of things. Jontaveus passed it on that your brother has been invited to go along when they visit the White House. Apparently, the word on your new veteran's foundation is spreading. He thought you might be interested—"

"Isaac?" I interrupted.

Jones groaned. "Why would your brother have *me* say that? Stick with me, Buttman."

"Meaning?"

"Meaning Manaforte wants you to know, yet he does it through Jontaveus. Has Isaac said anything to you?"

"No…"

"Again." He let the air stratify a little longer. "Also, Manaforte has had Josef do some personal security work for him lately. Know anything about that? I don't mind my guys doing some side work so long as I know about it. Word?"

"This is the first I've heard about it. Doesn't sound like something Josef would do," I said out loud, wondering.

"Maybe, but money talks and Manaforte has money. The question is why not just hire Josef full time? I know Manaforte has his own guys, so—"

"Josef needs money?" I asked, more thinking out loud.

Jones laughed, but not in a kind way. "Every person who ain't a millionaire needs money, Buttman. Are you busy tomorrow?"

"I got time," I assured him.

"The usual place?"

I assumed he meant the Manifesto. "Sure."

"Good. Jontaveus wants to talk. Bring Isaac. See you then, Mr. Buttman."

"Mr. Jones." I hung up and relayed the conversation to the detective sitting across from me.

"Interesting. Why don't we give Tasabian the copy tomorrow as well?" she asked.

"Yeah, why not." I was staring at my glass. It had ice, but no whiskey. The ice was melting. What was Josef up to?

"Sunshine?" I looked over at Agnes, who had her arms crossed. "What's on your mind?"

"Nothing. You better call the Tool," I told her.

"Me?"

"Yeah, he likes you better," I laughed.

"Yes, he does," she said with a smile.

While Agnes annoyed Tasabian, I annoyed my younger brother. He was surprised to hear from me.

"It's no big deal," he said, lying to me.

"Uh-huh. You lie to Moses like that?"

"When I need to," he laughed.

"We're meeting with Mr. Montgomery and Mr. Jones tomorrow. They requested you join us."

"I don't know, might have a date with Natalya tomorrow." I noted the mischievous tone in his voice.

"Not tomorrow. In fact, why don't you stop by the house tonight? You and I need to talk a little about Natalya," I told him.

"Natalya can do what she wants," he chided.

"So can I. Seven-ish, Mr. Bohrman. Bring some wine for the lady," I chided, before hanging up. Agnes, having completed her annoying Tasabian, was smirking at me.

"Again, what's on your mind, Sunshine?"

I shrugged. "Not a thing, beautiful, not a thing. The Tool?"

Agnes shrugged. "He didn't care for my tone, but he'll be there tomorrow."

We both laughed at that.

·　·　·　·　·

Isaac arrived as I was preparing the steaks. I'd made a quick run to the store while Agnes grimaced through a phone call with Denise.

"Problems?" I asked as she put down the phone, frowning.

"They want to talk some more, maybe come over here. I said I'd think about it." The frown did not abate.

"It took that long to say that?" I'd been gone a half-hour.

"*I* wasn't talking," she huffed as the doorbell rang. "I'll get that."

I watched as she headed for the door. Isaac was in kiss-ass mode as he first complemented Agnes on her attire and then me on mine before admiring the steaks as I put them in the oven. Agnes produced a crooked smile that she gave to me, and then Isaac.

"No need for the charm, loverboy," I said. "Have a seat."

"Be nice, Monk," Agnes said, still half-smiling.

"I'm always nice. That's what gets me in trouble." I reached for the bottle of wine in Isaac's hand, and watched the two of them watch me as I opened it. I placed the bottle on the table. "It needs a few minutes to breathe."

"Don't we all." Agnes had taken her glass and was running her finger along the top of the rim.

"What's on your mind?" Isaac asked. Third time's the charm.

"Natalya," I said. "You know her history?"

"I know a little," he said with a coy smile. I didn't like it.

"Well, I know a lot, and because I know a lot, I'm very protective of her. You need to understand that. I also know, so you don't have to remind me, that she can do what she wants; she's a big girl. But I want *you* to understand that if you're just fucking around with her because you can, you can also return to the farm and help Moses with whatever Sterling is up to."

"And Xavier?" Agnes added unhelpfully.

"Xavier is Natalya's headache. Again, be mindful of using that just because it might seem like a good way to pass the time while you're bored in LA." I tightened my eyes so Agnes would get the point.

"What if I'm serious about Natalya?" he asked, a nasty smile on his lips.

"Yeah, Monk, what if he's serious?" Agnes has the same nasty smile.

"Then play the long game. Now about this trip to the White House..." I didn't have to wait long for the confused looks.

After a moment, Isaac leaned forward, mostly addressing Agnes. "Jon Montgomery got me in to see Mr. Manaforte, so I pitched him on the foundation, and he asked if I thought it would help if I could say I had talked to the President about it. I mean, how do you say no to that?"

"Did he mention that he'd already had a meeting with me about the foundation up at the big house?" I was curious.

"No..." Isaac said this mostly to himself.

The wine was ready enough. I poured each of us a glass. Isaac took a sniff, swirled the wine in the glass before taking a drink. Agnes kept an eye on Isaac over the rim of her glass.

"I know you consider yourself a wily guy, Isaac, and I'm not saying you aren't, but be mindful around people like Delton Manaforte. There's a lot of smoke around the guy right now and I'd be very careful with my fingers if I were you."

Agnes rolled her eyes. "Oh, brother."

"You don't think I should go?" For once, he wasn't so self-assured.

"I'm not saying that. If you want to go, go; just be careful. We're going to meet with Montgomery and Mr. Jones tomorrow at the Manifesto. They'd like you to be there."

"Yeah, ok..."

"And no Natalya. Save that for another time."

He grinned at that. "Alright."

The rest of the evening was spent bemoaning family and their demands, be it Moses, Sterling, Denise, and by association, Jerry. Or me. I was ok with that. Towards the end of the evening, as he helped me with the dishes, he confessed that Africa was a bit of a dodge.

"Meaning?" Agnes asked. She was in her accustomed place at the kitchen table, watching her millionaire husband doing the dishes with his younger half-brother.

"Meaning I just wanted to get away. Allison was fun, and we had a good time for the most part, but she wanted other things, serious things. That and she was hanging with this guy, Toule. He had that French accent some of them have..."

"And you?" Agnes was smiling. "You don't strike me as the type to wallow in his miseries."

Isaac shrugged. "Maybe. I don't find it hard to meet women. I used to laugh at Jacob about that. Women would moon over him and he'd get all embarrassed. I told him he was never going to get laid that way, but..." Isaac got quiet. I handed him the last of the silverware to dry.

The last of the evening was spent in the backyard, drinking wine, and listening to the world around us. Isaac would make a note or two of the differences, whether between LA and the farm, or LA and Africa. Rather than have him drive off half in the bag, we rolled him into the guest room and bid him goodnight. The next morning, we fed him and sent him on his way.

•   •   •   •   •

I continued to worry about the car and the detonator on the gas tank.

28

"After tonight, we get rid of the detonator," I said, as Agnes drove us to the Manifesto. "I don't care if Aaron Alan, or whoever the fuck he is, finds out. I don't want to be riding around in a car that might go boom."

"Yeah, it's starting to get to me, too." She was driving more cautiously.

The only plus, to my mind, was that the tank was less than half full.

We decided to leave early. Agnes wanted some time with Anna, and that had to happen before the evening rush. Mikal had enthused that more people were coming in just to watch and listen; it was becoming more than simply a hangout for indigent musicians and singers. That brought more traffic to the faux food trucks in the dining area. Anna's business was continuing to improve, and bringing in some real money. I passed that on to Macklgrew.

"Maybe it's not a waste of money," I kidded him.

"It's just one quarter, Monk. Let's not spend what we don't have." He said to a guy who couldn't live long enough to spend what he already had.

I asked Agnes to park the 500 across the street, where there were driveways on either side. That way, no other cars could park close, just in case. The buildings were set back, so hopefully if the stupid thing went off, there wouldn't be a lot of damage. I carefully opened the trunk. I hadn't actually looked in some time to see if the copy was still there. If someone had time to plant a detonator, they had time for other things. The trunk was undisturbed. I put the 45 in my pocket and called Bernie to let him know we were losing our nerve.

"I agree. Bring it in tonight," he said. The fun had worn off for all involved.

"Once we're done here," I assured him. I set the fob so the detonator wouldn't pop. I hoped Javier had it right.

I let Agnes know.

"Shouldn't we take in the book?" she asked.

"No. I want whoever's watching to see us turning it over outside."

"I don't know about that, Sunshine..."

"Me neither."

Anna was in the middle of prep with a culinary student named Blanch. We stood by idly as they went about their work. After a few minutes of being ignored, I wandered off and found a table and a measure of quiet. My departure must have caught Anna's eye. She turned and smiled at her mother, lifted the index finger on her right hand, and hastily finished what she was doing.

As I was watching from a safe distance, Mikal snuck up on me. I nearly fell out of my chair when he tapped me on the shoulder. I must have cried out because Agnes and Anna were staring at me and Mikal was trying to both apologize and stifle a grin.

"Are you alright, Monk? I didn't mean to frighten you..."

"It's just the brace. I didn't see you, no worries," I assured him while slowly getting back in my chair. He sat down next to me, half-smiling.

"I wanted to thank you for getting Joanie down here to sing," he said. "She even mentioned that she'd like to sing with us regularly." His eyes were twinkling.

"Yeah? You ok with that?"

"Yeah, it'll be good for her. She needs to sing, don't you think?"

"I suppose she does, and she hinted she was getting a little bored out in suburbia, but that's the life she thinks she wants, right?" I was rambling.

Mikal shrugged at my feeble attempt at mockery. "There's always time for the things you love, Monk." He got up and waved at Anna and Agnes. Agnes furrowed her brows. Mikal and Anna ignored her. "The students are playing in the theater tonight. Are you going to stay?" he asked after turning back to me.

"It's possible, but first I have a meeting with Mr. Jones."

"Please give him my best," he said, affable as always. I nodded and off he went.

Agnes, with two plates in her hands, came over and sat down. "New stuff to try," she said, less than enthusiastically.

"What is it?"

"I don't know, food!" She wanted to frown, but knew better, so she pinched her lips and continued to furrow her brows.

"Really? Anna said here, have some food?"

Agnes sat down and handed me my plate. "Yes she did, mister smart-guy."

I looked at the plate. It appeared to be a Thai inspired dish with chicken, fried cut potatoes, red peppers, and peanut sauce on top of jasmine rice with a miso salad on the side. "And the talk?"

"She told me to be nice in so many words," she grumbled.

"Sounds like something I would say," I smirked.

"Not in the mood, Monk!"

"Fine, be a jerk," I teased.

Jones and Montgomery showed up as we gingerly tasted Anna's new dish. I thought it was pretty good. Agnes didn't seem as impressed, but stayed quiet. Once they got our attention, they went over and ordered something to eat. Isaac showed up a few minutes later, and seeing Jontaveus in line, joined him.

Mr. Jones was his usual stoic self, while Jontaveus and Isaac were more animated. Small talk ambled to cars, and then guys who like old cars, and finally to the car this old guy's wife was driving, though he was perfectly able to drive, thank you.

"Geez, Monk, not that again," groaned the old guy's wife.

"I saw a guy admiring your car," Isaac said.

"Yeah?" I asked.

"Yeah, little guy with glasses. He was running his hand along the edge of the fender, then walked off. Maybe he had one once." He smiled at that.

"There were a few of them manufactured in the day." I smiled back. Blanch brought over the food.

"What did you want to talk about, Mr. Montgomery?" I was done with my dinner.

"I wanted to know what it is you think it is I might be getting myself into." He looked up as he took a bite. "I don't like it when people think I don't know anything or am some wide-eyed dupe to be played."

"I feel the same way and yet here we are; people asking about you, and no doubt people asking about me. Mr. Manaforte, for example. He did inquire, did he not?" I looked at Isaac, who looked at Jontaveus Montgomery.

"He did," Montgomery admitted after finishing a mouthful. "What's the big deal, and don't tell me it's some assassination thing."

"That was Carmichael's tell," I said. "It's a great conversation starter. Just ask Mr. Jones here—" I noted the frown on the delightful man in black. "That said, I don't think Carmichael said it just to be shocking, just as I don't think it's a coincidence that you two are being invited to go along with Manaforte to the White House."

"Point, Buttman!" Agnes was leaning back in her chair, a frown on her face.

"Am I boring you, my dear?" I knew I was.

"You're boring all of us, Buttman, so get on with it." Mr. Jones was finished with his dinner and was staring at me with his arms crossed.

"As to what's going on, I don't know, other than it involves a small group of very rich people and a slim book that argues that democracy is futile." Agnes opened her mouth, but I cut her off. "Now before anymore whining, I would point out that the members of that small group are dying off, rapidly, as if someone might be on to their little game. Manaforte is among that group. Who's to say he isn't a wee bit concerned for his safety?"

Agnes was still bored. "We know that part, Buttman. Don't forget the Tool—"

"Who's the Tool?" Isaac thought that was funny.

"Loran Tasabian. Shyster," Jones answered. "Known for dragging people through the mud to collect. He's not particularly well liked."

"He'll be here in a little while to collect a copy of Carmichael's book. He thinks it'll save his ass, but I think his ass is already cooked," I said.

"What about our asses, Buttman?" Agnes was on a roll.

"We're the wild cards, my love, as are these two." I waved at Isaac and Jontaveus.

"Do tell."

I smiled at that. "We got involved because Xavier Dunkle thought it'd be cute to show me the book he nabbed from his uncle, but he wasn't supposed to; he was supposed to keep it to himself. Instead, I, and then Agnes, got dragged into this, and we're like a bad dream because we're not supposed to be in it. And now people are dropping dead, or are fearful of dropping dead, or are threatening us with ending up dead."

They were all blankly staring at me.

Agnes tilted her head towards Isaac and Jontaveus. "And these two?"

"I don't know," I admitted.

Jones set his plate aside. "Then what do you know, Buttman?"

"That what we're in the middle of won't reveal itself right away." I leaned in and tapped the table with my finger. "And maybe it's nothing, just a sign of the political climate these days. People are angry and on edge, but it reminds me of another mess I got into that was a struggle between people who weren't terribly concerned with whether we'd come out of it ok, and that's what I want you two to be wide-eyed about. Anything that seems wrong or weird is. Don't get talked into anything. Nothing. That's what I have to tell you. Be smart."

"That's all you got, Buttman?" Jones was unimpressed.

"It's enough. Is Josef still gigging with Manaforte?"

Jones nodded. "He said it was something he had to do and apologized for keeping it in his pocket. Said it wouldn't be for more than a couple weeks. What does that say?"

"That it'll be over in a couple of weeks," I answered. It was my turn to smile.

"And our trip?" Montgomery was ready to leave.

"Have a good time," I told him. Over his shoulder I noticed the Tool come in.

Jones looked at Tasabian and shook his head. "We got to split. If something comes up—"

"It comes up."

Isaac went with them. As they walked away, Loran Tasabian approached us. His appearance had not improved.

"You don't look so good, Mr. Tasabian," I said.

"Save the chit-chat, Mr. Buttman." Tasabian glared at Agnes. "Your wife told me you'd have the book."

"I have a copy. The original is locked up," I told him.

"I want the real thing. Ms. Duquesne, you said it would be here." He was visibly shaking.

"I told you it was a copy," she corrected him, "and you agreed to that."

"It's a complete copy," I said. "I won't turn over the original, but if what's in it is what you want, and that's what you intimated, then the copy should satisfy that need."

The Tool sat there, his shaking hands knotting into and out of fists.

"Who is pushing you on this, Mr. Tasabian?" I asked.

A thin smile came to his thin lips. "Nobody pushes me, Mr. Buttman."

"Uh-huh. Then it's normal for you to look like death, shake like a willow, and not seem like you know what you're doing." Tasabian tightened his already tight face. I thought it might crack. "You look scared to death, my friend."

"The copy then, Mr. Buttman. I have other things to take care of. Please give it to me."

"It's in the car, in the trunk," I said.

Tasabian turned to the window and the red Galaxie 500 in the distance. "Why didn't you bring it in?" He turned back to me. "Why leave it out there?"

"Why not?" He looked back at the car. "They want to see you receive it, don't they?"

"Who?" If he was trying to be dismissive, it wasn't working.

"The people you promised the book to," I said, tapping the table.

"You promised the real thing, didn't you, Tool?" Agnes was leaning back in her chair, a look of satisfaction on her face. "What happens if all they get is a copy?"

"It'll do for now," he sneered. "They just need to know you have the book, that it's not a scam."

"And you would know about scams, eh, *Mr.* Tasabian?" I asked.

"Spare me the humor, *Mr.* Buttman. The book?" His hands continued to shake.

"Alright. Agnes, you stay here." Agnes frowned at that. I stood up and gestured towards the door. "Mr. Tasabian..."

He slowly rose. More people were entering the building and he acted as if he had to examine every face. We let the group pass. I followed him to the door. He waited till the street was empty.

It was nice and quiet.

The car exploded as we stepped to cross the street, knocking us to the ground. For once, I was glad my neck was in a brace. The explosion blew the trunk lid into the air as the back of the car was engulfed in flames. It landed just a few feet from us. Tasabian shrieked as it landed. I sat up just as the rear tires popped and burned. The door windows turned to black, and the white convertible top caught fire. The shyster tried to get up. As I reached for him, he slapped away my hand and took off down the street, falling two times. Each time, it took longer for him to get up and get to his car. People pushed past me as I watched him drive off. He sideswiped three cars as he barreled down the street.

I pulled out my phone and called 9-1-1.

I wasn't the only one who called.

Agnes joined me, her arms holding tightly to mine. She, too, was shaking. We stared at the carnage in front of us.

"Tool took off?" she asked.

"Tool took off," I answered.

· · · · · ·

On the plus side, nothing was damaged other than my car. On the minus side, I was down three classics in less than a month. The building had emptied as people came out to watch the car burn, and then the fire department as they flooded what was left of it with water. I approached the lead firefighter once the flames were out. Agnes went back into the Manifesto.

"It's my car," I told him.

"Too bad," he replied. "It looked like a nice one."

"It was."

I answered his questions and the cops' after they arrived, but decided not to say anything about any detonator; might be hard to explain. The crowd thinned once the fire was out. Since the street was blocked, most went back inside to hear the students perform. I waited outside. Agnes came back out, as did Anna and Mikal. Agnes shook her head, but otherwise seemed indifferent to the smoking hulk. Anna and Mikal were shocked, offering sympathy and thanks that we weren't in it.

"Yeah," was all I could say.

"No more heaps, Monk," was what Agnes had to say.

"No promises," I told her.

"You have a perfectly good Mercedes," she harrumphed.

An idea came to me as we stood there. I took out Bernie's magic phone and sent him a text telling him the car was toast and asking for a picture of Aaron Alan Sobeski. He texted back, asking if we were ok, and that there were none that he knew of. Why he asked. I wanted to know what he looked like. Aaron Alan was a small guy, with light blond hair, he answered, and often wore glasses. Why? A guy like that was admiring the 500 before it went boom, I told him.

Be careful, was his last text.

Agnes went in to help Anna. She was our ride to the big house and the Mercedes. I hung out with the firefighters and the cops as the street was cleared and the tow truck arrived. I gave them Bernie's address.

"We might want to have our fire investigator look at it, so tell who's there to lock it up," the fire captain told the tow truck driver. He nodded and grunted. "Probably just a fuel leak, but you never know," he said to me.

I thanked him and texted Bernie the car was on its way. He sent me an emoji with no expression.

I went in and listened to the last of the performers. Anna took us to the house in the hills. It was a beautiful night. The city sparkled, and the ocean glistened in the moonlight. I drank till I couldn't keep my eyes open and wandered off to bed.

• • • • •

Mallory called the next morning.

Early.

Tasabian was dead.

29

As he had before, Mallory arrived promptly at ten.

Agnes handed him a cup of coffee as I let him in. He didn't appear to be particularly cheerful.

I didn't feel particularly cheerful either.

We sat in the kitchen.

"What happened to him?" I asked. My head ached from too much whiskey the night before, and my hands were having a hard time holding onto the coffee cup. The further removed from the explosion I was, the more freaked out I became.

"We found him hanging by a belt in his closet," he said, his voice steady. I noticed him watching my shaking hands.

"He killed himself?" Agnes asked. She seemed amused by that.

"It looks that way." Mallory took a slow sip of his coffee. "He was with you last night, correct?"

"Yes," I said.

Mallory took a longer drink of his coffee. A quiet smile came to him. "Your coffee is much better than what we have down at the station." His eyes brightened just a touch as he looked over the rim of his cup. "I heard your car caught fire. Was Tasabian with you when it did?"

"He was. We were going to the car just as it exploded. It's as if it was..."

"Was what, Mr. Buttman?" He was still smiling.

"It was as if it was planned that way," I said.

"Why do you think that?"

"Because there was nothing wrong with the car, and if we were meant to go up with it, why didn't we?" I took a drink of my coffee. It was getting cold. "It struck me as very convenient, that's all. Could be my imagination. Maybe it was just a coincidence. Maybe, as the fireman suggested, it was just a fuel leak. It *was* an older car."

"The term is heap, Buttman." Agnes felt compelled to add her two cents.

"Why were you and Tasabian going to your car?" Mallory had taken out his notebook and was writing in it.

"He wanted a copy of a book Monk had in the trunk. Thought it was important," Agnes answered for me.

"Was this the book you mentioned the last time we talked?" Mallory looked up at Agnes.

"Yep, Carmichael's book," I said. "He was pretty freaked out after the car exploded, just took off. He smacked a couple of cars on the way out."

"And you, Mr. Buttman, were you freaked out?"

I held out my shaking hand. "Not at all, happens to me every day." I got up to warm my coffee in the microwave.

"What did you talk about before you went to the car?"

"Just whether I had the book. He didn't seem interested in small talk," I said.

"How did he appear?" the detective asked.

"He looked like he hadn't been sleeping, and was more than a little anxious to get the book, as if it was the answer to his problems. Then again, maybe it wasn't if he hanged himself, huh?"

"Maybe," he said. The smile was long gone. "You said a copy of the book. Didn't he want the original?"

"He did, but all I had was the copy." I put the coffee cup in the microwave.

"Where is the original?"

"It's locked up," Agnes said, "at Aeschylus and Associates."

Mallory looked at me. "Durant has the book?"

"No," I said. I took out the coffee.

Mallory noted that. "I might need it at some point," he said.

"Why would the book matter in a suicide?" I asked, knowing why.

Detective Mallory sat back and finished his coffee. I had returned to my seat. Agnes, having said little, stared at the detective. "It matters only if it played a part in his death," he answered.

"So, while it looks like he killed himself, he might not have, much as the accident with his two punks looked on the surface like bad brakes. Is that it?" Agnes leaned in, her eyes alight.

"His hands had been bound and yet he was able to untie them after he'd hanged himself..." He let that hang in the air.

"Then he was murdered, and the attempt to fake a suicide was as amateurish as the cut brake line." Agnes was on her game.

"Possibly." Detective Mallory rose. "We'll want to look at the car and I may want to look at this book. You'll let me know if it gets moved, won't you, Mr. Buttman?"

"I'll let you know."

We walked him to the front door.

He turned to the two of us. "If someone blew up your car as a message, it might not have been just for Tasabian's benefit. I'd be careful if I were you two."

"We will," Agnes told him.

I wasn't so sure he believed her.

· · · · ·

The Mercedes purred as we motored towards the house in West Covina. Since it was more comfort oriented than the classics, I was driving. That and I was too frazzled to endure another road race with the woman next to me. Agnes, unconcerned, spent the first part of the drive smirking at me. "I told you this was better!"

"I don't remember that at all, and whether it's a better choice doesn't mitigate the fact that a detonator could be put on this car just as easily as the 500," I smirked back.

"Maybe, but other than someone trying to blow us up, it's far safer than your collection of heaps."

"Maybe, but it doesn't have the cache that the heaps had."

"Then you admit they're heaps?" she laughed.

"I admit nothing!"

"Typical Sunshine."

"There's always the Jag," I teased. The Jag was Judith's pride and joy, and as such, Agnes was less inclined to use it.

"Yes, but it's just a two-seater," she lamented. "We might need more room. Plus, it's a classic, unlike your heaps. No need to put it in harm's way."

"Uh-huh."

Agnes was laughing when her phone rang. "Yes?" she answered. "I see. Yes, of course, we can. We should be home in a half-hour. We'll see you then. Bye." She returned the phone to her purse. "That was Becky. She has some work to do and asked if we could watch the kids. Apparently, Zachary is being a pest. I wonder where he gets it from?" She smacked me lightly on the arm.

"Probably *his* father. We should ask." Zachary was the product of an affair Rebekah had while still married to Farrell, her first husband. She never told the man she was pregnant or revealed his identity.

"Let it go, Monk. It is what it is," she said, knowing it bugged me.

"Uh-huh."

Rebekah Montaigne was waiting for us as we pulled into the driveway of our quaint little home. Lizzy was in her arms and Zachary was sitting on the front porch with a scowl on his face.

"He's mad at me for taking his stuff."

"Not the stuff?" I said in mock desperation.

"Dad?" My daughter was glaring at me.

"What?"

"Not now!" I shrugged as much as I could with the brace around my neck. "He's been a pain in the ass all day. I need to get a few things done and he won't behave. What is it with boys?" She handed Lizzy to Agnes. "Anyway, he's still in a timeout, so no pool, ok, Dad!"

"No pool," I said. Zach continued scowling and kicked his feet.

"And no stuff, either," she said, mainly to the peeved little dude at the door.

"That's not fair!" he shouted. "Lizzy was bad too!"

"Yes, but Lizzy listens, mister, and you don't!" Lizzy was laughing at her brother, which only deepened his scowl. "I really appreciate this. I do. I promise not to take too long."

"Take all the time you need," Agnes assured her.

We watched her drive off to the house down the street.

"Alright, little dude, let's find you a chair," I said sympathetically.

"It's not fair!" he once again shouted. I noticed Agnes trying desperately not to laugh at Zach's anguish. Zach noticed too. "It's not funny, grandma!"

"No, it's not," Agnes said, laughing.

Lizzy was laughing, too. Zach began crying.

"Now, now, he's already miserable. Let's not rub it in, Elizabeth. And you too, Grandma." That got Grandma's attention. Agnes didn't like to think she was old enough to be a grandma; it was her turn to scowl. "You should have thought of that when you had kids as a teen."

"You're in the same boat, Grandpa," she muttered.

"Call me Gamps," I said.

"Yeah," said a less aggrieved Zachary.

"You sit there," she demanded of him, pointing to one of the chairs in the kitchen.

His scowl returned.

It was a quiet afternoon punctuated by phone calls and a whining three-and-a-half-year-old. "No playing if you keep whining," I warned him. He sat there brooding.

The first call was from Natalya. "Mr. Manaforte would like to see you at the house in Beverly Hills. Tomorrow if convenient," she said.

"Certainly. Did he suggest a time?" I asked my executive assistant.

"One o'clock," she answered. "Mr. Monk?"

"Yes?"

"Did you say something to Xavier recently?" There was a slight rise in the tenor of her voice.

"It's possible. Why do you ask?"

"No reason," she lied. "Would you like me to have lunch prepared for your meeting tomorrow?"

"That would be lovely, thank you."

"You're welcome, Mr. Monk. Goodbye." I pictured her smiling at me as if she knew more than I ever would.

"Goodbye."

The next call was from Mr. Jones. "I heard your car blew up. That's not good, Buttman."

"Yeah, I didn't enjoy it either."

"Save the humor, man. Do I need to have someone keep an eye on you?" I was touched by the concern coming through the phone. Mostly, I just annoyed Orville Riley.

"Might not be a bad idea. I'll let you know; I might have a trip coming up soon. Maybe Josef will be available," I kidded him.

He waited to answer. "Funny you should mention Josef. He came in earlier and said he was done with what Manaforte needed. Coincidence, Buttman?"

"Maybe. Either way, it works out. I'll be at the big house tomorrow afternoon. I'll keep in touch." I could hear Mr. Jones grumbling to himself.

"I heard about Tasabian too. This ain't a joke, my friend."

"No," I agreed, "it's not, but hiding won't stop anything. Any idea when Jontaveus is heading back to DC?"

"Day after tomorrow, I think. Do I need to nail it down?" The concern was growing in his voice.

"No, that's close enough. Thanks."

"I worry about you, Buttman, I really do," he said.

"Not to worry," I noticed Agnes coming into the kitchen, "I got the hard-boiled private dick with me. What could happen?"

"Great! Now I got the two of you to worry about. Goodbye, Buttman."

"Mr. Jones." I pictured him shaking his head as he ended the call.

"Should I ask?" Agnes was smiling at me. Zach was close to tears again. "Alright, you can get down, but any trouble and you're right back in this chair, capeesh?" She hardened her face. Zach frowned, but nodded his acquiescence.

"Pool?" he inquired of me.

"Don't push your luck, little dude," I admonished. He frowned, but said nothing. We watched him go to where his box of stuff was. "Soon, there'll be three of them," I said to Agnes.

"You don't fool me, Buttman, you're loving every minute of this."

"Maybe," was all I'd admit to. "As to your earlier question, Mr. Jones is concerned for our safety and suggested someone keep us company and surprise, surprise, Josef is available."

Agnes furrowed her brow. "Yeah, you mentioned that yesterday. Do you think Josef is up to something?"

"I think Manaforte is up to something. He wants to meet us tomorrow at the big house," I said.

"Does he?" The wheels were whirling in my beloved's head. "You think he's scared?" A broad smile crossed her face. "Or behind all this?"

"Makes you wonder, doesn't it? Maybe it's your ultra-secret gubmint hit squad?" I raised my eyebrows just because.

"Maybe," she said.

The last call was from Bernie. "They've impounded the 500, hauled it off on instructions from Detective Mallory."

"I'm not surprised. The pace has picked up. Manaforte wants to meet, Jones wants me to have protection, Tasabian is dead, and the boys are heading to DC the day after tomorrow to visit the President of the United States."

"President, huh? Interesting. The news said Tasabian was a possible suicide. Evidently Mallory disagrees."

"He does. Apparently, dead men don't untie their hands. Has the same amateurish elements as the car crash that killed Tasabian's two goons. Think it's the work of our bomber?"

"If he's trying to throw a little shade, maybe, assuming it's even him. Who saw this guy by the 500 yesterday?"

"Isaac," I said.

"Alright. Maybe we get together after your meeting with Manaforte. Go from there."

"I'll call you tomorrow." I pictured Bernie smiling and shaking his head.

I got up and went through the pantry, wondering what to make for dinner. Agnes was lost in thought. Zach was in the living room and Lizzy was taking a nap. The kitchen was flooded with sunlight.

"How about fried chicken for dinner?" I asked out loud, in case anyone was listening.

"And fries, Buttman?" Agnes smiled when I turned to her.

"Sure. Would you let Becks know dinner is over here?"

"Sure."

Rebekah and Fidel arrived a little before seven. I made plenty, which was good because everyone was hungry. After dinner, we gathered to watch a few Disney movies. I stood by the entrance to the kitchen watching this family of mine and worried there might not be too many of these kinds of evenings left to enjoy.

30

Agnes thought it over, with no real thought involved, and decided we should go for it.

"It's a death wish, isn't?" I countered. I wasn't convinced the plan had any reason to be successful; it was us playing detective and foiling the bad guys even though we weren't sure who the bad guys were.

"That doesn't make any sense," was how she greeted my concerns. "We know who the bad guys are, and you know it. You just like to hedge your bets. Besides, what's the worst that could happen?" She had that nasty look in her eye and a smirk on her face.

"They find me with my head blown off and you hanging by your sweet little neck," I said.

"That already happened. I'm sure we'd get something different." She thought that was a cute thing to say.

"Well, when you put it that way, why wait? We just need to gas up the car!" I bellowed.

"I'll start packing," she said, glibly.

All this because she didn't want to see her father!

•   •   •   •   •

The meeting with Manaforte was at one o'clock. With a little encouragement, Agnes got me out of bed and on the move such that we made it to the big house a little after ten. The car bombing continued to haunt me. It was all clever and fun until the blast knocked me to the ground, which, since then, seemed less and less firm. Agnes, more and more, began plotting.

"He probably doesn't want me in on the meeting, right?" A coy smile accompanied her tilted head.

"Probably not."

"Then maybe I'll play the jaded ingénue, drinking early and being insouciant. It'll be fun," she said.

"Insouciant fun," I answered.

"I even have the right dress for it." Her smile widened. "You know the one, it's the silvery one, goes almost to the floor and," she shook her breasts, "shows off a little cleavage."

"I know the dress." It shows off a lot of cleavage. She bought it for laughs, something for when we wanted to spice things up and pretend it was the 1940s and I was picking up a hot dame. "It'll be interesting to see what the others think."

She winked at me. "It might be interesting at that."

Natalya arrived at noon. Her practiced business face gave way to a large, toothy smile as she took in Agnes and me. I had on a smart double-breasted gray suit with a silver dress shirt; no tie due to the brace, silver socks and gray suede shoes. Agnes stood next to me, shimmering in her silver dress; her breasts strategically held in place by two silver straps that started wide and narrowed to the clasp at the back of her neck. A diamond necklace and a diamond bracelet completed the look. Her hair was up and her toes poked out from silver heels just below the willowy dress.

We were ready to hit the town.

"Very nice," Natalya said. "Will there be drinks later?"

"One would hope earlier, my dear," Agnes answered, deep in character.

"I also brought some papers for Mr. Monk to sign. I hope there's time?" She held out a large envelope, just in case I wasn't paying attention.

"We can do that now," I said.

"I'll set it up in the library," and she was off.

The caterer laid out the spread at a little before one and our esteemed guest arrived promptly at one. Like Natalya, Delton Manaforte was amused by the finery Agnes and I were wearing.

"If I didn't know better, I'd swear it was the late Fifties or early Sixties."

"Goes with the house," I said.

Agnes wandered over. "I understand you and Monk have things to discuss?" A wan smile accompanied the question.

"I do. I hope you don't mind the inconvenience."

"Why would I mind? Lunch?" We nodded, and she led the way to the dining room. After lunch and business talk, mostly between Natalya and Manaforte, Agnes got a drink, and he and I retired to the library. Natalya went back to the office. We sat facing one another by that part of the table shaded from the afternoon sunlight.

"What's on your mind, Mr. Manaforte?" Time to get to it.

"Threats, Mr. Buttman. The kind that make people anxious; the kind that make them do foolish things. I assume you heard about Loran Tasabian?" He was staring out the window, facing the city.

"I heard. Hung himself. Was he working for you?"

A rueful smile caught the edge of Manaforte's lips. "Peripherally. He was working for Seymour Dunkle and evidently felt the need to subtly inform me that he'd have something of great value to me, assuming I was willing to part with a fair amount of money..."

"Did he say what?" I had an idea.

"The book, of course." He was amused that I'd even ask. "Isn't that what he wanted from you?"

"He did. Unfortunately, it was in the car when it exploded. I thought he was freaked out by the explosion, but maybe it was all that lucre going up in flames."

"Then the book is no more..." Manaforte continued looking out the window.

"The copy I had, yes."

He began lightly tapping his finger on the table. "Maybe that will end all of this. The book's been more of a nuisance than anything else. People get foolish ideas and—"

"Have the threats to you been about Carmichael's book?"

"Among others, yes." He smiled at that. "I accept that threats go along with the businesses I'm in. People get stepped on and pushed aside. They don't like being marginalized or ignored, so they make threats, mostly of the legal variety. And there are some who threaten bodily harm. I don't worry too much; I can afford a very high level of protection, but when others, with as much protection as I have, begin dropping dead, it becomes concerning." Maybe that explained Josef's working for Manaforte.

"How does any of that involve me, other than having a minor connection to the book and its author? I hope you don't think I'm behind any threats."

He turned to me briefly before returning his gaze to the window at the end of the room. "I try to be careful in the assumptions I make, and as I said at our first meeting, I don't go in uninformed. I think there are areas where we see the world in the same vein, in its truer nature, and I admire your somewhat jaundiced views of wealth. To answer your question, no, I don't believe you to be behind the threats. My interest goes beyond what, as you say, is your minor connection to those of us associated with Mr. Carmichael's book." He continued tapping the table.

"What interest then?"

"A meeting has been proposed, but the place and time are in dispute because of fear, of being seen connected somehow outside of our usual business interests. Unfortunately, even men of wealth and privilege are creatures of habit and limited vision and therefore susceptible to foolish beliefs. However, certain recent events have given me an idea, and I think you can help."

"How so?"

"I understand you have a home in Michigan along the lake?"

"I do."

"I also understand it's secluded."

"It is." I'd only see pictures, having never been there, but I felt no need to say that out loud. "How does that help if you believe you're being watched?"

"There's a rather large conference taking place in Detroit in ten days, concerning business, technology, and how it can best be integrated into cities like Detroit that are transitioning from manufacturing to service-based economies. It's the kind of event where we would all logically come together, those of us associated with the book."

"Then why not get together in Detroit?"

"Because they, whoever they are, will be watching to see if we do just that, but if we break up and go our own separate ways and just happen to come together at your house along the lake, it would be more private."

"That it would be."

"Would you be willing to host us?"

"Let me talk it over with Agnes. I don't think she'd object, and she doesn't need to know the specifics, but I don't generally take off without saying anything. How many guests should we expect?"

"Ten," he said. "Can it accommodate that many?"

"For a meeting, yes. For an overnight stay? No, I doubt it's big enough. There are only three bedrooms."

"It's unlikely any would want to stay, anyway. I hope that doesn't offend you?"

"No, it's a fairly rustic place," I was trying to remember what the place even looked like, "so I wouldn't expect it to be up to their standards."

Manaforte laughed and began to rise. "Probably not." For the first time during our talk, he looked me in the eye. His were shining. Odd, I thought, given the nature of our discussion. "I appreciate this, Monk." He reached in his pocket and handed me a card. "This is my private number. It's secure and encrypted. I expect to hear from you soon."

"Of course."

Agnes joined me as I walked Manaforte to the door. It was then I noticed the men at the gate. He thanked us for lunch.

"Well," my beloved asked after Manaforte was out of sight.

"He wants to meet in Michigan in ten days at my rustic little place along the lake."

Agnes raised her eyebrows. "How'd he know about that?"

"He likes to be informed."

"That doesn't answer the question, Sunshine."

"Then either he had the records checked or someone told him about it."

"Who?" Agnes had a lot of questions.

"The only people who know are me, you, Ms. Lagenfelder, Mr. Macklgrew, and," I looked at the nails on my right hand for no reason, "Xavier Dunkle II."

Agnes smiled. "Figures. Did you agree?"

"I said I'd have to pass it by you, but I promised to be discreet..."

"I imagine you did, Buttman. Have *you* decided?"

"I wanted to know what you thought," I said, pulling her close. The dress, soft, frictionless, and designed to highlight a woman endowed as Agnes was, tempted fools like me. I kissed her neck just below her ear, the earring tickling my nose.

"What's on your mind, Sunshine?"

"Sex," I whispered as I continued kissing her.

"I see..."

It should have been how stupid this whole meeting business was.

•　　•　　•　　•　　•

That came after a very delightful afternoon of personal debasement, as I assumed my mother would chide me about running around half-naked and fornicating on the couch. Knowing me, I would have cavalierly mentioned that the couch was more than large enough for proper fornication. I wondered if she and Moses ran around naked up at the farm before she went back to God.

"Whatcha thinking about, Mr. Sunshine?" My half-naked wife was running her fingers along my unclothed thigh.

"What my mother would say to sex on the couch."

Agnes sighed, but not in a terribly condescending way. "I'm glad I didn't ask before we started."

"So am I." I reached down to the floor and picked up my pants. "The more I think about this business with Manaforte, and no, I wasn't thinking about it while we were doing it—"

"What were you thinking about when we were doing it?" I noted the sneaky little twinkle in her eyes.

"Where MaryAnn might fit in," I said, letting my own eyes twinkle a bit.

"I imagine you were. Should I ask who you were fucking?" At least she was smiling.

"A gentleman never tells, but as that's just a flight of fancy, maybe it would be better to talk about this meeting Manaforte wants—"

"What about it?" She was having a wonderful time interrupting me.

"It doesn't smell right." For some reason, I was having a hard time getting the pants to zip; it was hard to look down, so I'd become more adept at doing it by feel, which wasn't working.

"Here, let me." She zipped them after fiddling along the left crease for a moment. "Why do you think it should smell right?" Agnes stood, allowing the dress to cascade back down her legs. She also reattached the clasp behind her neck; her delightful breasts now more properly contained. I sighed. "Were you sucking on Maryann's tits, too?"

"A gentleman, my dear." I patted the seat next to me and she sat down. "Are we going to get deep into our MaryAnn fantasy? If so, I'd be curious what you two were up to, or are we going to return to the real world and the real possibility that we might be walking into harm's way?"

"You're probably right. It would just turn you on." She put her hand ever so lightly on my thigh. "Why would they want to harm us?"

"Seems to me the reason is irrelevant, as they've already tried a number of times."

"I think if they truly meant to harm us, they would have. They certainly had the means and opportunity. We were alone in the desert. How long before anyone would have found us if, say, they chose to shoot us? And the car? They could have blown it up anytime it was moving, or we were in it, but they didn't."

"No, but that's because they want it to look like something other than straight up murder. Maybe they're simply waiting for the right time," I said.

"Is there a right time for murder, Mr. Buttman?" Agnes moved closer to me.

"That depends on who you ask, my dear. Personally, I'm opposed on ethical and moral grounds. You?"

She smiled and kissed me lightly on the cheek. "That depends on what you're up to, my love."

"That's rather subjective..." I turned my shoulders so I could return her kiss.

"No, that's whether you behave..." She had wonderful lips.

"I'm hopelessly devoted to you, my dear; you know that..." Sweet, wonderful lips.

"Yes, I believe you are..." There was one last long kiss. "I expect nothing less in the future; you know that, don't you?"

"Yes, dear."

Agnes fell back onto the couch. "Maybe we should ask Bernie what he thinks. It's too bad Johnny's not here. He'd be a good guy to bounce this off. And Mr. Jones..."

"I don't think he likes it. I don't think he likes any of it."

I pictured Mr. Jones shaking his world-weary head at me for the umpteenth time. "I worry about you, Buttman, I really do!" I could hear him say.

I was beginning to worry, too.

31

The next day was one of seeking advice, receiving a call Agnes didn't want, and lining up our ducks. It was just a meeting, I continued to tell myself. We were secondary characters; hosts, and nothing more. Yeah, well, I counter-argued, hosting a group of people who may be planning to subvert the democratic process is still wrong and illegal.

"You're overthinking this, Sunshine." Agnes was at the kitchen table, drawing up a list of things to do before we left. "Are we flying or driving?" She looked up from her notes.

"Driving."

"Which car?"

"The truck," I said, knowing it would annoy her.

"If we have protection, there won't be enough room in the truck. Remember how cramped it was coming home from Oklahoma?"

"I thought it was rather pleasant," I lied.

"Ha-ha, we're taking the Mercedes," she decided. "How many days to get there?"

I had no idea. "Four or five, depending on how many stops we make. There's a town called Lautenberg in Idaho. I'd like to stop there..."

"Isn't that where you went with Moses after Jacob died?" Agnes narrowed her eyes. "What's up there?"

"Ghosts," I said.

"Ghosts?"

"That's what I said. Anything else?"

Agnes slowly shook her head. "With you, there's always something else."

I decided we should let everyone and their dog know we were heading out and to where. I also wanted to go back over what Judith had on this place in Michigan in her files at the big house.

"When do we leave?" she asked.

"As soon as we can. Hopefully, the day after tomorrow. There might be things to do once we get there, but before the hoard arrives."

"For someone who doesn't want to go, you're in quite a hurry," she laughed.

"Uh-huh. Start making calls," I huffed.

I called Bernie. We'd be out this afternoon. He would be there, he said. Next was Jones.

"You're driving halfway across the country to some secluded house you've never been in before, for a meeting with a group of crazy rich guys who may be up to no good, *and* who have been dropping like flies?" I couldn't tell if he wanted to yell or laugh.

"Something like that. Josef available?"

Jones sighed, "I'll find out. I'm in the will, right, Buttman?"

I laughed, "No."

Ms. Lagenfelder was her usual upbeat self, thanking me for informing her and wishing us a pleasant trip. Macklgrew was no different, mentioning how he loved going out on the lake as a kid.

"Get yourself a boat," he advised. "You can afford it." This from my fiscally conservative moneyman.

I thanked him.

Last was Moses. They were on the way, and we hadn't been up in a while.

"Michigan? What the hell are you going to Michigan for?" he bellowed. I wondered if he was sober.

"Big meeting. A bunch of us rich autocrats are taking over," I said, perhaps a little too sprightly.

"Figures. When will you be here?"

"Day after tomorrow. Are you behaving yourself?" I knew that'd piss him off.

"I don't need any keepers," he grumbled and hung up.

Agnes let the family know. Rebekah wasn't thrilled; her easy access babysitters were abandoning her. Anna wished us well and asked her mother to call her mother. Agnes lied and said she would.

"I don't want to talk to them," she said when I called her on it. "Oh, I called the doctor and got you an appointment after we go see Bernie."

"I don't want to go to the doctor!"

"I don't care." She had her hands on her hips, having risen from her seat. "Let go, Buttman, we're burning daylight."

Oh, brother.

.   .   .   .   .

First stop was Bernie's. Car needed to be swept and a few devices added. "For your safety," he assured us. "What do you know about this place?"

"Never been there before," I said, "but I think Judith has some info on it. I'll check."

Both Agnes and Bernie looked at each other and grimaced.

Javier checked the Mercedes, it was clean, no bugs or bombs. I didn't ask what was added on Bernie's end.

"Send the address," he said after I confessed I didn't know it. "If Sobeski is a part of this... keep your eyes open." Lovely. He promised to keep an eye on us.

Of that, I had no doubt.

The doctor's visit, much to my surprise, was quite wonderful, mainly because I was told things were looking up; I was healing faster than expected, and I could start taking the brace off periodically when I wasn't doing anything where rapid movement was involved.

"Can I go skydiving?" I thought it important.

The doctor, expressionless, looked me in the eye. "No!"

I thanked her nonetheless.

Next was the big house and what Judith had on this place of hers along Lake Michigan that I had so impulsively offered up. It had been a while since I'd ventured into the safe room off the garage. Agnes was right behind me when her phone rang.

It was Denise.

She wandered back into the house, grousing.

The information on the house was in its own folder in the upper drawer of Judith's filing cabinet. I lingered a few minutes on her other files, running my fingers along the face in the pictures. Put it back, I told myself, focus on the house.

Located outside Traverse City, where the wealthy kept their summer homes, the house was set on a quiet five-acre lot. Built in the early Twenties, it was bigger than I had at first thought, and though not large enough for ten, it was large enough with five bedrooms, five baths, and many more rooms throughout. It had a boathouse and a pier and was built in the Manor style. A large lawn stretched from the house to the lake. I looked through the pictures of the house and the rooms and wondered why Judith had the house to begin with.

She never mentioned it. The only times she even mentioned Michigan was to say she was born there and to lie to me when she was going through cancer treatments, saying that she was there to see her father, who I came to find out she had disowned.

I knew the house had a caretaker, and that funds were set aside for the upkeep of the house. I assumed it was, in fact, being cared for. I guess I'd find out.

Agnes came in, muttering to herself, while I went through a pile of papers on the history of the house.

It had quite a history.

A man named Haney had it built as both a summer retreat and as a way-station for moving high-end Canadian booze during prohibition. A shipping magnate, he, apparently, had major connections between the Canadian distillers and the mobs running Chicago. While the poor had to make do with suspect moonshine and coppers set to keep the county dry, the rich had the money and the private clubs that kept the locals out and the proper alcohol in order to lubricate their social predilections.

The house also had a few quirks due to its use as a way-station: namely a series of trapdoors and a secret passage through a floor that led to a cavern built under the house, and a tunnel that ended up at the boathouse. I made a mental note of where they were and how they worked, if they still worked.

Haney sold the house after prohibition ended, and a family named Monroe owned it until it was sold to one Judith Louise Taffy Delashay. Martin's name was nowhere on any legal papers concerning the house in Michigan.

Agnes leaned in and I handed her the pictures. I watched as she looked them and me over. After a few minutes, she smacked me lightly on the head. "You've had this place all this time?"

I shrugged. "How long have I owned any of these places?" I slowly rubbed my neck. I'd taken the brace off and was surprised how weak my neck felt. The doctor's assistant had given me a list of easy stretching exercises and a reference to a physical therapist, something I probably needed, but wanted to avoid.

"Look at this place, Monk? It's beautiful!"

I carefully nodded. "It would appear so." I slowly rotated my head. "What did your mother have to say?"

"They want to come over," she whined, "which is why we have to get the hell out of Dodge!"

"Dodge?"

She smacked me again. "No time for Mr. Funnypants, Buttman, we got things to do..." She looked over my shoulder. "What else is in here?" She reached for one of the binders.

I grabbed her hand and took the pictures. "More ghosts," I said, as I put the files away. Agnes snorted, but withdrew her hand. There was no need to delve into Judith and her history. I wrote down the address of the house in Michigan.

Josef was more than willing to go. Jones passed that on in his own unflappable way, assuming I would get the point. I did. The next day we packed and plotted how we'd make our way to just outside Traverse City. First, we'd spend a day at the farm, then on to Lautenberg. From there, we'd cross through Yellowstone up to I-90, and head to the Upper Peninsula and down to Traverse City.

"Still got your Comfort Inn card?" Agnes was grinning at me as we discussed accommodations. I nodded. "You know, with that wad of cash burning in your pocket, we could find a few nice places to stay?"

"The Comfort Inns were just fine," I said. "I don't know if I want Josef thinking this is a vacation."

"Right. Being cheap, with millions at your disposal, isn't particularly flattering, Mr. Sunshine." She wrote CHEAP in big letters on her list.

Jones delivered Josef to the big house. We offered to feed Jones, too, as the extended family was joining us in a goodbye dinner. He demurred, even as I tried to entice him with steak and beer and big screen basketball.

"I have a date with Coretta," he admitted. Josef smiled, but said nothing as I teased the man in black. "Be careful, Buttman, this ain't no game." He looked at Josef. "Remember what I said."

Josef nodded.

"What was that all about?" I asked my keeper after Jones left.

"No worries," was all the big man said.

Zach made a beeline for the pool the minute he stepped through the front door. His mother bellowed at him, but he paid her no mind. Apparently, he was informed that this might be his last trip to the big house in a while, and he intended to make the most of it. Fidel shrugged when his wife admonished him for letting Zach ignore her.

"It'll be ok," he assured her.

"Dad!" she bellowed at me as I tried to stifle a laugh. She then cocked her head and appraised her old man. "Where's your brace?"

"As long as I'm not in a moving vehicle or participating in vigorous activity," I winked at Agnes, who ignored me, "I can go without it. Doctor's permission, Mom!"

"That's not exactly true, Monk. She said you could take it off every once in a while," Agnes chimed in.

"See," I said.

She frowned at me, but held her tongue and handed Lizzy to me. Lizzy, noting that Gamps no longer had the big plastic thing around his neck, decided to see if my neck was still interesting, feeling it here and there. I kissed her neck, which made her laugh.

We dragged Zach out of the pool when dinner was ready and ate at the dining room table. Zach and Lizzy were mesmerized by the large, mostly quiet, Josef, who found his own entertainment in both ignoring and then focusing on them with his stony business face. I had questions for him, but they could wait for the long drive ahead.

Agnes cajoled Fidel into spilling as many beans as possible about the big shoot his company was a part of. They had landed a contract with an Internet giant that was now into "content," which Fidel said was just a silly word for movies and television series. However, he admitted, that had led to bigger stars and bigger budgets and business was good, so good that they were actively seeking more employees. This explained the rather rushed Montaigne household, and the exasperated pregnant woman trying to keep it organized.

"I don't want to hear it!" Rebekah barked at me, even as I had barely opened my mouth. "And where are you guys going, anyway?" she demanded.

"Michigan. I own a house just outside Traverse City," I said.

"When did you buy that?" I found her shock endearing.

"Judith bought it about fifteen years ago. It was part of the estate. Unfortunately, I haven't had a chance to check it out." I noticed that my neck was sore and tired. I rubbed it for effect.

Agnes tapped the back of my shoulder. "You need to put the brace back on, Sunshine."

"No," I whined.

My daughter continued to frown at me, ignoring my obvious suffering. "Why wouldn't you check it out if you knew about?"

"I wanted to, but I was needed here to look after my grandchildren." I nodded at Zach and Lizzy, but they weren't paying attention to us; they were in the midst of a winking contest with Josef.

"Ha-ha, Dad!"

"Just saying…" I slowly rotated my head in a circle. I noticed Agnes staring at me.

"Are you doing that on purpose?" She was tapping her plate with her fork.

I was doing a wonderful job of annoying two of the three women at the table. "I'm merely stretching out my neck muscles, the doctor said—"

"I know what the doctor said, Monk Buttman!" Agnes turned to Rebekah. "He didn't bother to tell me about it either until just a day or two ago." They were both now staring at me.

"I don't have to tell you everything," I mused for the purposes of being aggravating. Fidel kept his head down, trying very hard not to laugh. "But if you must know, I offered to host a gathering of some rather well-to-do individuals concerning a grave national matter which I can't discuss here. Nor can you, my love." I wagged my forefinger at Agnes, knowing she didn't care for that.

Agnes wagged her finger right back. "Keep it up, Buttman, and you'll be needing that brace even longer."

"I'm shocked you would say something like that if front of someone as impressionable as the fine Mr. Rostikov here."

The fine Mr. Josef Rostikov offered a thin smile before returning to his antics with the kids.

"I may have Mr. Rostikov help me, if you don't behave!" Agnes poked me with her finger, just in case I didn't get the message. I looked over at Josef, who shrugged.

"Really?" I said to him.

"She has money too," he answered, then shrugged again.

I looked back at Agnes, trying to act shocked, but I couldn't hide the smile, which got Fidel laughing, which got the kids laughing, which even got a smile out of the exasperated pregnant woman.

All in all, a good way to say goodbye, just in case it was goodbye.

I let Manaforte know we were in. I also called Bernie. An idea had come to me. He told me to call Art Devaney.

32

Moses was sitting on the front porch, looking past us. It was evening, and the sun was setting beyond the far side of the small house he shared with Meredith, casting us in its shadow. He shifted slightly as we got out of the car, but did not rise to greet us as he had in the past. What little attention he gave was directed at my brace and the large man walking behind us. Not until we were on the top step and staring down at him did his eyes grow clearer.

"I see you're important enough now to warrant a goon of your own," he muttered in as condescending manner as was possible. "What's with the neck brace? Life in the fast lane too much?"

"You're in rare form," I said as I started to remove the brace. "This is Josef." Josef nodded as I introduced him. "Josef," I pointed to the crank on the porch, "this is Moses, my father."

Meredith opened the door and scowled at her husband.

"They're here," he monotoned.

She, too, took in the large man beside us.

"This is Josef," I told her, a little more spritely than I had Moses, "he's our goon." I was still fiddling with the brace.

Agnes sighed. "You have to keep it on!"

I frowned at that. "I had an accident awhile back, which accounts for the brace."

"Are you alright?" she asked.

I smiled at Meredith's concern.

"That depends on who you ask," Agnes answered, Josef smiling behind her.

"Looks like it's open mic night at the comedy club," I said, rubbing the brace; it was itchy from the long slog north.

"Why isn't Isaac with you?" Moses was back to staring past us.

"What made you think Isaac was going to be with us? Did he say he would be?" I looked at Meredith.

"He said he might," she answered.

"He's in DC, late invite from a friend of his. They're going to meet the President," I said.

"The president?" Moses shook his head. "Why the hell is he meeting with that bastard? What the hell is going on with the lot of you?" He got out of his chair and stomped down the front porch.

"Moses, where are you going?" Meredith called after him.

"What the Goddamned hell does it matter now?" he howled as he walked away.

"Moses!" she shouted in vain.

Moses continued down the road.

I turned from Moses to Meredith. "Should I follow him?"

Meredith wiped the tears from her eyes. "I'll leave that up to you."

Agnes put her arm around Meredith and motioned with her head that I should take after the moody Moses Bohrman. Josef took a step as I did before stopping.

"Come along," I told him.

We caught up with Moses by the gate. He stared at the two of us, his eyes wet, his face tired and worn. The light was fading as we stood there waiting for the world to change into something than didn't ache so badly. Moses ran his hand along the metal post of the gate. I put my hand on his shoulder and he flinched, looking directly in my eyes. Without thinking, I drew him in and held him. He wrapped his arms around me and began to weep. It took all my strength to keep us from falling over. After a while, he stiffened and let go of me. I led him back to the porch. Josef stayed a respectful distance behind us.

Agnes came out and had Josef join her inside.

Moses and I sat as the sky darkened.

"It's Sterling," Meredith told us as we were cleaning up after dinner. Josef was merrily helping with the dishes in the kitchen as Meredith, Agnes, and I sat at the big table in the community-dining hall. Moses had gone to bed early. "If it's not one thing, it's another." She looked tired and worn.

"Should I ask?"

Sterling, the oldest of Moses and Meredith's three sons, had been the only one of us boys to stay. I ran off after James was murdered, Isaac fled to Africa, and Jacob joined the Marines. Sterling became the farm's liaison to the local wineries. The farm had transformed over the years, with grapes being their stock in trade, from hippie commune to a source of varietal specialties. As business grew, Sterling moved to Napa, got married and became more and more his own man, spending less time at the farm.

Apparently, he was always an odd duck, but I only learned of it after returning and then only a little at a time. Moses, Meredith, and Isaac come to think of it, would make vague asides about Sterling, but then leave it at that.

Meredith shifted uncomfortably in her chair. "He..." She looked about the room. It was empty apart from us. The others were in the kitchen finishing the evening's chores. "It's just too much, with losing Jacob, and Isaac being too clever for his own good, and now Sterling is..." She put her head in her hands, the tears streaming between her fingers.

Agnes, alarmed, slid her chair over and put her arm around Meredith. Josef, drying his hands, came out of the kitchen, took stock of the situation, and slowly turned back.

"Felicia is worried," Meredith said at last. Felicia was Sterling's wife. "Something is wrong with Sterling, but neither he or Felicia will talk to me about it, other than to say they're unhappy. She says he goes away, sometimes for days, and won't explain where he's been or what he's doing." Agnes handed her a napkin to wipe her eyes. "He gets visibly upset, but tells me it's nothing and we need to leave him alone and mind our own business."

"Is it affecting business?" I needed something to say.

"It was, but Andrea has been helping out. She's been something of a God-send around here..." An odd smile crossed Meri's face. "The

Mackinaw's brought it up. They'd been hearing from the vintners that they were having trouble getting a hold of Sterling. Andrea volunteered to help, and I was worried Sterling would become even more defensive, but he seemed relieved, which only heightened my concern." She continued wiping her eyes. "I can't do this anymore, Monk."

Agnes kissed Meredith's temple. "It'll be alright, Meri. You need to rest."

"It's been a stressful time, this last year," I told her. "Jacob's death affected all of us, you and Moses most of all, but I think it also made you worry too much about the rest of us and not enough about yourself. Sterling is going through his own thing right now, whatever it is, and, though you may not want to hear this, it's not your job to make it right. That's something he and Felicia will have to work out. And I'm keeping an eye on Isaac, so don't worry about him."

"Really? He's a handful," she said, trying to smile.

"Yeah, I picked up on that, and if he's up to some kind of mischief, I'll hear about it," I assured her.

"Let's get you to bed," Agnes told her.

We got her up and moving, with Agnes taking her home. "I'll join you in a minute," I said. I had things to discuss with Josef, who had poked his head out of the kitchen. I waved him over. The dining room was empty save for us.

"Have a seat," I said. Cautiously, he sat down. Josef had a masterful poker face, something I assumed he'd perfected over the years of being in the service of people like Big Mike Kovalenko. I was tapping the table. A bottle of Riesling and three unused glasses were between us on the table. I poured wine into two of the glasses and handed him one. "We have an interesting situation here, my friend."

Josef raised his eyebrows a hair. "Do we?"

"We do, concerning our dear Mr. Delton Manaforte. You've been working for him on the side, no?"

Josef shrugged his large shoulders. "I have obligations. The extra money helps."

"No doubt." I took a sip of the Riesling. It was good; not too sweet, not too dry. I motioned that Josef should take a drink. I watched as he did. "I'm not going to pry. It's not my place or my business, but I think we both know we're playing this a little too close to the flame. I have my suspicions as does our good friend, Mr. Jones, but at this point we have to see it through, correct?"

He nodded while continuing to drink.

"Mano a mano, my friend." I noted the confusion on his face. "It means we watch out for each other. The place we're going to has a few interesting features that might come in handy. We can work that to our advantage, yes?" I smiled and took a nice, long drink.

Josef smiled back.

"Ever been to Idaho?"

"No."

"We're heading there tomorrow. I'm not expecting any trouble, but one of the locals, a dude named Jay Lautenberg, might try to be a problem."

"No worries," the big man said.

Indeed.

Agnes was sitting in the small living room of Moses and Meri's house. The only light was from a lamp on the table next to her. I had taken Josef to the old bunkhouse. He wanted his own space, and for reasons of his own, found the bunkhouse charming.

"Like kid again," he said.

"We're leaving early," I reminded him. He merely shrugged.

Agnes patted the spot next to her on the couch. I sat down and put my arm around her. "I'm worried about them, Monk."

"Yeah, but we have our own worries right now, beautiful. One worry at a time."

"And what worries might those be, Sunshine?" She grinned at using my childhood name.

"Surviving the meeting," I said.

"Why wouldn't we?"

"Something Manaforte said to me about doing his research, knowing the people he was getting involved with—"

"People like us?"

"People like Aaron Alan Sobeski," I said. "I asked Bernie about that, about the possibility that Sobeski might be tied in with Manaforte or one of his associates in this Carmichael thing. Bernie said if Sobeski was actually involved, then we all needed to be careful..."

"Because he's a killer?" For some reason, she smiled at that.

"No, though he is that, and apparently quite good at it. No, it's that he's too much of a wildcard. Bernie said that's what got him kicked out of the government game, and it's why he's made a name for himself in circles where certain people might find that charming."

"People like Manaforte?"

"Or people like Loran Tasabian. It's possible the shyster bit off more than he could chew with Sobeski. Bernie didn't discount that when I suggested it."

"That just makes it more intriguing," she said, the light dancing in her eyes.

I frowned. "This isn't a game, Agnes, with us romping around with a martini glass in our hands!"

"Oh, stop being so dramatic," she chided. She mocked my frown with a faux frown of her own. "Besides, we have Josef with us."

"Josef is working for Manaforte, not just us."

Agnes' frown evaporated into actual concern. "How do you know that? Did he say that?"

"Our Mr. Jones admitted as much when he said Josef was more than happy to go with us, even as he was moonlighting for Manaforte. I don't think that's a coincidence."

Agnes pondered this new information. "So maybe you think Josef might sell us out?"

"It's something to be mindful of."

"Wow." The wheels were spinning wildly in Agnes Duquesne's head.

"Wow indeed," I said, slowly loosening the brace.

"I still say it exciting, even a bit of a turn-on, don't you think?" She was running her hand along my upper thigh as I removed the brace.

"Is sex all you think about?"

"I like sex." She leaned in and kissed me. "Especially with you."

I carefully shook my head. "I think you need some serious therapy."

She laughed before leaning in for a kiss. "You always think that."

"Because it's true."

Agnes shrugged and led me to the bedroom.

. . . . .

The next morning was bright and airy, and some of the angst from the night before had been expelled by sleep for some and sex for others. We rose early to help with the morning chores. Josef was already up and in the kitchen, helping prep for breakfast.

"Like kid again," he said, grinning, something I'd never seen him do before.

Moses, for his part, was more composed and affable. He gave me a hug and a kiss on the cheek. Meri, too, had perked up. Calista came over and said hello.

"How's Emily doing?" I didn't see her the night before.

"Emily is with her father for the summer," she said. It was then I noticed the bump in her mid-section. She noticed my noticing. "Baby's due in November."

"Congratulations."

She smiled and left to set the tables. Agnes, having also noticed that Calista was pregnant, grinned and winked. "There's still time, Buttman."

"You're already enough trouble, and the last thing I need is three grandkids *and* a baby. Makes you wonder who the father is," I said in my usual veiled reference to Zach's biological father.

"It's none of our business, and Zach's doing just fine with Fidel. Let it go, Monk."

THE FIST INSIDE THE GLOVE

"No," I pouted.

"Looks like I'm not the only one in need of some serious therapy, eh?"

"You got that right," I answered. "Most of the people in this room do."

Breakfast went quick and after a promise to stop for a longer stay on the way back, Josef, Agnes, and I were on our way to Lautenberg and destinations further east.

33

The town was as I remembered it; small and claustrophobic, cloistered between the river on one side and the trees on the other. The woman at the motel was as perfunctory as the last time, but I was no longer persona non grata in Lautenberg, Idaho, thanks in part to a compromise I helped engineer between old man Lautenberg and Sergeant MacMillan. The sergeant now used his property to help vets in need, in the name of Lautenberg's son, Franklin, who had been killed in Vietnam. I hoped it would work without interference or intimidation by the Lautenbergs directly, or the town via coercion by the Lautenbergs, particularly Jay.

It was their town, after all.

Jay Lautenberg, who had made an ass of himself, as well as falsely claiming MacMillan had assaulted him, was lying low and licking his wounds. It didn't hurt that the administration was gung-ho on opening the forests to more logging, which was allowing the Lautenberg mill to reopen.

People were getting back to work.

"Here are your keys." Heidi, the delightfully grumpy hotel manager, handed a pair to me, and a pair to Josef. She looked him up and down as he took the keys. Not too many six-foot-four square jawed Russians passed through Lautenberg. For his part, he kept his face quiet and his eye hidden behind thick dark glasses.

"This is it, huh? No Comfort Inns?" Agnes was not impressed by the accommodations as she looked around our room.

"It'll do for a night," I said. "We have places to go."

The entrance to Macmillan's property was still hard to find, though there was a small sign just inside the drive. I had called earlier in the day to say we'd stop by. Macmillan, like everyone else we'd come across since departing LA, took note of the brace on my neck and the big Russian exiting the Mercedes.

"If I didn't know better, I'd say you and I have crossed paths before... Russian Army Intelligence?" MacMillan was smiling ever so slightly.

Josef countered with his own slight smile before shaking his head no.

And to me, "What happened to your neck?"

"Sorry, need to know," I said, echoing military parlance.

Agnes rolled her eyes as MacMillan nodded.

Awestruck by the vastness of the meadows before us, and the mountains in the distance, Agnes was walking in slow circles, taking it all in.

"Monk didn't give you fair warning about our rustic little hideaway, did he, Mrs. Buttman?" MacMillan was standing behind the awestruck Mrs. Buttman.

"Mr. Buttman tells me very little, and I, for obvious reasons, did not take his surname. Please call me Agnes." Mrs. Buttman offered her hand.

"My apologies, Agnes." Macmillan nodded as he shook her hand. "I assume, then, that Mr. Buttman didn't tell you much about the measure of his business here or the events leading up to them." He looked over at me. I simply shrugged.

"He told me a man was killed here and that you'd had some trouble with the locals, but that was water under the bridge and now, through the foundation, this beautiful country was being used to help veterans work out their problems..." Agnes scowled at me for a moment. I shrugged again. It was mostly true.

"I'd like to think it's water under the bridge, but while better, it's not where I'd like it to be. Then again, I thought, given what happened with Corporal Cameron, there was no way for me to stay or have any kind of life here." The sergeant's eyes grew distant. He turned towards the mountains. "The cabins are down this way, or will be; they're only now being built."

We walked down the road, newly cut into the pasture that followed the tree line down the hill to a flat area where several foundations had been poured. A young woman was talking to a pair of grizzled construction workers who appeared to be finishing up for the day. Her name was Jenna Thalken, a former Marine, and the person in charge of the Franklin Lautenberg V Veterans Center.

MacMillan waved to Jenna. "I figured it'd be better if someone less polarizing was running the show. No matter what old man Lautenberg tells people, there's still a lot of suspicion. No doubt Jay's work."

"I heard of a guy who's good at getting rid of troublesome individuals in ways that don't arouse too much police interest, eh, Josef?" I smiled at Josef, who raised his eyebrows above his sunglasses.

"There are days that might be tempting, but I want nothing more to do with death," MacMillan said.

We greeted Jenna as the two workers drove off.

"This is Mr. Buttman and his wife, Agnes," MacMillan told her as she offered her hand. "It's his foundation that's paying for all of this."

"It's a pleasure, Mr. Buttman." I noted how her smile grew a little more animated at my peculiar name, and how she slightly cocked her head while appraising the large Russian.

"This is Mr. Rostikov," I said, motioning towards Josef. "He's here to keep me out of trouble."

"I see. Do you find yourself in trouble often?"

"It's his default position, Ms. Thalken." Agnes thoughtfully added, "Buttman has the uncanny ability to find himself in awkward situations that require assistance."

"I beg to differ, but we're not here to delve into my presumed deficiencies," I said. "Perhaps you'd be so kind as to show us around?"

"Certainly."

Jenna Thalken walked us through what would be a small camp able to accommodate up to thirty people when completed. There were plans for ten cabins built in a large circle with a common area at the center and a fire pit as the focal point. At one end would be the communal kitchen, and at the other would be a lodge for activities.

"Is this open to any veterans or just those with... issues?" Agnes asked, before adding, "I mean, I guess we all have issues, but..."

I smiled at Agnes' momentary discomfort. She frowned at my smile.

Jenna put her hand on Agnes' shoulder. "It's ok, Agnes, and to answer your question, it's open to all veterans. A lot of us who come back and separate find it a different world after so many years in the military. It's really a place to decompress and reacclimate to civilian life. It would be nice to dedicate some of this to really troubled vets, but given the concerns of the people in Lautenberg, we thought it would be best to try to keep any foolish beliefs about veterans being crazy to a minimum."

"Yeah, after what happened, you can't really blame them for being wary, and God only knows what Jay-Jay been telling everyone," I added.

Jenna laughed at that. "Yes, Mr. Lautenberg is something else, but I've known guys like that and you can't be intimidated, and you can't fight them with anger. Charm and good humor go a long way with people; that's my game with him. Work the people around him, especially his cousin—"

"His cousin?" There were more of them?

"Mr. Lautenberg's daughter. She came back after hearing what happened with Cameron, and Jay's interference with the sheriff's investigation," MacMillan answered. "She and Jay don't get along. I got the impression she doesn't particularly like it here, but I only talked with her a few times. Jenna knows her better."

"Yeah, Valerie's a handful; all the Lautenbergs seem to be, but at least you can talk to her, and I know she really likes the idea of honoring her brother's service and sacrifice."

"Well, that's something," I said.

We walked around a little more before wandering out into the meadow that opened up to the vista of the Bitterroot Mountains. It was a clear day, and the mountains rose high in front of us. There was no sound save for the birds and the soft rustle of the grass. In the distance, a deer scampered along the meadow near a grove of Aspen trees. An eagle soared in the distance.

"It's too bad Judith didn't leave you a place out here, huh, Monk?" Agnes gave me a soft elbow just because.

"Be happy with what we did get. Besides, there's the place on Lake Michigan we haven't even seen yet," I chided.

"I suppose. What do you think, Josef?"

We all turned to the Russian, who had said next to nothing to this point. "I wish I was U.S. veteran. Is nice, very nice."

"It's definitely that," I said.

Sergeant Angus MacMillan and Jenna Thalken thanked us for our support and for coming by. I said we'd stop on the way back if there was time.

"Why wouldn't we have time, Buttman?" Agnes and Josef were both staring at me.

"Because I have a frazzled pregnant daughter who can only go so long without her free babysitters," I answered. Everyone thought that was cute.

·　·　·　·　·

"So, what really happened here, Buttman?" We were sitting on the bed in our motel room and Agnes was running her fingers through my hair.

"Didn't I already tell you?"

"I mean the truth, not your usual evasions and lies."

"Lies? Wow, that's pretty harsh!"

"Really? That's your defense?" She was mocking me.

"It's always worked in the past," I lied.

"Spill, Buttman."

"It's not a pretty story, Mrs. Buttman..."

She tapped the brace. "I assumed that. Now talk!"

I sighed and gave her the unabridged version. I didn't care to be drawn back into that night, and the hideous sound of MacMillan's bullet tearing off the top of Cameron's head, of Moses weeping, of so many young lives senselessly lost. I wondered out loud whether Jasper was still alive. He was probably drunk behind the bar after being turned out by Dahl, the taciturn bartender. I explained how the sergeant fit in and of the two dead Marines in LA. I finished with what started it all, the murdered Afghan family.

"Now you know. Feel better?" I asked.

"No." She slid down on the bed and rested her head against my chest. "I hate to say this because I know you, but maybe the evasions and lies are better."

"Maybe."

. . . . .

We took off early the next morning, with nearly two thousand miles between us and Traverse City. Our first destination was Missoula; there we had lunch. I kept my eye on Josef for no other reason than to see if his demeanor ever changed. Agnes peppered him with questions, most of which he chose not to answer.

"Kids?"

"Two boys," he said.

"Wife?"

"Yes."

"Pictures?"

Josef took out his phone, and after fiddling with it, turned it our way. He and an attractive blond woman and two young boys were smiling. They were at the beach.

"Is your wife from Russia?" I asked.

He stared at me for a moment before looking back at the picture on his phone. "Yes," he said in a whisper.

After lunch, it was back to the Interstate and the long drive to Bismarck. Josef and Agnes marveled and then grew bored as the Rockies receded and the expanse of the Great Plains kept on going and going.

"How much more of this is there?" she whined.

"Another three hundred miles," I said.

Bismarck was just a place to stay. By the time we got in, it was already dark. Agnes was too tired to snark about another Comfort Inn and I was too tired to tease her about it.

The next day, we made our way to Minneapolis. It was a shorter drive, only eight hours. After dinner, we retired to our rooms and the quiet of our expensive hotel.

"Oh, stop, daddy cheap-bucks, so it was six hundred dollars? So what? You can't afford that?" She was both mocking and teasing me. I noticed her blouse was unbuttoned well below the underside of her breasts and she had removed her bra.

"It's not that," I grumbled.

"Then what?" She took off her slacks and sat down beside me on the bed.

"I was going to ask you that?" I ran my finger along her thigh.

She smiled and ran her hand along my leg. "Whatever do you mean?"

"If I undid the rest of the buttons on your blouse, you'd be ok with that?"

"Let's find out," she whispered in my ear.

I followed through and was soon running my fingers along her exposed nipples, something I knew she liked. "Why don't you get on top of me?"

"Let's take these off first." Together, we removed the brace and then my pants, and she straddled me, making sure her breasts were very close to my mouth.

"Something I can offer you, Sunshine?" She leaned in.

She moaned as I kissed and sucked on them. I pushed my hands underneath her panties, pressing my fingers against her, slowly moving them back and forth. She reached down and put my finger inside her before pulling at my cock. My finger and her hand moved in tandem. Soon we were kissing, and I was inside her. I wanted it to go on and on, but could only last a few minutes. The orgasm was so intense it was painful. Agnes shook as she came. She rolled over, pulling me on top, so I could keep going as long as possible. My neck was sore, but I didn't care. It was incredibly wonderful to be able to fuck without that goddamned collar. Exhausted, I rolled off her.

"Are you ok?" Agnes was tracing the edge of my neck and chin as we lay in the dark.

"I'm ok. Maybe a little sore, but I'm good with that," I said, pulling her closer to me.

She ran her fingers through the hair on my chest. "That was really intense, don't you think?"

"No need to think, it was." I kissed her.

"You know how much I love you, Sunshine?" she asked between kisses.

"As much as I love you, beautiful."

She put her head against my shoulder. "You think it's because someone might try to kill us like Idie and Ash? Certainly makes it more immediate, doesn't it?"

"There's that. I don't know if that's a good thing..."

"Yeah, but we have Josef with us," she said, pulling up the sheets.

"Yes, we do," I agreed. Whether that was a good thing, I chose to keep to myself.

It would take twelve hours to get to the house on the lake. So, much to Agnes' dismay, we had to get up early. I wanted to get to the house before the sun went down.

In the early evening, a man named Gale welcomed us. Gale Thomas was the caretaker. Ms. Lagenfelder had called ahead to let him know we were coming. He was a weathered-looking man with sharp gray eyes, a thin crooked nose, and wisps of light brown hair going gray. He was a little shorter than me, wiry, and duly impressed with the size of my personal goon.

"It's nice to finally meet you," he said in a clear, high voice. "I was beginning to wonder if I was keeping the place up for a ghost."

"No ghosts," I assured him.

Not yet anyway.

34

Gale led us into the house. It was more impressive that the pictures indicated. A large hall greeted us past the foyer, beyond which was a large sunlit room with views of Lake Michigan stretching off to the horizon. Dark oak panels and wainscoting adorned the hall, and the coffered ceilings were adorned with intricately carved wood. Ornate Oriental rugs covered the hardwood floors. Light floral wallpaper covered the walls in other parts of the house, with works of modern art placed here and there.

"The house is mostly original," Gale told us as we wandered through the place. "There were upgrades to the plumbing and electrical some years ago, I think after Mrs. Delashay bought the house, and the kitchen appliances have been reconditioned. I guess she likes that old look." The kitchen was to the far side of the house, behind tall swinging doors adjacent to the dining room. "So, she sold it to you, Mr. Buttman?"

"I got it from her, yes," I said. Apparently, word of Judith's death never made it up here, but as I didn't say anything, and I doubt Ms. Lagenfelder had, how would they know?

The upstairs comprised five large bedrooms and four baths. Downstairs was the great hall and living room, a library, music room, billiards room, and a sunroom. A door off the pantry led to the wine cellar. In the basement were the storeroom and the utility closet.

"How long have you been caretaker here, Gale?" I didn't actually know.

"Bout ten years, I spose. First heard about the job from Mrs. Delashay's father. They live over in Traverse City."

"I understand the house was used to move high end liquor during prohibition. There should be a false door around here somewhere."

Judith's notes said the door was behind the north wall of the wine cellar, a latch under the third shelf.

"I heard that too. House has a lot of local history. I think that's why Mrs. Delashay spent the money to keep it up. I guess she liked it growing up," he said with a sparkle in his eyes, "and when she got rich, she bought it. Do you know where the door is?"

I moved to the north wall and ran my fingers along the underside of the third shelf. The latch was above the fifth bottle. I pulled on the latch and felt the rack of shelves give. "It's right here. Would you give me a hand, Josef?"

The big Russian took hold of the two upper shelves while I, and an excited Gale, grabbed the two below. The large, heavy door slowly opened. Inside the door was an old rotary switch. I turned it but no light.

"We'll need a flashlight," I said to no one in particular. "The bulbs are probably long burned out."

"I can go grab one," Gale said, still visibly excited.

"It's late, Monk," Agnes was less excited. "Why don't we do this tomorrow? I'm tired and hungry."

The three of us men mumbled, but it had been a long day and my neck was stiff and sore. "Yeah, that might be best. We'll do this tomorrow." Josef helped me push the door back. We left it open just a little. "We should lube the hinges, so it's easier to open."

"Don't worry, I'll take care of that," Gale assured us.

Gale helped us haul our suitcases to our rooms and promised to be by early the next day.

"Where's a good place to eat, Gale?" Agnes was still hungry.

"Barnaby's is good. It's just off Main and Third, you can't miss it."

We thanked him and followed him into town.

· · · · · ·

With the flashlight from the Mercedes, I pulled open the secret door in the wine cellar. Josef and Agnes were upstairs. Agnes was exhausted and Josef wanted some alone time. The room through the door was large, probably thirty by thirty feet. Four light fixtures hung from the ceiling. The room was musty and covered with more than a few cobwebs. No one had been in it for some time. With a broom from the utility room, I swept away the cobwebs and kept the flashlight on the ceiling. At the far end of the room were two ladders rising to two trapdoors. Ten feet from there, in the middle of the room was a third trapdoor. A series of cables and pulleys stretched from the doors to the wall by the ladders and up through two metal pipes. The large trapdoor had two swivel blocks bracing it. I reached up to see if they would move at all.

They did!

The two smaller trapdoors had metal latches but no blocks.

I pulled on the cable attached to the smaller trapdoor on my left. It gave, and the door swung down. I climbed the ladder, which, as I suspected, led to the large pantry next to the kitchen. A mat was covering the two small trapdoors. After climbing back down, I went to the utility room, looking through the cabinets. In one was a can of lithium grease. I went back and lubricated the latches and pulleys. The lights were standard pan fixtures with incandescent bulbs. Using a stepladder, I replaced the bulbs using spares found in another cabinet. If nothing else, Gale was organized.

I headed upstairs.

In the pantry, I lifted the floor mat, exposing the trapdoors. Each had a rope pull drilled through a metal plate in the door to pull it back up. Between the two trapdoors on the wall, was a heavy ornate metal hanger shaped like a wolf's head. Where the hanger was attached to the wall was a linchpin at the top, locking it in place, and through the nose of the wolf's head was a thick metal hoop. I pulled up on the linchpin, unlocking it, which took a while to give. A small amount of grease allowed it to move more freely. The note in my pocket told me, with the linchpin up, to turn the hanger, using the hoop, in the direction of the door I wanted to release. Turning it clockwise, the trapdoor to the right of it fell open. Turning it counterclockwise did the same to the door to the left. Pulling the hanger forward, away from the wall, released the large trapdoor. It moaned as I pulled the hanger down; I could hear the latch disengaging; the door, still blocked, stayed closed. The only indication it was even there, below its own floor mat, was the slight unevenness of the mat.

I returned to the secret room to inspect the latches and hinges. The latch on the big trapdoor had not quite closed. I pushed on it with all my back could give me to get it to latch. It wasn't helping my sore, not entirely healed, neck, even with the brace on. It was nothing if not solid.

Satisfied, I returned to my sleeping wife. Before that, however, I needed to have a few words with Josef.

•   •   •   •   •

The next day brought sunshine and our caretaker. True to his word, Gale showed up early. Smartly, we had stopped at the local grocer after the previous night's dinner to shop, as there was no food in the house.

"Coffee?" I offered a cup to Gale. He seemed surprised.

"Thanks."

Agnes and Josef, amused, were sitting at the small table in the kitchen that looked out on to the stand of trees just north of the house.

After coffee, it was back to the secret room downstairs. Agnes was more sympathetic to our interest now that she'd had a little sleep.

"It a dark, damp, empty room, Buttman!" she barked when I teased her about it.

"That's the spirit!"

I confessed to coming down late last night when Gale asked about the lights. I also pointed to the trapdoors. "The two on the end work, but the big one has been blocked shut."

At the other end of the big room, were a pair of thick wooden doors. They, too, took a considerable amount of effort to open. Gale, having grabbed the can of lithium grease, lubed the hinges and the door handles, working them till they moved more easily. Another light switch by the door produced nothing for the same reason the other hadn't. Ever mindful, Gale retrieved the stepladder and the box of bulbs and relit each fixture as we move down the dark, damp, empty corridor. There were twelve fixtures ten feet apart. At the end of the corridor was another ladder and trapdoor, roughly four feet by four feet. To the side of the ladder was a length of chain and a handle next to two old trolleys.

I pulled on the handle after Gale sprayed the hinges and latch.

It took three pulls before it popped open.

Above us was the boathouse. The trapdoor was in the storage bay under a large straw mat. We climbed up and looked around after Gale turned on the light.

"Well, I'll be goddamned," he said. "I can't tell you how many times I've been in here and never knew there was a door there."

"It's what makes life interesting," I said.

Since we were out and about, we wandered around the boathouse. No need to buy a boat. There was one already here. A nice mid-century Chris-Craft was set up on the lift.

"It's ready to go if you want to take her out for a spin?" Gale was patting the side of the boat. It was white along the sides, with a dark mahogany deck and an enclosed cabin. Looked to be about thirty feet long.

"Why not? It'll give us something to do till the others arrive," I said.

Gale, a big grin on his face, fired up the lift motor and slowly lowered the boat into the water. "The only time the boat ever sees the water is when it needs maintenance, and it hasn't needed that in years. I did bring over some gas just in case. It's over there." He pointed to a metal cabinet that had danger-flammables stamped into its door. "Here's the key." He handed it to Josef. Josef, a smile on his face, unlocked the door and took out the gas can. "Not a lot of gas, but enough to get over to the marina. They got a place to gas up there."

"We'll do that," I said.

The gas was poured in the boat's tank. We got on the boat and Gale handed me a set of keys. The third one fit in the ignition and after a few cranks, the motor fired up. After the idle settled in, Gale disconnected the power line from the boathouse.

"Might as well motor into town. Get some lunch. What do you say, Gale?"

"I'm in."

"Aggie?" I was feeling good enough to annoy Mrs. Buttman.

Aggie was not amused. "You know how to steer a boat, Buttman?"

"How hard can it be?" I said. "Cast off, Mr. Rostikov."

He did, and we were off to the marina for gas and lunch.

Among the other perks that came with the Manor house on Lake Michigan, was a membership to use the local marina. Several people in the marina were surprised to see the boat, the *Judith Louise*, on the water.

"Hey, *Teddy's Retirement!*" One guy called out.

"That's what it used to be called," Gale helpfully added.

The guy at the pump remembered too. "Nice old boat," he said. "It's good to see her being used. Too many times these boats get fixed up and the people never go anywhere with them. They become investments. It's a waste."

"I agree," I replied as we waited for the tank to fill.

Lunch was at the marina, which, as Gale said, was a pretty fancy place.

The rest of the day was spent on the water, tooling along the shore of Lake Michigan. For an old boat, it handled well. It was warm, even on the water, and the sun rolled languidly across the sky with high white clouds shuffling by. There were darker clouds to the west. We'd dropped Gale off after returning from lunch; he lamented there was work at another place he was responsible for. We took turns steering the boat and were out so long that we had to return to the marina to refill the tank.

"It's nice up here," Agnes said as she sipped her glass of wine.

We were out at the west end of the lawn, not far from the boathouse, watching the wood burn in a large granite fire pit. Gale had set eight teak Adirondack chairs around it and stacked more wood than we'd ever need. Josef was in the boathouse, sitting on the dock, staring at his phone. He had gone quiet, more so than usual, which was saying something. Earlier, after I started barbequing the steaks for dinner, his phone rang and he left for a moment.

He had not been the same since.

Agnes had turned her phone off. "I don't want to ruin this wonderful day with people I don't want to talk to," she said when I asked her about it.

The fire was going out.

The phone Bernie had given me buzzed as I added more wood.

Your brother's on TV, the text said.

I had no idea where the TV in the house was. I didn't watch much TV to begin with, and Gale hadn't pointed it out.

Bernie then sent a link to an online news site.

"A plane from Davos, Switzerland, has gone missing over the Atlantic," the headline read. Further on the article noted, *"on board were a group of wealthy individuals heading to a conference in Detroit."*

Be very careful, was the last text.

We found the TV in the billiard room, behind two sliding oak panels.

All hell had broken loose at the White House. A secret service agent had attacked the president, who was saved by two quick thinking young men, the breathless reporter said, but admitted that had not been confirmed at this point. What exactly happened, no one knew. The White House wasn't talking, other than to say the president was safe and unharmed. The reporter noted that whatever happened occurred while the president was conducting a private meeting with his personal friend, the financier Delton Manaforte, and the two men identified as Isaac Bohrman and Jontaveus Montgomery. The TV continued playing a loop of them taking pictures with the president just prior to the meeting.

"None of the men, as of yet, have spoken to us," the reporter continued.

"Wow," was all Agnes could say.

We watched for another half-hour before coming to the conclusion that nothing more would be forthcoming anytime soon. Josef joined us as we turned the TV off.

"It's time," I told him. Agnes stared at me as Josef nodded.

"What does that mean?" she asked.

"It means, Detective Duquesne, that it's time to earn your money," I said, kissing her cheek.

She still didn't get it.

By the time we returned to the fire pit, only glowing embers were left. I raked the coals around before pouring water on them. A plum of steam and ash rose against the twilight to the west, which continued to darken.

A small motorboat was puttering off in the distance.

The house was quiet. Josef stood in front of the large plate-glass windows of the great room, staring out at the dark. Only a hint of moonlight escaped the slow-moving clouds. Agnes was asleep on the large couch across from me. A long eventful day and three glasses of wine had done her in.

I called Art Devaney.

It was late, but I didn't think that would matter.

He answered on the third ring.

"Monk, so good to hear from you," he said, jovial as ever.

"I would think, given what's been going on, that you'd be more worried."

He laughed. "No one is dead, and intrigue is as pure an adrenaline rush as you can find. Are you calling about your brother?"

"No. I assume Isaac and Jontaveus are alright. Hopefully, I'll hear from them soon."

"Hopefully? Should I ask?"

"It ties in with one of the others in today's intrigue, Mr. Manaforte."

"Ah," he sighed, "in what way?"

"He has a problem he means for me to solve one way or another. Ever heard of a man named Aaron Alan Sobeski?"

"I know of him by reputation," Art answered. His voice had lost its exuberance. "I thought Sobeski was working for the Russian mob, or one of their variants?"

"That I don't know, but recently people have been dying in ways that Bernie says suggests this guy is back in business..."

"And you think he's tied in with Manaforte?"

"Yes, but my interest is in Manaforte's relationship with the president and a Secret Service agent named Nakatomi."

"I see." The line grew unusually quiet. "I'll look into it," he said at last, "but with the events of the day, it might be a little tight-lipped around here."

"Just a thought. Thanks, Art."

"Be very careful, Monk," he advised, before hanging up.

Where had I heard that before? And how did he know it was me when he answered? I was using a different phone.

There was one last thing to do.

I quietly left Josef and Agnes and went down to the hidden room under the pantry. There, I adjusted the blocks on the large trapdoor.

I went back up to get my sleepy wife to bed.

35

They were waiting for us by the stairs. Somehow, they had gotten in undetected. I recognized the two motorcycle punks right away by their smart-assed grins and stringy hair. Both had guns out, pointed in our direction. The third member of this little party was the man Isaac saw walking past the 500 the night it exploded. He was trim, maybe five-eight, with thick-framed glasses and sandy blond hair. He was wearing a rather nice gray silk suit.

"Mr. Rostikov," he said, "we'll take it from here." Josef, looking at neither us, or our three callers, walked towards the door leading to the great expanse of lawn and the lake beyond. "This won't take long, Mr. Buttman." He pointed towards the kitchen. "This way, if you please."

"So, you're Aaron Alan?" I said. "People hold you in high regard."

"Save the flattery, Mr. Buttman." His eyes were small and there seemed to be no light in them. The punks continued to grin.

We were led through the kitchen to the pantry. The mat covering the two smaller trapdoors had been pulled away.

"You have a decision to make, Mr. Buttman. As I'm sure you're aware, we are here to hasten your journey to a better life, and, as you've no doubt been told of my interest in variation, please stand, each of you, on one of the trapdoors."

Agnes, still half in the bag, grabbed onto me.

"And the decision?" I asked.

"What's he talking about, Sunshine?" Agnes looked at the three of them. "Who are you?"

"I'm your executioner, Mrs. Buttman. Now stand away from your husband."

Agnes held me closer, but the punk with the ratty brown hair pulled her away. The other punk moved in with his gun pointed at my head. When I offered no resistance, he returned to Sobeski's side. Agnes and I were both on top of a trapdoor. The punk with the brown hair remained close to Agnes.

"The decision is a simple one," he said. "As you know, the trapdoors you are standing on will drop you fifteen feet and probably break your necks, something of an irony, don't you think, Mr. Buttman?" I rubbed my neck to indicate I did. "If you survive the fall, we'll break them for you in as quick and humane a fashion as possible. So, I'm going to have to ask you to remove your brace."

"And the alternative?"

He smiled at that. A grim, ugly smile exhibiting ugly white teeth. "The alternative is that I put you in that chair," he motioned to a stool in the corner of the pantry, "and I let these two fuck your wife in any fashion they choose, after which we beat her to death, then we hang you. Slowly. Painfully. One is quick. One is not. I'm not squeamish, Mr. Buttman, and I am aware, as you are, of your wife's painful history. Do you really want her to go through that again before she dies? Are you willing to watch something like that?" The smile faded. "I've witnessed many terrible things. One more won't do me any harm." Sobeski thrust his hands in his pockets. "The decision, Mr. Buttman?"

"You're a clever guy, Sobeski—"

"Save the talk, Mr. Buttman. Bernie Schoor will not be riding to the rescue this time."

"No?" I wanted to make certain.

"No."

I looked over at Agnes. She was crying, her face in her hands. "Can I at least kiss my wife before we do this?"

"Be quick about it," he said.

I took the four steps and put my arms around her, kissing away the tears. "It'll be quick, my love." I patted her on the ass, noting the sap in her back pocket. "I love you, Agnes Jean."

"I love you, Sunshine." She then winked, startling me.

"Alright, move away," Sobeski demanded. I returned to my spot above the door. "The brace, Mr. Buttman."

"Yes," I mumbled. I slowly removed the brace, casting it away.

"Good. Now pull the lever, Mr. Buttman." The smile was back on the killer's face.

I hesitated. "I don't know if I can…"

"Save the Games, Mr. Buttman. I know the trick to the handle. Left for one, right for the other, or," he motioned with his hand downward, "straight for both."

"You sure?"

"Little birds," he said.

"Or big Russians…"

"Straight down, if you please."

I grabbed the hanger with the ornate wolfs head, and jerked it straight down, praying the latch would give.

Sobeski and the Blond punk fell through the floor as the thin mat and the large trapdoor gave way. A sickening thud followed. The brown-haired punk stepped toward the large opening in the floor. Agnes pulled the sap out of her pocket and smacked him on the back of the head. He fell to the floor, groaning. I picked up the gun. Agnes kicked the miserable fucker three or four times before I stopped her.

Josef was next to Sobeski and the punk in the room below. "This one," he tapped the blond punk with his foot, "is dead. The other…" Sobeski was trying to crawl away from the big Russian. "Time?" He was looking up at me.

"Time," I said.

Josef lifted Sobeski up by his neck. Sobeski flailed as Josef tightened his grip. He quickly broke Sobeski's neck.

"This one's next," I said. I grabbed one arm as Agnes grabbed the other. We pushed the punk through the opening, head first. Another sickening thud filled the space below as he struck the concrete floor. "Is he done?"

Josef moved his head before looking up. "Yeah."

"Let's get the trolleys; there's still work to do."

We loaded the three dead men in the trolleys and took them to the boathouse.

"What was the original plan?" I asked Josef. He sheepishly pointed to the Chris-Craft. "Damn!" I said.

Agnes was confused. "Why don't we just put them in their little boat?" She pointed to the small skiff tied up on the other side of the dock.

"You'll see," I told her.

Once the dead were in the boat, I fired up the engine. Josef untied the lines, and I turned up the throttle and barely made it back onto the dock as the boat took off. I did the same to the skiff. The Chris Craft moved in a mostly straight line towards the western horizon. The skiff veered off to the south. We stood in the faint light of the dock, watching nothing so much as the dark western horizon. A light rain began to fall. We continued to wait. A bright light lit up the far end of the lake, followed by a muffled boom some seconds later.

"Oh my God!" Agnes cried out. "That was planned?"

Josef and I nodded.

We returned the way we came, making sure the doors, trap, or otherwise, were closed, latched, and covered. What little blood there was in the secret room below the pantry was cleaned up. I put the blocks back where they had been originally. At Agnes' insistence, I retrieved the unloved brace from the pantry.

"I don't like it," I whined.

Agnes groaned at my whining. "I don't care, Sunshine. You still have another two weeks."

It was four in the morning.

• • • • •

Gale was quick to inform us the boat was missing when he arrived later in the morning.

After a few confused minutes, I owned up. "I must have left the keys in it."

"Better let the police know," he said.

They already knew something was up. Others, too, had noticed the light and the boom earlier in the morning. The Coast Guard had been called. Debris had been found, along with a few body parts. I woke Agnes and Josef and we told our tale, such as it was: After returning from the marina, we docked the boat, had dinner, built a fire, went inside for a few drinks, and went to bed. It was as simple as that we told them. I admitted I probably left the keys in the boat, foolishly forgetting that someone might try to steal it.

"Well, something was going on last night," the sheriff's deputy said. "Another boat was taken as well, but it washed up about ten miles from here."

We thanked him for his time and assured him we'd be here for a while longer if they needed to talk with us. I told Gale he didn't need to stick around.

"If you need me, you got my number," he said.

Once he was safely in the distance, it was time to talk. Agnes had questions.

·　　·　　·　　·　　·

The boathouse wasn't the same without the boat. It looked sad and purposeless. I'd need to get a new one. Or another old one, which made me think of the Falcon. We sat in the Adirondack chairs, burning more wood, drinks in hand. The rain had cleared, and the sun was back in the picture, warming us up.

Agnes was tapping the arm of her chair, staring at me and Josef.

"You both knew what was going to happen, and you didn't tell me?" Agnes was kinda pissed. The shock of the night was waning with anger taking its place.

"I only had a suspicion," I admitted. "I thought Manaforte was setting us up as chumps for the Secret Service with his bogus meeting, but Mr. Rostikov here made me wonder. It was all too pat, his working for Manaforte just before enthusiastically, well, for him anyway, agreeing to keep an eye on us."

"What does that mean, Josef?" Agnes turned her attention to Mr. Rostikov. Mr. Rostikov didn't want to talk. Agnes turned back to me. "Well, Buttman?"

"I only know it has something to do with his, or his wife's, family, probably those still in Russia," I told her.

"Is that true, Josef?" she asked.

He looked at her. "Yes," he said in as quiet a voice as possible.

"They knew we were here, and you knew they were going to kill us, yes?" Agnes was almost yelling.

"Yes," he said, "but hopefully not."

"Hopefully not? What the fuck does that mean?"

"Agnes..." I foolishly open my mouth.

"You're next, Monk Buttman! Well, Josef Rostikov?"

The big man stared at his glass before speaking. "Sobeski was the target, not you, but..." He looked at me.

I took a turn. "But if we didn't make it, well..." There was no easy way to say it.

Agnes frowned. "So, if we didn't take him out, the boat would. Is that it?"

"Yes," I said.

"And the trapdoors? You got it all rigged up without me, didn't you, Buttman?" Her frown had not abated.

"Yes, but in my defense, I thought it better if only Josef and I knew, that way—"

"That way what? What are you saying here, Monk Buttman? That I can't keep a secret, that I can't be trusted when our lives are on the line?"

"Umm, kinda," I admitted.

Agnes shook her head. "You two are something else. If it weren't for the fact that I was watching you all the time, I'd really be angry!" It was then she cracked a rather nasty smile.

"What?" For once, I was floored.

"That's right, smartguy. I followed you the other night while you were sneaking around. The only reason you didn't figure it out was because you went in to talk to this goombah before coming to bed." She derisively shook her hand at Josef. "I also watched you sneak off last night, too!"

I was still shocked by the hard-boiled private dick playing me like a well-worn card. "So... you weren't out of it... you were..."

"I was *hoping* your little plan would work," she said, mockingly. "I assume Josef told them about the trapdoors, or do we have to bump off Gale?"

"I told them what Monk told me," Josef told her.

"How did you know about all the trick doors anyway, Sunshine?"

"They were in Judith's files on the house. How she knew, I don't know. I didn't even know she owned the place under after she died. Maybe she planned to use them to kill Martin." I could see Judith dragging Martin up here for the purposes of finishing him off. "Any other questions, detective?"

The detective shook her head. "Not at the moment."

Josef stood and looked at the slow, easy waves lapping at the shore. We watched as he stood there. After a minute or so, he noticed us watching him.

"I think I'd like to go home," he said, mostly to himself. "I have things to do now."

"No worries," I told him.

36

A kid picked him up that evening, some rideshare thing. He had an overnight flight booked out of Detroit. Whatever deal he'd made with Manaforte, I hope it paid off. I sent a text to Jones, thanking him. He didn't bring up Jontaveus, and neither did I.

Agnes turned her phone back on and called her mother.

"I said they could come over when we got back," she groused when I asked.

"I promise to behave," I said helpfully.

"You're a jerk, Buttman."

"Yeah, but whatcha going to do? I'm *your* jerk." I smiled and blew her a kiss.

I got a minute to enjoy my reverie before the doorbell rang.

It was quite loud, booming through the house.

A thin older man and his wife were at the door. Their faces were drawn and their eyes moist. They looked much as they had in the pictures I remembered from one of Judith's photo albums, only older.

"Come in, Mr. Taffy, Mrs. Taffy." I opened the door wide enough so there was room between us. Agnes eased up behind me. "This is my wife, Agnes."

"We came about Judy," he said.

"What would you like to know?" I asked as I directed them into the living room. The sun was falling behind a layer of dappled clouds along the water's edge, filling the room with a soft, diffused light.

"Why are you in my daughter's house, sir?" Robert Taffy was looking around at the splendor of the house more than he was looking at me.

"Because she gave it to me."

"Gave it to you? Why on Earth would she do that?" Barbara Taffy had the same dark countenance her daughter had when she was angry.

I tried to see Judith in them. "For one last nasty laugh, I suspect. She didn't tell me anything about this place. I only learned about it after she—"

"After she what?" Mrs. Taffy's eyes hardened.

"I'm sorry. I forgot that you weren't to be told. Judith died a little more than two years ago from ovarian cancer," I said.

"Why weren't we told?" he asked, but his eyes betrayed him.

"You know why."

"And how would you know, *Mister*?" Barbara was having none of it.

"My name is Buttman, Monk Buttman. Judith Louise Taffy Delashay was my lover, and I know because I read the summary decree cutting you out of her life. She also gave me her money and property, which I came to learn included this house."

"I don't believe it," she said, turning to her husband.

Mr. Taffy looked more worn than he had just a few minutes before. "Then it's true. She is gone."

"I don't believe it," Barbara Taffy continued, despite her husband. "It's just another goddamned trick she playing." She scowled as she appraised my unfitness in all of this sordid business. At least that's how I chose to look at it. "I don't believe it and I don't believe you, *Mister Buttman!*"

"It's not a matter of what you chose to believe, Mrs. Taffy," I said in my most soothing voice. "Is there anything else I can do for you?"

"You can get the hell out of my daughter's house, and if she is dead, then it ought to be my house. That's what you can do." The veins in her forehead were making their presence known, much like the angry redness enveloping her tight, hard face.

"Anything else?"

Robert Taffy had tears running down his face, which only angered his wife more.

"Goddammit, Robert, the last thing we need is you crying." Barbara Taffy wagged her finger in my face. "This isn't right, *Mister Buttman*, you'll hear from my lawyer, goddammit." She turned and walked back to the front door. "Let's go, Robert!"

Robert Taffy wiped his eyes. "She didn't die alone, did she?"

"No, I was with her."

"Robert!" his wife bellowed.

"Goodbye, Mr. Taffy."

The perfect end to a perfect day.

· · · · ·

We stayed another two weeks, bought another boat, played tourist, enjoyed the quiet, and the fact that it was just the two of us. Agnes, oddly, wasn't particularly interested in the Taffys, or any of Judith's family drama other than they did not get along.

"Maybe I should do that," she said when I told her how Judith had settled with them and promptly cut herself off from her goddamned family.

"All of them?" I countered.

"You know what I mean!"

I did.

The police and the Coast Guard had a few questions, but we didn't know anything we were willing to admit to, and, apparently, there was little left of the boat, or those on it, to help with any investigation.

Gale was sorry to see us leave, but I assured him we'd be back, and we'd bring the kids and grandkids next time.

"Too bad about the boat," he said.

Yes, too bad about the boat.

Other than Rebekah calling and asking when we'd be back, there was no rush, especially since Agnes was not looking forward to an exciting evening with the Jerr. I assured my daughter we were on our way.

I was very assuring.

• • • • •

We spent two days in Lautenberg, mostly hiking about Sergeant MacMillan's property with him and Ms. Thalken. With Jenna there, he felt he could go back to Virginia and repair his relationship with his wife. We wished him well.

The last stop before getting back to LA was the farm. I didn't want to, but I'd stupidly promised, and if Agnes had to put up with the Jerr, I had to put up with Moses.

He was not on the porch when we arrived, but there was no big Russian to gawk at this time. It was, however, noticed.

"What, no goon this time?" At least he was smiling.

"Don't press your luck, old man!"

"What does luck have to do with it?"

I shook my head and gave Meredith a hug.

Emily was back. It was good to see her and hear about all the things that were interesting and complicating to a fifteen-year-old.

"Mom's pregnant, you know?" she said, stating the obvious.

"Yeah, I noticed. What do you think about that?" We were out by her garden, absentmindedly pulling weeds.

"It's ok, I guess. They think it's a boy..." she laughed at that. "I'll have two step brothers..." She looked over at me and smiled, a little too mischievously. "Maybe now I can talk her into letting me come live with you?"

I shook my head. It was a sore subject that hadn't come up since the détente after Jacob's funeral. "We might want to hold off on that," I said.

Emily frowned at me. "You're a coward, Mr. Sunshine."

"You got that right!"

The talk at dinner continued, as I was to learn, the conversation about the imbroglio in DC and Isaac's role in it. While the specifics were still being withheld due to a special investigation, they had come to find out that a "rogue" Secret Service agent had attacked his partner, or the other guy who was with him protecting the president, or something like that and Isaac and another guy...

"Jontaveus Montgomery," I said.

"Yeah, that was it, and they knocked the guy down or protected or shielded the president, or something like that." As Brewster Mackinaw said, the details were a bit sketchy.

I thought the whole thing was sketchy, but I kept that to myself.

"Anyway," Moses said at last, "Isaac will be home in a few days and we can hear what he has to say."

"Sounds interesting," I agreed.

What happened in Michigan or what was up with Sterling wasn't discussed. I did, however, assure Moses and Meredith that if I saw Isaac, I'd remind him to drag his sorry butt up here.

• • • • •

Two days later, I was home, sitting in my little backyard watching Zach splash Lizzy, who laughed and splashed him back. Rebekah was glad to see us, if for no other reason than to get a break from her boisterous children.

"How much longer?"

She was annoyed that I couldn't remember. "Six weeks, Dad. I've told you that many, many times."

"Yeah, yeah, yeah," I said.

Zach laughed while his mother glared at me. You can't win everyone over, I told myself.

"And your neck? How much longer?" she asked, mocking me.

"My esteemed quack says another week," I groaned.

"Good!"

Rebekah returned to the house as Agnes was coming out, nursing a glass of wine. She, too, was frowning, but for her own reasons. "They'll be here Sunday," she whined.

"It'll be fun," I assured her. She didn't believe me.

• • • • •

Manaforte called the next day. He was ready to talk. I told him I'd be at the house in Beverly Hills. I forgot to mention Agnes would be there, but I wasn't worried. He arrived at one. I ordered a couple of pizzas for the occasion. They arrived just before Manaforte.

"Have a slice," I said.

He looked at Agnes, who was staring back at him.

"I assume your wife will join us this time?" He smiled as he took a slice from each pie.

"Goddamned right," she said.

"You missed the meeting." I thought that was a good starting point.

"Yes, I had my own adventure."

"So we heard." Agnes poured him a glass of wine. "What did Agent Nakatomi tell you?" she asked, knowing that Art had informed me that Nakatomi had worked for the Secret Service before joining Manaforte's security contingent.

"The same thing Mr. Rostikov did, that the job was finished," he answered.

"You do this often, Mr. Manaforte? Seems a little sinister for a venture capitalist?" Agnes was on a role.

"I agree, but sometimes mistakes are made. Sobeski was mine. I trusted someone I shouldn't have, and it complicated an already complicated game."

This from a man known for carefully vetting those he deals with.

"Oh, I think he was doing exactly what you wanted him to do," I countered. "That he was exactly what Carmichael suggested. The problem with Sobeski, as I came to find out, was he played his own games with the people he worked for. It's what got him kicked out of the CIA. It's what made him so many enemies over the years, but he had people like you to hide him, to shield him, and I can imagine how over time that can, as you say, complicate an already complicated game." It was my turn to roll.

"Very good, Mr. Buttman, very good. And the rest?"

"The government thing? That was already in the works; *that's* the complicated game," I said. Manaforte smiled at that.

"Spill, Buttman." Agnes poured herself a second glass of wine.

"Someone has to be in charge, someone has to lay down the law. The members of Carmichael's little group, the people whose activities are opaque to most of us, but not to people like Mr. Manaforte here, need to understand that. Fear is a powerful tool, so is death. Even presidents of the United States sometimes need to be reminded of that. That reminder has been handed out to a lot of important people lately, people who are never otherwise troubled by social niceties like the law. That was Sobeski's part in this. Terror being a hallmark of authoritarian rule."

I grabbed another slice of pizza.

"I dislike the term authoritarian," Manaforte said. "But, as you say, someone needs to be in charge. Decisions, important decisions, can't wait for consensus from a public that is easily distracted, or politicians primarily concerned with their own well-being."

"Yes, Carmichael's book said as much, that while democracy is a nice idea, men, and women, are easily manipulated, and a truly informed electorate is a pipedream. It's better for everyone if their roles in society are known early on, as they had been for millennia. And we've reached the point where disinformation and propaganda are the norm, whether we know it or not. Why not use that to further dissatisfaction and fuel demand for a better order? And Mr. Manaforte, with his connections through ownership and influence, is in the perfect position to direct and exploit that." Moses would be so proud.

Agnes smirked at my self-satisfaction.

"Nice, Buttman, but that doesn't excuse our guest here from having no problem with our being murdered by his rogue assassin, just so he could be dispatched afterword." Agnes directed her glass at

Manaforte. "I don't like the idea that we can so easily be sacrificed for a more perfect union run by a dictator."

"Perhaps I had more faith in you than you suspect, Agnes," Manaforte said.

"Save the BS. I've spent a lot of time around gangsters and those types. The only difference is you're not a social lowlife."

Manaforte laughed at that. "I like you, Agnes. You're brighter than most of the people I deal with, and for all intents and purposes, you're right, I'm no better than a gangster. That doesn't bother me. I think the world can be a better, more organized place. But that also means that a certain order has to be maintained. I mean to direct my energies and wealth to that end, and if some sacrifices must be made, so be it. Besides, I don't believe that you two were unaware of the situation to be begin with. You could have hidden yourself away like that little troll Dunkle—"

"Or those on the plane that supposedly disappeared crossing the Atlantic? I assume, now that Sobeski is no longer hunting them down, that they're back in the light and their disappearance was a technical problem or something like that," I said.

"Yes, they turned up in Bermuda, I believe."

"I still don't like it," she huffed.

"I'm not saying you should, but it's obvious that, far from being terrorized by the experience, you found it exciting." He tipped his glass towards Agnes.

"That's not the point!" though she and I knew better.

Manaforte snorted. "I disagree. I think the opposite is true. You find, as I find, that life is more interesting when you take chances. In that, you're no different than I am." Manaforte finished his glass of wine and rose. "I think that's enough for now."

"How do you know we won't tell the world about you?" she asked.

"Tell them if you'd like. I have people who can spin with the best of them, and at the end of the day, there has to be proof enough to warrant a proper investigation. Do you have any proof, proof that can't be spun a hundred different ways? Are you willing to sacrifice

Mr. Rostikov? Will Xavier Dunkle rally to your side? I think not. And for every Bernie Schoor you throw my way, I have an equal counterpart in the same agency to dispute them."

"You have it all worked out, don't you?" Agnes didn't want to let go.

"This country was built around wealth and those who possess it. My advice is you take advantage of that." He took out his phone and looked it over. "Thank you for lunch."

We walked him to the door.

37

For the remainder of the afternoon, Agnes said little, preferring to sit out by the pool. She played with her phone for a moment before putting it away. It was a hazy day, warm, with a light breeze rolling along the hills around us. It was a good time for a nap. When I awoke, the sun had receded and Agnes was standing over me.

"Do you think there's something wrong with me?"

"You're asking me that now?"

"You know what I mean..."

For some reason I wasn't connecting the dots here... "You mean beyond the fact that we were nearly murdered and you thought it was exciting and fun?"

"Well," she huffed, "you didn't seem worried..."

"I was plenty worried. I just hoped the trapdoor worked and Josef kept his end of the bargain."

"See, it was all ok in the end." She smiled at that.

"Yeah..." What was going on here?

"Oh, MaryAnn will be here shortly. You should get cleaned up."

It was then I noticed she had changed her clothes and was wearing drawstring pajama bottoms, a loose, nearly see-through blouse, and no bra.

"Why do I need to clean up for MaryAnn?"

"Because a gentleman cleans his cock before offering it to a lady, that's why." Apparently, she had changed her mind about a threesome.

"Well, we certainly don't want that." As I got up, she patted me on the ass.

Once cleaned, I waited nervously as Agnes read a magazine.

The doorbell rang.

MaryAnn was smiling.

.   .   .   .   .

"Well?" Agnes was curious.

"Well, what?"

"You know very well what," she said.

We were at the door watching as MaryAnn drove away in her car. It was morning and there were dishes to clean.

"It was very interesting," I said. "And you? Are you worried now that MaryAnn has sucked my cock? You mentioned that earlier as a reason we should not do what we just did."

"Is she better than me?"

"No better than Judith, and doing it out by the pool was very much in her style, but to directly answer your question, no, she's not a better cocksucker than you."

Agnes kissed me on the cheek and slapped my ass. "Good answer. And the rest?"

"Like I said, it was interesting, and I'd be lying if I didn't admit it was very erotic, but it was also very weird to have you kissing me and playing with my ass while I'm fucking your best friend."

"Maybe we could try it with your best friend?" She had a big grin on her face.

"Well, turnabout is fair play, but until recently, the only person I could call my best friend was Joanie. I don't think that's quite what you had in mind, and while I wouldn't be surprised if Joanie has been with other women, I don't think she'd go for it. Other options... Mr. Jones? Knowing him, I don't think he'd be interested, nor do I think Coretta would let him. There's Mikal. I don't know him that well, and there's the possibility by fucking him you'd be fucking your daughter's lover, but he might be game. Maybe Xavier—"

"Stop!" Agnes put her finger to my mouth. "I'm not fucking Xavier Dunkle."

"That's all I got," I had to admit.

"I'm not surprised," she said, though she was smiling.

The threesome was in some ways a diversion from the dismal prospect the coming day held. Jerry and Denise were expected at the house in West Covina that afternoon for dinner and drinks and some quality family time.

It was Agnes' turn to be nervous.

After our recent adventures, I thought it quite comforting in an odd sort of way.

For dinner, there were steaks and potatoes and wine. The house was clean, and the weather was its usual agreeable self. There was nothing beyond that, other than four decades of anger and discomfort, to look forward to. Anna was busy, so Agnes only had me as a buffer and maybe her mother. We'd see.

They arrived at four-thirty. Jerry bitched about the traffic. "It's terrible every goddamned minute of every goddamned day anymore," he lamented.

I had to agree.

We talked about our trip to Michigan and showed them pictures of the house. I gave a short history lesson on the place. I decided not to mention killing Sobeski and the punks.

"It looks lovely," Denise exclaimed.

"There's plenty of room," I said. "It's built for vacations."

"Maybe next summer, huh, honey?" She put her hand on Jerry's sleeve.

"We'll see," he said.

For dinner, we sat outside beneath the neighbor's tree. Jerry talked about work. Griped might be more accurate. Denise thought it was so nice that we were sitting here enjoying dinner together.

"It is," Agnes said. Whether she meant it or not was another matter.

After dinner, we returned to the living room so Jerry could watch the Angels game. They were hosting Seattle.

Agnes and Denise went into the kitchen, and I kept Jerry company. Little was said, which was fine by me. I was tired of talking.

At nine, Jerry announced it was time to go. "Some of us got jobs to get to in the morning," he muttered.

As we saw them to the door, Jerry Fannis gave his daughter a hug and thanked us for dinner. Denise echoed his sentiments.

"It's a nice house you got here," he said, "but I think the TV is better at your fancy place."

I nodded, thinking it was better than nothing. Agnes, looking over at me, one of her more curious habits, smiled.

"Now you know how I feel," she said.

I smiled back. "Do I?"

Agnes pulled the sap from her pocket. "How's that neck feeling, smartguy?"

I rubbed my neck to find out. I had taken off the brace for our get-together.

"So far, so good," I said.

"That's good to know. I'd hate to have to use this..." I appreciated that she was smiling as she said this.

The last thing I needed was any more adventures.

That's when Felicia called.

Read on for a look at the next exciting installment in the Monk Buttman Series:

THE OBJECT OF OUR DESIRE

I looked at the woman. She was a light-skinned black woman, a few inches shorter than me, heels and all, with dark hair that she wore loose, so it fell on her shoulders. Her eyes were a soft brown highlighted with blue mascara that matched her dress.

"My name is Monk. Sterling is my brother." I noted the confusion on her face. "You asked who the fuck I was."

The confused look morphed into a more knowing one. "Yes, I did."

We stood on the sidewalk. People walked by, occasionally glancing at the woman beside me.

"What's your name?" I asked, though from the investigator's report I already had a name.

"Aisha."

I pointed to the diner across the street. "Well?"

Aisha looked at me, then the diner, before following me across the street. Once inside, we were taken to a table in the back. Aisha kept her head down. I took the chair that allowed me a view of the entrance and the people around us. The incident in Michigan continued to haunt me even though nearly a year had passed, but that's what you get when you don't pay attention, when you let your guard down. I thought of Josef. What would he think? I should ask him when I got back.

Aisha fiddled with her purse, her shoulders hunched, like she was trying to be smaller, less noticeable. I ordered a whiskey, Aisha a daiquiri.

"Is this what you do, Monk, spy on people?" she asked.

"Apparently."

Aisha grimaced at that. "You think this is funny?"

"Do you?"

Our drinks arrived. I ordered the split pea soup and a salad with bleu cheese. Aisha ordered a veggie burger with sweet potato fries. It was a perfectly ordinary meal between a spy and his brother's lover. Little was said.

Midway through the meal, I spied Sterling and Felicia leaving Aisha's building. Sterling had his hands in his pockets and his head down. Felicia was walking in front of Sterling, her expression still tight and angry, stared straight ahead.

"You can go home now," I told my dining partner. "They've left."

Aisha turned around, craning her neck. Sterling and Felicia were out of sight.

"Any reason I should stay?" She gathered her purse.

"No."

She got up and weaved her way between the tables until she was free of us.

I finished eating and paid the bill. It had been a long day and there was still the drive back to LA.

Aisha stood in the doorway of her building as I left.

About the Author

An engineer for 40 years, Mr. Pearce, following open-heart surgery, decided to pursue his muse and write. He is the author of the *Monk Buttman Mystery* series. When not writing, Mr. Pearce is the accomplished recording artist, Mr. Primitive. He and his wife live in Kenmore, Washington.

Note from the Author

Word-of-mouth is crucial for any author to succeed. If you enjoyed *The Fist Inside the Glove*, please leave a review online—anywhere you are able. Even if it's just a sentence or two. It would make all the difference and would be very much appreciated.

Thanks!
David William Pearce

Thank you so much for reading one of
David William Pearce's novels.

If you enjoyed the experience,
please check out where it all began.

Where Fools Dare to Tread by David William Pearce

It's easy to be a nobody when you've got nothing to lose, but with his
life and potential redemption on the line, can Monk be a somebody
people will remember?

We hope you enjoyed reading this title from:

www.blackrosewriting.com

Subscribe to our mailing list – *The Rosevine* – and receive **FREE** books, daily deals, and stay current with news about upcoming releases and our hottest authors.
Scan the QR code below to sign up.

Already a subscriber? Please accept a sincere thank you for being a fan of Black Rose Writing authors.

View other Black Rose Writing titles at
www.blackrosewriting.com/books and use promo code
PRINT to receive a **20% discount** when purchasing.

www.ingramcontent.com/pod-product-compliance
Lightning Source LLC
Chambersburg PA
CBHW010727100726
47899CB00009B/2959